To the Gohelman Family,

You gave love to Paula as tho she was yours --- What greater gift _can_ be given?

Jesus gave us love first + you share it.

David F. Barr

This Very Day

This Very Day

David F. Barr

Herald Press
Scottdale, Pennsylvania
Kitchener, Ontario
1977

Library of Congress Cataloging in Publication Data

Barr, David F   1931-
   This very day.

   1. Dismas, Saint—Fiction. 2. Caleb (Biblical
character)—Fiction. I. Title.
PZ4.B2658Th   [PS3552.A7315]   813'.5'4   76-48111
ISBN 0-8361-1803-0

THIS VERY DAY
Copyright © 1977 by Herald Press, Scottdale, Pa. 15683
   Published simultaneously in Canada by Herald Press,
   Kitchener, Ont. N2G 4M5
Library of Congress Catalog Card Number: 76-48111
International Standard Book Number: 0-8361-1803-0
Printed in the United States of America
Design: Alice B. Shetler

This book
is dedicated
to the unfortunate people who
will read in its pages only
the misadventures
of a thief
without
seeing
in the
story
a ray
of hope
for all
of us.

1 SUNDAY MORNING

Those who knew him considered Dismas to be the vilest man ever to walk the streets of Jerusalem. Today he was only drunk—so drunk that he sat sprawled on the dirt floor of Aram's dingy inn, propped against a mud back wall.

Layers of smoke, which came from the kitchen's fires, hung like cobwebs in the dark room's air. The fires contributed to the morning's heat, adding smoke and the smell of burning grease to the already rancid odors which clung to the room's murky walls.

Chunks of plasterlike mud, which originally provided a smooth cover for the pockmarked handmade bricks, had partially fallen from the walls years before. The type of customers this inn drew would not notice its dilapidated condition anyway.

Aram, who slouched against the doorsill near the small

portal connecting the large, low-ceilinged main room with the kitchen, allowed his squinted eyes to slide over the room's few customers to the drunken pair lying against the wall. The fat innkeeper sucked on a bone, which had once been the graceful hind leg of a lamb.

Aram paused in his watchfulness long enough to examine the bone over which his large wet lips slurped as they sloppily caressed it.

He checked for any tiny slivers of meat he might have left on it. Finding none, he jammed the dirty little finger of his right hand deep into the end of the hard tube to loosen the marrow, almost dropping the prize as he did so. Withdrawing his finger, he quickly stuck the end of the bone into his mouth and sucked deeply on it. His mouth suddenly full of moist marrow, Aram fell back heavily against the doorsill once more. A few moments later, after making another fruitless try to draw more marrow from the femur, the dark-skinned Syrian simply dropped it on the floor and wiped his grease-coated hands, front and back, on his tunic, which already showed evidence of weeks of careless eating and drinking.

Finally Aram pushed himself away from the door and heaved his way across the room to stand, fists on hips, looking down disapprovingly at the snoring thieves lying on his floor. Although he greatly disliked Dismas and Caleb, Aram's fear of the merciless thieves, especially Dismas, gave him caution enough to not waken them.

That Dismas was drunk was nothing unusual, but that Aram had not thrown him into the street, once drink took the thief's consciousness, was a near miracle.

Beneath the filth-starched tunic covering his bulbous body, Aram had the heart of a ruthless businessman. He knew that Dismas' love of wine and his talent for stealing

8

from the pilgrims who now streamed into Jerusalem for the Passover would provide him with some extra income. He could afford to be patient with Dismas this particular week.

○   ○   ○

The spring rains stopped earlier than usual. The flowers, which just a week before had made the countryside look aflame, now drooped and were changing color. The heat and floral death, which sometimes claimed the land in spring, had settled early over Judea. It came quickly as the countryside was baked by the annual sirocco-like desert wind from the south.

Instead of the cool, moist freshness of winter mornings, Jerusalem's brilliant dawns were now dry, hot, and oppressive. This morning the usual gentle and swift lifting of night's silence had been greeted with the swelling roar of wide-eyed pilgrims pressing through the city's gates.

The eight-day Passover celebration brought excitement to a fever pitch inside the city each year—and thousands of visitors. Hebrews, Romans, Greeks, Egyptians, Syrians, and Galileans arrived from all parts of the world. Even Samaritans came when their clothes indicated they possessed sufficient gold and silver to allay Hebrew disrespect. Old hatreds, such as existed between Hebrews and Samaritans, always seemed to fade a bit when money was involved.

Merchants of every description, selling anything which could be carried, screeched their sales pitches into the faces of passersby. There seemed to be no lack of pilgrims willing to purchase anything which was for sale. Many had walked mile after scorching mile. All were either determined to cleanse their soul at the great temple or erase their debts at the expense of others. Each year the crowds came, and each year they left with the feeling that their goal had been met.

Atop Mount Moriah, known as the Holy Hill, which lay in the eastern part of the city, work was still under way on the huge temple of Herod Antipas. The awesome edifice, which many hoped would be a satisfactory replacement for the one designed by King David and built by his son Solomon was started by Herod the First, father of Antipas. During this particular week its priests would again become wealthier than the richest merchants in the land.

Each year at Pasah (the local name for the Passover season) pilgrims came to purchase favor from Yahweh through the bloody sacrifice of helpless, screaming goats, sheep, lambs, and birds. It was God's requirement that it be done, but with each bleat or scream of the sacrificial animals, which were slain in many sections of town, more gold and silver entered the already bloated temple coffers.

Like the holy men they were, and according to religious doctrine, the priests inspected each animal to insure its perfection before it was accepted for sacrifice. Like the good businessmen they were some of the priests found it convenient to discover blemishes of varying kinds in all of the animals not purchased from temple stock. The same priests were strangely blind to the imperfections in animals purchased from within the temple walls. In either case, with parts of the sacrifices available for their personal use, priests ate well.

For many months the temple hirelings had gathered and penned great quantities of animals and birds for this season. During this single week more than 250,000 hapless creatures would scream their lives away—throats cut,

10

fulfilling a promise made centuries before by Abraham, ancestor of the Jews. Animal blood would run so thick that, in the main temple, deep grooves had to be carved in the marble floors. Through these grooves a red stream flowed out special holes cut through the temple wall. Night and day it gushed into the Kidron Valley below.

The chief priest, Caiaphas, who frequently paced along the upper balcony of the temple, had long looked forward to Pasah. In these days he would become rich. Today, however, he was not on the balcony looking contemptuously down on the people. Instead, before dawn, resplendent in his tasseled robe with the delicate tinkling of tiny silver bells sounding from the hem, Caiaphas walked along the damp floor of the subterranean treasury room, which ran the length of the temple. He had come to inspect the piles of money bags stacked and waiting along the dank walls. As he checked the small sacks, he frowned and thought, *It is wrong that I, Caiaphas, priest of all of Israel's children, should be limited to a single annual reaping of my golden harvest. Why must I wait for this holy week each year to gain what should be mine— while that pig, Herod, gathers a daily fortune? He commands but three territories and I am the spiritual leader of all the Jews.*

Despite the disadvantage of gaining most of his wealth during only eight days each year, Caiaphas compensated by arranging to take as much money from the pilgrims as possible and as fast as the flexible law would allow. Caiaphas not only sucked dry the people in Jerusalem, but he had Pharisees in many countries doing the same there, and each of them sent tribute to the wily chief priest's treasury. For this brief but heavy rush of incoming coins, many arrangements had to be made.

In past years Annas, the dried-up, but still powerful

11

former chief priest, who was Caiaphas' father-in-law, had failed to have a sufficient number of money bags for the Passover collection. Because of this, Annas had stored thousands of coins in unsealed earthen pots each year. Caiaphas, then an upcoming priest, had frequently "borrowed" what his fellow priests jokingly referred to as "holy money for holy men for holy causes" from the open pots. Over the years Caiaphas and the other priests had relieved Annas of whole purses of gold and silver shekels, as well as coins from as far away as Rome itself.

As he picked up first one empty bag, then another, tugging at their stubborn seams as he went, Caiaphas smiled. Throughout the winter he had two eunuch slaves, provided from among Queen Herodias' personal attendants, cut and sew money bags made from the scrotums of gelded camels and specially tanned for this purpose. Caiaphas even arranged to have far more than his share of these bags affixed with the royal Roman seal. He did this because it meant guaranteed safety from the limber fingers of his fellow priests. To steal anything under the imperial seal was to invite a lifetime chained to a galley oar. Further, he arranged for Roman soldiers to move the heavy bags from the temple to his summer home, which was just outside the country village of Geba. Caiaphas, a deep smirk now on his face, was ready for the riches he knew would come.

In the heart of the holy city, Passover noise blared like the king's trumpets—first rising to a dull roar, then subsiding, only to rise again to a new and louder level. Day by day, as the crowds grew, the city's noise level grew also.

Adding to the din of the excited visitors were the monotone screeches of vendors. As they tried to out-scream and out-lie each other, the vendors worked from any space they could find—small shops, back packs, from baskets at their feet, or even from baskets teetering on their heads.

For visitors with money there were thin loaves of tough bread, dates, olives, incense, goat and sheep meat cooked in hot oil, wines of all qualities, dried fish, or water by the cup.

Along most of the city's walls sat beggars, each with his or her own affliction and plaintive wail, but all filthy and strangely alike. The bent limbs, sores, missing eyes, and other deformities were all displayed at best advantage for begging and gaining the sympathy necessary for generous donations. Frequently the "blind" glanced at their bowls to check how lucrative the day was, or the ones with sores sneaked a dirty finger to their open wounds long enough to scratch away scabs to insure a colorful display of blood. This too was an annual part of Holy Week.

The squeals of darting, dusty children playing tag and shouting insults at passersby sliced through the street noises. Many of these lice-ridden urchins were abandoned or orphaned. Others, although no cleaner than their companions, were from established families. Whether they were from warm, loving homes or the cold, uncompromising streets, life at this time of year was demanding. All of them were caught up in the electric excitement of Passover.

°   °   °

Dismas, choked by a swallow of spit which accidentally went down his windpipe, coughed noisily before drunkenly falling to one side. In doing so, he bumped against his companion, knocking him over onto his face without waking him.

"Oooh," Dismas groaned, clenching his eyes tightly together, hoping the racking, throbbing pain in his head would quit.

The man now lying on his face was young, well muscled, and obviously strong. He too was a thief—Dismas' student. His skin, which was naturally light in color, was made even more pallid in appearance by the black beard, moustache, and hair, which covered his head and face.

Dismas was older. He too had dark hair, but unlike his companion, Dismas' hair was flecked with silver.

The older thief's knees slowly rose upward and he allowed his head to droop onto his arms, which were gently folded across his knees.

Both men had been riotously drunk the night before and had sat against the wall since being dumped there by Aram.

Dismas knew by the swelling on the side of his head that he had either been in a fight, or Aram, as usual, had enlisted the aid of several of his stronger patrons to beat him into unconsciousness. He concluded that both of these probabilities were wrong, since his companion appeared to be equally drunk and was unmarked. As his head whirled faster and faster, Dismas gave his injuries no more thought. Instead, he slipped back into oblivion.

Hours passed, but the air of Aram's inn was still foul. It smelled of soured wine and stale smoke. An even worse odor, that of long-unwashed bodies and vomited wine, rose from the awakening pair of men. Their smell and ruthless reputations caused other patrons to sit as far from them as possible.

The older man snorted sharply, startling his companion. As soon as the sound's effect faded, Dismas slowly lifted his head, his face pinched by pain. His clamped eyelids looked like the skin of a prune in the

14

dim light of the inn. Tiny crusts of dirt flaked loose from his nose as he wrinkled it, trying to keep the pounding in his head under control.

As Dismas stirred gently, the younger man, with a grunt, pushed himself off the dusty floor and into an upright, but still seated position. Caleb had not yet opened his eyes. He sat resting his head against the cool mud wall, his face taking on the relaxed appearance of someone in a gentle sleep.

Caleb slowly rolled his head toward Dismas. The exaggerated gentleness of the move gave the impression that any quick movement might cause his neck to crumble and drop his head from his shoulders. When his face finally completed the turn, tiny wrinkles appeared around eyes which had opened as nearly unnoticeable slits.

"Are you alive?" Caleb inquired thickly, his voice stringy and harsh. His tone indicated he did not necessarily expect an answer. Without waiting, and with another equally gentle move, he closed his eyes and rolled his head back until he was once more resting it against the wall, his face toward the ceiling again.

The older man, hearing his friend's voice, grunted, but did not relax his heavy squint until his head was fully tilted toward the sound. Then he opened his red, watery eyes. As he blankly stared at his young student, his face relaxed. Without thinking, he stuck his tongue out to lick his parched lips. Instantly the squint reappeared. Like a fish, he began opening and closing his mouth, making smacking sounds as he tasted the slime which coated his mouth and tongue.

Weakly, as if all strength was gone, he raised a bruised, scraped, and limp right hand as he loudly mumbled, "Aram, bring *yayin* before we die," then dropped his seemingly dead arm into the dirt. The foul-smelling

15

thief, in his pain, had used the Judean word for wine rather than the more common Roman *vinum*. Roman soldiers, demanding wine all over the world in their native Latin, had made the word vinum widely understood, but also widely hated by the Jews.

Aram, a Syrian from Cadasa, wore the dress of the Hebrews, but shaved his head as did the Egyptians. He did these things because he did not overlook the smallest detail which could earn him financial favor from any quarter. Hearing the call for wine from the two drunken thieves, he looked toward them in disgust and snorted half through his nose and half through his mouth. He retreated through the much scarred doorway and soon reappeared with two huge earthen cups of frothy, fermented wine. Instead of delivering it himself, which he felt to be beneath his position as owner of the inn, he jerked his head toward the servant girl, who obediently took the wine and glided toward the smelly pair.

Dismas was around forty-five years old, but the blackness of his hair, despite the gray now starting to show, made him appear younger than his years. He had young ideas too. His face and hands were pocked by many tiny scars, souvenirs of the warfare of lust. His fights came from a too deep love of wine and a somewhat lessened involvement with headstrong women, who felt payment for their favors should be a thing of the night, and not of the next day, or next week.

Dismas always discovered the damage from his fights the morning after each encounter. He vaguely remembered most of them. Sometimes he recognized that he had been fighting through aches, pains, and blood on his woolen cloak. At other times, when the damage was less and he had a full night's sleep, he was told by his woman of the moment. After many years of tavern brawling with men and waking to find a strange woman sleeping next to him, Dismas had learned that many women equated bravery with the amount of damage done. For this reason, the more enthusiastically the women spoke of his bravery, the more desperate and determined Dismas was to check for wounds.

Aram's servant girl, Miriam, was Dismas' friend and his most severe feminine critic. She seemed to delight in telling him, when he suffered most, that had he remained conscious but few minutes more, instead of being instantly bludgeoned into insensibility by a Phoenician galley timer, who disliked being called a webfooted boat herder, his appearance might have been altered enough to be acceptable. Ridiculing him seemed, to Dismas, to be Miriam's favorite pastime.

Regardless of the damage, comments of supposed friends, or soreness, Dismas would flex his limbs, examine his torso for punctures, then laugh uproariously before exclaiming, "I must have had a wonderful time last night."

This particular day was not one for drinking, but for work. The two men, both suffering severely from sluggishness and headaches, drank their cup of wine to steel themselves for what they knew lay ahead. In their line of work they needed a clear head, a steady hand, fleet feet, and glib tongues. Dismas and his young protégé were not just ordinary thieves, but the master thieves of Jerusalem. They had a reputation to uphold.

Passover was the highest of the religious holy days celebrated in Jerusalem. It honored an event more than three hundred years before which had saved the Hebrews from the Egyptians. It recalled how Moses led God's children out of Egypt after the death angel had respected the gory signs left outside all homes of the

17

faithful. In the middle of Pharaoh's mistreatment of them, Moses said that an angel was coming to destroy the firstborn of all living creatures in the land, but would not enter the homes which had a lamb's blood smeared above the doors. Just as God had promised, it happened. That night echoes of mourning came from all parts of Egypt—even the palace of Pharaoh was not spared.

Now, centuries later, the occasion was still celebrated, but as had happened to so many other religious holidays, commercialism gripped the holy and revered city and its citizens. It clouded the actual meaning of the festivities. In their urge to celebrate, many of the people involved remembered to enjoy the special day—but forgot why.

The pilgrims, rich and poor, came each year. Most of them had saved their money throughout the year and their purses were fat with the coins needed to cover expenses for weeks of traveling and food and lodging.

Beggars, prostitutes, thieves, merchants, and a multitude of scoundrels in a variety of deceptive businesses had also come. These men and women did not have religion in mind; they were in Jerusalem to relieve the pilgrims of the burden of their hard-earned money. For Dismas and Caleb it was the season to harvest that which had never been planted.

As the two men sipped their wine, both of them dreaded the hour when they must leave their cool mud wall and enter the heat and noise of the street. As they sat quietly, waiting for the pounding in their heads to subside, Caleb finally raised his cup and motioned it toward the door.

"You know, Dismas. Those stupid people out there come here every year. Some travel for weeks just to celebrate something about which they know little, if anything at all."

"Unh-hunh," Dismas grunted, agreeing without interest.

"They are not even sure when or where it happened in Egypt."

"Unh-hunh," Dismas again agreed.

After a short silence, Caleb snorted, "They can't even name a single kinsman spared by that so-called 'death angel,' which no one ever saw."

Dismas did not bother to respond. His head hurt too badly.

"Imagine!" Caleb paused, then gently shook his head as if he were thinking of something which needed pitying. "Imagine celebrating being alive." Caleb drank deeply from his cup.

The young man's last remark had struck a minor chord in Dismas. The older man turned toward his friend and, as he carefully picked his nose, asked, "What's so unusual about that?" He examined the end of his finger before wiping it on his cloak. "If I'd been spared from death, I'd celebrate the day too."

Caleb, seeing he finally had Dismas' attention, took advantage of it to press on. He squinted his eyes slightly as he stared at the closed door, looking as if he could see through it.

"Spared from what, Dismas?" Caleb let his question settle slowly on his friend. Timing it so he would not lose his lead, Caleb snapped his face toward Dismas and allowed fire to enter his eyes.

"Roman soldiers swarm through our land. They demand taxes for every product and every job we do and what do we get for our money? Nothing!"

Caleb saw that Dismas could not disagree with him so he raised the level of his voice a little and continued. "No, we do get one thing for our taxes—more Romans.

We also get higher taxes the next year and less of every-thing else, unless you want to count a few useless aque-ducts in places where the Romans want water." Caleb spat between his feet. "If God had intended water there, He would have planted springs."

"Yes, but. . . ." Dismas was about to ask what all that had to do with the Passover, the pilgrims, and to point out that the Romans, with their laws, had made the Jews easy prey for thieves, such as themselves. But Caleb, still a little drunk, would not be so easily interrupted.

"Hear me out, Dismas. The Romans not only infest every part of our lives, except our useless religion—they even named our last three kings."

Dismas suddenly came wide-awake. Mention of the king in any way other than favorably could be very dan-gerous. He quickly looked around the smoky room to see if hostile ears were listening. The inn's only other cus-tomers were departing. Only Aram and his servant girl remained, so he did not bother to muzzle his friend.

"Herod and his family turn our own people against us by making them tax collectors. They relieve us of our own law. They even bring graven images into this holy city." Caleb had suddenly become piously indignant too.

"That was just Pilate," Dismas retorted.

"True, but what the Romans don't steal from us, their royal jackals, the Herods, do."

"Watch your tongue, Caleb," Aram warned from across the room. "If the wrong person hears you, you will quickly gain an intimate acquaintance with Roman law and justice. If not Roman, Herod's." Aram laughed loudly at his own words.

"Don't associate Roman law with justice," Caleb shouted at the still-smiling innkeeper.

"Enough," Dismas bellowed as he climbed to his feet.

20

Once up and balanced, he stretched his arms widely and emitted a roaring yawn. "We should be on our way."

Caleb looked up at him, his face plainly showing that he did not like the idea. He made no move to rise. "I still say, these pilgrims are stupid to feel they are spared." He drained his cup. Caleb knew he was about to anger his friend, but since there was no one in the inn, and Dismas had not started to leave, he continued, "Just think, Dismas, Romans take most of what we have for that pig in Rome. And Herod, the king inflicted on us, takes half to build a temple which will only steal from our people for all time to come." Caleb violently jabbed his finger toward the ceiling and shouted, "We can't even call our souls our own!"

Dismas grabbed the pointing finger and pulled his friend to his feet. "Stop your confounded shouting," he grumbled. Once he had Caleb on his feet and stood facing him, Dismas began tapping a taunting forefinger against the younger man's chest. "Do you go to the temple to worship? No! Do you pay the Roman taxes about which you complain? No! Do you pay taxes to Herod? No! Do you even have a soul to claim as your own? I doubt it." Dismas took a deep breath. "I do know something you have and use too much—your big mouth!" With that Dismas turned to leave, but hesitated long enough to spit out, "Besides, if you do have a soul, you probably stole it from someone."

At that Caleb broke into a gale of laughter. Dismas smiled wryly as he turned toward his friend. "Caleb, we have had the Romans longer than I have lived—the Herods also." Shrugging his shoulders, Dismas lifted his eyebrows and nodded his head as he mused, "Who knows. Maybe this is because we Jews are not able to rule ourselves."

"That's not true and you know it," Caleb snapped. Dismas had touched a tender spot and it was Caleb's turn to complain again. "Saul ruled our people, as did David and Solomon and Josiah and Hezekiah and many others."

Just to irritate his young, and now incensed friend, Dismas facetiously said, "True, but who among them was as powerful as Rome? Who have we today who could bring pilgrims to Jerusalem as do the Herods and their obedient priests?"

Having caught the joking tone of Dismas' voice, Caleb again chuckled, clapped the older man on the shoulder, and roared, "You're right, oh rabboni of thievery. We have all been spared by the love and benevolence of Rome, the Herods, and the most holy priests—each selected for power by the other." Caleb laughed so hard at his joke he rocked back.

As the laughter faded, both men steadied themselves, then weaved toward the door which led to the street. As they made their way among the stools and benches, Aram, who had returned to his place by the kitchen door, slipped in front of the pair. He stood wordlessly, his hand upturned and outstretched. Dismas, now but inches away from Aram, looked blankly at the palm of the dirty hand. His eyes slowly met those of the innkeeper.

"I suppose you want four coppers for our drinks?"

Aram did not answer, a wet smile plastered on his mouth. His eyes were narrow black slits. The greasy innkeeper knew Dismas was dangerous and not to be angered, but Aram also knew his inn was one of the few in the city still open to the two rowdy thieves. He chanced upsetting Dismas by flatly stating, "No, I don't want four coppers. I ask fourteen silver shekels for your night's drinking." He lowered his voice to add, "If you

want, I will accept fifty drachmas or fifty denarii."
Aram's alternate offer was of no benefit, since fifty
drachmas or denarii were of the same value as fourteen
silver shekels.

Dismas was about to object, but Aram quickly added,
"And you still owe Miriam."

The innkeeper nodded toward his busy servant girl. "I
doubt if either of you remember, but both of you used
her last night." A sneer came to the fleshy mouth of the
Syrian. His eyes darted from Dismas to Caleb as he
continued, "First you, then you."

"Both of us?" Dismas asked, hoping the innkeeper
would deny it.

"Both of you."

Caleb, his feelings hurt more by having been second
with Miriam's favors than by the absurdity of the situation, countered, "Didn't she object to such an arrangement?"

"Not when each of you offered a silver mina."

"A silver mina!" thundered Dismas. "Why I would
not pay that for ten women, much less for a public
wench." As he spat out the last statement he jerked his
arm up to point at the now glaring Miriam. When she
saw that her two customers might leave without settling
their account with her, she ran across the room screaming, "Pay me, you lusty goats. Pay me! Pay me!"

Acting out of instinct, Dismas snatched his purse from
his girdle with his left hand and stuffed it into the waiting hand of Aram. In the same movement, his right hand
shot back, grasped Caleb's sleeve, and the two men
bolted for the door. As they dashed into the noise, dust,
and the heat of the day, they faintly heard the crash of a
wine cup as it shattered against the wall near the door.

Caleb groaned as he thought of the wine which might

have been in the cup. "I hope it was empty," he said. Caleb's respect for the blood of the grape was too much for Dismas.

Although he had run only a few strides from the inn door, Dismas stopped and, in spite of the painful throbbing still pounding inside his head, leaned against a wall to laugh. Strangers in the street stopped to stare at what they presumed to be a madman. They saw a vomit-caked man, his hair and beard matted in great, twisted strands, holding his stomach with one hand and his head with the other. They heard him laugh as only a madman would. Soon his mirth gave way to a gurgling "Huuch, huuch," as Dismas began to spew out his excesses of the night before.

Caleb and Dismas made no effort to cleanse themselves—partly from laziness and partly from their knowledge that an unkempt appearance was a natural disguise. Dirt, they had both learned, was an excellent cover for scars and other identifying marks. Additionally, most of the people of Jerusalem's streets looked much like them in dress, color, and appearance. All looked as though they had rolled in the city's dirt—and many had.

Despite their appearances, Dismas and Caleb were talented. Dismas was not only an accomplished thief in his own right, but was a teacher of thieves. For this reason, Caleb frequently called him "rabboni" (a more honorary term than "rabbi"), which was reserved for only the most respected teachers.

Caleb was not just Dismas' friend, but was his most receptive and proficient student. Caleb believed himself to be a master thief. Since his childhood, when Dismas bought him out of the pitlike prison into which his mother had sold him, Caleb had remained at Dismas' side.

To the aging thief, his purchase of the skinny boy from the prison keeper was just a case of a heavy drinker wanting someone to look after him when wine had relieved him of the ability to think or stand alone. At the time of the purchase, he reasoned that if he had a strong young boy on whom to lean, and who would see him to a warm, dry spot before he fell to harm, things would be a lot better.

In reality, Caleb's mother had not sold him into prison, as he repeatedly claimed. Dismas knew the boy was the result of a commercial union of two unknown night people. He knew Caleb had spent his entire childhood with his wits for a father and the streets as his mother. His jail sentence, when Dismas purchased him, came when the boy was caught stealing food. Caleb, knowing his new master was a great thief, always felt that any admission of being captured while stealing would lower him in the eyes of Dismas, so through the years he stuck to his story.

As the vomiting stopped and the pair recovered from the fit of laughter brought on by Caleb's concern over the wine which might have been in the cup Miriam had thrown at them, they moved on. If there was to be any sanctuary in Aram's inn later, they would have to pay the price asked by the owner and his serving maid. Worse yet, Dismas did not know if the purse he passed to Aram contained money or not. If not, the financial injury they inflicted on Aram and Miriam was compounded. It was obvious to the men that the most direct solution to their problem would be to "borrow" what they needed as soon as possible.

It was the third hour and already an abnormal heat had settled over the city and suffocated its streets. Dust was being kicked up by hundreds of feet shuffling through the streets. It hung in the air, untouched by even the most gentle breeze, choking everyone.

Taking long strides, even through the thin crowds on a street which ran up and down hill, the pair quickly made their way to the Pool of Siloam, built years before by King Hezekiah as a water source during a siege of the city. They knew that caravans of wealthy merchants arriving for the Passover would be filling their waterskins after having spent the night outside the high walls and locked gates. Caravans headed for surrounding countries with wares from Judea would also be filling their waterskins.

As the pair turned the corner to enter the street which led directly to the pool, they were forced to leap back out of the path of a string of heavily ladened camels.

Disgruntled, Dismas and Caleb impatiently watched the plodding, bulky animals pad along, each camel's lower lip quivering with every step. Some of the beasts rhythmically dropped dung onto the streets while others grunted and belched bile from their stomachs, their contributions adding to the vile odors already in the air. Dismas knew the answer to the question, "Why do camel drivers all walk barefoot." Camel droppings, and the driver's disdain for them, argued against wearing expensive shoes or sandals.

As the two men waited for the camel train to pass, a finely dressed big-boned, darkskinned Hittite approached. He walked beside the caravan.

The Hittite's shouting at the camel drivers clearly identified him as their leader. From his walk—the throwing of his legs outward and the frequent jerking shifting of his buttocks as he came—Dismas and Caleb assumed his ride had been long and extremely uncomfortable. Other signs were also apparent to the thieves' experienced eyes. The size of the purse swinging from the Hittite's belt said none of the drivers, herders, or bearers had yet been paid. Dismas and Caleb decided that none would be.

Caleb dropped back several steps into the side street, where he and Dismas had retreated from the camels. As the Hittite neared Dismas, Caleb, coming at a full run, darted past the older thief and slammed clumsily into the caravan leader.

When the two men collided, the suspicious Hittite caravan leader whirled, grabbed Caleb with one hand, and with his other hand felt for his purse. Having assured the safety of his money, the big man released the purse to grasp Caleb with both massive fists. As he cursed the young thief, the Hittite shook him as a dog would shake a rag. His head jerking back and forth, Caleb, in his most humble Hebrew, tried to gasp out an apology directed at the Hittite, his family, his ancestors, and even to his men and camels.

Dismas, as if just another member of the forming crowd, stepped up to watch the beating everyone assumed was sure to follow. Instead of just watching, however, with the speed of a striking cobra, his hand darted under the big Hittite's muscled arm and, in a single flowing move, removed the heavy purse and stuffed it inside his own cloak. As soon as the bulging moneybag touched the tender skin under his arm, Dismas put his other hand in the small of the back of a man standing next to him and shoved. A look of surprise appeared on the innocent bystander's face as he hurtled headlong into the now furious Hittite caravan leader.

With a roar, the big man dropped the hapless Caleb, who was totally aware of every move which had taken place. When the big Hittite whirled to face what he believed to be a new assailant, Caleb shot between the legs of nearby onlookers, jumped to his feet, and with a yell ran in the opposite direction from that being taken by Dismas, who was several hundred feet away by the time Caleb disappeared into the crowd.

Instinctively the Hittite again felt for his purse. Just as his eyes snapped to the part of his belt where the missing moneybag had hung, he heard Caleb's yell. He instantly tried to push through the crowd, but by the time he roughly shoved his way through the complaining men, women, and children, all of whom were disappointed that no fight had taken place, Caleb's young legs had proved their value. He had not only bolted more than forty feet from the Hittite, but by turning his dirty back on the big man, he was only one of dozens of other dirty backs shuffling through Jerusalem's main streets.

Twenty minutes later, at the door which led from the street into Aram's inn, the pair of successful thieves met to share nervous laughter and begin complimenting each other on their performances.

"Ah, my little fox, not only were you convincing in your act of fear in the face of the camel driver, the way you ran told me that what you did was no act," said Dismas. He clutched the swollen purse against his side with his right hand and wiped sweat and spit from the corner of his mouth with the other. A grin covered his face.

"Fear?" Caleb questioned in mock indignity. "Fear, you say? Was it not I who faced that demon eye to eye? Was it not I who led him from the thief he could so easily have squashed? Fear? Dismas, I risked my neck to save you and you don't even recognize my bravery."

Dismas' eyes rolled upward as Caleb's reference to bravery reminded him of their coming trial. "Speaking of bravery, as you do," the older man said, "I . . . I think it

28

is time we faced our biggest test of the day."

"What do you mean, Dismas?"

"Aram and Miriam."

Caleb smacked his lips when the subject was mentioned. Almost immediately he pressed his lips tightly together as his eyes looked toward the inn's door. He sighed, "I guess you're right. We'll still have a roof over our heads if they give us a chance to heap gold or silver in their hands. If they don't, well, we'll be orphaned again."

Without further delay the two men nudged the rough-hewn door open, stepped into the darkness, and quickly shut it behind them.

Coming from the burning brightness of the sun, they might as well have been blind. As they groped their way toward their favorite spot near the back wall of the familiar room, Aram spotted them.

"You damned among the damned! Get out of here! Begone, vermin, you scum of Jerusalem!" Aram's voice roared like a freshly castrated bull camel. Before the irate innkeeper could shove them onto the street, Dismas pulled the bulging brown moneybag from his cloak and held it high above his head. He could still only see little more than the faint outlines of a few objects, all of which were slashed through with the silver bars of sunshine which gouged its way through cracks and was accentuated by the smoke which hung in the air. Dismas knew Aram would see the moneybag. He also knew that even if Aram could not see it, he would surely smell it. Not a single wedge of a coin entered the inn without Aram's knowledge.

As the purse in Dismas' hand swung around the thief's wrist, Aram's screaming stopped as suddenly as it had begun. In its place, the pair heard him give orders to

Miriam to pour three of the inn's largest cups of wine and bring them to the back table.

As their eyes became accustomed to the dingy room, Dismas and Caleb strode to the back of the room and sat down, allowing the purse to slam heavily on the thick, heavy tabletop. Since they had no idea how much money was in the bag, they quickly stretched open the neck of the pouch and poured its contents out noisily. As the coins rolled around, a startled Caleb whistled softly and reached out to catch a coin which was about to fall off the wooden slab.

Reacting from instinct, just as his friend's arm quickly stretched out, Dismas' had streaked out slamming Caleb's hand hard onto the unyielding top. Both men gasped slightly and withdrew their hands. Dismas' eyes darted to Caleb's hurt face and back down at the money before grunting what passed for an apology.

Turning again to their new wealth, both men noticed there were several gold pieces among the small pile of Hebrew and foreign coins. His voice barely above a whisper, Caleb said, "Dismas, look at that. I see Babylonian shekels, two Phoenician tetradrachmas, some gold shekels, and twenty or thirty silver minas. Dismas!" Caleb shouted as a grin spread across his young face, "We're rich!" His uncontrolled shout in the quiet of the public inn returned common sense to the furtive conversation.

"It is true, Caleb, but do you notice anything strange about all this?" Dismas hissed.

"The only thing odd about it I see is that we have a larger fortune than we usually get."

"Of all the money we took from the Hittite, there is not a single Hittite wedge among them. We have coins from three countries, but not a single coin of the land of the man from whom we took it." Both men puzzled over this.

Just as they began to count the coins, the thieves heard the soft pad of Aram's footsteps. The nature of their livelihood had sharpened their hearing to a keenness not known by most men. They had heard Aram, despite his walking barefoot on a dirt floor. Since they were unable to hide the coins, both men leaned back and turned to face the innkeeper. Aram's smile was at its widest, which allowed the gaping hole on the left side of his upper teeth to show, along with one in the middle of his lower teeth. Dismas held back a grin. He had removed Aram's upper tooth during a night of trying to prove his manhood by challenging all patrons of the inn to a fight. No one dared undertake the task, so Aram, with all good intentions had walked up to Dismas to invite him to drink instead of fighting. Dismas had not given the innocent innkeeper time to make the offer. Snatching a nearby stool, he had smashed it soundly across the Syrian's face, instantly removing the tooth and leaving him unconscious.

"My friends," Aram beamed, his eyes never leaving the pile of coins on the table. "I pray you did not take my childish fit of misunderstanding seriously. Even as you closed the door this morning, Miriam and I were sorry we had screamed at you so. No sooner had the door closed than she all but burst into tears for the way she had treated her two. . . ." Aram's voice quieted into a tone of confidence as he chuckled the way a man would do when sharing an intimate secret with a close friend. "Heh, heh . . . her two nearest and dearest friends." Aram emphasized the words "nearest and dearest."

As he talked, Miriam, still unsmiling, walked up with three cups of wine. As she put them on the table she saw the money too. Her black eyes flashed up to Aram's, and

31

a wide smile spread across her face.

"Yes, you slut among whores," Dismas taunted. "You will have your money, and now." He started counting the smaller coins as he asked, "How much do you say we owe you?"

Miriam's eyes jerked back and forth as she watched Dismas' hand sort out the various coins. "It was—four silver minas," the teasing girl exaggerated without hesitation.

"You lie," Dismas said as he fished four silver coins from the table and tossed them into the air for the girl to catch. Dismas knew she was not telling the truth, but he understood and appreciated her gall. Had she told him two minas, as had been the original agreement, he was prepared to argue the point. "Now you," Dismas said as he turned to look sideways and up at Aram. "How much do you say we owe you?"

"I did not keep close count last night," the whining man said, "but I know the amount was very, very much. Possibly more than you now have on this table. . . ."

"Now wait, you flea-covered jackal," said Dismas in protest. "We do not mind being robbed, for that is part of life, but to try to take our skin as well is beyond my patience."

Caleb directed his attention to his wine cup. Between deep swallows of the cool, stinging drink Caleb glanced askance from the corner of his eye to examine the figure of Miriam as she weaved around the room picking up cups, stacking them unwashed along one wall to be used again.

Returning to the matter at hand, Caleb's attention was drawn to the animated conversation continuing across the table from him.

"All right, you–you swine-loving Syrian, take all the

money, but remember one thing." Dismas did not continue until he grabbed the front of Aram's tunic and yanked his face to within inches of his own. Even then, he growled, "If we ever . . . until our dying day . . . come to you for help, or to be hidden, and you so much as wave away a fly before you jump to assist us, I will personally reach my fingers in and rip your eyes from their sockets and squash them like grapes. Do you understand?" As he spoke the last three words, Dismas tightened his grip on the tunic, twisting it until it choked the greasy innkeeper.

"Yes, gracious one," choked Aram. "I fully understand. Have no fear, it will be as you say. You are more than generous."

"Come, Caleb," Dismas said, not bothering to hide the revulsion he felt. "Let's get out of here before I vomit into perfectly good wine." As the pair headed for the door, Caleb smiled as he saw Miriam look first at her coins, then at him. Instead of returning his suggestive smile, Miriam pursed her lips and threw him a kiss.

Miriam was in her mid-twenties, but the hard life she lived made her look much older. She kept her inviting figure hidden beneath the loose-fitting feminine Hebrew tunic, but Caleb knew it well. He knew her breasts did not sag, but were like fully ripe pears. However, her slightly overwide hips confessed of children she had borne, but never raised. Miriam was one of many such women in Jerusalem. Scorned by everyone, she and her sisters of circumstance were kept as necessities, as were the dogs which roamed the city's streets at night consuming carrion.

The Miriams of Jerusalem pacified the animal lusts which dwelt in soldiers, thieves, and other unscrupulous men of the city, keeping harm from the city's high-bred ladies. To men like Aram, such women attracted money-laden men. To goldsmiths and silversmiths, these women were purchasers of rings, bracelets, and dowry coins—a source of great profit.

They were forbidden to improve themselves, worship God in the temples, or even obtain their water from public wells during the cool morning or evening hours when "respectable women" filled their jars. None of the city's citizens would recommend that these women stay, but none would even hint that they leave.

Miriam was different from most of the night ladies. She shared her favors just as they did, but to her it was not a cold affair. She either had a genuine fondness for her customers, or they were not customers. In Dismas and Caleb, her attraction came from a respect for their free spirit. Not only were these two thieves free of the suffocating laws which bound Judea, they were free of giving respect to the undeserving. Miriam felt that through Dismas and Caleb she contributed to the withholding of a measure of comfort to people who had enjoyed comfort unjustly all of their lives. It was her way of striking out at the rich and the Romans.

From the commercial side, Miriam knew she would always receive a fair price from Dismas and Caleb, no matter how long it took them to pay. For thieves, and in their own peculiar way, Dismas and Caleb were very honest.

From the customer's standpoint, the pair of thieves made a point of complaining about Miriam's heartlessness. They could not acknowledge, even to each other, that she was probably the one person in Jerusalem to whom they could turn when there was no other. They knew that whether they had money or not, Miriam would provide a warm bed and a cup of wine.

Both men saw her in the double image of a friend and a partner in lust, but they felt a real affection for her in

34

both roles. Dismas, when in the depths of loneliness, or when he doubted his waning manhood, turned only to Miriam. After they had enjoyed each other's bodies, and as his strength returned, Dismas had more than once told her, "Miriam, if I were sentenced to spend all my days with but one person, it would be with you." These words, from Dismas, were more than complimentary. Miriam knew she had the nearest thing to love that Dismas was capable of giving.

Caleb, on the other hand, saw her primarily as an older woman and regarded her as he would a cup of good wine—something to be consumed and paid for—little more, nothing less.

As the men were about to open the door, Miriam put her hand against it and held it shut. Close enough to be heard only by them, she whispered, "You two have bragged of your ability to steal a wart from the face of the high priest. Now I no longer doubt it."

Aware that Miriam was courting Aram's displeasure by talking with them in the drinking room, Caleb smiled at the girl, but murmured to Dismas, "You see, my friend, our severest critic recognizes our prowess." Dismas gave him a look of mock anger as Caleb continued, "She knows that in bed you have all but lost your touch, but as a thief your hands prove you are still the master."

"What do you say, you worthless scum? In bed I satisfied her before you even approached her. With the Hittite you were little more than a diversion for my work of art."

Caleb was stung gently by both statements because he knew they were true. To get even with Dismas, without seriously hurting his feelings, the younger man quickly glanced at the girl, but retorted to Dismas, "All of that is true, Miriam, but I did it in the tradition of a faithful

Jew—in deference to the elderly."

"Liar!" Dismas flung back, shattering the quiet. He quickly lowered his voice to a whisper again, "Caleb, I will admit you are a good thief, if you will admit my ability as a lover has not yet departed." He showed his teeth as his gray-splashed beard parted in a smile.

"Done," Caleb conceded.

Miriam, afraid the men would leave, and not wanting them to go, motioned for them to sit at a nearby table. "I will bring another cup of wine," she tempted.

Since the heat of the day held no enticement for them, the men sat down.

When she returned, and had set the two tall cups on the table, Miriam picked up a small three-legged stool. With the grace of a woman in her ninth month of pregnancy, she fell on it, knees spread wide. As she did so, she said, "If I were a master thief, such as you, I would go out there," she jerked her head toward the door, and gather a fortune." A slight frown crossed her face and she bit her lip before adding, "I don't know—it is Passover and possibly an unlucky time for such things."

"Unlucky? Woman, of what do you speak? No time is 'unlucky' when it comes to gathering money," rebuked Dismas gently. "Passover festivities last a full week and, unlike farmers, we harvest best at this time." He added, "Well, not exactly at this time of day. In the mornings people are too alert, so night is best for us." Thinking about this, Dismas made a decision.

"I'm not talking about the usual Passover," Miriam explained. "Just this one is unusual. Have you not heard that the greatest prophet since Isaiah is coming to the city?"

"Do you speak of that small-town carpenter who has the priests so angry?" Caleb asked.

36

"I hear he will be here today—with hundreds, even thousands of followers," the girl said. With an enthusiasm the two men had never seen before in Miriam, she continued, "I also hear he teaches a whole new idea of what religion should be. Dismas, Caleb," Tears welled up in her eyes and her voice softened. "He even holds out hope for me—and for you too," she added.

"I'll bet the priests appreciate that." Dismas snickered. To punctuate his statement he followed it by barking out a single, humorless "Ha!"

"Yes," Caleb added, "I'll bet those pious heaven merchants up on the hill enjoy someone telling them that they have been spreading the wrong line all the time."

"Oh, no," Miriam defended. "It is not that way at all. Jesus doesn't say the old teaching was wrong. He just says that what once was, is now no longer necessary because it has been fulfilled. From what I hear, he may be the Messiah we have waited for who will free us from many of the things we have put up with for so long."

Dismas tugged at his beard thoughtfully, "Maybe she's right," he said. "With those thousands of followers, he could be the Messiah. But they may not be religious followers at all. Perhaps they're an army in disguise. Maybe he's coming to Jerusalem when both Herod and Pilate are in town for the festivities to overthrow the government."

"I doubt that," said Caleb. "From what I hear this carpenter teaches men to give up, not fight; to run, rather than resist; to quit, rather than do anything worthwhile. No, Dismas, this can't be the Messiah our people dream of."

"Oh, Caleb, how stupid can you be? Did we not fool the Hittite using a diversion? This Jesus may be doing the same thing."

"That could be true," conceded Caleb.

"Oh, you rascals," chided Miriam. "All you think of is fighting and war. You are like most men, all muscle and no feelings. Don't you see? If he brings hope for people like us. . . ." She pointed a forefinger first at Caleb, then Dismas, then allowed her hand to fall on her breast. "We are no longer condemned to despair. Jesus says God loves us. He will give us new life if we allow Him to change us."

"Woman," Dismas responded, "I cannot see this God these holy men speak of. He doesn't give me food, I steal it. He doesn't free me from the law which says I may be pressed to do anything a Roman says I must do. No, only a forceful person like Jesus Barabbas and his cutthroats can free me. Heaven is only what I make it—what I can touch, that which makes me happy, such as a full stomach, good wine, a loving woman. These are heaven."

"Do you really think so? What of when you die?" asked Miriam incredulously.

"I will simply be dead. I will exist no more. No one will care then, so why should I care now? Today I belong to myself. I am determined to find some measure of happiness while I can enjoy it. When I enter the grave, I will provide food for the worms. That's all."

"Oh, Dismas. Poor Dismas," Miriam whimpered as she looked down into her lap.

"Confound you, woman. Don't pity me when you don't know what you're talking about yourself. Tell that carpenter, if you see him, that if he will fight with his thousands, I will fight alongside him. Otherwise, tell him to keep one hand on his purse or, there too, I will join him—long enough to steal it." Dismas had enough of such talk. "In either case, with the followers you say he has, Caleb and I can stand by the gate and lift a thousand purses as they file into the city."

At this, Caleb's interest in the conversation picked up. "Yes, we can play the role of grape farmers with a new method of harvesting. Instead of us walking along rows of vines and picking the fruit, we will let the rows walk past us as we pluck them clean." Caleb began to chuckle.

"Miriam, stealing is an art to be practiced, much like the playing of the Hebron zither or the blowing of the ram's horn. An art, an art," Caleb said.

Miriam would not give up. "I hear this Jesus teaches that stealing is wrong—that poverty is better than wealth gained by theft."

"Then he's more stupid than I thought," Dismas challenged. "Or maybe he's just feebleminded. Either way, if his followers believe him, our job will be easy because they won't resist."

"Yes, foolish one. But if they have discarded all worldly goods, as he told them to do, what will there be for us to take?" Caleb now showed concern. "We rob from those who have much to take, not the poor. If they believe in poverty, why bother them?"

Dismas' brow furrowed. He could only nod in agreement.

"You may be right, Caleb. At least partly right. However, if his followers listen, but do not do as he says, it might be simple to relieve them of what they have kept for themselves."

"Perhaps, but that is yet to be seen," Caleb conceded. "There's another consideration, old thief. If he's, as some say, the Messiah. . . ."

"Yes," Miriam interrupted, "if he is really the Messiah, your act of stealing could bring a curse on us."

Dismas pinched up his face and weaved his head in frustration. "Not you too, Miriam," he admonished. "All

Judea seems to have suffered a measure of madness since this carpenter began performing his magic." Dismas' tone took on a sarcastic ring. "I'm anxious to see for myself what hold he has over so many people."

Angry at his having poked fun at her, Miriam taunted spitefully, "And how are you, a common gutter thief, so sure he is *not* all that they say he is?"

"Common gutter thief!" Dismas sputtered. "If he were the Messiah, would Pontius Pilate have his golden images in this holiest of cities? No! Would the Romans be walking our streets instead of fighting for survival along its walls? No! Would the Messiah be strolling through the land mingling with beggars, tax collectors, whores, and lepers? No! He would be at the head of the mightiest army ever seen, riding on a white stallion, indestructible." Dismas was so wound up the two listeners did not interrupt him. "The Messiah would command his men to put Roman heads on pikes along all Judean roads, instead of telling his followers to be— poor." Disgust filled Dismas' voice.

Miriam could stand no more. "Shut your hell-bound mouth before your serpent's tongue decides to bite you. I have heard him teach. Two years ago, north of here, I heard him and if he is not the Messiah that you expect, he is still a wonderful rabbi and does no harm. I heard it explained that he walks among the sinful and sick because it is they who need his help most."

Impulsively reaching out she grasped Dismas' hand before saying, "Oh, Dismas. He talked to *me* then. He did, really—and when he did, I knew there was hope for my soul; that I need not continue in sin. No one has to."

"Is that why you slept with Caleb and me last night?"

"Damn you, Dismas! I do what I do because I know of no other way. Jesus can teach me differently though. He can show me—or you, another way."

Caleb grinned and broke in, "Maybe I should cut this Jesus' throat before he talks us out of future nights of pleasure."

Before Caleb could turn his head from Dismas to Miriam, the girl snatched his wine cup and threw its contents into Caleb's face. He sputtered as he staggered to his feet. Both men bolted for the door. They had experienced Miriam's wrath before.

Once more outside the inn, the pair again squinted in the late morning sunlight.

"I hate that man," Dismas said idly.

"Man?" Caleb asked, wiping the wine from his face with the front of his cloak. "It's the woman in there who's face I'd like to smash. Which man do you mean—that Jesus you spoke of, or Aram?"

"Aram."

"If you hate him so, why did you give him all our money?"

"I did it because he said we would no longer be welcome there unless we made the nuisance of befriending thieves worth the risk."

Caleb was confused. "What if he did deny us use of the inn? There are other inns in the city."

"That is true, but Aram's is the only safe one—and the only one to befriend us. If he denied us, where would we go?" Dismas did not give his friend a chance to answer. "Besides, that's not the real question." Dismas began slowly shaking his head as he lamented, "Oh, the dishonesty in this wicked city."

"Thank God for that," Caleb mocked, a serious look on his face.

"What? Oh, yes," Dismas agreed. There was no zest in his voice.

As they turned to walk down the street, Caleb still wiped at the sticky wine on his face. Out of the corner of his eye, he saw Miriam standing in the doorway of the inn. "Miriam," he yelled, "I still think your loving is the best in the city, but your brains have turned to slop."

Instead of the uproar he expected from Miriam in response to his taunting, all he heard was Aram's laughter as it wafted into the street from deep inside the inn. Miriam simply shut the door.

The heat of the day had arrived. It was early afternoon and the two men sought what little relief they could find in the narrowing shade along one side of the street. It offered little, if any, respite from the glowing orb hanging brilliantly in the sky.

Before long, the two thieves found themselves muttering and shoving like the rest of the crowd. Accustomed to dark, quiet nights and the dim, sparsely patronized inn, they were irritated by the rudeness of those around them.

Several blocks from the inn, as they wandered south toward the city's Zion Gate, Dismas saw a skinny, withered merchant selling figs. The man leaned over one of the baskets in a way which exposed the neck of a small, bulging sack of money neatly tucked inside a fold of his wide girdle. The merchant sold his wares from a narrow stall along the street. Working with the emaciated old man was a boy about fourteen.

Dismas thought, *No man this old could have such a young son. The boy is probably a slave or works for practically nothing*. As Dismas watched the merchant check and fuss over the arrangement of his figs, he heard him harping at the boy, no matter what the lad did. After sizing up the situation, Dismas decided to rob the irritable old man. Looking up and down the street, and at the man's stall, Dismas made sure all would go smoothly.

With an instinct possessed only by thieves, Caleb realized that Dismas had something in mind. He knew it even though the master thief's face had shown no indication at all. When he felt something was about to happen, Caleb stopped pushing against the crowd, and instead, eased over against a far wall to wait and watch.

Caleb had learned years before that when his help was needed, he would be asked. Otherwise, his efforts to aid were just hindrances to Dismas.

Taking his eyes from the merchant long enough to glance over his shoulder into the crowd passing by, Dismas saw a large woman about to pass on his right side. She had a basket, half full of melons, balanced atop her head. As she passed, Dismas took careful aim and shoved her directly into the upturned posterior of the fig merchant, who in turn, dived headlong into the unyielding mud wall of his stall.

As the woman's melons rained down onto the dazed man, Dismas innocently leaped into the stall to assist the still tumbling pair to their feet. The young boy watched as Dismas helped the man and woman up, but he did not see Dismas lift the merchant's moneybag from its girdle pocket. Caleb, a look of awe on his face, followed Dismas' hands throughout the entire drama. He saw the master thief take the purse and, almost as an afterthought, relieve the woman of two of five silver bracelets about her wrist. Three of the five bracelets were left to allay immediate suspicion by the woman.

The most startling part of the theft came when Dismas quickly extracted a silver shekel from the stolen purse before stuffing the remaining money inside his cloak. As the merchant looked around the cluttered stall and wailed at his misfortune, Dismas handed the boy the shekel and apologized, "Boy, I'm afraid this trouble was all my fault. You help your master repair the damage I have caused and I will pay you for your efforts."

The boy grinned broadly at the coin, which represented many days' wages for him, and quickly began straightening up the small stall—which would have been his job anyhow. Dismas mumbled his apologies to the complaining man and woman before stepping into the flow of pilgrims once more. He quickly blended into the surging masses.

Again without urging, Caleb fell in step beside Dismas. Neither man looked at the other for several minutes. Finally Caleb could no longer contain himself and blurted proudly, "That was the most wonderful piece of work I ever saw!" Taking a deep breath, he gushed on, "Dismas, do you know what you just did?"

"I should. I did it," the older thief said confidently, trying to contain his self-satisfaction while enjoying Caleb's admiration.

"But—but you just robbed two people, then, with the money you stole, paid a third person, who had stood watching you from less than four feet away. Oh, rabboni, rabboni. . . ." Caleb, in his excited admiration, could not find the right words.

"Oh, shut up," Dismas snapped, pleasure showing plainly on his face.

Without further conversation the men pushed and elbowed their way to the Zion Gate. As they came near it, the crowd became even denser. Finally, in a small side street, which was scarcely as wide as a man's height, they stopped to wait. Looking around, they found a small ledge along the wall and sat down.

"Dismas."

"What do you want?"

"What if this fellow leads his people in through the

44

Dung Gate? It's a shorter route to the heart of the city."

"Why would a messiah enter through the Dung Gate and into the poorer section of the city, when he could come this way, through the houses of the wealthy? If he plans to make a show of strength, he could do it best by parading past the house of Caiaphas, which is not far from here. The high priest not only hates him, but would see that King Herod and Governor Pontius Pilate heard of his entry quicker than you or I could spread the news. Besides, you know what a liar that Caiaphas is. A thousand men, ha! By the time he gets through telling it, it will be ten thousand."

"That is true," countered Caleb as he thought over what Dismas said, "but the other route is still the most popular one."

"Besides," continued Dismas, as if Caleb had never spoken, "it is more pleasant sitting here smelling the odors of the city rather than sitting at the Dung Gate— smelling dung."

"True." Both men settled back to wait.

As they sat, a drop of sweat trickled down Caleb's forehead and into the dirt on his nose, forming a tiny drop which clung tenaciously to the end of his nose. Using his woolen sleeve, Caleb wiped the drop away. As he did, his eyes wandered along the street behind him. There, he noticed a farmer. He was not one of the men of the soil who gets it under his fingernails, but one who has others do it for him. Caleb nudged Dismas and nodded toward the finely dressed farmer, never taking his eyes from him. Dismas gently tapped Caleb's knee as a signal of approval.

The farmer was just completing his bargaining with a seller of wax, when Caleb edged toward him. The young thief, having been well taught by Dismas to watch for a victim's idiosyncracies, surveyed the man. Where one man hooked his purse string to his cloak with a thorn, another might have it sewed into his girdle. This man simply allowed his girdle one large, sagging fold into which he could lazily drop his purse without looking.

Caleb maneuvered through the pressing throng until he was snugly against the farmer, who did not notice him. The thief then watched and listened as the farmer paid the wax merchant. As the farmer was about to drop his moneybag into its familiar fold, Caleb raised his hand and cupped it inside the open fold. When the farmer relaxed his grip on his purse, it dropped into Caleb's waiting fingers, which in turn dipped heavily, giving the farmer the familiar feel of his money falling into its customary place.

When Caleb started to edge away, the farmer turned to face him. As he did, the pilgrim acknowledged Caleb's presence by mumbling the same traditional blessing he meaninglessly gave to everyone.

Caleb responded with a short, nervous laugh and thought, *You'd better bless others, old man. Bless them as you have just been cursed, measure for measure.*

Since the noise around them made conversation difficult, and to congratulate Caleb for what he had just done would court disaster, Dismas just smiled and nodded his head. Just then above the shouts and clatter of the street, far to their left and coming from a much wider street, Dismas and Caleb heard the rumblings of an even greater chorus of voices coming toward them from the southeast, along the city's wall nearest Hinnom Valley. Judging from the level of the shouts, the two men first thought it announced the approach of a royal person.

Cupping his hands, Caleb shouted, "Who could that be?"

"Maybe it's that carpenter."

"I doubt it. Not with that much cheering," Caleb screamed as he shrugged to show that he did not rule out the possibility. Dismas knew that to his followers, the carpenter was far more than royalty.

Caleb and Dismas tried to move closer to the excitement.

The loyalty of the dignitary's followers became more evident when the two men saw the people not only laying palm fronds down in the street, an act reserved for kings, queens, and other highly placed persons, but the people were even removing their precious robes, something almost revered in Jewish families, and laying them in the street too. This, thought Dismas, was going entirely too far—unless these people knew something he did not.

What was even odder was that such respect was not just being shown by only a few—the fanatics who always followed the false prophets who invaded Jerusalem from time to time. It was being done by almost everyone.

Their cloaks are valuable, Dismas mused. He knew some of them were made of rich wool and highly prized. Some had been tenderly woven by mothers, sisters, or aunts; all were made by loving hands and were all but priceless to their owners. Exchanging looks of wonderment, the two thieves were visibly impressed. No words passed between them on the matter.

Moving to the wide street, they stood staring at what they knew to be either men of insight or fools—all shouting with excitement. Dismas leaned his head toward Caleb, cupped his hands, and said, "Maybe we were wrong. Maybe it is Herod—or Pilate." Caleb laughed, but the sound of his laughter was lost in the noise around him. He cupped his hands to his mouth and shouted back, "Maybe it is Caesar himself." Dismas made a face,

47

signifying he had no idea. They did not have long to wait.

After shoving their way near to the street through the yelling, grumbling crowd, and by standing on tiptoes to look down the street, the thieves could see only hundreds of heads bobbing and weaving. Occasionally people jumped as high as they could trying to see what was happening further along the street. Oddly, despite the press of the mob against itself, on both sides of the street, people kept a clear path down the center. The thieves knew that whoever came had to be royalty, certainly not a common country carpenter.

From a distance came an impromptu chant, "Hosanna to God in the highest," followed by other phrases normally heard only around the temple. Even when the people used the phrases nearer the temple, they were reserved for God or other persons felt to be among the mightiest of the mighty.

As the noise grew louder the two thieves saw more people with palm fronds dropping them immediately in front of a surging mass of people. As the jam of bodies broke, Dismas could hardly contain an exclamation of surprise, disappointment, and disgust. Although it was not a total surprise to them, Dismas finally blurted, "Would you look at the guest of honor? I'd wager it's that confounded carpenter—and he's just a lump of a man. Why, he doesn't even wear decent sandals." A nearby follower of the man being honored by the people suddenly began shouting, "Jesus! Jesus! Jesus!"

A silent Caleb nodded his shaggy head in agreement toward Dismas before adding, "What more could you expect from these idiots?" As he asked the question, his eyes slowly surveyed the crowd, a scowl of disapproval on his lips.

48

As the parade made its way closer, the crowd squeezed together more tightly. Finally, the man who was the undeniable center of attraction came into clear view. He sat on a young, small, and skittish white donkey.

Leaning over until his mouth was just inches from Dismas' ear, Caleb grumbled loudly, "At least, since he pretends to be a king, he chose an appropriate color of beast. The white donkey of royalty at least comes closer to what I expected than anything else I see."

Noticing his friend did not smile, Caleb waited for a comment to his observation.

Finally Dismas declared, "One thing, Caleb. Did you notice that the animal he rides has no marks of binders? Caleb, I don't think that colt has ever been ridden before."

"Ridiculous!" countered Caleb. "Have you ever tried to steal a young, unbroken donkey? I did once and before they are broken to the load, donkeys have the wrath of the wind within them."

"I know," Dismas snapped, "but that animal hasn't a single mark on him." He nodded his head toward the animal as it neared. There was no look of fear or wildness in its young eyes.

Seated on the donkey was a man with straight brown hair—not long, as was the custom in Galilee, but just touching the back of his neck. Covering his chin and upper lip was a full beard of almost red hair. The man appeared to be oblivious to the near hysteria going on around him.

He rode the donkey awkwardly. It was obvious he was no horseman and was not accustomed to the animal's side-to-side swaying gait. Adding to the rider's discomfort was the fact that the donkey had to pick his flat-footed way over Jerusalem's cobblestone streets. This deliberate gait caused the ride to be much bumpier than it had been on the dirt road from Bethany, from which the rider had evidently come. Even the path around Jerusalem's wall, taken by the rider before entering the city, was not as difficult.

The man sitting on the small donkey did not look up. Instead he stared sadly at the back of the donkey's pitching, jerking head. In the midst of all the noisy joy being expressed around him, he looked as though he had just received the worst possible news, as though he knew of a great tragedy and could not share it.

As the one-man caravan arrived directly in the front of the two thieves, the donkey stopped. When this happened, the crowd's roar dropped to a reluctant whisper.

In that instant, as Dismas stared transfixed, a frail old man dressed like a beggar clutched at Caleb's sleeve.

Seeing that the old man wanted to tell him something, Caleb leaned over and turned one ear toward the shriveled, toothless mouth. Before the man could speak, his foul breath caused Caleb to jerk upright once more. Undaunted, the old man whispered, "Marvelous, isn't he?" Caleb signaled that he had not heard and hoped the old man would give up his idea of whispering to a stranger. Instead, he leaned even closer. Then in a louder whisper, he repeated what he had said before.

It was then that Caleb noticed that the watery old eyes of the ancient speaker, like Dismas' eyes, had never left the face of the Galilean. "Some say he is Elijah, the prophet. They say he is Elijah returned," the man fervently confided.

"Elijah! Don't be stupid, old man," Caleb mocked, his voice louder than those around him. When he saw several heads turn his way, Caleb turned to the old man, who now stared at him incredulously.

50

More softly and thickly, Caleb muttered, "Just look at his rough clothing and his ragged, filthy followers. Why, just look at the terrible way he sits on that beast!" Caleb took time to turn his head to glance derisively at the silent rider, who was still the center of the milling, but quiet crowd's attention. "Elijah, my hind leg. He doesn't even look like a decent carpenter, much less a so-called prophet from God."

The old man, who quite obviously could not believe what he heard, gasped, "May God forgive you such blasphemy." Taking a wheezy breath, he pressed bravely on, "You see him and then mock the Lord God, as well as this great man. Oh may God forgive you." Then as an afterthought, he added, "Or strike you dead." With that, the old man would no longer speak to him.

The young thief, however, was not about to let an old beggar of the street have the last word. His pride would not permit it. Leaning over, he taunted, "I see in this country chap nothing more than a Galilean who lacks even the most basic riding knowledge. The man is so mighty he attracts the trash of mankind, just as garbage attracts green flies." After having spoken words he knew would knife deeply into the old man, Caleb smiled evilly.

"Shame! Shame!" chastised the old man as he pushed away from Caleb. "What you have spoken," the old man added in a tone sounding much like a curse, "you shall regret longer than time itself." He shrilled on, "he once told his twelve that as they spoke of him, so would he speak of them. You have hurt him," the old man screeched, pointing a bony finger at Caleb, "and he will surely do the same to you." With that, the old man disappeared in the sea of dusty woolen cloaks. Caleb tried to dissipate some of the hostility which had obviously sprung up in the crowd because of his comments by tilting his head back and laughing aloud.

Dismas and Caleb had made fun of the carpenter each time they had heard of him. From the stories of his love of children and animals, the thieves had conjured up an idea of a feminine, frail, little man too cowardly and timid to defend himself even in an argument with a woman. From what they now saw of Jesus, he was not as they thought at all. He was clearly a muscular and powerful man.

He was not tall by Hebrew standards. Even seated and slumped on the donkey's back, dressed in the sacklike robe and mantle common to Galilee, it was easy to see his broad shoulders, which set above a large and muscular chest.

From beneath his garments, the carpenter's legs, from which a pauper's sandals hung, were not spindly, as sometimes was the case with men having big torsos. Instead, they too were as massive as the rest of his body. As the two thieves made their observations, it became clear to them that no man who worked as a carpenter, lifting, prying, using the adz and heavy hammer, and loading and unloading rough timbers, could have the willowy physique they had pictured of him in their minds. Both men flashed an embarrassed smile as they realized how stupid their mental pictures of him had been.

Dismas had ignored his companion's harangue with the old man. Instead, he had concentrated on the carpenter. Less than a minute had passed since the straining little donkey had stopped in the street, but to Dismas it seemed much longer. The older thief had not only examined the magic carpenter's physique and clothing, he had closely scrutinized the man's sad face too.

Dismas' first thought was that, even if the man was a

fraud, he would certainly be a good man to have at your back in a fight. Further study of the rugged and muscular features drew Dismas' attention closer and closer. The man astride the donkey had not looked up, had not acknowledged the crowd, but Dismas felt the carpenter's awesome presence demanding undivided attention.

Amid the honor being given him by his followers, in spite of joyful shouting which went on around him, a deep, fathomless, heartbroken sadness seemed to radiate from the silent man—a sadness almost beyond belief, Dismas felt in his marrow.

In addition to the flash of compassion which swept over him for the man, Dismas sensed that this man could be trusted—not as he trusted Caleb, but in a way Dismas had never trusted anyone before. The old thief's eyes jerked to a squint and his head cocked, movements noticed only by Caleb.

Dismas thought, *What a man of contrasts this Galilean is. He has strength, but appears to be above using it against anyone. He ignores adoration—which creates more adoration. He could have the wealth of these multitudes simply by asking, yet has nothing—nor does he seem to want anything.* Dismas took a deep breath and muttered to himself. "He is a man of contrasts." He paused and corrected himself, "No, he is a madman."

Try as he might to ridicule the humble man seated before him, Dismas was drawn to him. He found himself consciously aware of the emptiness of his own life. This man, and several of his followers around him, seemed to enjoy a completeness not possessed by most of the crowd.

Suddenly Dismas shook his head violently. He leaned toward Caleb, who stood waiting for some signal from the master thief, and muttered, "I don't see how such a man could ever hope to be the Messiah, the deliverer named by Isaiah. But I do know that if there is ever to be such a person, this man could be the one, if he so desired."

"Dismas, has he cast his spell on you too? Are you now as crazed as these fools?" Caleb impulsively blurted out. Dismas ignored his young friend.

The hush of the packed crowd deepened as the man who had been looking only toward the donkey raised his head slowly to face Dismas. The eyes of both men locked. There was no smile. No obvious recognition passed between them.

Without a word, the carpenter almost imperceptively nodded his head several times, as if in agreement with some unspoken point Dismas had made. Dismas caught himself nodding in return. The old thief was an absolute prisoner of the eyes which did not look at him, but deep into him. In those black piercing eyes Dismas saw something he had never seen before—and he did not know what it was. The eyes seemed not to be those of a man, but were like the glowing embers deep inside a burning log.

"Soon," Dismas finally whispered, a heavy fatigue coming over him.

"What was that?" Caleb chirped loudly.

Whipping his head around angrily, Dismas snapped, "None of your business." When he looked back at the Galilean, the carpenter was once more staring sadly at the donkey's head and moving on down the street. The rumbling cheers of his admirers once more echoed from the high walls lining both sides of the thoroughfare.

Dismas glanced at Caleb, who saw Dismas' embarrassment at being caught talking to himself. Dismas could see that Caleb was obviously hurt by his verbal attack. "Caleb, I am sorry. You did me no wrong. I don't know what came over me."

Dismas knew Caleb was not angry at his unprovoked outburst when Caleb, a small smile spreading across his broad face, clapped him on the shoulder and, in the usual companionship they shared, quipped, "Another sign of old age slipping up on you?" Happy that his young friend was not offended, Dismas did not bother to answer the jibe.

They turned back toward where the carpenter had been, but by this time he had moved on. The crowd was disappointed at not seeing a miracle performed. Their disappointment did not last long. Almost as if directed by a leader, they reverted to their previous holiday spirit and again picked up their sing-song chant, "Hosanna to the Son of David, Hosanna in the highest. . . ."

With the thinning of the crowd, Dismas and Caleb turned and started walking eastward, up the narrow street.

The aging thief did not like the way he felt. Instead of stalking insolently along, or blustering as he usually did, he walked quietly. He tucked his lower lip between his teeth and began scraping the wine scum and dust from it, spitting occasionally to rid himself of the results of his efforts.

As he did so, he asked himself, *Why did I blurt out what I said? What did I mean by the word 'soon'? Why did I feel a warmth for a man I never saw before? Why should I feel anything but contempt for such a spineless clod?* Dismas didn't realize a deep frown was on his face.

"What's wrong, Dismas?" Caleb gently asked.

Snapped out of his reverie, Dismas quickly rallied his thoughts and answered, "Nothing. Why?"

"Oh, the look on your face. Your quietness. That isn't like you, you know."

"I was just thinking about that man."

"The old one?" Caleb was still irked by the old man who had rebuked him.

"No, the carpenter." Dismas decided to confide in Caleb. "Also, I was wondering about what I said."

"It was strange," Caleb agreed. "Out of nowhere you said, 'Soon.'"

"I know." The frown deepened across Dismas' face. "Worse yet, Caleb. I felt his magnetism. You know, like he was talking to me without even opening his mouth."

Caleb shoved a small boy away who had run into him while darting from a playmate, then asked, "Do you really think he's genuine or accursed? I have heard it said that he was one, then the other, then both. What do you really think?"

"I have no idea about that. I only know I felt something when he looked at me and I don't know what it was," Dismas replied in a serious tone.

Both men now breathed heavier. They had completed their climb up the street and had reached a series of steps, which also led upward. Caleb had seldom heard his master in such a talkative mood and pressed on, "When I heard you say 'Soon' back there, my first thought was that you meant the two of us would soon start plucking the onlookers of their wealth."

Dismas, hoping to change the whole distasteful conversation, forced himself to laugh curtly and exclaim, "An example of your lying tongue, Caleb. You probably thought I was possessed of a devil, you filthy harlot's spawn. You know full well that I am not in league with any devils, even if they exist at all. The real lunatics who talk to the unseen are priests—and I would make a terrible priest. After all, as a self-confessed thief, I am entirely too honest to be a priest." Both men laughed heartily as they panted their way several more steps before stopping.

The sun was high and the unseasonal heat caused perspiration to trickle down the sides of their faces and into their beards. Both men used the sleeves of their heavy robes to wipe the dripping saltwater from the hair on their faces. Both men squinted and took time to look back down the street they had just traveled. Looking back, to them, was as necessary as looking ahead, for a thief had to know, if anyone, was following him.

2 SUNDAY AFTERNOON

Having reached a level stretch of street, the two men, still laughing loudly at their little joke, stopped to catch their breath. Ahead of them, leaning against a wall and talking with two of his comrades, was a Roman soldier of the lowest rank. When he heard the two Jews laughing, he was irritated.

Turning to the other soldiers, he snapped, "It isn't right for us to be stuck in this forsaken land where even the gods cannot find us, only to have to listen to such rot as those two giddy Jews." He paused long enough to look the gleeful thieves up and down arrogantly, head to foot, before saying, "Laughter in a conquered country belongs to the conquerors—to us Romans, along with everything of any value. Let's teach them a lesson—that only what we cast off belongs to them." His two friends, sensing what was coming, chuckled with amusement.

Dismas and Caleb had not seen the soldiers. As they climbed the steps, they watched their feet. Arriving at a small landing, they were completely absorbed with each other. Turning, they labored up the inclined street, seeing only small dust swirls beneath the feet ahead of them. Without any warning, they found themselves staring at a pair of neatly constructed sandals planted firmly in their path. From the construction and the lacing of the shoes, which ran from the top of the feet upward, the men knew they belonged to one of Caesar's soldiers.

With an instinct gained from years of adapting to practically any situation, the men instantly put a humble look on their faces, even before looking up at the man before them. From the way his feet were spread, they knew a difficult time lay ahead of them, unless they used every ounce of wit they had rehearsed and used so often before on so many Romans.

"By the gods, what makes you so happy?" the Roman snarled. Both men looked up as if in awe of the person before them. As soon as their respectful glances hit his youthful face, both took on the next stance needed for talking with a Roman. Raising one cupped hand toward the soldier, who was barely in his twenties, each assumed an imbecilic look.

The man's armor, worn and tarnished, showed he had been away from his homeland for more than a year. From the mixture of Latin and Hebrew he spoke, they surmised from his Jerusalem accent that he was untested in battle, that his whole time on duty had been spent in the city.

Squinting into the soldier's crystal blue eyes, and in an idiotic tone of voice, Dismas stammered, "Excellency, we were just laughing at our fellow countrymen. Today we watched a parade given in the honor of a poor carpenter who comes to this godforsaken city from an even worse place—they said from the hilltop village of Nazareth. The parade was given for him by my countrymen. The . . . ." Dismas stopped long enough to allow a low chuckle to roll from his mouth. "Heh, heh, heh. The carpenter they so greatly honored was dressed in rags and riding a donkey. We laughed because this was the kind of man Jews could be expected to adore. What dolts we are—heh, heh, heh—we are not at all like you powerful and magnificent Romans."

Again Dismas chortled before allowing his tongue to ramble on—as though he was not too bright. "Look at you, oh mighty one. So far from your home and family, a conqueror, and even here, in this stinking crotch of humanity, you have the best that life can offer. What do we Jews settle for? A failure of a carpenter from a wilderness mud village riding on a donkey. Heh, heh, heh, don't you think this a bit strange, a bit funny?"

The young Roman could not withhold his smile as he considered what Dismas had said. He had heard that such a man was expected to come to the city before the Passover was completed, but from what he had been told, the man might be a political threat and certainly not the type of person this beggar described. The reception given the carpenter, if as this oaf said, was a gala affair, but of no consequence in terms of a threat to peace and order.

Suddenly embarrassed at dropping his guard, even temporarily, the smile that flitted across his face while Dismas was talking disappeared. The soldier remembered he was being watched by his friends and had already lost his advantage to the beggars by listening to their senseless chatter.

"Do you scum think such things give you the right to

laugh so loudly, especially before Roman soldiers, disturbing me and my friends?" he growled.

Caleb, shuffling slightly as he bent over sideways, stepped in front of Dismas, apparently prepared to flatter the Roman out of any harmful intentions he might be forced into to maintain his dignity before his friends.

"Oh, centurion," Caleb began. Before he could continue the soldiers' outburst of laughter cut him short. Caleb allowed a false look of bewilderment to come over his face.

Dismas knew Caleb's remark about the young Roman being a conqueror had been well received by him. The laughter, which also came from the young man's friends, was evidence that his calling the rankless soldier a "centurion," or the leader of a hundred men, had been far more successful.

As if he was innocent of the cause of the laughter, Caleb continued, "If you could but see the idiocy of these people through a Jew's eyes, you'd laugh too. We. . . . " Caleb gestured toward Dismas and himself, "We are much more intelligent than the average Jew, so we saw how ridiculous the parade was."

At that, the Romans broke into laughter. From behind the young soldier who had challenged them, came a deep voice, "Indeed, the Jews are stupid. Look at these two examples of the more intelligent ones." Again the trio of armor-clad men began to laugh. Chuckling as a man with manners would do at a joke they did not understand, Dismas and Caleb joined them.

To insure that the young soldier did not have a chance to collect his wits to punish or belittle them, Caleb began again, "Just compare you brave Romans with those you rule." Caleb's sarcasm was totally disguised. "You have strong armor and we but woolen rags. You enjoy the finest foods; we eat the bitterest of lentils. You savor beautiful temple maidens: we have only dirty wenches—which is even against our narrow-minded laws. You ride fierce stallions and swift, mighty chariots, while we only have leather-bound bones called donkeys. And we. . . ."

Dismas interrupted by throwing back his head to laugh noisily before bubbling, "We. . . . " He acted as though his laughter would cause him to faint. "We call ourselves the chosen ones."

At that not only did Dismas and Caleb roar with laughter, but they were joined by all of the Roman soldiers.

Throughout the entire discourse between the pair of thieves and the arrogant soldiers, only Dismas saw Caleb extending his hand closer and closer to the soldier who had originally challenged them. In this movement, Caleb had repeatedly tapped the young man on the breastplate of his armor. Caleb insured that none of the touching motions were offensive or even greatly noticeable. He had done it so swiftly and repeatedly that the Roman had finally begun to ignore it. As the laughter subsided, the soldier, still chuckling, smiled faintly and said, "As admirers of Rome, go your way and I will say no more of the incident. But," he warned, "go quietly."

Caleb, still acting the fool, flamboyantly imitated the desert nomads by bowing low before the soldier. As he straightened up, Caleb touched his heart, his lips, and his forehead with his right hand. As he did, Caleb's left hand snaked out in a wide arch, then back to his waist.

The young soldier did not see that as Caleb's arm swung wide in front of him, the young thief's fingers had moved in to steal his meager purse from the wide leather strap which crossed his armor. Caleb had made sure the Roman stood between him and the other two soldiers so that they would not see what happened. Once Caleb had the small purse in his grasp, he deftly inserted it into the folds of his wide Hebrew belt and turned to leave.

Dismas was already walking away quickly. He began his exit as soon as he realized Caleb's dangerous ploy.

Turning once more toward the three soldiers, who now jerked their thumbs over their shoulders, pointing at the "crazy Jews," Caleb gave a series of jerking, shallow bows as he backed down the street. Soon he whirled and strode after Dismas.

When they were a safe distance from the military trio, Dismas growled, "You fool! You crazy, wonderful fool!" He had to clamp his jaw tightly to keep from once more bursting out in laughter.

"What if he had caught you? You forgot my first rule of thievery: keep a way out of all situations. If he had caught you in that act, you would have been too close to him and his companions. You left yourself little running room. Caleb, believe me, I was afraid for you."

"I know," Caleb reasoned, "but I could not help myself. That arrogant peacock was standing there just begging to be plucked, so I did it."

"But if you had been caught, your position left you not only defenseless, but needing to escape uphill. I couldn't have helped you either."

A sober look came over Caleb's face. "I didn't think of that."

"Well, you'd better think of it next time," Dismas said.

At the top of the incline, the two thieves looked back at the three soldiers. Still unaware of what had happened to them, they were strolling to the bottom of the street.

Caleb spat contemptuously. then he muttered, "Walk with your gods, my blond-haired, blue-eyed Roman.

Walk arrogantly—because arrogance is all you have now. I have your wealth."

Later, after a delayed and lazy lunch of cucumbers, tough bread, and strong cheese, Dismas and Caleb reclined under a solitary, gnarled tree, which was all but nude of leaves. They had wandered the city streets, finally strolling out the Water Gate. They were eating their lunch in the city's burial place, their favorite quiet spot for relaxation. All around them were the graves of the dead of all ages.

The men's eyes grew heavy after their meal. They closed them to hold back the glare of the searing sun. With their legs extended in opposite directions, both men lay with their faces clothed in the meager shade of the tree's trunk.

Although their lunch had not been large, even by Judean standards, it was enough to make them drowsy. Occasionally each of them made weak and futile efforts to drive away the persistent flies which stalked over their faces. The unrelenting insects seemed determined to keep the drowsy men from dozing off.

"Dismas." Caleb sighed, as if the effort exhausted him.

"Huh?" Dismas grunted absently.

"What do you think of the Galilean?"

"Who?"

"That carpenter—the one at the head of the parade this morning. Do you wonder about him?"

"What am I supposed to think of him?"

"You know. Do you believe he could be the Messiah everyone hopes for?"

"I don't know."

"Oh." Caleb considered Dismas' answer a few seconds before beginning again. "He could be, you know."

"Who could be what?" Dismas asked, his voice tinged

with irritation directed almost as much toward Caleb as the bothersome flies.

"The man we saw this morning could be the Messiah."

"Confound these flies. Why do you think that? He doesn't even look like a messiah."

"Have you ever seen a messiah?" Caleb retorted, waving helplessly at a fly buzzing noisily near one ear.

Dismas didn't bother to answer Caleb's question. Instead, he raised his hand and weakly waved it several times in front of his face.

Caleb shoved a blade of grass into his mouth and chewed on it vigorously. Then he snatched the blade out and tossed it away. He raised himself on one elbow and commented, "I talked with Korath. You know, the blind beggar who sits outside the home of Hiram the merchant. Korath says it is possible."

Dismas' mouth twisted with disgust as he forced one eye open and looked scornfully at Caleb. "Pray, tell me my gullible friend, from what heavenly revelation does the holy beggar get that information?"

Ignoring Dismas' sarcasm and testiness, Caleb responded, "Korath spent much time near the temple area, back when he pretended to be a cripple." Caleb was taking heart at Dismas' interest. "He said that when alms stopped coming his way he would sometimes listen to the rabbis. He said even the prophets of old revealed that the coming Messiah would be from Bethlehem, which they say was the carpenter's birthplace. They said he would be of the house of David, and it is said the carpenter is from that line. And, listen to this one, Dismas, they foretold that he would come to claim his kingdom riding on a white ass." Caleb spoke the last three words slowly and with exaggerated emphasis, to give them an ominous sound.

He stared anxiously at his master and waited to see if the older man would be excited by these things. Seconds passed before Dismas turned his head, spit, then, in a bored tone, snorted, "So?"

"So! So the carpenter fits the predictions." Caleb was disappointed at his friend's lack of enthusiasm.

"Ha!" Dismas exclaimed, "That stupid Korath probably heard them say the Messiah would cause bedlam—not be from Bethlehem—would again raise the house of David and that this Galilean was an ass—not that he would be riding on one." Dismas had a stern look on his face and spoke in a tone which left no doubt in Caleb's mind that he wished to be left alone to sleep.

But Caleb would not be put off. "Just think. If he is the one, we can look for the uprising any day." The young thief took a deep breath, smiled broadly, and his eyes took on a look of excitement. "Maybe even today."

"If that man is as sleepy as I am, the only uprising he wants is after his nap, which his friends are probably letting him enjoy right now."

"Don't misunderstand, Dismas," Caleb continued as if he had not heard the retort. "I don't say this man is the Messiah, I just say. . . ."

"Is there anything that you do *not* say? What do you know about the Messiah anyhow?" Dismas was becoming angry. He propped himself up on one elbow, whirled over onto one side to face the troublesome Caleb, then snapped, "You asked me what I knew of the Messiah, and you say this country field mouse could be the one. What in the name of Isis do you know of such matters?" Dismas' reference to the god of the Egyptians came from his frequent association with the desert people, who traded heavily with Egyptians. He frequently mingled with caravan members to steal their coins or wandered

66

among the many baskets brought into the city by the heavily ladened beasts of the desert.

"The priests say he is the one who will someday set us free," Caleb defended.

"The priests say! The priests say!" By now Dismas was all but seething not from his disturbed sleep, although that had set the mood, but from Caleb's show of respect for a class of men Dismas loathed above all men—even the Romans—men Dismas equated with swine.

Dismas' voice reeked with hatred as he continued, "By all the Roman gods, have you ever gotten anything from priests but empty words?"

Caleb's mouth opened as he prepared to reply. Dismas cut him short.

"No, and you never will!" Dismas' eyes were wild as he spoke. "In my entire life I never saw a priest do anything but talk and take. Talk and take." He took a deep breath. "Even the high priests dressed in their fine clothes, a thousand bells on their garments to draw attention so the simpleminded will give them the respect they demand. These high and mighty 'holy men' people think talk face-to-face with a Yahweh no one has even seen."

Caleb saw that Dismas' tirade was as much worry and concern as it was hatred by this time. A deep frown had come to the older man's forehead and drops of saliva flew from his lips. The younger man was deeply shocked and his face showed it.

"Caleb, these godforsaken priests that you talk of are thieves, just like you and me. The difference is—and it's a big difference—that they steal according to laws they themselves had the Sanhedrin, the lawmakers, create. Then they live like pious kings. You and I, at least, have the honesty just to take the fruits as we find them, and live as best we can. What we steal is only what a man can

67

carry and replace. The priests take what a man carries, frighten him into giving what is yet to come, and even destroy his peace of mind—and that is the real sin."

Having run out of wind, Dismas' last few words trailed off and he had to gulp for air.

Dismas took a deep breath and was slowly calming down. "No, Caleb, priests only talk, abuse people, threaten, and take, take, take, take."

During his tirade, Dismas had almost constantly waved his arms. In doing so, he had become so incensed and heated that a drop of perspiration snaked its way into one eye, causing him to blink rapidly. As he batted the offending eye, he fell back heavily, taking another deep breath after he had thudded into the dirt.

An oppressive silence came over the two men. Caleb knew he had touched some tender spot—a spot never before irritated by him. Even Dismas knew it. He felt shamed. For some unknown reason, he had objected too much about the priests and the Galilean being called the savior of the people. Caleb finally broke the silence. "Korath said the priests are afraid of the carpenter."

When Dismas did not respond, the young thief continued, "He said he heard the priests whisper among themselves that Caiaphas had, on several occasions, sent his keenest priests and scribes to hear this Jesus teach. Korath said Caiaphas wanted to trap the Galilean into saying something against the temple, the law, Rome, or if possible, against Caesar himself."

"Did they trap him?" Dismas asked with new interest. As Caleb told of the attempt to trap Jesus, Dismas turned his head to study Caleb's face. Seeing the interest on his master's face, Caleb grinned and proudly snickered, "Never. The carpenter has wits about him, even if he is from the country."

A pleased snear crossed the older thief's mouth, but his eyes remained hard. "So the carpenter beat them at their own game, did he? If that is true, Caleb, he just might be a better rabble-rouser than we suspected. He might even be a messiah." Dismas' eyes squinted as if he was thinking deeply. "Those men of the temple are not only sneaky, but shrewd. It is said they have trained men, educated men, whose job in the temple is to trap even the most brilliant people, if the high priest wants it done. I have heard they sometimes do this just as an example for others. It is supposed to keep all Jews in line, so they will do what the priests tell them to do."

"Korath said the Galilean would never be trapped."

Dismas, deep in thought about how the scholars were unable to snare the serene man he had seen on the donkey, did not answer Caleb. Finally both men lay back, less tense than before. As they finally began to breathe easily, they closed their eyes, each man deep in his own thoughts.

Almost an hour later Caleb awoke from the nap he thought would never come. Putting his fists against his chest, he stretched both elbows upward, loosening his shoulder and arm muscles. Squinting his eyes against the blazing sun, he sat up, pulled his knees high, then leaned forward into a stoop-shouldered position. Draping his arms easily around his raised knees, he put his head forward, trying to rest his still groggy head until his mind cleared.

With the passing of time the sun had moved the shadow of the scrawny tree away, leaving Caleb's face bare to the searing sun. As he leaned forward he could still feel the heat radiating within his beard and on the skin of his face. Lifting his head again, the sleepy man blinked his eyes into focus. Suddenly he realized his companion was no longer beside him.

"Dismas!" he shouted, his voice pitched higher than normal and tinged with a note of panic.

From about forty feet away, and in a tone which was almost paternal, the familiar voice of his master came back at him, "It's all right, Caleb. I'm here."

The young thief looked over his shoulder toward the sound. Dismas was leaning comfortably on one of several burial vaults built above ground of the cemetery.

Dismas' elbows rested atop the mausoleum, and one of his feet was propped casually on the small building's protruding stone base. The older thief's eyes slowly wandered along the rim of the city wall, which stood towering above him.

The wall rested on the edge of a small cliff and, because the sun raced to disappear behind it, seemed to divide the day from eternity. Jerusalem was an ancient city. In fact, it was a number of cities, each built on top of the other over the centuries.

As Dismas' head slowly lolled around, allowing him to scan the full length of the wall's top, he paused to look over at where Caleb now sat.

When Dismas saw that the younger man was staring at him, he turned and, with deliberate and lengthy steps, walked over and sat heavily on the ground near him.

"Didn't you sleep at all?" Caleb asked.

"No."

"Are you feeling sick?"

Letting his head droop wearily, Dismas replied, "Yes, that's it. I'm sick. I'm sick of never being sure what the day will bring. I'm sick of always wondering, as I grow older, when I will be too slow and someone will feel my fingers as they lift their purse."

Staring at the ground between his legs, Dismas rocked

70

his head dejectedly and slowly from one side to the other and back again. "Caleb," he said, then paused.

"Yes," the younger man softly responded.

"Caleb." Dismas now groaned without lifting his head. "Ever since I looked into that carpenter's eyes I have wondered where I'm headed and of what value my life has been." Suddenly he looked up and almost shouted, "Where am I going?"

Startled by his master's sudden outburst, and seeing that he was extremely despondent, Caleb forced his brightest smile and matter-of-factly stated, "It's just this place where we sit. This place with its dead and its silence is enough to make anyone sick. This place. . . ." He slowly waved his arm around to point toward the sea of graves around them. "This place can be very depressing."

"Maybe what you say is true," Dismas agreed meekly.

Placing both hands against the ground and pushing himself upward, Dismas stood, then hesitated long enough to place his hands in the small of his back, leaned back and stretched mightily. Without warning he straightened up and boomed, "Let's be on our way and see if we can 'borrow' the price of some of Jerusalem's finest wine."

"An excellent idea, my friend," Caleb responded happily as he bounded to his feet.

Dismas beat the dust from the back of his dirty clothes, then, like a pair of children on their way to steal grapes, the pair linked arms and strode off toward the noisy city.

The sun was turning into a bright red ball as it enjoyed its final hours of the day. One of the greatest days in history was coming to an end, but few persons realized its significance.

3 MONDAY MORNING

The red and gray layers of dawn sliced bloody gashes across the blackness of a dying starlit night. After their evening of drinking, belching, exchanging tales of personal prowess, and embellishing each story with whatever words were needed to top the story before it, Dismas and Caleb spent a cool night huddled together atop a house. Despite their discomfort, they were safe from the scavenging dogs which roamed the streets in packs each night.

Before the sun's warmth relieved them of the chills which had disturbed their sleep throughout the night, the men rose, scratched, then made their way to one of the low walls which lined the roof. There they urinated over the edge and into the street below.

Their plan was to return to Aram's inn, but both men knew that if they did, they would probably be drunk before the day had really begun. While the thought of the inn was most alluring to them, Dismas and Caleb realized that the hangover they had now would only worsen after a morning of drinking in the heat at Aram's.

"What do you think, Dismas?" Caleb asked, knowing full well the older man had no more idea of where they should go than he did.

Instead of answering immediately, Dismas sat on the low wall, then swung his legs out over the edge to dangle over the street. He ran his tongue over his coated teeth several times, coughed, spit, then mumbled, "I don't know." Dismas looked out across the rooftops surrounding him. He was trying to decide what to do and in what direction to go. "I heard last night that the Galilean is going to be at the temple today. That could be interesting. If the priests are out to shame or trap him into something, and if he is as shrewd as you say, that could be very interesting."

"I didn't say he was shrewd—Korath said it." Besides, if we turn our attention to him again today, you may get as upset as you did yesterday."

Dismas, somewhat hardened from the day before, pursed his lips and indignantly retorted, "When the day comes that I become upset over some common country lump and rabble who gather around him, that is when I will get a job." To Dismas and Caleb manual labor was unthinkable.

After a few minutes of silent pondering, Dismas swung his legs back to the roof, stood, and began to scratch again. Raising one arm to examine his hairy armpit closely, Dismas looked up and around, then once more went back to his scratching. "Someday, Caleb," he mumbled, his chin pulled so far down by his dedication to his scratching he could hardly talk.

"Someday what?" Caleb asked.

"Someday," Dismas mumbled, still searching among the oily hairs under his arm, "someday we'll not wake up at all. It will happen because the confounded lice will have eaten completely through our bodies and devoured our hearts."

Caleb moved out of Dismas' reach before snickering. "Not you, smelly one. The lice couldn't survive that much of you." Caleb ran across the roof as if playing a game. Dismas did not try to give chase, but did give up on the irksome louse.

"We don't fill our bellies standing here scratching. We need to eat," the older man said. "Let's be on our way," He threw his cloak over his head and strode down the stairway. Caleb followed.

The crushing crowd of the day had not gathered in the street yet, due to the early hour. But the early opening of vendor's stalls seemed to indicate that the crush this day would be worse than on others. With the coming of Passover in just three more days, Dismas and Caleb knew the ocean of humanity would soon be nearly unbearable—except to thieves.

Giving in to hunger and thirst, they made their way to Aram's inn. Before opening the splinter-covered door, Dismas withdrew his purse and checked to make sure he had sufficient money to pay for their meal. Drawing the purse strings and leaning toward Caleb, he said, "Whatever we do, we must not get drunk. No, we must have no more than a single glass of wine. Today will be a rich one for us, but only if we keep our wits and nimbleness of fingers."

"Agreed," Caleb concurred. This day they would need all of their keen talents to avoid trouble.

Inside the smoky, dank room, the men stood to one

side as their eyes adjusted to the darkness.

"Why doesn't Aram put windows in this room?" Caleb muttered.

"Because," Dismas explained, "if he did, and the Romans or the law-enforcing Sanhedrin saw what went on in here, and who his customers were, his business would be branded for what it is—the city's most festering sore. They might just burn him out of business as they would a plagued house."

Caleb grinned at his friend's joke, even though he knew there was truth in what he said.

Soon they were accustomed enough to the dim light to make their way to the rear of the room and a small table. Once seated they could faintly make out Miriam as she approached them.

"Greetings, my unholy pair. Where have you been that you could do without free wine and food?" she teased.

"Ha, wench!" Caleb laughed. "Do you think this pig sty is the only place where two highly talented artisans would go?"

"No," Miriam taunted, her voice dropping to a whisper and a false seriousness spreading over her face, "but I did not think any pig, even Aram, would allow the likes of you in his sty at all. You might taint each other, you and Aram."

At that, both men laughed loudly and asked for the biggest portion of wine that Aram had to offer.

"I have instructions to serve you anything for which you have money," the girl announced, holding her hand out for advance payment.

"By the gods!" Dismas bellowed. "That grease-soaked, sow spawn of a Syrian has the gall to say that we—" He gestured frantically from Caleb to himself and back again. "We, who have made him wealthy as recently as yesterday, will only be served if we have money in advance? Does that ungrateful boor think we are anything other than honorable men?" As he shouted he pulled the recently stolen purse from his sash and let it fall noisily onto the table. Hearing the telltale clank, Miriam rushed away to bring them food and drink.

There were no other customers in the large room yet— the hour was still too early for the type of patrons Aram attracted. Looking around the darkest parts of the room, the men realized they were, indeed, alone.

Because business was dead at this time of day, Miriam sat with them after she had brought several bowls of fruit, two big flat loaves of fresh bread, the remains of a leg of lamb, two doves, cooked the night before, and a small bowl of curd.

After he stuffed his mouth full of food, with some of it protruding from his lips, Caleb turned to Miriam. Half-slobbering and half-spitting particles of food from his mouth, Dismas swallowed deeply several times as he tried to clear his mouth to speak. Finally, with an explosion of half-chewed food, he mumbled, "You know somefing, Murum. . . ." Dismas' speech problem was compounded as he stuffed more food into his mouth. "I fink fhat corpunder is smart."

Caleb almost choked when he heard this. Taking no chances, he spit the entire contents of his mouth onto the floor then blurted out, "Miriam, Dismas has taken your carpenter to heart."

Dismas turned and cuffed Caleb on the back of the head as he too sputtered, "That's a baldheaded lie!"

Caleb, stung by the blow, swallowed deeply as he rubbed the back of his head. He then mocked, "If it's not so, why are you so quickly angered at what I say?"

76

Dismas didn't bother to answer, but scowled and raised a bunch of dark grapes over his head. He tilted his head back and nibbled at them, starting from the bottom.

Miriam, sensing that the two men were serious, and herself curious about the carpenter, asked, "Did you see his entry into the city? I hear it was as majestic as any king who ever arrived here. Did you see it? Tell me about it."

Since Dismas was busy with the grapes, Caleb took time to tell of the people, how they shouted, put palm leaves in front of the donkey which carried the stranger, and how some of them even removed their cloaks for the donkey to walk on.

"It is just as the prophets said it would be," Miriam gushed. "Surely this must be the one."

"You had better pray it isn't," Caleb said. "If the prophets were right, and if this Jesus is the Messiah, he has come not just to free us, but judge us as well." He stuffed a piece of bread in his mouth and mumbled, "I'm sure you wouldn't measure up."

Miriam stared at Caleb silently and seriously. Her eyes moistened. Finally, as a teardrop ran down her cheek, she looked at her rough hands and softly said, "I know."

Caleb, sobered by the girl's seriousness and obvious concern, and touched by the unnecessary hurt he had caused, reached across the table and placed his dirty hand on hers. "Miriam, you must also know that if he is the Messiah, he will forgive the wrongs we have done. If he is the one, he is supposed to be able to forgive all." Smuggly he added, "In your case, I'm sure he would."

Dismas looked first at Caleb, then at Miriam. He had heard Caleb's rare apology and saw that the soft-hearted, but tough appearing woman was crying. "Miriam," he said softly, "this man is not the one. Don't worry about him. It is as Caleb says. If he should be the Messiah, he will not only judge, but forgive." Dismas' own doubts had again surfaced. To keep them from showing, he once more donned his hard look. "Besides, I still say he is no messiah. It is as I said before. He's just a smart operator." After repeating his remark, Dismas glared at Caleb to see if his slight admiration of the carpenter would bring another sarcastic remark. It didn't.

Dismas turned again to the girl. "You have no doubt heard of his teaching in the old temple when he was but a boy, twelve or thirteen years old, I believe. The man knows his holy teachings. From these he has made sure every detail foretold of the coming Messiah fits him. Such things swing gullible followers to his side before he meets the priests head on. By that time he cannot only quote from the prophets, telling what they foretold, but he will be able to apply all of them to himself. He is smart, I tell you—and not your average messiah." Dismas' last word was spat out with all the disbelief he could muster, including a distended jaw and a mouth twisted in sarcasm.

"My filthy friends," Miriam said possessively in a voice more intimate than they had heard from her in a long time, "if this man is the Messiah, I must find some way to see him and talk with him. I have heard from the other girls, those at the well, that one of our own, a girl of the north, near the Lake of Galilee and of the village of Magdala—Mary, by name—has received his forgiveness. He is said to have wiped her record clean and given her a new outlook on life. My friends say this Mary had been scraping the bottom in life. But now she radiates like the sun. She follows her new master, this Jesus, wherever he goes."

78

Hearing this, Caleb, always the doubter, chimed in, "See there, Miriam. You have no reason to worry about this man judging you. He's just a man like Dismas and me. This Mary is undoubtedly his woman like you are ours. Would a holy messiah do such a thing?" Caleb tried to be gay about the whole situation, but his bid fell flatly on deep silence. As the quiet intensified, Caleb turned to look at Dismas, who stared stonily at him. The young man's head turned to Miriam. She stared vacantly at him. "What did I do? Did I desecrate something holy? No! I just said what I think."

The thick silence hung like a heavy weight. Stung by the chill aimed his way, Caleb slammed the flat of his hand heavily onto the top of the massive table. "Stop looking at me like that!" He rose to his feet. "If my presence or words anger you so when I have said nothing you yourselves have not said before, then . . . then. . . ." Caleb snatched his empty cup from the table and stalked across the room to the two huge kegs of wine which hung from ceiling ropes. Dipping deeply into one of the barrels, he filled his cup and broke his promise of minutes before by quickly drinking a second cup of wine. He dipped again and angrily glared across the room at Dismas and Miriam.

The older man was bothered by his own disapproval of what Caleb had said. He wondered, *Is now the time for Caleb to leave and make his own way?* He had known for several years that the young boy he had acquired was no longer a boy. Caleb had passed the awkward stage, had learned nearly all the aging thief could teach him, and had recently shown evidence that Dismas' decisions were not necessarily those he, himself, might have made. Dismas knew that even though he had purchased the lad from prison, he could not hold Caleb as a bond slave effectively. When the younger thief finally decided to leave, Dismas would be powerless to prevent it. That was a day Dismas could never be prepared to face. It would be like the death of a loved one and the older man knew it. Now, as Caleb showed open defiance, the gnawing fear reared its ugly head and once more faced the old man. Dismas had nothing to say to his student. Now he could only sit and wait.

In an effort to rid himself of the unpleasant thought, Dismas quickly forced the prospect from his mind and, instead, turned to look at the girl seated across from him.

"Dismas," Miriam grimly murmured.

"Yes."

"Is he the one?"

Dismas knew what she meant. "Miriam," he said with an intensity she rarely heard from him, "I don't honestly know. Yesterday morning I would have said it was all just one big pile of rotten garbage. You know, what the people say. Today I feel as if I'm full of that garbage. I'm completely mixed up inside." Dismas frowned and Miriam impulsively put her calloused hand gently on top of his.

"Why do you speak so, Dismas?" she asked softly.

"I saw him, Miriam." Dismas' eyes met hers and both of them felt an unusual closeness. The harlot of the inn and the unwanted thief felt they had a common bond in the man Jesus. Neither of them knew what that bond was. They were two pieces of human driftwood drawn together by something they did not even understand. In their closeness both felt a touch of unreasonable panic.

"I saw him and he just looked at me," said Dismas. "He was—well, different from anyone I ever saw before." Tossing his head to one side in obvious frustration, Dismas went on, "I can't explain it. I just looked at

80

him and his eyes looked right through me and into my soul—if I have one." Dismas glanced at Miriam and saw that she was listening intently. "Miriam, am I going mad?"

"I do not think so, Dismas. I've heard from others that his eyes often speak sorrow and compassion—a strange mixture of feelings. I'm told he speaks to great crowds of people in scarcely a whisper, and yet all can hear him clearly."

Dismas studied the tired face before him. Miriam's hair hung down in wild wisps and beads of dirt had built up in the tiny folds of sweaty skin around her neck, the wrinkles made the dirt look like tiny strings of black pearls. Dismas looked for mockery in her eyes, mockery at what he had said, but there was none. "How can it be? Where did you hear of his eyes speaking?"

"From almost everyone who has seen him. At the well, where Aram sends me to get water two or three times each day. There everyone I've spoken to says they felt more than they heard what the man had to say. They say that as he talks, he urges people to believe. Even his most impossible words seem to be truth of a kind most people are incapable of telling."

"How strange, Miriam! It was like that with me, even though he said nothing at all. He sat silently on a white donkey and I heard him. I don't know what it was, but I just felt something happening inside. I can't understand that man."

Dismas clenched his eyes, pushed his fists deep into their sockets, and rocked forward. He bowed his head and huskily grunted, "I hate that feeling. No, I—yes, I hate it. Confound it. I hate it!" Dismas looked up at the ceiling of the inn, his eyes a little wild. "I can't stand believing in something I can't understand. The magic done in the square by men for money, I know is a trick, not fact. I learn how they do it and I appreciate their skill. This man's magic—I don't even know if it is magic—haunts me. I don't understand how he can reach deep into my inner being with only a look—not even a word—and demand a response. Yes, I hate what I feel!"

Jumping to his feet, his nose flaring like that of a terrified horse, Dismas all but screamed, "Caleb! You ungrateful whelp! If you're ever going to amount to anything, you must work for a living." Dismas took a deep drink from his remaining wine before he added, "And if you expect to work with me, you will come—*now*!" With that, he whirled and strode across the room, threw open the door, and went into the street without even bidding Miriam his customary farewell.

Outside, the heat was once more beginning to fill the streets. Dismas hesitated, pretending to examine the streets when in reality he waited for the now tipsy Caleb to catch up.

Bowing low before Dismas, a stupid grin smeared across his broad face, Caleb exulted in mock adoration, "Oh mighty and now holy one, shall we go where the purses hang like dates from the palm, or—" He giggled like a young girl. "Shall we simply go up into the sky as the prophets say your newfound friend will do?"

Dismas smiled at Caleb, "I think the first thing we should do is find you a nice, cold well in which to soak your dizzy head."

After roaming around the city more than an hour, the suffocating heat had baked most of the wine from Caleb's head. During that time Dismas had not slowed his pace, intentionally denying his suffering friend of rest. He hadn't even given Caleb time to stop for a drink of water. Throughout their walk, they had not left the old part of the city, but instead stopped to talk with beggars they knew. The stops, according to Dismas' plan, were not stops at all, but pauses only long enough to link arms with the other thief and continue walking. Dismas gave Caleb no chance to sit, but kept him on his feet and moving from place to place.

Along their circular route, both men had repeatedly been told that the man Jesus, who was the topic of conversation everywhere, was going to visit the temple. Most of their informers said he had been seen coming from the small village of Bethany, which was but a short distance east of the city, past the olive grove on the other side of the Kidron.

Jahuad, who carefully cultivated running sores and scabs on his body, just as a farmer would raise grapes, said, "I hear this magician of Nazareth learned much about wizardry when he lived in Egypt as a child. With luck, he will place the evil eye on the Pharisees and they will withdraw the Sanhedrin from the persecution of beggars. Did you know the Sanhedrin was trying to have us classed as lepers by temple law?"

A dog, with ribs showing through his mange-spotted fur, strolled over and began to lick the sores on the beggar's leg. Jahuad made no move to stop the dog because he knew such canine licking sometimes created even better sores than could be made by an ambitious fingernail. Bigger sores brought bigger donations.

From under his filth, Jahuad whined, "What does the Sanhedrin have against us? Have not the poor been with Israel since before the great slavery under Pharaoh?"

Dismas did not look at the man, but kept a wary eye out for soldiers or Herod's guard. He retorted, "Maybe the Pharisees try to have such laws passed because they like no one of a lower caste than they."

Caleb injected, "They need not fear for that—they should fear only what is possible." He followed his statement with a shallow chuckle.

Dismas ignored the interruption and continued, "Maybe they dislike you simply because they know you receive what might have been theirs if it were not given to you." He raised his arm and wiped his lips on his sleeve, "Probably, they know you will give nothing to them. Of what use is a dry well to them, and to them you are but a dry well."

Jahuad chuckled and, with blackened fingernails, picked more scabs from the sores on his arm. "You are probably right, Dismas, but still, it seems they would have better things to do," he whined.

"Maybe they will have, when this Jesus arrives at the temple," Dismas snorted grimly.

"All right, master," Caleb surrendered, "Let's join the others to watch this carpenter be made the fool."

"I didn't say I wanted to follow him," Dismas retorted. Then, embarrassed, he became angry. "Caleb, you know that if I wanted to go there, I would have gone. Besides, if I do go, it will not be just to watch a man be carved into small pieces; I will leave the temple a wealthy man."

"Dismas!" Jahuad exclaimed in mock surprise, "You surely wouldn't rob a man who stands on holy ground, would you?"

"Hear me, you pus-covered vermin," Dismas snarled, "I'd rob Yahweh Himself, the God of gods, if He had a fat purse and was as stupid as these lost pilgrims." Dismas waved his arm down the street toward the thin crowd, which wormed its way toward the temple.

Taking notice of how few people were left on the street on which they stood, Dismas snapped, "Come, Caleb.

We're going to the temple where the shekels hang heavily from walking, breathing trees ready for our harvest." Without waiting, he strode quickly away.

Caleb winked at the festered beggar as he assumed the gruff tone his friend had used and mimicked, "Come, Caleb!" Still grinning, he looked at Jahuad and said, "Gold and the Galilean. Dismas is interested in both."

From ahead of him, Caleb saw Dismas pause, take on a bored look, then put his fist on his hip as he shifted his weight to one leg and waited.

The streets leading to the temple led upward and the thieves' progress, especially since they joined the now thick flow of people going that way, was slow. For Caleb, even in his youth, it was irritating. Dismas found the frequent pauses in the mob's forward movement to be an occasional chance to regain his breath.

After what seemed like hours of pushing and being pushed, the pair began to snatch random pieces of fruit from the baskets which teetered atop hapless persons' heads. To do this in a crowd was a test. Each fruit could bring the dreaded cry, "Thief!"—and jail. This had never happened to Dismas or Caleb, but it was an occupational hazard they dared not ignore. Soon they saw the gleaming, massive walls of the temple ahead of them.

"Herod's masterpiece," Caleb snarled bitterly. "In those giant stones are Hebrew tribute, Hebrew sweat, and even Hebrew blood—all for the glory of that swine who switches from Roman friend to Roman friend, just as we would change clothes."

Dismas laughed at his friend's eloquence. "And when did you ever change clothes?" he asked.

"Well," Caleb was embarrassed at being caught by his own words, "it would be so if I had another change of clothes to put on."

As they neared the towering walls, the men could hear shouts coming from far ahead of them. The din did not come from the temple, although the temple had a noise of its own inside. The noise they heard came from the northern corner of the wall surrounding the courtyards and holy area.

From the excited talk they had heard while coming up the hill, it was obvious that the carpenter was about to arrive. It was equally evident that the crowd with him was not of the same temperament as those who welcomed him into the city yesterday morning. This crowd sought blood, and it appeared not to care if it was of the priests, Sanhedrin, temple guards, or even of the man they followed. They were looking for excitement, and it seemed to lie in tormenting this man.

Although most of the crowd entered the temple courtyard through the North Gate, behind the procurator's fortress, the Galilean was apparently going to enter through the small gate at the southern viaduct, which led to the courtyard set aside for Gentiles.

"That proves it," Caleb said loudly to Dismas, shouting to be heard above the din as they made their way ahead. "If he was any kind of Hebrew messiah, he certainly would not enter the temple where the Gentiles are. If he were even remotely a holy man, that is the last place he would go. Even the money-grubbing scribes only cross through the warning wall they built to keep Gentiles separated from Jewish holy ground when there is profit in it."

Dismas took time from cursing the pulsating, pushing mob to agree with Caleb. No sooner had he done this than they saw they had reached a fork in the street. One branch led sharply east along the temple's south wall. Both men saw that the crowd was practically nonexistent along this rough, narrow street. "Let's go this way," Caleb urged, grasping Dismas' arm. "There are fewer people and we can circle around and come in the Beautiful Gate on the east wall." After he said the name, Caleb quickly asked, "Do you know why they call it the Beautiful Gate? It looks just like the others to me."

Dismas had no answer for the question. Despite this, the older thief quickly agreed with the idea of going where fewer people could push him, so the pair began trotting along the narrow street.

After all but running the length of the south wall, then going northward along the east wall, both men paused before the Beautiful Gate, then strode through the wall and into the adjoining Court of the Women. There they stopped to catch their breaths.

The Court of the Women, while beautiful in its unpolished white limestone magnificence, was built to correspond with the Hebrew law regarding the subservient station of women in life. It was beautiful, but nothing when compared to the nearby Court of Israel, which belonged to the men. The Court of Israel stood between the Women's Court and the warning wall, which kept the holy areas from the desecration of Gentile feet.

In the men's portion, all structures were finished in gleaming marble, brought all the way from Carrara, just north of the Roman village of Pisa. This part of the temple's beauty attested to the extravagance of Herod in his expansion of the temple. Great stacks of similar marble, some polished and some waiting to be, were stacked along the Israel Courtyard's west wall, near the entrance of the Council Chamber.

When the two thieves had caught their wind, they made their way southward along the east wall of the court, passing stall after stall of bleating sheep and goats.

Mixed among these were stacked cages of cooing doves. All were destined to be sold at great temple profit as sacrifices during the Passover season.

Greedily the two men's eyes passed over the many stacks of gold and silver coins piled atop the massive wooden tables of the temple money changers. As if of a single mind, the look on their faces said they wished but for thirty seconds of blindness to strike everyone in the courtyard so they could apply their trade.

Money changers in the temple had been a common sight for many years. Hebrew law did not permit graven images of any sort to be part of Jewish life. For this reason, Jewish families did not have paintings of loved ones—only designs to decorate their walls, clothing, and money. Because other lands did not believe as they did, much of the money which found its way into Judea had images of various foreign leaders imprinted on it. For this reason, temple scribes exchanged such "unclean" money for Judean coins, which were completely acceptable inside the holy city, or exchanged the foreign coins for temple money, all at rates which gave from one third to one fifth of the actual value of the money being exchanged.

Further, if the sincerely pious of Judea wanted to purchase sacrificial animals at the temple, the law stated that the sacrifices could be purchased only with temple money—further profits for the holy men.

The two thieves knew the blindness they wished for the money changers was not to be, so they continued along Solomon's Porch, where the changers' tables were located to shade them from the sun, toward where they knew the Galilean would appear.

Speaking in tones so low that only Dismas could hear, Caleb muttered, "If the magician from Nazareth will but draw enough attention, or will start a fight, possibly you and I could relieve some of these money changers of the labor of counting so much at day's end."

Dismas' frustration at what he knew to be impossible was evident as he shook his head to show his disagreement with Caleb.

"God's blessings on you, gentlemen," spoke a piercing, high-pitched, and nasal voice. It came from behind the last stall and startled both men to an immediate stop. Looking down and to their left, they saw the "blind" beggar, Korath.

"What in Caesar's name are you doing here?" Dismas hissed. "You have claimed space before a merchant's door, not here."

The blind man, still habitually raising and lowering his beggar's bowl, causing its two tiny coins to jingle, stared at what seemed to be a single spot far in the invisible distance. He grinned, "That's true, but from what I've heard, the events here today will be too interesting to miss."

"What do you say, Korath?" Caleb encouraged. "Will there be an uprising today? Is the mob we hear in truth this Jesus' army? Speak up, man!" By this time Dismas and Caleb had squatted on their heels, a sitting posture popular throughout the land. It had been picked up wherever Egyptian and Babylonian empires traded, for it was their favorite resting position.

Korath quickly tucked his begging bowl beneath his leg, tossed his shawl over his head, and for the first time allowed his eyes to focus on the faces of the two men. The fellowship of lawbreakers knew no secrets, and with these two, Korath realized his guise as a blind man was transparent. As a wise man would talk to the ignorant, he began. "Caiaphas is going to unleash his legal jackals on this prophet today. He tried it before, during one of the man's talks out in the countryside, but the questioners failed. Today Caiaphas sends only his best."

The beggar licked his lips, glanced around, and continued, "Not only that, I hear that Caiaphas, the high priest himself, and his father-in-law, the old high priest, Annas, will be among them. Naturally they will ask no direct questions. To do so and have this Galilean best them might be more than the people would stand. This is what is being said. If the two high priests do show up, it will be a real test of tests. I hear from one of this prophet's followers that his leader, when he was but twelve years old, taught from the Scriptures, even explaining obscure passages to the temple rabbis here in Jerusalem. If that is so, my friends, this should be a most interesting day." Korath stopped talking to lick his lips once more and await some response to what he had said.

Although extremely interested in what he had heard, Dismas replied flatly, "We have heard too many times of this man teaching in the temple when he was a boy."

Dismas looked into the beggar's eyes and Caleb stared, fascinated, at where the man's front teeth used to be. Finally, Caleb asked, "Is that all?"

Hurt that his information had not fired his listeners to great excitement, Korath sputtered, "Is that all? Is that all? Isn't it enough?"

"But . . . but I thought this man was to be the Messiah. He was to be the one to free our people from Rome, the Herods, and all other oppression." Caleb's voice was fading with disappointment. "I thought you were going to tell us that he was planning to call down God's wrath, kill all the Romans, and then—then—oh well, I just hoped for more."

Korath, seeing Caleb's disappointment, and in an effort to cheer him, chirped, "That too may happen today, who knows?"

Dismas had not spoken much, but now blurted, "Caleb." He forced his attention from the beggar to his companion. "If what Korath says is true, it may be exactly what you expect, but done with an intelligence beyond your and my understanding."

"What I say *is* true," Korath whined when he heard Dismas cast possible doubt on him.

"But I thought this was to be a fight," Caleb protested. "How could an overthrow of the king and the Romans be otherwise?" Caleb was completely puzzled.

Dismas explained, "This Jesus could strike the priests dead and they would just be replaced by others. However, if he totally discredits them before all of Israel—" Dismas looked over his shoulder toward the Gentiles standing in the courtyard set aside for them, "No, even before the entire world, he will have destroyed them forever. If he does that, everyone who worships in any temple anywhere in the land would overthrow the Pharisees, the Sanhedrin, scribes and elders, then would turn to him—" Dismas' face broke into a full grin as he realized the magnitude of his own words, "The great messiah." Sarcasm fairly dripped from Dismas' last two words. the grin remained as he continued, "After that, every Hebrew in every land would know that Herod and Rome would face combat with God through this man—and any battle, especially the one you look for, would be assured."

A look of understanding slowly crossed Caleb's and Korath's faces. Caleb's previous discouragement was now gone. The look of a man who feels he knows some deep secret spread across his face. In his newfound enthusiasm, Caleb blurted out, "Come, Dismas. Let's place ourselves near a temple guard. With my talent for taking that which was never mine, if this man does what you say, I want to be where I cannot only disarm an enemy, I want a weapon with which to dispatch him to Hades."

"Not so fast, my young friend. Let's first gather the cost of the midday meal. That sun is already past where it should be when it is time for us to eat."

Dismas and Caleb rose to their feet and once more walked carefully and slowly across the Court of Israel. They weaved among the hundreds of men already there, all of whom stood in clumps of three or four, talking in muffled voices.

Before the two thieves had gone more than a hundred steps, Dismas stopped, his elbow catching Caleb in the pit of the stomach and causing him to gasp slightly.

"Caleb. Look at the huge pouch hanging from the waist of that fellow standing with the two old men. If it holds half as many coins as it appears to, we'll have enough money for a month's food."

After he scanned the courtyard several times, Caleb finally noticed the man about whom Dismas talked. The bulging coin purse was something to get excited about. "True, but how do you remove such a heavy adornment without the man becoming aware of it?"

"We don't," Dismas announced, startling Caleb with his negative answer. "Do you have the small knife you have tried to hide from me for so many years?"

"Yes," Caleb answered without thinking, excitement rising in his voice.

"Good. I'm going to embrace that fat pig and in the same move, you must slice the bottom of the bag enough to spill its contents. Then we'll be the instant neighbors the man needs to retrieve his coins. One for him and two for us," Dismas said, grinning broadly at Caleb.

In less than thirty seconds, Dismas' plan had gone exactly as he had described it. The only difference was that as the master thief embraced the man with the big purse, he exclaimed, "Cousin!" as he enveloped the man. Almost instantly, Caleb did his part of the job and before the first coin hit the stone courtyard, Dismas backed away apologizing as he did for his mistaking the man for some long lost relative.

As the old man, Dismas, and Caleb were on hands and knees searching for the coins, the two thieves kept muttering such things as, "It's disgraceful how dishonest men are today," and "Even the men at the temple are no longer to be trusted," and "Surely a good sacrifice will force God to replace your fortune." All of this they said loudly enough to impress their victim with their honesty and pious intentions. From the man's complaining company, the two thieves next made their way to a food stand, where a priest's helper charged three or four times the normal cost for such foods.

Moments later, leaning against a stack of tiles, they munched on sweetmeats and dipped their blackened fingers into a small pot of honey. As they noisily slurped at the tasty treats, their fingers slowly took on a cleaner appearance. Neither man noticed, however, for they were busy looking around them.

King Herod had begun work on the temple several years before. One arched bridge in the main court was built of a single piece of marble eighteen feet long, nine feet wide, and around nine inches thick. Dismas and Caleb heard men who should know look at the bridge and remark, "A true wonder. I don't see how they did it." The huge stone from which the bridge was made had been brought to the holy place by the sweat of borrowed Roman slaves, each cursing it with every straining, staggering step from the sea, across plains, and up hills and mountains to Jerusalem.

The rest of the temple was equally majestic, but Dismas considered it a waste of good money. "It's just something to glorify Herod and with which the priests can impress those whose money paid for it. That way they can squeeze even more money from them," he complained. Dismas did not realize that in addition to the temple at which he looked, the Herod family had built sports stadiums, and even cities elsewhere. Even if he had known, Dismas' next statement would have expressed his opinion of the other Herod accomplishments as well. Spitting and drawing the disapproving glares of those about him in the temple area, Dismas concluded, "If it were made of camel dung, it could not be less holy."

Finishing the last of the honey, Caleb casually rolled over, spotted the big-mouthed drinking jug of a country man who sat near him. After making sure the jug's owner was not watching, Caleb dipped first one hand, then the other into the man's drinking water. After doing this, he rubbed his hands together to make sure all of the sticky substance was gone. He then wiped the remaining moisture on the front of his already crusty robe.

From across the courtyard came a great shout. It was not a sudden thing, but rose gradually from the throats of a massive wave of hundreds of men, all pushing and shoving their way across the wide marble courtyard.

Rolling his head to one side, Dismas, in a tone which indicated total boredom, said, "Well, it looks like the miracle worker has finally arrived. Apparently something delayed him. Now let's see if he can indeed conquer with love—and cunning."

4 MONDAY AFTERNOON

Leading the crowd, his eyes furrowed with the look of a man who has just seen something take place which disgusted him, strode the man Jesus. He seemed oblivious of the men scrambling along behind him. For the first time since they saw him sitting quietly on the small donkey, the two thieves got a good look at him. It was obvious to them that while it was the same man, this time his mood was entirely different from what it had been the day before.

He was not tall—no more than five feet four or five inches. Although his height was not impressive, both thieves were amazed at the massiveness of his heaving chest and the naturally strong legs supporting him. The Jesus they saw today was an offended and angry man. His steps were the long, strong strides of a powerful and determined man.

As his cloak pressed against him in his headlong plunge through the quickly parting crowd, which seconds before had just milled around in the open area, Dismas and Caleb saw muscles ripple as the man's fists clenched and unclenched. When he neared Solomon's Porch, where the money changers were hard at work, he paused, looked up and down the line of tables, and his breathing began to get deeper and heavier.

Approximately halfway from the far wall where he had entered the temple courtyards, and without even looking at what he did, the Galilean allowed one hand to snap out and grasp several thin, tightly woven ropes from the hand of the young temple goat herder.

With his eyes glued on the long row of tables at which the money changers sat, he hesitated and then began his determined walk again. Without breaking the unyielding stride he had set, the man began quickly and deftly to braid the small tough ropes into one large one. The larger rope took on the thickness and stiffness of a flexible staff, but it was a whip. Not once had he looked back, to either side, or even down at the strips of hemp he swished back and forth as he braided them. His entire attention was now focused on the stalls ahead.

Within seconds the money changers looked up to see Jesus coming at them. "A madman," one of them screamed, setting off a scramble to gather up the many stacks of gold and silver coins on the massive tables behind which they sat. There was no time for them to protect themselves or their money from the swiftly approaching and vengeful man, but they tried. The look in the carpenter's eyes made it plain that money would give no protection from his wrath.

The two experienced thieves knew that trouble of a magnitude they had never before seen was about to

96

erupt. With a cunning born into them, they wanted to be around to act as scavengers of any spoils which might result. With equal cunning, they would make sure they could in no way be blamed for what took place.

Quickly Dismas and Caleb darted into a tiny staircase and up from the courtyard to the sheltering roof which protected the money changers from the sun.

As the carpenter reached the exchange area and came almost directly below the two thieves, they heard him shout in a voice more authoritative than Dismas imagined possible from such a person, "It is written—" The Galilean's muscular right hand slipped under one of the massive tables. My house shall be called the house of prayer." With those words the man's muscles suddenly flexed and the table went end over end, coins and men scattering in all directions. A roar of approval went up from the crowd.

"Caleb!" Dismas screamed over the noise of the mob, "Did you see that?" Dismas excitedly inched forward to get a better view. He could not believe what he had just witnessed. The brute strength of the Galilean seemed to be that of twenty men. "That table and the money—he just cast them aside. They must weigh three hundred pounds!" Both men were mesmerized by the drama which was unfolding below them.

The carpenter's voice once more knifed through the pulsating roar of the stunned crowd. "But ye have made it a den of thieves." His Galilean accent added massiveness to his voice, and again he overturned a table—with one hand. It was apparent through the man's fiery eyes that what he did was not from hate, but from disgust and hurt. Regardless of the attitude of the money changers or the mob, which cheered his every move, he paced his way along the rows of tables, each waiting its turn to be the victim of his righteous wrath.

At the end of the row where the money changers sat, a knot of temple Zealots ran forward to stop what they felt to be sacrilege. The carpenter all but ignored them. He began swinging the whip he held in his left hand, slicing the air with sharp snapping arches. The hissing tips of the thongs swished past the intruder's faces by scant inches. Still, he did not stop sliding his hand under table after table, and with what appeared to be little strain now, threw them into the air. As quickly as they had charged, the Zealots retreated, their bravery melting with the sound of the rope slashing past their faces.

Jesus scarcely hesitated as he kicked the three-legged stools from beneath dove sellers and sheep tenders. He intended no harm to the men who watched the sheep and fowl; his act was done only to make sure they did not interfere with his central purpose. As each tender lost his seat and fell backward, animals and birds found freedom from the terror they had known just seconds before. The sound of goats, sheep, and the loud stir of flapping wings added to the confusion which echoed back and forth across the temple court.

Curses, screams of fear, threats, and even cheers came at the man from all sides. The carpenter chose either to ignore them or simply didn't hear them in his intense concentration. He continued his righteous rampage.

As the Galilean's one-man skirmish proceeded against the sellers and money changers, Dismas and Caleb saw several temple guards armed with swords, shields, and spears try to force their way through the tightly packed crowd. They also saw that the same guards, Roman soldiers hired by the temple, were not particularly interested in what they were doing. The guards worked for the priests only to earn extra money, not to risk injury.

The two men also saw that Jesus' twelve closest followers were stationed at strategic points in front of the crowd. They did not take part in what their master was doing, but they made sure the crowd did not surge forward and that the guards did not advance on him as he went about his dramatic job.

"Incredible," Dismas said.

"The man is mad," Caleb echoed.

"Mad as a fox," Dismas gleefully replied through clenched teeth. The older thief was not even aware he had used the word "fox," King Herod's despised nickname. The older thief swelled with enthusiasm. "He has now forced the detestable priests, Sadducees, Pharisees, and the Sanhedrin to recognize him," he gleefully yelled. "And look at those stupid priests running in circles shouting for help from people who are enjoying this as much as I."

Dismas went on, "He is no longer just another fanatic, but one who challenges God's thieving temple crew. He is no longer the teacher of love and telling people to kiss the feet of the powerful. Caleb—" Dismas slapped his young friend soundly on the back. "He has challenged Rome itself and announced that he is the one to reckon with. Not even Jesus Barabbas and his cutthroats ever dared to do what this man now does."

"Yes, but all that this can gain is trouble," Caleb moaned, shaking his head sadly, "just trouble. He didn't even take the money—just threw it away."

With this realization, both men involuntarily snapped alert. They turned to face each other, their faces ashen and a look of horror on them.

"The money," Dismas blurted out. "I forgot all about the money."

Both men dropped from their perch, which was more

than ten feet from the courtyard floor, fell to their knees, and ignoring the jostling they got from the staggering, kicking, darting legs, began frantically scrambling around the floor in search of any coins which may have rolled their way. But all they received for their efforts were mashed fingers and hands. Not one single coin was to be found. Both men' were slightly sick at their stomachs when they finally stood.

The milling crowd moved like the waters of the sea at high tide—surging inward as the carpenter moved toward the wall, and rippling back as if they were attached to each other when he turned toward them to make his way to a different area.

In the midst of the confusion caused by the rising and falling of the noise, which came with each new move of the determined Galilean, the darting sheep and goats grew thicker. Their bleating and butting added even more chaos to the already unbelievable uproar.

Several priests, standing clear of the source of their problem, ran from place to place. Each gestured wildly and repeatedly shouted, "Stop the madman! In the name of all that is holy, stop him. Let the guards through. Arrest him."

From nearby, another priest, much younger than the others, heard his senior priests squawking pleas for help and became even more adament in his demands, "No!" he screamed, his voice pitched high and shrill like that of a terrified woman. "Seize him and kill him."

The malice of the priests' words was wasted. Their shouts were all but drowned by the excited clammer of the crowd. Even the centuries-old barrier which divided Gentile from Jew in the holy temple had lost its importance. Gentiles, laughter booming from their throats, mingled freely throughout the courtyard areas. All that the Hebrews held sacred and inviolate was crumbling before the eyes of Caiaphas, who stood on the balcony overlooking the crazed mob below.

Caiaphas was a tall man, much taller than his fellow Jews. But his face had the palor of one who seldom, if ever, allowed the hot sun to touch his skin. His paleness, which stood out when he mingled among those he sometimes called "the faithful fools," was overshadowed by the flabbiness of his skin, which bagged under his eyes and swung in folds below his chin. As was the custom of the high priests, his dress was garish, but did not hide the fact that under it was the paunchy body of a man whose most strenuous exercise was an occasional walk in King Herod's palace or a rare appearance at the temple. Today he had come to estimate the wealth, from sacrificial animal sales, which would be his by the end of the week. He had heard that the "so-called messiah" would make an appearance and that the people of Jerusalem expected him to match wits with the carpenter prophet. The thought had amused him.

This violent man, this worker in wood, this Jesus, had been a mild thorn under Caiaphas' skin for almost three years. Now the priest of priests was anxious to see how the man's Passover temper tantrum would affect the people, particularly his own followers.

Though this man's popularity grew even greater, he would still not be as well liked as that odd man, John, who ran around trying to get everyone to jump into the river with him.

Caiaphas' first encounter with the man some people called John the Baptizer had been a funny one. The wild-eyed man had walked around in the skins of animals. The skins had been properly cured, but looked as if the animal might still be in them. For people to follow such a person was highly unlikely, but it happened. At that time Caiaphas took heart in his ability to milk the people of gold and silver. If people were gullible enough to follow a wild prophet, they were ripe to accept any tale as fact.

In the past the high priest was confident the carpenter could be caught violating one of the hundreds of contradictory and interlocking Hebrew laws. However, try as his men might, the man had escaped every trap they set for him. Looking down at the chaos below him, Caiaphas knew one of two things would happen. Either the people would turn on Jesus as a mad man for violating what they had been taught was holy, or the man could no longer be considered just another passing false prophet, and would have to be crushed, one way or another. Caiaphas would not allow himself to consider the third possibility—that the claims of the Galilean's followers were literally true.

As the minutes passed and the destruction became more widespread and financially disruptive, Caiaphas seethed in helpless anger. In his wildest nightmares he could not have imagined the destruction of temple trade as he now saw it in the yard below. This lone man was accomplishing what even Rome had never dared to try.

As the high priest watched, Jesus overturned all of the twenty-four money tables, sending their scribes scurrying in all directions. He loosed more than two hundred sheep, a hundred and forty goats, untold numbers of doves, and was thrashing wildly at a large herd of oxen, forcing them to crash through the gate which locked the pen holding them.

As the minutes passed, Caiaphas watched the total disintegration of the temple marketing system, as well as the attitude his priests had taken weeks to instill in the people. This man had wrecked it all. The climate his

102

priests had so carefully molded to inspire greater Passover contributions, was gone. From his high perch, Caiaphas glared at the destroyer below him. The muscles in his jaw flexing and relaxing, Caiaphas reflected a hatred he seldom allowed to show.

Caiaphas knew that to salvage anything from the remainder of what he called his "Pasah Harvest," he would have to find a way to squash Jesus like a detested bug.

Caiaphas took consolation in this thought, but he could not stop pacing along the balcony in furious frustration. With each step the tiny bells along the bottom of his robe tinkled and jangled noisily. Several times, when he saw one of the guards looking up toward him, he would point at Jesus and shout, "Seize that man."

Each time the guard just shrugged his shoulders as if to say, "What can I do when I can't even get through the crowd?"

The guards knew better than to spill the blood of a Jew when he stood on holy ground. Violation of the law of sanctity would have worse consequences than what now took place. Rumor was that Governor Pilate was already in trouble with Rome for having killed three hundred or so people from the small district of Samaria. To kill Jews right on the temple ground could bring much bad feelings—worse because it would be a Roman who violated the law, and more so for the guard because of what his centurion would do to him later.

Dismas, now packed among the rest of the crowd, shifted to his left for a better view between the heads and shoulders of the pressing masses. As he did, he bumped into someone. Intending to intimidate the person, he whirled to glare at the man. Instead of looking into an excited face, he found himself staring at a hairy chest, exposed through the open neck of a rough woolen mantle and cloak. As Dismas tilted his head back to look at the face of the huge man, his gaze met a broad face surrounded by sun-bleached hair. The face was smiling and looking down at him.

"Impressive, isn't he?" the big man asked, his voice more of a rumble than a normal speaking voice.

"Impressive is hardly the word I would use," Dismas responded apprehensively. "I'd say he's either one of the bravest men in all Judea or completely mad. Either way, he'd better be one of the fastest. After all of this—" Dismas jerked his head toward the overturned tables and destroyed stalls. "He must run like the wind and expect death or worse from Roman or Hebrew justice."

The big man responded with booming laughter. "Death holds no fear for him. As for being mad, he is mad all right." The big man's grin broadened even more as he looked over the destruction and back at Dismas. "Yes, he is mad—and his madness comes straight from God. It is a madness given only to one—to him chosen of God."

The hulking man paused and looked deeply into Dismas' eyes before continuing, "Don't worry about him, my friend. Anything that happens to him will be because he allowed it to happen. If it appears to be otherwise, I and others like me are prepared to defend him." Then the big man asked, as if expecting only one answer, "Are you one of his?"

Dismas, never one to be pinned down by question or deed, quickly stepped away from the big man before answering.

"I'm, not sure I know what you mean by 'one of his.' I do know, however, that the steel of the temple guard is Roman steel. I also know that this stranger has broken

104

the flow of gold to the priests, and I know they have destroyed other men for much less." Dismas took a deep breath. "And I know that with a man of your obvious strength at the side of any man, he is equal to ten. But ten men may be too few after all of this." Dismas squinted his eyes as he added, "What do you mean when you ask if I'm one of his'?"

The smile left the huge man's face. "Friend, if you must ask, you are not. I beg you to listen to his teachings, then you will no longer need to ask."

"Are you also a Galilean?"

"Yes, even though the color of my hair, as light as it is, says otherwise.

"I thought so. You have the accent. Are you one of his twelve?"

The man's face creased in another smile, "Yes."

With the news that the big man was an associate of the man purging the temple of what he said was the corruption of holy ground, Dismas frantically looked around to see if anyone had watched him talking to the man. The old thief knew he was in no position to be connected with lawbreakers.

As he scanned the area, he saw that the carpenter had stopped his rampage. The whip he had made and used so effectively now lay at his feet. He stared at the marble slabs which made up the floor of the courtyard, and his chest heaved heavily. He was spent.

Aware that all eyes were on the carpenter, Dismas made no move to flee from the big man. He finally realized that the giant was the one called the Big Fisherman by the people

His real name was Simon Bar-Jona, but the twelve referred to him by the new name, Peter, given to him by the carpenter.

Before Dismas could turn to continue his conversation with the fisherman, he felt a huge hand on his shoulder. Out of instinctive reaction, the thief immediately shook loose. It was Peter again. He quietly rumbled, "The man you see is not actually a destroyer, as you said. Really, he is not. Before he began all of this," Simon Peter gestured toward the chaos around him, "I heard him say that this place had become a den of vipers. No, he is not destroying, but building—building what Almighty God originally meant true worship to be."

Dismas grunted disrespectfully, but did not dispute the matter. Instead, he turned, as had the rest of the crowd, to watch Jesus. He felt it would be but a matter of minutes before the temple guards rushed up and, with one or two strokes of their swords, traded the man's blood for the spilled coins. Dismas did not know the guards had already decided against such a thing.

Before the thief could completely visualize what would happen, a lone temple guard pushed past him on his way toward the carpenter. With the speed of a striking cobra, the foot of the big fisherman snapped out in front of the armor-clad guard, causing him to topple into a noisy heap. Instead of the guard falling gently, as they were taught to do in combat, he fell abnormally hard. The big man's foot had powerfully lifted both of the soldier's feet from the ground, causing him to land awkwardly on his face.

Dismas turned to the big man with admiration and said, "Good for you! Good for you!"

A man standing on the opposite side of the fisherman, a man with curly black hair and a serious look on his face, said in a quiet voice, "What you did was not good, Peter. The man may be injured."

At that, Peter seemed to awake from a bad dream. He

106

too suddenly became concerned. The pair knelt beside the fallen soldier as Peter mumbled, "You may be right."

While Peter and the black-haired man checked to see if the soldier was hurt seriously, Dismas continued to back away. When the men were assured that little more than the guard's pride and forehead were damaged, they too melted into the milling mob.

Seconds later, Dismas' grin, caused by the guard's fall, grew even wider when he saw Jesus and his twelve gathering together. He thought to himself, *There will be one big battle now.* Dismas knew the carpenter and his fisherman, alone, could put up a good fight. With eleven more, most of whom were muscular men, the scrap would be a spectacle to watch.

Instead of a wave of metal-wrapped guards sweeping down on the man, only three temple priests appeared, each dressed in the best clothing a priest could wear. The trio started talking heatedly with Jesus and his men. *They're probably trying to talk him out of destroying the whole miserable place,* Dismas thought happily.

Dismas could not hear the words being said, except when the carpenter pointed a finger toward the temple and clearly and emphatically said, "No." The priests made no move against him.

The old thief was astonished at the way this man, who had previously been so docile, stood up to the temple officials most people looked upon with awe. Although he would not bend to their will, seemingly he had a sincere sympathy for them.

The three priests gestured frantically as they argued among themselves. Dismas saw something about which he had heard, but had never before seen. While the three priests agued among themselves, Jesus drifted a few feet closer to Dismas. As the carpenter waited, a man whose leg was badly bent and shriveled crawled to within five or six feet of the Galilean. Pitifully, like a tiny child begging for candy, the cripple extended a scrawny arm, his hand open limply. On his face was the pleading look of a man who saw in Jesus his last hope.

Again Dismas could not hear what was said when the Galilean approached, leaned over the lame man, and talked with him. The thief could see that the man on the ground looked intently into the carpenter's face. As Jesus spoke softly to him, and without lowering his weak arm from its pleading position, the cripple slowly nodded his head in agreement with whatever was being said to him.

Instead of pulling away, as the priests would have responded, the carpenter reached out both hands, placed them on the head of the cripple, then closed his eyes. It was obvious to Dismas that the carpenter was praying—not as the priests, the Pharisees, and the elders did, for they often went into the streets to pray loudly, beating their chests to gain attention. This man prayed in silence.

With his eyes still closed, Jesus turned his rough features directly toward the sun. standing thus he took on an added glow. Dismas was not sure if what he saw was real or only his imagination. He felt that possibly what he saw was caused by staring at a sunlit object too long. But he thought he saw a circle of light, brighter than any reflection coming from the sun off anyone else in the crowd, was surrounding Jesus' head.

The radiance seemed to flow first along his neck and shoulders, then down both arms, until it reached his hands. At that point the glow spread to the bowed head of the invalid crouched on the ground.

Dismas saw that Jesus' lips, which had moved ever so easily, were no longer moving. Instead, a gentle smile enveloped his face, like that of a man who, for the first

108

time, looks on his newborn child. As the Galilean stood with his hands on the man's head, the cripple realized something was happening to him—something miraculous—so he remained absolutely still.

For the first time since childhood his leg slowly began to move. At first it jerked spasmodically. Then it began to inch its way from the cramped, crooked position. The leg continued to straighten out until, like the normal leg, it was straight out before him.

When it was fully extended, the man jerked his head away from Jesus' hands. His face lurched up to where he could look directly at that of the man who had done this wonderful thing for him.

"Praise God!" he shouted through a grin of bewilderment and awe. "Praise God! Praise God!"

Jesus opened his eyes to look into the man's face. He was not startled by the man's shouts. He knew the sounds were not from terror, fear, or any of the other things which excite men to such outbursts. He knew the shouts were an expression of absolute joy released from the deepest depths of the soul.

"Your sins are forgiven," Jesus said calmly.

The cripple looked deeply into the carpenter's eyes as he more softly and clearly said, "Praise the living God!"

What had happened brought a deep hush over the crowd, even over the gawking priests. Everyone, even Dismas and Caleb, stopped moving and stood still, almost afraid to breathe.

Instead of the man leaping to his feet, as Dismas had heard many of the healed ones did, this man sat staring at his shriveled, but now extended leg. The miracle Dismas had seen was not yet complete. It was clear to all of the men standing around that it was still in progress.

The cripple man again shouted, "Look! Praise God!

Look at my leg. Oh, Master! Look at my leg!" His rav-
ings were not without cause. Like a wineskin being filled
from a fountain, the leg was expanding. Where before it
had the look of a bone covered tightly with nothing but
leathery skin, it now slowly swelled, filling with muscles
and sinews.

The men nearest the healer and the cripple, along with
the priests, gasped in terror, then drew back as if to escape from what they saw. None but the carpenter's
regular followers understood what was taking place.

As Dismas stared in disbelief, along with dozens of
other onlookers, Jesus extended his hand. Now silent and
exhausted, the crippled man reached up, took Jesus'
hand, and carefully, ever so carefully, pulled himself
erect.

A sigh came from the crowd and a look of fear and astonishment crossed the cured man's face. He looked
around in awe and Dismas realized that the man had
never before looked at people from eye level. For the
three or four decades of his life the man had viewed
everyone from two or three feet off the ground. He had
seen adults face-to-face only when they lay sleeping or
languished on the ground. Now, as a whole man, he saw
them as they saw each other.

"*EEEeeeyahhh,*" the man screamed, both of his hands
whipping up to clutch the sides of his head hysterically.

Jesus stepped back away from him. The carpenter's
eyes never left those of the standing cripple, his arms and
hands extended outward as if he were calling the still
shaky man to him. When he was nine or ten feet from the
man, Jesus began beckoning, using only the slightest
movements of his fingers. Next he smiled the same smile
he had shown before, and a message seemed to pass
between the two men even though no words were said.

110

Without any further hesitation, the man took a short, jerky step. It was like the step of a baby letting go of his mother's fingers for the first time, but it was a real step—the first the man had ever taken in his life. After looking down in disbelief at his feet, the man looked up again at the still-beckoning carpenter and took another step, then another, and another.

As the full realization came over him that he could walk without the fear of falling, the man almost ran toward the Galilean. Once there, he intentionally fell at his healer's feet, clutching him around the knees and sobbing.

Again Jesus tenderly leaned over and lovingly stroked the man's hair as he whispered something in his ear.

The man released the carpenter's knees, but could not raise his head because of his uncontrollable weeping. Slowly the tears gave way and the cripple bowed his head to the ground before the man who had healed him. The gesture was one of absolute gratitude and subservience.

Raising his head only a few inches, the man crawled forward. This time he kissed first one, then the other of the dusty feet of his benefactor. No one who watched doubted that the carpenter had won another staunch and devoted follower.

Dismas found the entire episode almost more than he could bear. Around him he heard men whispering. One hissing more loudly than the others caused him to look over his shoulder.

"I tell you, he is either a god or a devil. Here in the sanctity of the holy place that he first wrecks, he destroys what is God's. Then he cures a lifelong affliction with but the touch of his hand."

Another man, listening to his neighbor's whispers, responded, "It is certainly the work of the devil. How

111

else can you explain his mistreatment of God's holy place?"

The first whisperer retorted, "But it must have been God's will that this be done, or God would have stopped it."

"Maybe so, maybe so," the second man agreed with a puzzled look.

Confusion was thick throughout the temple courtyards. But the confusion, especially that of the three priests, turned to horror when the formerly crippled man reverently gasped, "Praise God! Praise you, oh, master. You can be no other than he which hid himself from Moses—the one who blessed Abraham's wife, Sarah, with child when her insides were shriveled with age. You—" The man stood completely upright, threw back his shoulders, and loudly proclaimed, "You are the living God. The one without beginning or end. The master of all time and all things."

A silence almost beyond description fell over everyone who could hear. Their astonishment was broken only by the irritated and blustering shouts of Caiaphas high above them. The high priest's words were only sounds. None of the people below could understand him, but he was obviously beside himself with rage.

At the cripple's declaration of faith, the carpenter's expression of love did not change. Dismas thought, *If ever a man looked beyond what can be seen, this man is doing so now.* He sees within—not as I do. Dismas, like the men around him, was utterly confused.

His confusion, as befuddling as it was, would soon be magnified, for as Jesus looked at the former cripple, a blind man came staggering out of the crowd. He was young, perhaps twenty or twenty-one. With a steady cadence he swung his outstretched arms stiffly from side

112

to side. In seconds, apparently guiding himself by sound, he touched the carpenter with his clawlike hands. The Galilean slowly turned to face the young man.

Just as with the cripple, the carpenter seemed to know what was expected of him, but instead of healing the man immediately Jesus softly began asking questions. Again, as before, the man to whom Jesus spoke nodded vigorously in agreement. Jesus continued to lean forward to talk with the blind man, who kept nodding.

Then the Galilean put one hand on one of the man's eyes. Slowly he placed his other hand on the other eye. After he had done this, he took a deep breath, as if what he was about to do would take much strength. Then he closed his own eyes and the same glow as before began to come over him.

This time Dismas moved closer to see better what was taking place. Dismas saw Jesus' lips moving gently. The blind youth's arms slowly dropped to his sides.

There was no doubt in Dismas' mind that this young man was truly blind. Dismas had seen him many times over the years. Each time, he was led by a boy Dismas guessed to be the sightless man's younger brother. Both had curly black hair and wore robes obviously made from identical thread.

Now the Galilean allowed his hands to drop from the blind man's eyes and rest easily on his shoulders. Neither man moved. Jesus whispered something to the man, who continued to stand motionless, squinting hard. He was trembling with fear.

After Jesus coaxed him several times, the young man slowly relaxed his eyelids, then opened them wide—only to stare sightlessly ahead as always. After a brief pause, a hiss went up from the expectant crowd. Several hundred mouths whispered in disappointment at not seeing a second miracle unfold before them.

The Galilean did not flinch. Instead he stood perfectly still and stared—almost glared—into the unseeing eyes. Dismas moved even nearer, and he too stared at the blind eyes. As he did so, the realization hit him that he was not just curious, but actually expecting to see this country carpenter cure a lifelong blind man of his sightlessness. That Dismas, the thief, would find himself believing in this Jesus, just as the pilgrims did, was more than he could take. Shaking his head as if warding off a slight dizziness, Dismas hardened his heart, but remained to see what would happen.

From the blind man came a slight groan. Dismas leaned forward to get a clearer look at the man's eyes. He saw new life begin to come into them. The vacant stare gradually took on expression and life.

The blind man's mouth dropped open and his face suddenly went pale. His sightless eyes widened until, holding back a sob, he exclaimed, "I'm— I'm beginning to see!" He shouted it twice more, then screamed, "I can see!" Then, without even thanking the man who had healed him, he turned his back on Jesus and shouted again, this time into the faces of those who were behind him when he was cured, "I can see!"

As Jesus hung his head, members of the crowd began patting the newly sighted man on the back and congratulating him on the wonderful good fortune that had befallen him.

"What a bunch of pigs," Dismas mumbled. He thought, *This man does these great things and only one or two even recognize their miracles for what they are.*

As if aware of Dismas' thoughts, Jesus turned and looked directly at the old thief. For the second time in two days, Dismas fell under Jesus' burning gaze and

114

knew why others respected the man so. Not a word passed between them, no move was made, and yet Dismas felt naked before the man. It was as if Dismas looked deep into his own conscience, rather than into the burning brown eyes of a man radiating love. From Miriam, Dismas had received passion and care. From Caleb it was respect and fondness. From this man it was a love which was not frivolous or sentimental, but intense, deeply caring and incomprehensible. Dismas could almost feel Jesus telling him, "I can give you what no other force on earth can provide. I can give you peace—contentment beyond what your mind can even imagine." The feeling all but suffocated the old thief.

"No!" Dismas suddenly screamed as he whirled and raced through the crowd, bowling men over as he went.

Dismas was terrified beyond reason, terrified of something he could not understand. He knew the carpenter was asking him a question. He was equally sure he did not want to answer it. He was being called to a new life, and he did not want to respond. Dismas was afraid. He knew he had been dealt a blow from which he would never recover.

Dismas ran. He left Caleb far behind, but pursuing him.

By the time he reached Hezekiah's Pool, another of the small watersheds built by the old king to help the city if it came under siege, Dismas had run many blocks without stopping. He had run until his legs would no longer carry him. Despite the stares of the women there to fill their earthen jars, the exhausted and frightened thief fell at the water's edge and desperately splashed the cooling dampness onto his face and into his hair. That the water also drenched his clothes did not concern him. He had escaped from the madman at the temple, and that was reason to be thankful.

After the third dip of Dismas' hand into the brackish water, Caleb caught up with him.

Breathing heavily and with his legs spread, the young thief was unable to speak for several seconds. "You ran— like a lion—was after—you." Caleb paused in his gulping long enough to take a deep breath. "What caused you to run so?" He took another deep breath. "Did you see something dangerous?"

Dismas, his nostrils flared wide, looked up from the stones on which he lay. His face showed the terror he felt deep within. "Caleb, you saw it. Did you see the way he looked at me? The man is a devil—or a god. Caleb, that man, for the first time ever, left me cold with fear— afraid to the marrow of my bones."

"What did he do, master?" Caleb was completely puzzled. "He is just a strong country carpenter who plays tricks on the senses of people."

"How blind you are, Caleb. He is more than a carpenter. Far more."

Caleb, feeling that his master was somehow ill, tenderly put his hand on Dismas' shoulder and gave it a slight squeeze.

Fear still in his eyes, Dismas violently jerked away. As he did so, he stared hostilely at the young thief's hand, as if it had offended him.

Dismas knew he was overreacting, but he could not help himself. Caleb was still trying to regain his breath, so he made no further moves to touch his friend. Instead, Dismas clenched his eyes tightly and shook his head. He was trying to stop a dizziness which had come over him.

Taking a deep breath and letting it out with a loud "Whew," Dismas tried to get a grip on his shattered nerves. As the tenseness slowly lifted from his arms and

116

shoulders, he looked up at Caleb. "You're right. I am foolish for acting as I do. He is just a man." Dismas looked down at the stones beneath him, then mumbled, "But Caleb, how do we explain the cures we saw today? Can we say they were just tricks? No. The lame man was crippled for years. We know the blind man was, indeed, blind." He looked away, across the water, then wearily added, "Were his miracles simply like the lakes that nomads see in the desert? No, they actually happened."

Caleb, wanting to ease his friend's mind, said, "Maybe it's as I have heard, my friend. Maybe this man is the world's greatest magician. Maybe he just made us see what he wanted us to see."

"Maybe you're right," Dismas conceded, not believing it.

Dismas arose and the two men stood beside each other a few seconds before the other thief led his student toward a nearby stone wall. Soon they were seated and leaning back against the wall staring across the pool. Each man was deep in his own thoughts as they watched the women dip the water. Dismas was still deeply disturbed by what he had seen, and even more worried by the unspoken words communicated to him by the Galilean.

Caleb sat playing a simple guessing game with the women as they went about their chores. First he would imagine what they looked like shorn of the bulging, flapping clothes they wore. Then he would try to imagine the many uses of all the water being dipped. He guessed that most of it would be used as drinking water, but he also pictured in his mind the various kinds of stews or boiled vegetables it would help cook over small, but efficient fires in odor-filled kitchens. Caleb's imagination had few bounds—and held nothing sacred.

When the shadows had lengthened until they fell well out into the water, the two men rose, and without even brushing their clothing, moved toward the center of town.

It was time to retire to Aram's inn again. This time, instead of abstaining from the wine, as they had so weakly done before, Caleb was determined to get his nerve-wracked friend and teacher as roaring drunk as possible.

It had been an exciting and tiring day. Now it was time, as the Greeks and Romans said, "to eat, drink and be merry, for tomorrow they might die."

Arm in arm they went to the security of their own haven, Aram's inn, and the blackness of intoxication.

5 TUESDAY MORNING

No sooner had Dismas opened his eyes than the sharp pain slashed through his forehead, forcing him to squint.

When he finally forced both eyes fully open he knew he had been sleeping on the cool roof of a building—one made of palm-leaf walls, which sheltered him from view from other rooftops. Judging by the smell, which draped the air like a stale fishnet, he was on the roof of Aram's inn. Dismas knew he had been very drunk; in fact, getting drunk was the last thing he remembered of the night before.

In the agony felt only by men drunk from bad wine, Dismas put the palms of both hands against the sides of his head and pressed hard. Nothing, it seemed, would stop the pounding inside his skull.

As the suffering thief tried to roll onto his side, he touched something soft and warm. He gently turned his head, trying to keep from causing more pain, and saw that the warmth came from the body of Miriam. She was not in the rough clothing she wore when serving customers downstairs, but was naked.

She lay on her back, still sleeping. With no show of feeling on his face. Dismas allowed his eyes to wander over her. From her open mouth came the low purr of a near snore. The woman's long black hair lay across her face and down both sides of her neck.

Unsure of what he should do—or even of what he had or had not done, Dismas reached for her robe and covered her and then decided that it would only be proper to waken her with a kiss. With great effort, he forced himself to one elbow, then leaned forward, his lips pursed for the kiss. As he neared the girl's face, she sighed gently and Dismas' head jerked back as if he had been slapped. The smell of soured wine, either on her breath or his, almost made him sick.

One of us will surely die, he thought. If it is my breath I might kill her with it. If it is hers, it could be the death of me. Dismas gave up the idea of kissing her and, instead, pushed himself to his knees. He struggled to maintain his balance. Once more he squinted his eyes shut tightly, which gave him the appearance of a man about to have his head publicly removed. He remained still until the throbbing in his head forced a low moan to come from deep within him.

In slow, easy moves he planted first one foot flatly on the floor, then the next. With the mightiest effort of all, he pushed himself up into a squatting position. The move caused his face to redden and the blood to roar through his temples. The girl still had not stirred.

After locating his mantle, which lay in one corner of the room, where he had carelessly tossed it the night

120

before, he slipped into it. taking no chances on waking the girl, Dismas picked up his cloak and sandals, then tiptoed down the mud stairway leading through the roof and into the main room of the inn.

There, behind the small counter, stood the obese. monster of a man, Aram. The greasy innkeeper grinned as if the secrets of the universe were his, and his alone.

"Good morning," cooed Aram cheerfully.

"Good? *Good?!* I am dying, and you say the morning is a good one. Aram," Dismas whined, "you are more cruel than the Romans ever were."

Like a man talking to a novice, Aram pulled out a huge wineskin and replied, "This will dust the cobwebs from your throat and brain. It will scrape the slime from your tongue and steady your most talented hands once more."

At the thought of wine, Dismas felt the churning again in his stomach.

"It is a strange thing," the innkeeper said, "the same liquid that puts the torments of hell into you is the very thing that snatches it from you." As he talked the fat man poured a cup of blood-red wine into a wooden cup.

Dismas knew what he said was true, so he snatched at the life-saving liquid with both hands. As fast as his constricting throat would permit, he swallowed its contents in large, noisy gulps. As he drank, he thought, *If I must be as sick as I know I will be, let me at least be sick with the taste of fresh wine, not the rotten stink with which I awoke.*

Contrary to his expectations, Dismas' stomach did not revolt against the cool, fresh wine. Instead, the turmoil he had felt before began to subside. Even the pulsating knife which kept jabbing his brain slowly left him—not completely, but enough to permit him to look around the dim room with just a slight squint.

As the wine spread comfortably throughout his arms and legs, Dismas felt it warming him. It was as if he was once more on the way toward intoxication. When Aram offered a second cup, Dismas had regained enough sense to decline.

Still somewhat sensitive to light, the older thief decided that the dim coolness of the inn was more to his liking than the noisy, shoving crowd he knew would soon be milling in the city's streets. Besides, Caleb was nowhere around, and his absence would be the perfect excuse for waiting. With this thought he struggled to a far corner and slowly sank to the dirt floor. Settled against his favorite wall, Dismas tilted his head back, then turned it to permit the mud wall to cool his face.

To himself he muttered, "I have said it a thousand times, and I say it again. If I survive this hangover I will never, no never, allow wine to conquer me again. I vow this before whatever gods there are in the heavens." Dismas was totally sincere. The old thief had made this pledge many times before. As his muscles relaxed, he once more slipped into a gentle sleep.

Several hours later he was awakened by someone kicking his leg. A familiar voice was chiding him.

"Arise, oh king of the grape. Awaken to a world of ripe purses, sheep waiting to be shorn, women to be comforted, and other such lively events."

"Speak softly, Caleb—I beg you," Dismas whispered as he licked his lips. "Caleb, my friend. You now see the resurrected dead before you." A sickly smile slowly spread across Dismas' face. "What part of the day is it?"

"Just past midmorning," Caleb said, plopping himself down beside his ailing friend. After a few silent seconds, Caleb asked, "Do you remember what took place at the temple yesterday?"

122

Dismas frowned as he tried to remember what had happened. He was not entirely sure he understood Caleb's question. Finally, he said, "Temple . . . oh. If you speak of the carpenter, and what he did, yes, I remember it." Quickly he added, "I remember, but only vaguely, that he put some sort of curse on me. He tore the whole city to hell, then wanted me to follow him—no, he wanted to own me, like a slave. He wanted me voluntarily to be a slave to him. Yes. I remember that best."

With an understanding nod, which indicated he understood more than he actually did, Caleb grunted, "Uh, hunh."

"Not only that," Dismas' face took on a serene look "I actually cheered for him when he wrecked that wicked place. He was certainly wonderful then."

"He must be," Caleb responded. "The priests are still trying to recapture doves, goats, and sheep from all over the city. You wouldn't believe the priests' anger."

"I can imagine it," Dismas chuckled before quickly grabbing his head with both hands. "You should have heard those pious dogs cursing when he upset the tables of the money changers."

"I did," Caleb blurted, his bubbling laughter about to double him over. "I'll bet the temple lost a fortune yesterday afternoon."

Now beginning to sober, Dismas said , "They deserve it. Tell me, Caleb, did you ever hear tales of their profit during Passover?"

"Me?"

"Well, I never did either," Dismas admitted before continuing, "until I overheard a pair of devout merchants talk about it once." Dismas' eyes widened and he gave Caleb a know-it-all look, "And believe me, those merchants don't miss much when it comes to money. I heard one of them say the priests charged twenty minas for a single dove, one you could buy in the city for one tenth that price.''

''I know. The best thing that could have happened was what the carpenter did.''

''Not only do those priests cheat the pilgrims when they sell sacrificial animals, but what about the business of allowing only temple money to be used?'' Dismas was really getting excited. ''They say they demand temple money because other money is tainted. But that's not the real reason. They force everyone to change money through them because there is profit in it. It is just another legal crime dreamed up by the priests. The rate of exchange is not fair but the only place pilgrims can secure temple money is through those contemptible priests.'' Dismas shook his head in disgust as he snorted, ''If the temple had more religion and fewer laws, the Messiah they keep talking about as coming, might be able to afford to come. As it is, he probably couldn't afford the company of such businessmen.''

Caleb, no longer smiling, agreed with his suffering master, ''Yes, it's a crime, but, unfortunately, a legal one. We have no way to ask for Rome's help, and even if we did, the Romans would just say they have no jurisdiction over religious matters. If you ask a priest about it, he just brands you a pagan, and might even have you stoned for—'' Caleb reared his head back and raised his arms toward the ceiling before intoning, ''Stoned for challenging the will of Yahweh. If you should ask another Jew, he will just shrug and tell you it's the way of Adonis, his god.'' Caleb took a deep breath and blew it out heavily.

After a few more seconds of silence, Caleb asked, ''What do you think will come of it all?''

''Well,'' Dismas began, his voice flat, as if he had little

interest in the subject now, "according to what the crowd said yesterday, this man just may be the Messiah. If what I felt is any sign, he just may well be. If it is true, he may have an army out in the hills."

Dismas shrugged. "If he does, that may be why he has so much courage. I don't know—no one seems to know for sure. The temple priests will try to get even with him somehow, though. He cost them a fortune in just one afternoon, and money is the one thing truly sacred to them."

"You are so right in that, Dismas, but he had no worry last night. As I chased after you, I saw him about to be questioned. After you had fallen into your usual after-drinking sleep, I went back into the streets. I saw him and his twelve take the road to Bethany."

"Maybe he'll be smart enough to stay away. The temple priests are bound to be in an ugly mood today, especially Caiaphas and his father-in-law."

Caleb looked at Dismas, then thoughtfully stuck out his lower lip as he began to shake his head. "No, he didn't stay away. He and his men passed Gethsemane this morning. You should hear the stories they tell about this Jesus and that place."

"Stories?" Dismas' attention was once more acute. "What stories?"

"I've heard it said—" Caleb paused to think. "I don't remember if it was today or before he upset the money changers. Anyhow, it was said he cursed trees and things, or something like that."

Not trying to hide his irritation, Dismas snapped, "Caleb, will you never get things straight? Now think. What did you hear?"

"I am not sure. They say he will be called before the priests, scribes, and elders this morning to be questioned.

Rumor has it he will once more challenge them, this time with their own Scriptures."

"How do such stories get started? How would anyone know what a man is going to do before he does it? How do they know who will meet with him?"

"I don't know, Dismas. I'm only repeating what is being said in the streets. Some say his twelve know what their master is going to do even before he does it. Others say it is in the stars. I don't know."

"Well, I'll say this, those no-good men from the temple had better watch what they say and do with that him. Jesus is a man to be reckoned with." Dismas looked toward the ceiling, his teeth gleaming even in the dim light. "I wouldn't mind hearing that encounter, if it really takes place."

Caleb jumped nimbly to his feet. "You can hear it if you'll do two things."

"What do you mean? Do what things?"

"First, don't get as involved with what goes on as you did yesterday. Second, you must hurry. I mean, you must come right now. They are meeting at the temple again."

Dismas climbed laboriously to his feet. He wanted very much to hear the battle, though he didn't know why.

Maybe I just like to be around where there might be a good fight, Dismas thought to himself. But he would not admit, even to Caleb, that his desire to be near the Galilean was a strong one. He even tried telling himself it was weak and foolish to want to be of service to a man many people felt to be mad. Despite this attempt at reasoning, he knew his logic was not logic at all—just wrong. His inner yearning to give something to the man—help, money, even himself—was against Dismas' basic nature. Although the feeling bothered him, he couldn't ignore it.

126

The two men shuffled between the inn's familiar tables and on out the door into the blinding sunshine.

As they pushed and sidestepped their way back up the hill to the temple, Caleb broke the silence by asking, "Tell me, Dismas, why do you hurry so? Is it just to watch this event or is it more?"

"Let me just say I want to see who tears whom into small pieces."

Caleb clapped his old master on the shoulder in acceptance of the answer, then jokingly responded, "Dismas, you're the most bloodthirsty thief I ever heard of."

Grinning crookedly, Dismas retorted, "It comes from my childhood. Remind me to tell you of the time I once relieved a man of his burden of life."

Caleb frowned and looked intently at his master without slackening his stride. The younger thief could not imagine Dismas as a dangerous man. He saw him as explosive and shrewd a man who occasionally permitted his temper to lead him into a fight now and then, but it was unthinkable to him that Dismas would ever take a life. No, he was too smart—too cunning. Yet he had just heard his master admit that he had killed someone. Caleb was disturbed by the thought.

The rest of the trip to the temple was made without further conversation between the two men.

When they were once more inside the temple walls, Dismas and Caleb saw that the mess from the day before had been cleaned up. They also saw that the animals were once more being sold and money was again being exchanged. The priests had been delayed in their business dealings, but not stopped.

After looking around and finding things back to normal, Dismas and Caleb searched for Korath, the blind one. Although what was about to take place was known

127

to practically everyone, the wary thieves wanted to learn the exact schedule of things. By knowing this, they could position themselves at the best place to observe what was going on with the least likelihood of personal danger and arrest.

"There he is!" Caleb all but shouted as he pointed toward Korath. As usual, the beggar sat on crossed legs wailing pitifully as he weakly bounced his beggar's bowl up and down. His simpering appearance was as contrived as his ruse of being blind. The men began nudging their way to him, sidestepping the faithful and curious as they went.

"Greetings, Korath," Dismas said cheerfully. The familiarity of one so widely known in Jerusalem's criminal world was great flattery to Korath.

"And greetings to you also," Korath replied, nodding ever so slightly toward Caleb. The eyes which were not supposed to see did not waver from the point in space at which they stared. Friendship or not, professional caution had its place first and foremost, especially inside the crowded temple. It was even more important during the high, holy, and profitable days.

"Korath, what do you know of today's events?" Dismas asked without trying to hide his curiosity.

"I hear that today will be a battle of words only, if that is what worries you. It will be between this Jesus and more of the holy men—the priests and scribes. To further reduce any fears you may have, I have seen no extra soldiers and have seen no runners sent to bring any."

"That's exactly what I wanted to know. Is there anything more?"

"Yes," blurted the blind man. "Don't expect a mild encounter today. I hear from all sides, from many sources, that Jesus came to Jerusalem from Bethany to-

128

day. It is said that he walked up to a fig tree that he did not know was barren to pick some early figs to eat."

"That's what I was trying to tell you before, but couldn't remember the details," Caleb interrupted.

Korath glared straight, his "blindness" still uncompromised, but the look on his face revealed his irritation at being interrupted just when his story was getting interesting. He spaced his words out, "As—I—was—saying. . . ." He waited for Caleb to burst in again. When he didn't, the blind man went on, "Anyhow, he didn't find any fruit on the tree. I'm told that when this happened, the carpenter cursed the tree. As the people around him looked on—" Korath again hesitated. "As they looked on, the tree just withered and died."

"Cursed it? The tree withered and died? Korath, do you mean he just used strong language and a tree died?" Dismas was about to become angry.

"No. That's not what I mean. He put a curse on the tree, just as it is said the Egyptian sorcerers can do. Then the tree died."

"You keep saying 'they' told you these things. Who is 'they'?" Dismas wanted to know.

"From what is being said, there were more than forty or fifty people following him at the time—not counting his usual twelve."

A disgusted grunt came from behind them, then a voice said, "Listen to a blind beggar and you hear what you can expect—nothing but lies."

Dismas and Caleb turned to see who owned the intruding voice. It was a merchant, judging from his clothes, and one who was none too prosperous. The stranger added, "What you just heard, I mean about the fig tree being cursed, I heard that tall tale yesterday." With no more words, the man turned and walked away.

"Korath, you camel dung. I used to believe most of what you told me, but how do you expect me to swallow this kind of nonsense?"

Embarrassed at possibly being caught passing unreliable information, the beggar allowed his eyes to flicker to Dismas' face, "By my mother's head, what I told you is just as I heard it—today. Not once, but many times in the last hour alone."

Although an oath spoken by Korath was usually meaningless, Dismas felt there was a ring of sincerity in his voice today. "That may be so, but if this man killed a fruit tree, I'm, certain he must have done it with more than just words."

Caleb looked at Dismas before soberly asking, "Why not? How did he, as a twelve-year-old boy, teach Scripture to scholars? How did he talk to you without using spoken words?" All three men became silent.

After watching the milling people for a few minutes, Dismas and Caleb rose from their squatting position and started to leave. Korath, having taken in no money while the pair sat in front of him, was glad to see them go.

"Go with God," the blind man bleated. The thieves did not bother to answer or even look back. Instead, they strode across the court toward a council room built off the thick wall of the ramparts.

As they walked, Caleb asked, "Dismas, the things taking place here today are scary. For some reason I have the feeling you and I should not be here, that we should get away as fast as we can—now."

"Don't be an old woman," Dismas chided as he shouldered scowling men out of his way. "This man is wise." He raised his eyebrows as he added, "He may even be almost as cunning as I am, but he is certainly no threat to anyone—at least, not to us."

130

"I didn't say he was the threat," Caleb defended. "I just have a feeling that whatever is about to go on here is something we do not understand and shouldn't get involved in."

"Who's getting involved in anything?" Dismas asked in the same tone used by merchants trying to weaken a buyer. "I just came to see this man spar with the priests. So far he has done well. It has been a one-sided conflict—he disrupting, and they muttering and sputtering. No, Caleb, in this man we have nothing to fear." The old thief looked up for an instant, as if in thought, then went on, "As far as danger goes, certainly he is stirring up trouble, but nothing of enough consequence to be dangerous to us. No. When his end does come, surely it will be entirely his—and very, very sudden. You don't anger people the way he does and then expect to live into the quiet, peaceful years." Dismas did not smile at what he said. He found himself oddly disturbed by the thought that the rugged-faced man from Nazareth would be harmed for doing what many people in Judea would do, if they had the courage.

As they neared the tightly pressed crowd by the west wall, it was obvious that the gathered people were listening to some speaker. Although a common occurrence in the temple courtyard, this group was uncommon in that the listeners were actually listening. Instead of the usual vocal agreements or disagreements, which created an almost constant hiss during normal speeches, this speaker some way awed the people. The man spoke in a low, soft, rumbling voice.

As they stopped to listen, both Dismas and his young companion were intrigued by the voice.

Squeezing past a few of the men on the outer edge of the standing mob, Dismas and Caleb stood on tiptoes to

131

see who the talker was, to no avail. It struck both of them as odd that although they could hear the man talking in a low, soft voice, they could both still hear him as distinctly and clearly as if he stood by their side.

After again trying to stand on tiptoes to see who it was, and failing, the pair began to push those standing in front of them to each side. Still the people remained quiet. Slowly they made their way until they were but four or five persons back from the one they wanted to see.

As he pushed a man away from a place he wanted to be, Dismas looked up and was startled to see that the speaker was the one who had cleansed the temple the day before. He was startled because after the exhibition of the money changers, Dismas felt that the man's voice just had to be as rough as his actions had been. It was not. Truly, it was deep, as he would have expected, but it was not rough, gravelly, or coarse. Instead, it was smoooth, low, and melodious.

As the Galilean talked, he occasionally gestured to emphasize a point. When he did, the muscles in his brawny brown arms rippled. Dismas could not help smiling when he compared the man's physical condition to that of the statues of various Roman heroes—statues carved in Judea or brought here to be mounted at the Roman baths.

Romans, Dismas thought, spend fortunes in their feeble attempts to create strong, virile bodies. This man, through the simple act of hard work, had bested all of them. Dismas was pleased at this.

As Jesus talked of the kingdom of heaven and God's true followers, a voice rang out, "Make way! Make way for God's emissaries." Several priests of high position, judging by their flowing, high-quality clothes, were strutting toward the Galilean, who now fell silent. The priests, as they always did when trouble loomed, walked behind armor-clad guards who pushed the faithful aside—those who did the tasks the priests felt to be beneath them or did not have the courage to do for themselves.

When the priests finally reached a prominent spot in front of the crowd and slightly to the left of the carpenter, one of them asked, "By what authority do you speak and teach here?" The priest raised his nose higher and haughtily asked, "Who gave you permission?"

Jesus, without raising his voice or changing his expression as any other man would have done, replied calmly, "I would like to ask you a question first. If you will answer me, then I will tell you by what authority I do what I do."

The Galilean had not affronted the priests, nor insulted or embarrassed them, but he left no doubt that he was not to be intimidated by their priestly behavior. A slight smile came to his lips like one held by a father as he teases his children, "From where was the baptism given by John?" He spoke of his cousin, who had recently been executed by King Herod. The priests knew of whom he spoke. "Was it from heaven—or of men?"

The priests were stunned. In less than ten seconds, this man had taken the initiative. They blanched when they realized they had been trapped by his few words.

As if by secret signal, the priests turned to form a tight huddle and, head to head, began whispering to each other. Dismas, who stood nearer to them than to the carpenter, leaned over to listen to their conversation.

"If we say it was from heaven, he will simply ask why we, the holy ones, did not believe him. If we say it was of men, these people who saw John as a prophet will tear us to pieces."

133

"You are correct, but what should we do?"

"We are the priests here, and have the authority. We don't have to answer his question. Let me speak to him."

The trio turned to face the carpenter. After an instant of silence, the leader of the priests all but shouted, "We cannot tell."

The look on Jesus' face reflected that this was the answer he had expected from them. In the same voice with which he had spoken to the crowd before the priest's arrival, he said, "Then neither will I tell you by what authority I do these things."

The three priests gasped. Again, with a few carefully chosen words, he had drained their authority from them. The carpenter's gaze was as steady and composed as his speech. Again he spoke to them. "What do you think?" He did not give them a chance to answer, but continued, "A man once had two sons. He said to the first, 'Son, go work in my vineyard today.' The son refused, but was later sorry for what he said and reported for work."

The carpenter paused to take a deep breath and to look around slowly. Dismas tried to edge closer to hear and see better, but was stopped by a fat man who smelled vaguely of sour cheese.

Seeing that his audience was hanging on his every word, the Galilean continued, "The second son was also told to go to the vineyard to work. He assured his father that he would go, but didn't. Which of the two sons, would you say, did what his father asked?"

By this time, the priests were dumbfounded. Their credibility was gone. Their dominance of the situation had melted with each word spoken by the man before them. Instead of dominating a simple country man they were forced to respond to his initiative. "The first son," they replied.

When they had answered, an even deeper hush fell on the crowd. The tiny smile on Jesus' lips disappeared. He resembled a stern judge. "Absolutely!" His eyes narrowed. "And that is why I now tell you, the men hired by the Romans to collect taxes, and prostitutes will enter into the kingdom of God before—" He pointed his finger at the leader of the trio of priests. "Before you do," he thundered.

Jesus now breathed deeply through his nose, causing it to flare as his massive chest expanded. "For John came to you speaking honestly and truly. You wouldn't believe him. Even after you saw for yourselves that what he taught was true, you would not change your evil beliefs and habits so that you could believe him."

Dismas was shocked, as was everyone around him. The man was not afraid of the temple priests. He was not the least bit awed by their finery or his surroundings. What he said had the ring of royalty speaking to disobedient servants.

Jesus, an indignant expression still on his face, took several strong steps toward the now cowering priests. "Let me tell you another story. A rich landowner put hedges all around his vineyard, dug a winepress, built a guard tower, and rented out his property. Then he left on a voyage to a foreign land." The Galilean turned slightly away from the priests and seemed to be talking to the crowd, who stood spellbound.

"When harvesttime came," he continued, "he sent servants back to collect what was due him in fruit raised by his tenants. Instead of honest payment, the tenants badly beat one of the servants, killed another, and threw stones at the third." A soft moan went up from the listeners.

"The landowner sent more servants, even more than

135

the first time, but they too were badly abused by the tenants. Finally, thinking the tenants would respect his son, the actual son of their landlord, the man sent his boy. Instead of respecting him, the tenants decided that if they could kill him, the landowner would have no one left to inherit the land. When he died, he would have to give it to them. With this thought they took his son to the fields—" Jesus lowered his voice. "And they killed him." Another gasp went up from his listeners.

The carpenter did not hurry to speak, but waited for the groan to die out completely. An air of expectation hung over the listeners gathered around him. Even disrespectful Caleb waited politely. Finally one of the younger priests could wait no more. He blurted, "What will the landowner do when he returns to his lands from his travels?"

Without giving the Galilean a chance to answer, the younger priest answered his own question, "I know what he'll do. He'll kill those who murdered his son, then he will rent the land to someone who will pay him what is honestly his."

Placing his hand over his heart, and giving the distinct impression that he spoke of himself, the Galilean responded in a firm and confident voice, "Didn't you ever read the Holy Scriptures, where it says, 'The stone which the builders rejected, the same is become the head of the corner?' " It was an ancient quotation which explained that that which was rejected by experts was often the very thing which was most important. A rejected rock would become the cornerstone of the structure. "This is the Lord's doing, and it is marvelous in our eyes. For this reason, I tell you—" Again the man's eyes narrowed and an impressive darkness came over his face. He once more pointed an accusing finger at the three robed figures who now cringed before him. "The kingdom of God will be taken away from you and it will be given to a nation willing to bear fruit."

Off to one side, Caleb nudged Dismas and asked, "Is he talking of stones or himself? Is he saying the blessings of God will be taken from all Jews unless they accept what he teaches?"

Dismas, astonished and mixed up over what had been said, just shook his head to indicate that he was not sure himself. Both men missed the next words spoken by the Galilean, so Caleb again leaned over and whispered, "You wanted to see someone cut into slivers. Look at those three priests and then laugh, my master." Caleb nudged Dismas disrespectfully and quipped, "This Jesus has just told the holy men that the vengeance-seeking hand of God is stretched out for them, and if they knock it away, they will burn in hell. Watch them, Dismas. Watch them with all the pleasure you have yearned for so long."

Although irritated at being distracted from what was being said by the carpenter, Dismas could not suppress the satisfied grin brought on by what Caleb said.

The quiet which hung over the huge courtyard was almost suffocating. An expression of disbelief appeared on the faces of the priests. How dare this sacrilegious country carpenter come into the holiest spot in Judea's holiest city to embarrass them and tell stories. They seemed not to recognize that his words applied to them.

The way in which the Nazarene condemned the priests was overlooked by them as the prattling of a madman, but his manner of speaking to them was a public insult and more than they could bear. Making choking sounds like lions with arrows through their throats, the three priests took several steps toward Jesus, their hands upraised as if to claw him. Their faces, despite their previous attempt to remain composed, were now distorted with rage.

As the priests made their threatening gestures toward the quiet speaker, a rumbling "No" rose from the several hundred persons looking on. Shaken back from their anger by the sound, the priests clearly realized that to his listeners the man was some sort of holy prophet. Suddenly the priests were afraid, and their fear stopped them in midstride. Without further word, they turned to leave, their steps quick and urged on by fear. But when they came to the edge of the crowd they paused to observe what Jesus would do next.

When Dismas saw the priests retreat, he knew that he, along with the rest of the crowd, had been tensed and ready to defend the carpenter if necessary.

But Caleb just stood and stared. He was puzzled at the way Dismas reacted. "Dismas, what's wrong with you? We can't afford to become entangled in the mess this man is making." The young thief glanced around to see if any temple guards were in sight. "Come on, Dismas," he said." "Let's get out of here."

But before Caleb could pry Dismas away, Jesus again began to speak. "The kingdom of heaven is like a king who had made a marriage agreement for his son. He sent his servants out to invite the wedding guests, but they did not come. He sent the servants out again with word that he had prepared oxen and the best calves for a great feast. This time they not only failed to come, they laughed and some wandered away—one to his farm, another to his shop. And the remaining invited ones first tortured the king's servants, then killed them.

"When the king heard of it, he was furious and sent his armies, which executed the murderers and burned their

138

cities to the ground." Jesus took a deep breath. "The king told his remaining servants that the wedding was ready, but the people who were invited had missed their opportunity. He told his servants to go into the streets and invite anyone, everyone, acquaintance and stranger alike, to come. This they did the good and the bad.

"The king noticed that one of the strangers did not have on a wedding garment, that his clothes were plain and much worn, so he asked him why. The king was angered when the man did not answer, so he had the man bound and thrown out."

The carpenter was now quiet and walked slowly inside the small circle left to him by the people crowding around listening to him. Caleb leaned over and asked Dismas the meaning of what Jesus had just said.

Dismas, without turning his eyes away from the Galilean, said, "That's not hard to figure out. He was saying that what the priests call worship is really a denial of God. God initially told Moses that we Jews were his favored people. We received the first invitation as a notice of what was to come and to get ready for it. The priests not only did not get ready, they even had God's servant—" Dismas allowed his eyes to look at Caleb for an instant before looking back at Jesus, "I guess he meant John, the Baptizer. They had John killed and the king—God—will destroy those who did not accept John's message."

"Why would God destroy all of us?" Caleb protested. "I didn't do any of those things to His servants."

"No, Caleb, we didn't do them. But did we follow John when the invitation came? We are guilty too."

"Well," Caleb defended himself, "if God is so merciful and full of grace and kindness, why did He, if He is as you said, the King in this story, why did He torture the man who did not wear his wedding clothes?"

"You know our custom. When we are invited to a wedding, we are given plenty of time to prepare ourselves. When the invitation comes on short notice, we must still do our best to get ready for it, and that includes wearing our best clothes. In this case, Jesus was talking not about clothes, but lives. When the invitation was given to go to God's home, our lives should be our best—not the same lives, with the same offenses as everyday before the invitation—but new and beautiful lives—or clothes, in this story. As for that king torturing the offender, I imagine God is like any master. When he says he wants something done, and it isn't done, he'll punish the offender."

Dismas' answer seemed plausible to Caleb, so he blankly looked at his wise friend and replied, "Oh."

Jesus paused in his walking and looked directly into the eyes of the priests who had ventured more closely again and said, "For many are called, but few are chosen." The carpenter then looked down, signaling that he had said all that he intended to say on the subject.

The confused priests, who wore the badges of office, were all members of the Pharisees. When Jesus stopped talking, they turned to each other and began to whisper. Finally one of them, with a smirk on his face, spoke a few words of cheap flattery to the carpenter before hissing, "Tell us, rabbi, do you believe it is lawful for a Hebrew, one of God's chosen, to pay tribute to Caesar, who by our religion, is a pagan?"

Jesus tilted his head forward, but continued to look at his questioners. His lips tightened as he considered the new challenge put to him. It was clear to everyone that he saw the obvious trap set for him in the question. If he said no such a statement could be construed as rebellion against Rome and a violation of Roman law. If he said yes it would indicate approval of paganism and would violate Hebrew law.

Looking up again he calmly replied, "Hand me a piece of tribute money." The priest failed to remember that Roman money was not to be on holy ground. But anxious to deliver the cunning carpenter to Caiaphas and feeling he had left the man no way out of breaking the law, he nervously struggled until he got his hand into his purse, which was carefully and securely hung by a long cord from around his neck. From the small bag he took the smallest coin and handed it to the Galilean.

"Whose face and words are on this coin?" Jesus asked.

"Why, Caesar's face of course."

Jesus looked at each of the priests, "Then give to Caesar that which belongs to him, and to God that which is God's."

After a brief silence, a roar of triumph went up from the crowd. The three priests all stood with their mouths open. The perfect trap had been sprung and their intended quarry stood not only untouched, but victorious.

Seeing that they were completely outmatched, the priests respectfully backed away several paces, then turned and left. They were beaten at their own game. They had been dumbfounded by the brilliant answers given to them. The logic of the Nazarene, his lightning fast crushing of their carefully set trap had left everyone in awe.

When the shout had gone up, Dismas could only stare along with the others. Caleb too had yelled and he still stood with a grin on his face.

However, instead of rejoicing, as the other people did, the carpenter had dropped his head as if in defeat. He stared at the marble under his feet. His pose reminded

141

Dismas of a gladiator he had seen once. The gladiator, although victorious, stood in a sagged pose, trying to rest before the beginning of another bout. This, in fact, was just what Jesus did. He did not have long to wait before the opening of a new bout.

From a small porch off the temple wall, a large group of lawyers, Sadducees, filed out to confront the lone man. When the people noticed that the Sadducees were coming, the men who had always followed the Galilean, the same ones who had shouted praise at him, all seemed to melt away. Out of habitual fear of the lawmaking Sadducees, they withdrew almost fifty feet from the Galilean.

Instead of retreating, Jesus turned to face the learned men who, as if they had been drilled for this one occasion, lined up in three semicircular rows around him.

Once in position, the Sadducees began to shout questions at him. Each question was rehearsed and geared to trap the carpenter into breaking any of the hundreds of laws. The breaking of even one would enable the questioners to take legal action against him. The questioners worked hard at what they had set out to do, but none succeeded.

Dismas listened intently and in awe as the man from Nazareth politely warded off the vicious thrusts of his tormentors. The master thief could hardly believe his ears. A country village carpenter, a man whose education in his small hill village could hardly have proceeded very far, was debating religious law with the top men of the faith—and winning. Despite his educational disadvantage, Jesus stood like a rock, responding confidently first to one questioner, then another. Dismas thought to himself, *Here in the capital city of Judea, in the holiest city of all Zion, this man is challenging the holiest men*

142

on the holiest matters. This carpenter is not succeeding by accident. His answers are as deliberate as a woodsman's ax felling a towering tree.

At one point, Dismas heard Jesus say, "God is not the God of the dead, but of the living." At this, he saw many members of the Sadducees turn to whisper among themselves. One of them, seeing that the lawyers were getting no edge on their opponent, asked a question no one before had dared to answer. "Galilean," he began. "Which is the great commandment in the law?" The look on the questioner's face made it plain that he had no respect for Jesus.

Without an instant's hesitation, the carpenter faced him, and in a voice which rang with authority, answered, " 'Thou shalt love the Lord thy God with all thy heart, and with all thy soul, and with all thy mind.' This is the first and greatest commandment. And the second is like it, 'Love thy neighbor as thyself.' " Coughing among the crowd kept Dismas from hearing all of what was next asked and answered. It irritated him, but to hear better he would have to expose himself and he felt that this would make him appear as one of the men with the Galilean. For this reason, he just cocked his head, cupped a hand behind his ear, and caught what he could.

No sooner had Jesus answered the questions put to him than he asked one of his own. Looking the full length of each of the rows of men, he finally asked, "What do you think of the anointed one? The one sent by God? Whose son is he?"

The lawmakers, the ones most knowledgeable of Scripture, talked among themselves before a spokesman—a small, weasel-faced man—called out in a high-pitched voice, "If you speak of King David's encounter, the anointed one was the son of David."

"If that is so, why did David call him Lord?"

The man standing next to Dismas snickered at the question, then tipped his head and whispered to the man next to him, "A shrewd question—no man would call his own son Lord."

The man's snicker and words had drowned out what Dismas was trying to hear, so the old thief jammed an elbow into the man's ribs before turning to him and growling, "Shut up, fool. We want to hear a master speak, not the braying of an ass." The man's smile became a scowl, but he remained silent.

Jesus continued talking to the Pharisees and Sadducees, "If David called him Lord, how could the anointed one have been the son of David?" At that the frustrated questioners gave up trying to lure their opponent into a breach of the law! A few of them, in disgust, left, but most remained to listen. They still hoped to hear words spoken which would break the law. If this happened, and they were the ones to catch the violation, each man felt he would gain favor and esteem in the eyes of Caiaphas and King Herod.

As the crowd pushed itself in closer again, Dismas made sure he was near the front, but not too far forward. For the first time since the two-way exchange began between the temple hierarchy and the Galilean, Dismas thought of Caleb. As the master thief moved forward, he grabbed Caleb's cloak and pulled him along. Caleb, not as deeply involved as his friend, found it all somewhat boring. However, he did not want to dampen Dismas' enthusiasm and went along.

"The scribes and Pharisees sit in the same position as that held by Moses. They are religious leaders."

As the carpenter said these words, Dismas caught himself frowning. Why does this man, this destroyer of

144

false holy men, endorse the position of the Pharisees?

"Every one of you, no matter what they tell you to do, you must do it. But do not do what they do. I say this because— " Jesus frowned. "I say this because they do nothing good."

Dismas began to realize what the speaker was doing. He was not saying that all that the priests taught was wrong. But the priests had strayed far from living as examples of the laws of Abraham and Moses.

"They create heavy loads, which are hard to live with, by constructing laws upon laws; but know that the laws they devise do not touch them. They demand the best rooms for feasting and the finest seats in the synagogues, and expect you to address them as rabbi, the most respected of names. I say, don't call anyone rabbi—or master—because you have only one Master, no others. You must all look at each other as brothers. And don't call anyone father. You have but one Father, and He is in heaven.

"The greatest among you will be servants, and the servants will someday be the greatest. I tell you that, the one who is great must be humble and the humble will be great."

Dismas knew that Jesus spoke of what actually is versus what will be. If a man thinks he is great on earth, only on earth will he enjoy greatness, unless—unless he is a servant of God on earth.

The old thief stood reasoning with himself. If that's the case, in heaven the earthly servant will be a master. Dismas knew he'd give that matter a lot of thought later.

When Jesus had said these things, he turned toward the remaining Pharisees, elders, and Sadducees. addressing only them, he almost growled, "But woe to you, scribes and Pharisees—hypocrites! You are not only blocking your own way into the kingdom of heaven, you are blocking it for others too. Woe to you!"

When the carpenter pronounced this sentence on the temple leaders, those around Dismas gasped loudly, drowning out what Jesus was saying.

Even though he could not hear the spoken words, their impact was clear to Dismas, as he watched the faces of the religious leaders change from passive to shocked disbelief. Even the crowd began to mumble its dissent.

Jesus turned to the watching people, which almost instantly became silent again. "Oh, Jerusalem," he cried out, lifting both arms and beginning slowly to turn in a circle. "Oh, Jerusalem, Jerusalem, you that killed the prophets and stoned those God sent to you. How often I have tried to gather you to me; yes, just as a hen gathers her chicks under her wings—and you would not even listen." He took a deep breath and left it out in a sigh. "Look around you now—your houses are empty."

Dismas, trying hard to hear what was unsaid as well as what was spoken, knew the man did not speak of buildings when he said "houses," but of lives—the lives of the chosen people.

Dismas saw tears coursing their way down the carpenter's cheeks. They were not tears of shallow sorrow or disappointment, but evidence of the soul-searing agony felt by this man for his people. As Dismas looked at the carpenter's face, he felt his own eyes filling with compassionate tears, something he could not remember happening before, especially not out of respect for a stranger's feelings. The Nazarene's voice quavered with genuine grief.

Dismas knew Jesus mourned deeply over what he seemed forced to say. "For the last time—I tell you. . . ." Jesus choked on his sobs. "You will not see me again until

146

you say, 'Blessed is he who comes in the name of the Lord.'" As if completely overcome by his grief, the carpenter began to walk away, wiping the tears from his face with his hands as he went. No one made a move to stop him. Instead, all stood in respectful and awestruck silence. Most of the listeners had no idea what Jesus meant in much of what he had said. But Dismas understood, as did a few of the priests and other religious leaders. The old thief knew the man's message was for him as well as for the priests. Oddly, the priests feared what he said, but sealed their ears and minds to it.

Jesus did not leave the temple area, however. Instead, he walked from the west wall to the center of the courtyard where he joined his twelve companions. They had remained away from him during his questioning, but had never been far enough away that they could not come if needed.

Before the speaker and his friends could leave, Dismas pushed his way through the crowd toward them. Again he had forgotten Caleb, who fought and pushed, trying to keep up with his teacher.

Dismas wanted only to congratulate the man from Nazareth for saying publicly what the old thief had felt most of his life. When he neared the cluster of men, however, he was afraid to say anything. Despite his outward display of superiority most of the time, Dismas felt naked each time he was in the presence of this Jesus of Galilee. To others, and even to himself, he referred to the man only as "the carpenter" or "the Galilean." Any other time, if he spoke the man's actual name, it was a slip of the tongue that startled Dismas. Even with the titles he used, he said them in half-sarcastic tones. Deep inside, however, Dismas knew the man was much more than just a carpenter or a Galilean. Some people called him Michael, the archangel, which Dismas felt just might be true. Others said he was the much heralded Christ, the Messiah. Dismas reluctantly admitted that this title could best fit the man if he would show more signs of strength, rather than knowledge.

To the master thief, this man, strong in features, strong in courage and heart, was not a man that Dismas could look straight in the eye without some resulting effect. He knew that whatever happened in that look, it would be merciful, and not harmful, but it was still something Dismas was not ready to do.

Dismas heard Jesus tell his friends, "Look around you, my beloved brothers. Do you see the majesty of this place?" Without waiting for a response from them, he went on in a voice now soft and personal, but containing a touch of sadness, "I must tell you. In a short time nothing will be left of this place. I tell you that what you see here will be so utterly destroyed that not a single stone you now see will be left on top of another."

Dismas heard several of the men, one in particular, grumble over what the Galilean said. The main dissenter commented that to destroy such a wonderful building would be an awful waste of money, especially since the structure was still in the process of being built.

It was past noon and Caleb strode up to stand beside Dismas. "Did you hear what this Jesus fellow said? He has sealed his fate now. The priests will take his life somehow." Caleb had not seen Jesus and his twelve standing nearby.

"Do not wager on that, my friend," Dismas retorted, a smile playing around his lips. "How do you kill such a one as he? No, Caleb, they must be much craftier than what we have seen, and I don't think they can do it." Dismas seemed confident, but not completely convinced of what he said. It made him strangely sad. He wanted to believe his own words.

As the carpenter and his small group of men walked slowly from the temple, they turned into a street which led out the city gate toward the Kidron Valley and the distant olive grove. Dismas stood watching them go.

Caleb is probably right, he thought, *and what a pity it is. The brave die because of their courage; cowards always seem to live until they can no longer tolerate themselves. Such will probably be the case with this brave man.* Dismas took a deep breath and blew it out as if he felt very tired.

It was again time to eat. He and Caleb still had plenty of money left in the several moneybags they carried.

6 TUESDAY AFTERNOON

The roast goat, dates, spiced cucumbers, and watermelon did not set well with the pair of thieves, who lounged near a temple wall. They had gone their separate ways to gather their meal. In doing so, neither man knew what the other was buying. The result, when combined into a single collective meal, was a sickening mess. They ate it anyway.

Since both men had frequently known times when they had no food at all, they were not willing to throw any of what they had away. Instead, they combined the sweet with the sour. They now sat belching, scratching, and nodding sleepily.

The heat of the day was oppressive, even in the shade of the scrawny tree under which they sat. They were sweating and their perspiration coursed its way down the sides of their faces, causing streaks in the dust and grime which covered them. Despite this, and the many flies which wandered excitedly over the filthy pair, the men continued to nod their way in and out of sleep.

Unlike the others who lounged around the temple courtyard, most of whom sat bolt upright, Dismas and Caleb were almost lying down. The only thing which kept them from stretching out was fear. To lie down outstretched on sacred ground for any unproductive reason violated temple rules and could bring punishment.

To make sure this did not happen, the conniving pair made sure their heads were held upright by propping them securely against the slim trunk of the spindly, sparsely-leafed tree.

Caleb scratched his beard as he slowly and lazily looked around the open terrace before him.

"Dismas?"

"Huh?"

"What in the name of Isis are we doing here?"

"Isis? When did you become an Egyptian?"

"Why not Isis? It just seems better to say Isis in this place. You know. More respectful."

"Respectful of what? Besides, speaking the name of a pagan god in a Hebrew temple doesn't sound right," the old thief mumbled, his eyes still closed. "What are you, anyhow? Are you too now a holy man?" With his eyes still closed Dismas smiled slightly.

"No," Caleb defended, "but I still don't see why I shouldn't appeal to Isis. Egyptian gods, Persian gods, even those of the Romans. What difference does it make?"

Dismas' eyebrows raised as he gave this bit of philosophy some sleepy thought. He didn't feel like starting an argument, so he just grunted to signify that he agreed.

151

From where Caleb was lying Dismas heard a rasping sound. The old man stirred and, with what appeared to be extreme exertion, opened one eye to look at his friend. He weakly snapped, "Stop that scratching, will you? Either your lice are jumping over onto me or you're making mine restless." Dismas heaved one arm overhead and with the other hand began to scratch the pit of his upraised arm.

"Why don't we go somewhere? Why are we staying here?" Caleb wanted to know.

"I don't know, but can you think of a better place to be at this time of day? We're at the highest, cleanest, sweetest-smelling spot on earth and—" He waved his scratching hand around the courtyard. "Except for God's favorites, it would be the coolest."

"God's favorites? God wouldn't claim these vermin," Caleb spat back.

Dismas saw that his young friend was about to launch into another political-religious tirade. The older thief was in no mood for it, but as usual, it was unavoidable.

Raising himself on one elbow, Caleb half rolled over to face Dismas. "Look at Herod and this—this—glorious bride to God that Herod calls his temple." Caleb was angrily shaking his finger toward the main temple building.

"Shut up, Caleb," Dismas hissed. "Either keep your voice down or pretend you don't know me. You may not value your freedom, but I value mine. What you say cost that madman from the desert, that John, the Baptizer, his life. From what I've heard, all he did was dip people in whatever water he could find and help his followers pray. Nothing went wrong for him until he said just what you are saying, and then—" Dismas made a quick gesture across his throat with one finger. "Then his head became a decoration on Herod's table."

152

"All right. All right, I'll keep my voice down. Will that please you, my terror-stricken master?"

"Yes, but don't be surprised if this, your fiftieth or hundredth telling of your useless opinion, puts me to sleep." Dismas hesitated in his taunting of Caleb, then added, "Come to think of it, please tell it again. It may, in fact, put me to sleep."

Undaunted, Caleb took a deep breath, looked up at the huge stones at the top of the temple, and listened to the stonecutters chipping away at the massive slabs.

"Naturally, the men working on the temple are permitted to work, even on holy days. All the priests have to do is arrange for another law to change the existing law and continue constructing their beautiful edifices— even on holy days."

"Caleb, will you please shut up?"

"As I was saying, you and I know the Hebrew God does not exist. Some people say to speak so is a dangerous thing, but if there were such a person as God, and He was as loving toward the Hebrews as it is written, why would we be so poor? There is much wealth in Judea and it lies in the hands of but a few—and stays there. The poor, like you and me, and the rest of these poor but hopeful fools, we give what little we have to the rich few, just so they can be richer. Dismas, it just isn't fair."

"What you say is true, Caleb." Dismas yawned. "And I do my best to change it each time I meet a rich man. I choose the richest I can find, take his glutted purse, then return the money to the poor—by way of Aram. All I ask for myself is a lusty woman now and then, an occasional glass of wine, and—rest."

"Idiot," Caleb laughed, nudging his groggy friend gently. "I look around me in this great theater and tell myself that the Greeks were right in acting out dramas

153

written by their ancestors. The difference here is that in Jerusalem we do not even realize we are but playing tiny parts in a drama."

The young thief seemed to be infatuated with his own voice. "To the Persians we Jews are businessmen, and it is true, I imagine. They respect us. The Romans, however, they conquer. Despite the Romans being conquerors, they exist in the eyes of the Persians as little more than turtles who wear deadly iron into the desert, where such armor will kill them as they try to conquer what is not worth going after in the first place—the desert. We all fear and respect each other at the same time. Oh, how it would amuse God to see it, if such a person really exists at all—you know, a messiah."

"Yes, Caleb. Yes, Caleb. Now let me hear the rest of your nonsense so I may have some measure of peace."

"You just don't see what I see, Dismas. If there was a real God, these miserable creatures around us, the faithful ones, would not be miserable at all. They would be His favorites and well treated. God must see us, the Jews, as real two-legged sheep. We are shorn of money by Romans to please their Caesar and other gods. Then when the Romans are finished, along comes that half-Jew, Herod, to shear us of all that is left. Herod then spends what he gets from us either to try to please that hyena in Rome, or this—" Caleb once more jabbed a finger toward the temple. "This faceless, nameless, helpless god."

Caleb turned his head and showed his contempt by spitting, then adding, "Oh, I forgot someone. He erects this useless holy fort for his even more useless priests, Pharisees, and any others hiding behind the cloak of religious dignity."

Dismas' head snapped around and his eyebrows

twisted in anger. He was incensed not by what Caleb said, but that the younger thief, in his exuberance, had openly and thoughtlessly broken the law by spitting on holy ground. Dismas had no respect for the temple or its guardians, but his respect for punishment was profound. Caleb had been unforgivably careless.

The younger thief had not even noticed what he had done, or the effect it had on his master. "Look at it!" the younger man almost shouted.

Without thinking, Dismas did just that. He looked around the crowded courtyard and at the gleaming, towering temple.

Caleb continued, "This is not a monument of marble and mortar. It is the bones of the Hebrew nation—the bones of all Judea. It is held together by the blood of all the living today and will be consecrated with the sweat of generations to come." Caleb noisily slapped the marble slab on which he sat. "Oh, if this Jesus had only been the man we hoped, instead of just another prophet, he could have done something about all this."

At the last statement Dismas opened his eyes wider, then immediately squinted at his friend. "Don't speak too hastily about the carpenter. From what you and I saw yesterday and today, we know he's not a weakling. He may not carry a sword, as we expected, but his knowledge and cunning tops that of the elders—yes, even that of the Sanhedrin and Sadducees." Dismas found that speaking in defense of Jesus came easy to him today. In just two short days his attitude toward the carpenter had changed greatly.

Dismas went on, "He's braver than the toughest Roman and, if he can gather and control an army as he does the twelve who follow him, our freedom may still be in the near future."

"As you said earlier, Dismas, he has turned brains to slop and I now fear for you too."

Dismas just chuckled as he lay back easily and again tried to sleep, or at least rest. He soon found that he could not sleep. Instead, his thirst grew as the sweltering minutes went by. The heat of the day was relentless, even the shadow of the rodlike tree under which they slouched did not help.

Incense from the temple, in the absence of any breeze, hung like a sweet cloud over the entire area. Jerusalem's aroma, because of the temple incense, could be detected as much as thirty-five miles downwind during the normal Pasah days. On days like this one, when the saving breeze failed, the same incense descended like a suffocating fog.

Because of his thirst and the smell where they were, Dismas suggested moving to Aram's inn. Caleb quickly agreed that anywhere else would be better than where they were.

They uncomfortably sweated their way past the Court of the Gentiles, then strolled across the bridge into the city. Despite the difficulty in breathing brought on by the sickening sweet air hanging over the city, they did not stop along their route.

They went past Pilate's aqueduct and through Jerusalem's ancient north wall gate, which was now within the city and never closed.

As they neared the huge amphitheater Herod had built as a gift to Pilate when he was the newly assigned governor of Judea, they saw a large crowd of people milling around in the open market area which lay before the huge theater. They stopped to stare.

"Caleb," Dismas cautioned as he touched his friend's arm. "Let's stand here for a while before we mingle with

156

them." The old thief's wary eyes had never stopped scanning the people who walked slowly around and none of whom moved more than a dozen feet before stopping to talk with another onlooker.

"What do you suppose is going on?" the younger man asked.

Just as Caleb asked his question Dismas saw the big fisherman standing near the far side of the mob.

"I believe it's that carpenter—that Jesus." His eyes darted to his friend's face. "If it is, this could be a risky place to visit. Not only did he set the priests off with what he did in the temple yesterday, but as you heard a while ago, he antagonized them even more by besting them this morning."

"Old friend, I'm not the one most intrigued by him, you are. We could just pass him by," Caleb jested.

Dismas turned back to the crowd. Besides Peter, he could make out several of the twelve whom he had seen before.

Finally he nudged Caleb with his elbow and began to walk cautiously toward the crowd, mumbling, "Let's go."

As they began stepping between and around the people who stood in huddled groups, Caleb nudged Dismas, then jerked his head toward four men who walked confidently toward them. All four were slightly taller than the men around them. Unlike the rest of the people, these men wore flowing, draped clothes, much like the Roman toga, except they wore no tunics under them, thus leaving their right shoulders exposed to the sun.

All of the men had strong, straight bodies accentuated by their broad bare shoulders. The youngest was in his late teens, his facial hair just beginning to fill out. The oldest still had completely black hair, but his beard had taken on a gray look. All wore laced sandals of colors which matched their robes. They were men of wealth and this interested the two thieves.

"Where are those men from?" Caleb whispered.

"They are either from Achaia or Macedonia. Probably either from Athens or Corinth," Dismas whispered in return. "I've seen men like them in Jerusalem during other Passovers, but usually they do not venture far from Joppa, Caesarea, and the other coastal cities."

"Oh," Caleb grunted. "I've head much of them, but these are the first I remember seeing."

The two men, openly displaying bad manners, stared at the four Greeks as they walked steadily toward them.

Afraid that they would become a center of attention if, for some unknown reason, the quartet stopped to talk with them, Dismas and Caleb started to turn to get out of their path. Instead, the four men walked only as far as another man, who stood between the thieves and the Greeks. Dismas recognized the man as Philip, one of Jesus' twelve. Quickly the thieves moved forward to hear what the Greeks had to do with Jesus or his followers. Dismas wanted to know because he was curious, and Caleb because his master was pulling on his sleeve.

As they inched nearer, Caleb hissed, "I wonder why they go to one of the magician's men rather than to this Jesus himself?"

"Who knows, Caleb," Dismas responded. "Maybe because this man's name is Philip, which is Greek. Maybe they feel that's a good omen for them."

Since Philip had his back turned as they approached, the Greeks did not get his immediate attention. This allowed the two thieves to reach Philip's side at the same time the four visitors spoke to him. All of them gave the traditional Hebrew greeting before beginning their conversation.

158

"Shalom, Philip," the older of the Greeks said, stopping a respectful distance from Philip, then stepping up to him. His three companions did the same.

"Shalom, brother," Philip responded before lapsing into an expected silence to await his guest's question.

"Your name is Philip?" the older man asked, even though he had already used the name to address him.

"Yes. Why do you ask?"

"Are you Greek?" The expression on the old man's face showed that he hoped he would get an affirmative answer.

"No. I am a Jew, but may I help you?"

"Oh," the old man said. He shot a glance at the Greek standing next to him then resignedly continued, "Well— We—" He waved one hand toward his companions. "We were in the Court of the Gentiles yesterday when your rabboni, with the strength of hundreds, did what no man before him ever had the strength, determination, or courage to do." The old man took a deep breath, then smacked his lips as if savoring some enjoyable flavor in his mouth. He continued, "Sir, we would like to speak with your Jesus."

Philip frowned as he realized these men, thinking him to be Greek, felt he was the one they should approach with such a request. It was equally evident that he didn't know what to do about it. He quickly mumbled, "One moment, sir."

Turning to grasp the shoulder of another of Jesus' twelve—one who stood less than two feet away but with his back turned—Philip gently pulled the man around and blurted, "Andrew. These Greek brothers have asked if they may speak with Jesus." His sudden pause after the statement was awkward. "May they?"

Andrew did not hesitate to answer. He softly, but

strongly said in thick Galilean, "But of course." He motioned to the men and said, "Please, come with me."

Philip evidently felt Jesus might be too tired after the morning's events, or too busy now to talk with anyone. Andrew knew otherwise. During the few years he had known his Lord, if nothing else, Andrew had learned of Jesus that any soul seeking him for any reason would never be turned away.

As the six men strolled toward the man Andrew called "Master," Dismas saw that he and Caleb could join the group without drawing attention. Again he grabbed for Caleb's sleeve and began walking behind the last of the Greeks as they crossed the open area.

After moving only two hundred or three hundred feet, the group stopped. The two thieves turned slightly to face each other as if holding their own conversation. Instead, they listened intently as the older Greek addressed Jesus of Nazareth.

"Lord, yesterday, despite guards, tradition, and a huge mob which could have torn you to pieces, you stood firm in your belief of what your God desires of men in His house—and you destroyed an evil that even I, a non-Jew, could see. didn't you fear for your life? Where did you get such bravery and strength?"

Dismas knew the answer to this innocent question might be all that was needed by the Pharisees or Sanhedrin to condemn Jesus. He couldn't help turning his head to face Jesus as the answer came.

Looking directly into his questioner's eyes, and seeing no guile, Jesus, his voice resounding like a drum and loud enough for all to hear, answered, "The hour has come that the Son of Man should be glorified." He hesitated to let his words take root in his listeners before going on. "This is the truth I tell you. . . ." Again he hesitated

160

briefly as he looked away from his visitors to the faces of the great crowd which now looked at him. "Unless a grain of wheat falls into the ground and dies, it remains alone; but if it dies—" he paused and looked around. "If it dies, it bears much fruit." Jesus turned again to his visitors.

"He who loves his life is losing it; and he who hates his life in this world will keep it to life eternal." He emphasized the words "in this world." "If anyone will serve me—" Jesus turned directly toward Dismas and repeated what he had begun to say, "If anyone will serve me, anyone, let him follow me; and where I am, there will my servant also be."

Dismas felt his knees go weak. It was not just that he felt Jesus had put out a personal call for him—Dismas, the thief—to become one of the followers. It was the meaning of what he had just announced.

The old thief was not a scholarly man, as were the priests and rabbis of the temple, but the meaning of what Jesus had said seemed clear to him. Jesus, in saying it was time for "the Son of Man to be glorified," was talking about himself. He had just announced that the cruelty and savagery and lack of hope of the ages past were gone forever because of him.

Daniel, the ancient prophet, of whom stories were recounted almost daily in one part of Jerusalem or another, had foretold that this would happen. Centuries before, when he interpreted the dreams of a Babylonian king, Daniel told of bears and leopards and unidentifiable beasts reigning over the earth, only to be replaced by "one like the Son of Man" who would be the master. He would be given glory and a kingdom—that all people, nations, and languages should serve him. His dominion would be everlasting and would not pass away, and his

161

kingdom would not be destroyed. It was prophecy repeated by Jews so often that Dismas remembered it well.

Jesus said this was no longer a thing of the future, as it was for Daniel, but that the time spoken of had now arrived. For several years Jesus had told people about the kingdom of heaven. Now he announced that this kingdom was at hand.

Turning to Caleb, Dismas huskily stammered, "Caleb, did you hear what he just said?" Fear and amazement emphasized the shock he felt.

Caleb was unimpressed. "Yes."

"Do you understand what he just said?"

Dismas talked, not really aware of Caleb. It was as if Dismas was in a fog talking to himself. "He just said that now is the time for all things of the past to be changed and a new life to begin. He just said that. . . ." Dismas almost used the word "he," meaning Jesus, but stopped in time. "He just said—a man—would give his life to establish the new kingdom. In fact, he said we all must die to ourselves in order to find new life."

"I didn't hear all of that," Caleb whined. He felt left out of something the older thief seemed to be included in.

"That's what I understood him to be saying."

"Well, I didn't—" Dismas put his hand over Caleb's lips to silence him as the older man turned to listen to anything else being said by Jesus.

Dismas knew that when Jesus talked of the wheat dying, he didn't mean wheat at all, but men. When wheat is stored in a sack, it lies dormant, Dismas mused. When it is planted in the dirt and dies, only then does it bear fruit. The Pharisees and other religious leaders lacked real greatness because, like the stored wheat, they try to

162

save themselves. If they buried themselves in service to others they too would blossom into life. Dismas understood that Jesus' brief words pertained to all people, big and small, rich and poor, young and old.

Dismas knew that Jesus had just taught a new view of life—that greatness, true greatness, was not in riches or fame or glory. It came from the giving of one's life to others, through service to others, through love of others.

Caleb had not understood any of this.

A dark cloud seemed to come over Jesus' face as he looked upward and said, "Now my soul is troubled. And what shall I say?" He turned away from the Greeks and pivoted to face the people turned toward him. Seeing that he had their complete attention, he turned once more and walked over to a low platform which was elevated by two or three stone steps. He climbed them slowly, as if carrying a heavy load, then turned.

He repeated, "And what shall I say, 'Father, rescue me from this hour'?"

Then slowly making sure each of his words carried the full weight of what it meant, Jesus strongly declared, "But it was for this reason that I came to this hour." He raised his face and both arms toward the sky and almost shouted, "Father, glorify your name."

"No!" Dismas shouted from the crowd. Faces turned to look at him, but he was unaware of them. Jesus also looked at him, smiled almost imperceptibly, and gently nodded his head understandingly. Dismas' shock was even greater than before.

"What is it?" Caleb urgently asked, his voice held low to draw as little attention as possible.

"He's going to die—by choice, Caleb." Dismas tore his eyes away from Jesus to look at his friend. His loud exclamation had brought him back to the reality of where

163

he was and he lowered his voice. "I don't know why, when, where, or how it will happen, but he knows it and plans to let it happen."

"The man is crazy then. He—"

"Hush. Listen."

From what seemed to be immediately overhead came the deep rumble of thunder. Many heads in the crowd looked up into a cloudless sky.

Suddenly Dismas and a few others bent over as if dodging something thrown at them. Their arms shot up in a gesture of self-protection. Others just turned to look at the crouching few curiously.

Those who remained upright had either heard nothing or, as did some, had heard only thunder. Dismas, in the midst of the thunder, had heard a mighty voice in the distance say, "I have both glorified it and I will glorify it again."

The old thief did not fully understand the meaning of the words, but looking at Jesus he saw that the one who needed to understand them—did.

Dismas could stand no more of what was happening. His mind was being bombarded with things about which he had no knowledge and the burden of understanding was more than he could bear.

He shook as if he had palsy, which terrified Caleb. The younger thief could see no special reason for Dismas to tremble.

When Dismas jammed both fists into his eyes to block out the sight of Jesus, then turned his back, Caleb rushed up and quickly grabbed the older man's arm to guide him away. What had taken place was understood by one of the men and feared—but was not understood by the other—and also feared.

By the time they plodded their silent way downhill

164

through the narrow, twisting streets to finally reach the familiar drinking room, Caleb had stolen two money-bags, but neither was from a wealthy man.

The events of moments before had quickly been forgotten by the younger man. It was not that way for his master. Dismas had walked deep in thought, his mind bogged down by what he had heard and seen. The old thief felt the voice he had heard might be that of the God he had so long doubted and he was dazed by the thought.

After they had sat down at a table near the rear of the inn and had dumped the stolen money on the table, Dismas' serious attitude began to change. He slowly returned to his old thieving self as he became more aware of the familiar surroundings. The tinkle of money and the sounds and smells of his past pushed his thoughts of Jesus away.

When Caleb opened and poured out the contents of his last purse. Dismas let out a whoop. Out fell two small lumps of cheese, a single mena, and a strip of twisted and dried meat.

"Caleb, you bungling whelp," the old thief hooted. "Can't you tell the difference between a man's dinner and his money?"

Embarrassed almost more than he could stand, Caleb laughed nervously. Finally he blurted out, "A Samaritan. By the stars, it just had to belong to a Samaritan. Who else would carry food so carefully hidden?"

Both men banged the tabletop several times as they roared with laughter.

Shortly after dark, several hours after they arrived in their wine-filled sanctuary, the inn was more crowded. Because the thieves were not enthusiastic about large crowds in an enclosed area, they decided to move as far back in the room as possible—into the darkened area, where they had a measure of protection from prying eyes. They claimed their favorite cool spot on the floor. Minutes later, as they sipped their third cup of wine, a short, slender man sat down on a stool near them. He had black hair and a black beard, which emphasized his rodent-like facial features, Dismas thought.

Dismas, never one to be shy, stared openly at their new neighbor. The man's nervous and irritated manner fascinated the old thief. Dismas found the man's impatience amusing, as he waited for the overworked Miriam to serve him. He watched as the man's bony fingers fidgeted with a dirty cup left behind on his table by a former customer. As the man twisted the cup, he stared at the moist circles left on the tabletop by the few drops of wine which had spilled down the sides of the cup. The man glanced out of the corner of his eyes, aware of other eyes watching him. Turning his head slightly to enable him to look sideways at Dismas, the man asked, "Do I know you?"

"No."

"Then why do you stare at me so?"

"I stare at you because you sat in front of me. I have the choice of closing my eyes and possibly falling asleep, or leaving them open and looking at you. I simply chose to remain awake," Dismas said with a smirk.

"You mock me. Are you sure you don't know me?"

"Aren't you one of the twelve which follow the man, Jesus?" Dismas vaguely remembered having seen the man at the temple. The thief's interest sharpened.

"How did you know I was one of the twelve?" the man asked nervously.

"I was there along with most of the city when he cleaned up the temple. I saw you there at that time."

166

"Ummm," the weaselly man mused.

"Which of the twelve are you?" Dismas asked. He had heard that among Jesus' followers were men of many trades, some of them, such as the tax collector, not far above Dismas' own low station in life.

"I am Judas Iscariot," the man replied cautiously. "Why do you ask?" Dismas heard fear in the man's voice.

"Are you the publican? The tax collector? I hear Jesus has a tax collector among his twelve."

At the question the man seemed to relax some. Dismas detected a slight smile at the corners of the stranger's mouth. "No, I'm not. I'm from Kerioth. You speak of Matthew, formerly called Levi. He's from Capernaum."

"It surprised me," Dismas mused, voicing thoughts he had not particularly intended to share, "that Jesus would have such a man with him. Oh, I assume it might be for the wealth the tax collector must have." Dismas looked intently at Judas and continued, "What's your job?"

Judas stared stonily ahead. Slowly his face darkened as a look of disgust came over it. "I'm the so-called keeper of our purse. The keeper over an always empty purse."

Assuming the statement to have been made for a reason, Dismas tossed a gold coin onto the table, then watched the man's greedy expression as the coin spun, pivoted, and glistened on its way to a ringing stop. For the price, Dismas now felt he had a right to ask more questions. "Would you tell me a few things?"

Still looking toward the coin, the man quickly muttered, "Yes. Certainly. What do you wish to know?"

"It is said that the man you call "master can work great wonders, even miracles. Is it really true?" Dismas knew the answer to his question. He was not sure, however, that he could trust this man, so he asked him the question as a test.

167

"It's true," the man responded flatly. "He works them for everyone except those faithful to him."

"You sound as though you're unhappy."

"I am. When I did as he said, and followed as he commanded, I expected to enjoy a rich life as the follower of one able to raise the dead. Instead I have no gold or silver. I go without. Even now, I have little more than the modest clothes I wear and the price of a single cup of cheap wine."

"Raise the dead? He can do that?" Dismas asked with surprise.

"Yes, I've seen him heal the lame with a command, lepers with a touch, the possessed with a caress and a command to the devils to leave, and raise the dead by taking them by the hand. I have seen all of this, and yet—" he sighed. "Yet he gives no blessings to us who serve him day after day. He pays us with promises of things to come, in a world beyond death—a place known only to him. I want to enjoy life now—the things I can touch."

"But what if he's telling the truth? I only say this because I too saw him cure the lame and blind."

"If you have seen him in action, why do you ask if he can work wonders?"

Dismas was not a man to lie when lying was not profitable. "To see if you were a liar," he said coldly. The man to whom he talked showed no emotion. "You spoke of his raising the dead. This I have not seen. How can such a thing be?" Dismas was intrigued by this totally preposterous story.

"I don't know how he does it. Some said the man, a friend of the master's, by the name of Lazarus, was not dead at all, but simply coming out of a fever. Others said he was just pretending, that it was a hoax from which the

168

master could gain fame through wagging tongues. None of these are true, I know it."

"How can you say that?"

"The dead man, Lazarus, had lain in that burial cave until the smell of rotting flesh came from his grave when the stone was rolled to one side." The sulking man almost smiled, "Oh, I'm sure he was dead all right."

Dismas could not contain himself. "Yes, yes. Go on. How did your master do it? Did he use exotic medicines? Magic signs? What did he do?"

The stranger's eyes squinted at the questions. Dismas had asked them so fast Judas was having difficulty keeping up with them. He had been given no time to answer. Finally Dismas ended his string of questions and waited.

"He simply walked to the cave's opening and, calling out in a loud voice, he commanded his friend, the dead man, to come out. As many people (including the dead man's two sisters) watched, Lazarus, still clothed in his burial rags, slowly walked out of the cave—alive and all by himself."

Dismas stared with his mouth open. Finally he nervously licked his lips and blurted out, "What about the stink? Was he rotting? Was his flesh sagging—or coming off in patches? Or did he look as healthy as you and me?"

"No. The man looked as though he was still dead. Not bloated or falling apart or anything like that, just pale and weak, and gulping for breath—but he was alive after being dead. Today he looks like you and me, however." Almost as an afterthought, the man hissed, "He's here in Jerusalem with the master, if you wish to see him yourself."

A silence fell between the two men as Dismas contemplated what he had just heard. There was no way for the dead to return—or was there? The Egyptians had believed for centuries that their dead did not die at all, but lived on in a new land beyond some river named Styx, wherever that was. They even buried servants, food, furnishings, and money in their tombs so that when their dead needed these things, they would have them. Some families, so Dismas had heard, even left the person's pets in the grave. Dismas considered these things. *Maybe life after death is possible*, he thought, *just maybe*.

Bitterness returned to the ratlike man sitting at the table. "Friend, I appreciate the marvelous things he does for others. I stand in awe of what he does for the dead, but I am well and alive *today*. What does he do for me? He speaks of another kingdom. I accepted his word because I have seen his truths become realities, but I need some of the niceties of life now. I have seen him conquer the impossible, but I have never seen him conquer men. If he would but do this, do you realize the position we twelve would have?" A fire now shown on the man's face; his eyes were ablaze.

The fire quickly faded as the man turned his eyes down to look once more at the empty cup before him. "Yet, he does nothing for us."

"I have never spoken with him, even though I have seen him," Dismas said. "He seems to live well for one, as you say, who has nothing. He does not appear to hunger. Those who follow him do not have the look of the hungry either."

"This is true. We do not lack for anything, but the same could be said for a landowner's sheep. We have what is absolutely necessary, nothing more." Anguish arose in the man's voice, "I am just sick to my soul at being the goat for him and still having that street rabble look on me as someone who is fortunate." As he spoke, he jerked his head toward the door. "We are fed—meagerly. Sometimes it is a gift, as if to the poor. At other times it is by allowing us to pick fruit, as is granted to widows by Hebrew law. As for the rest, we must do without even the most basic of comforts. Many, many times I have been forced to shiver through a night in an open field just because we had no money for lodging."

Dismas saw that the man's temper was rising.

"I have remainded poor month after month," Judas said, "but it doesn't have to continue that way. He could change it with a wave of his hand—but he won't." Without waiting for Miriam to come, the man rose from his seat, turned, and reached back for the gold coin. Excusing himself only with a nod of his head, the weasel-faced man left.

It was Caleb's turn to laugh at how quickly Dismas had lost the gold coin and at how little the old thief had received for the price. But Dismas felt he had received much. The more experienced of the pair watched as the stranger pushed toward the door. Dismas thought, *There goes trouble*. The master thief could all but smell disaster in the departing man.

"You know, Caleb," said Dismas as he watched Judas push the door open and step into the street, "I feel sorry for that man."

"Why? It was he who left with your gold coin, not the other way around."

"What is gold? It can be gathered just outside the door. I talk of his consuming greed. He's little more than walking, breathing greed."

"That's true," Caleb chirped. "It's an ailment we share to some degree." The younger man still felt in a happy mood from the laugh he had on his master. "Now, take me. I have a greed which is like the weather. Mine is predictable for the most part. That man's is not."

"True, he has it so badly, it's almost a madness—like a deep hate."

Dismas did not dwell on the stranger's bitterness. He chuckled. "You know, if all the carpenter's twelve are as strange as that one, Jesus had better take up the hammer and adz again. With twelve such helpers, he's in more danger from friends than enemies."

"True, true," Caleb nodded before he turned to shout, "Miriam! Bring some wine, you sweet hag."

Dismas winced at his friend's crudeness, slouched back against the cool wall, and closed his eyes to wonder about the carpenter. If he was as smart as many people seemed to think he was, couldn't he see that Judas was not to be trusted? Maybe he was too far above thinking of Judas. Maybe Jesus' mind was so occupied with deeper thoughts that he simply overlooked Judas' whole attitude.

Hours of drinking passed. Not the boisterous drinking the pair usually did, but slow and quiet hours. Neither man showed his usual symptoms of drunkenness. Each was lost in his own thoughts—Dismas with the strange carpenter, and Caleb with the flitting, adventurous dreaming of youth.

"Dismas," Caleb finally said, "I have an idea which could make us rich tonight." For the next several hours, far into the evening, Caleb explained his plan.

Night came slowly to Jerusalem. When it finally did settle in, the cool blackness was almost as thick as the day's heat. This particular night was no exception and was like many others except that Dismas and Caleb were about to do something they had never done before—rob a place instead of a man.

More than an hour later, from a rooftop, Dismas and

172

Caleb looked down into the courtyard of the home of Hiram, the wool merchant. Below them they stared silently as Hiram and his fat wife made final preparations before the whole family left to visit some other wealthy home. The watchful pair of thieves guessed that the family's late start meant they were probably going to visit the palace of Herod. They surmised this because the king's parties were known to last days on end, with entire families spending from one night to a month as the festivities went on. When feasts lasted that long, those who attended them had little reason to hurry.

After much scurrying around and shouting orders to servants, Hiram and his family, each person dressed in finery fit for presentation at the palace, gathered their escort guards and left. The guards, however, were not the mercenary men normally employed by the wealthy, but were guards from Herod's court.

Quiet descended slowly over the servants and other members of the household. Finally there was practically no sound from any part of the house. It seemed apparent to Dismas and Caleb that even those left to guard the house had made themselves comfortable and were now asleep. It was time for the thieves to go to work.

Stealthily and slowly they boosted each other up and over the high wall which surrounded the house, boosting from below for the younger of the two and a pull from above for the older. Once atop the wall, they hesitated only long enough to make sure all was still quiet. Then they stepped down onto a small guard porch and creeped down its tiny mud steps into the outer yard.

Crossing the yard in their bare feet, which they decided would be safer than taking a chance on wearing squeaky sandals, they came to the wide main door, which opened into the flagstone inner court of the large home.

173

Scarcely daring to breathe, afraid that they might awaken an unseen dog or a light-sleeping slave or servant, the pair cautiously peered into the house. By the flickering light of several small oil lamps placed on tiny ledges built into the court's support pillars, the men saw many doors leading from the court into various rooms. Judging by other homes they had been in during celebrations of circumcision or marriage, they guessed these rooms were those of the house workers, a kitchen, and probably one or two storerooms.

The thieves stepped onto the slate floor. The cold stone caused their feet to tense slightly. They hesitated briefly, intensely aware of the silence. In the distance, from one of the small rooms, they could hear the deep bubbling snore of a man in deep sleep. From a room to their left, past a curtain drawn across the door, came the high-pitched grunts of a woman as she restlessly turned over in her sleep.

All appeared to be safe so, with the wave of one hand, Dismas signaled to his friend that they should begin searching for anything of value.

With a silence surrounding them which made their own hearts sound like muffled drums, the two men slowly and ever so gently padded their way from doorway to doorway, hesitating each time to insure that the occupants of the room behind each curtain were soundly asleep.

After seconds, each of which seemed like a minute, the men reached a rough-hewn stairway which led to a narrow balcony, also made of the same rough wood as the stairs, and which completely circled the wall around the court.

The two thieves began their assent of the steps with a caution they seldom displayed. They were out of their normal element and both knew it. On the street they depended on noise and the jostling of people to cover their thievery. Now they found themselves depending on absolute silence and the absence of people. As dangerous as their normal feats were, in the open and frequently facing the man they robbed, in Hiram's house they felt their downfall might be nothing more than the tiniest of sounds. Each man wondered if that small sound would be the squeak of a stairway step.

With each slow, cautious step the men applied their weight to their feet as if they walked on hot coals. The slightest groan from the aged stairway could set off screams and shouts of alarm which could be their undoing. For the crime they were committing, they would lose their hands in Nubia. In Egypt, they would simply be taken into the wilderness and staked out for the jackals, ants, and scorpions to eat. Cilicia was even less gentle with robbers of homes. They tied them to a wall as if they were sheepskins. Each day a special torturer would remove one joint from a man's body. He might first take the joint of a toe, then, using a white-hot piece of metal, sear the wound to stop the bleeding. The next day, another joint would be severed and seared with the hot metal. On and on, day after day, the victim was tortured in the same manner. Travelers from Cilicia said they had heard of men living to see their legs removed to the knees and their arms to the shoulders.

Regardless of a less savage punishment of thieves in Jerusalem, Dismas and Caleb knew that if they were caught this night they would become slaves on the eastern salt flats near the Sea of Death, or made to work on one of Herod's many projects. Such punishment ended only when a man took his final breath. Hope for mercy did not exist. For this reason, caution was more important than gain. Both men were prepared to bolt from the house, run up the observation guard posts along the wall, leap into the street, and flee along a preplanned escape route. They had left little to chance.

Perspiration ran down the side of Dismas' face as he breathlessly eased up the narrow stairway. He swore to himself he would never again try to rob a home when so many rich men walked the open streets, all but begging to have their excess wealth taken from them.

After they reached the top of the stairs, both men flattened themselves against the cool mud wall to catch their breaths. After one or two seconds, and with a motion of his head, Dismas signaled they should again continue their search.

When they reached the door to the room that overlooked the street in front of the house, Dismas pointed to himself and then to the room. Caleb nodded. Dismas pointed toward his friend, then toward a second room. They knew the first room, the one on the front, was the largest and that of Hiram. The second room was that of his wife. In one of these rooms was whatever wealth was to be gained.

Before entering the master bedroom, Dismas knelt down, stretched far out over the edge of the balcony and carefully removed one of the tiny oil lamps from its perch on the support. Caleb saw what his leader had done, so he too took a lamp the same way. The men removed the lamps slowly, ever so slowly, to keep any sudden change in the room's lighting from being noticeable, especially to the sleepers below.

Once the men had sufficient light to see their way, they quietly entered the rooms. As Dismas held the palm-sized lamp with its tiny flickering flame higher, he squinted into the darkness, allowing his eyes to adjust.

Finally he could see enough to make out the room's furnishings and was surprised at its sparseness.

In the center of the large room was a table around which were placed four small stools. For an instant Dismas wondered just how many gold and silver shekels had been counted over that table. Quickly his attention snapped back to the business at hand. There was no time for dreaming.

Picking his way deeper into the room, he looked all around. In one corner, still rolled into a tight roll, was the thick straw mat and soft quilt Hiram placed on the nearby platform of hardened clay and used as a bed. Near the head of the platform was a pair of badly worn sandals, a pitcher of water, and a plate on which lay a small, unbroken loaf of bread. Dismas smiled as he thought, *How nice it would be to wake up each morning and eat, even before rising from your warm bed.*

Along the far wall he saw wooden pegs with clothing hanging from them. The clothes ranged from fine clothes designed especially for state occasions at the palace to a leather apron the rich man probably used as he counted goods being loaded on a caravan. It was commonly known that the miserly Hiram trusted no one with the loading and counting of his trade goods. He was heard telling his own brother, "My life lies in my possessions. In myself and my wares I have faith and security. What I own provides my happiness." Dismas smiled as he thought, *Tonight I steal not only gold and silver, but I take from Hiram his faith, security, happiness—what he feels to be his very life.* In the dim light of the small lamp held in the palm of his hand, Dismas grinned as he considered the stupidity of the man who based life and hope on things which could be stolen.

On the floor near the window lay a chest. It was almost

two feet long, with handles of carved ivory. Although Dismas was unaccustomed to this type of stealing, he felt that any wealth in the room would be inside such a chest. Quickly he padded his way across the room. In one motion, he carefully raised the lid, uselessly squeezing it in an unconscious effort to keep it from creaking.

When it was fully opened, the master thief began examining the contents of the chest. He tossed several pieces of clothing to the floor and felt growing frustration at not having found immediate riches. In his haste he yanked on one of the lower garments only to hear a loud clank. The noise snapped him back to exaggerated awarenes. Once more he began extracting items lightly and slowly—first a scroll; then two highly ornamented, but inexpensive, knives from some foreign land; and finally, the leather bag for which he and Caleb had come. Holding the lamp closer, Dismas awkwardly forced the pouch open with one hand. Inside were more gold and silver pieces than he had ever seen.

Without trying to count his find, Dismas pulled the string, closing the bag. He stood up gracefully, not bothering to close the lid on the chest.

Bending over and grasping the neck of the bulging moneybag, the thief was surprised at its great weight. Giving an extra heave, he straightened up and cradled the bag in the crook of his elbow in order to carry it as noiselessly as possible.

As he turned to leave the room, the form of a man standing in the doorway caused him to weaken and gasp. In an effort to hide his temporary fear, he hissed, "It's here." His young friend nodded his head.

As silently as they had come, the two men crept slowly back down the stairway, Dismas trying to keep the coins quiet by snuggling them close to his chest. In contrast,

Caleb fumbled every step of the way as he tried to aid his friend with his heavy, valuable load.

Their trip down the stairs became a desperate comedy as Dismas carefully watched exactly where he put his feet and grimmaced. Cradling the moneybag carefully in one arm, he had to balance an overly warm lamp with the other, all the while concerned with an overly helpful Caleb. His desperation was as much to keep Caleb from knocking the awkward sack from his arms as it was to keep the load from clinking and clanking.

Finally the pair reached the foot of the stairs where Dismas, for the first time, was able to lean back against the wall and safely push his zealous friend away. Caleb looked quizzically at his master, who, with a deep frown, shook his head violently to indicate he did not want help.

After a brief pause, the two men glided across the inner court, out the still unguarded door, up the guard platform, and prepared to go over the wall. At that point in their much rehearsed plans, things almost fell apart.

They had planned that Caleb, the younger and more agile of the two, would drop over the wall, take whatever had been stolen, then help Dismas down the steep wall. The first two steps went well, but Dismas, in his haste to leave the scene of his silent agony, failed to wait for Caleb to set the money on the ground and reach up to help him. Instead, the older thief placed the bulging bag in Caleb's eager hands, then leaped from the wall.

Instead of the continued silence, as they had expected, Dismas fell on Caleb, who in turn dropped the moneybag with a loud crash. On top of that, Dismas twisted his ankle so severely that both men heard the crunch of tearing tendons. Pain shot up the full length of Dismas' leg, but no sound came from him. The old and disciplined thief knew that even the slightest additional sound might bring pursuers and, with his injury, he would be brought down like an antelope by a leopard.

Instead of allowing himself to scream in pain, Dismas threw his forearm across his mouth and bit down as hard as he could. As if by magic, fresh perspiration sprang out in tiny drops across his forehead; his eyes bulged as the scream silently burst inside him.

As soon as he felt the coins lurch from his grasp Caleb fell forward to stop any of them which might have escaped from rolling noisily into the street. The instant he hit the ground the young thief whirled around to see if he had been struck by some unseen guard. As he turned he realized what had happened.

Caleb's face reflected that of the suffering Dismas. Like his master, Caleb made no new sounds, but instead, slowly raised to his feet and held out both his hands for Dismas to grasp and pull himself up. Once this was done, Caleb bent over, grasped the coin sack, and the pair set out slowly on the long trip back to Aram's inn.

It was night and danger lurked everywhere, but for these men the night and the darkness were their friends. As for danger, it had been a lifelong part of their existence.

As they limped slowly along the dark, narrow, alley-like streets, the men were comforted by the heavy load that Caleb carried—money—the largest haul of their sordid careers.

7 WEDNESDAY MORNING

Following a night of moaning and groaning over a leg which throbbed as if the muscles had been torn from it, Dismas was exhausted. He sat, as he had all night, on a stool at the rear of Aram's main room. He leaned against the back wall, using a table for further support. The injured and badly swollen ankle claimed a stool of its own in front of him.

The sun showed that it was slightly past midmorning. The smoke from kitchen fires once more hung in the air.

Despite a futile attempt to get drunk and forget the aching he felt, Dismas stayed in good spirits and was completely sober. His enthusiasm was dampened, as Caleb had expected, by an irritability mainly brought on from lack of sleep.

Caleb, clutching the heavy bag of money they had stolen from Hiram, had slept from shortly after their ar-

181

rival at the inn to less than an hour before. Since then he had talked with several men of dubious reputation who had stopped in to begin their day with a few cups of wine. Dismas had caught snatches of their conversations only to find the men almost as irritating as his throbbing ankle.

Finally Caleb returned from a talk with a man Dismas recognized but whose name he could not remember.

"Imagine it," Dismas said, repeating the conversation that he had heard. "He not only touched one of them, but he had the gall to stay all night in a leper's home."

Caleb made a face to indicate that the horror wrapped up in what he heard was sickening to him. Caleb picked up the ranting, "I don't think it was gall; it was an act of stupidity. Everyone knows that if you even breathe the air through which a leper has passed, you too are afflicted."

Dismas suddenly found his own and Caleb's words offensive. Instead of dwelling on them, he reacted as he frequently did when he did not want to expand on a topic—he responded in the traditional Hebrew dialect used in Jerusalem. "I have heard such things of those afflicted with the dread disease, Zara'ath. It is true they are cursed of God, but I also believe what the people say about Jesus cleansing Simon of it with nothing more than a single touch."

"I heard that too," Caleb scoffed. "And I also heard he walks on water. Ha!" Caleb turned to look at Dismas, lifting one eyebrow higher than the other to show he totally disbelieved these reports and was disgusted by such ridiculous stories. "I saw a young boy once—I was but a child at the time—who tried to walk on water. When I saw him, he was blue—very blue and very dead."

182

As if Caleb's doubt was contagious, the hardness of disbelief spread slowly through Dismas' eyes too. "That may be true, but what about this man's ability to raise the dead?"

Suddenly Caleb was the leader, "Have you ever seen such a thing? No. What's wrong with you, my friend? Is the thought of all our gold causing your brain to weaken?"

"What do you mean?"

"Less than two days ago you agreed with me about that magician from Nazareth. Today you talk as if he were more than a fraud."

"I did not say, others have, that he's some sort of savior." Dismas' temper was beginning to rise, but his voice betrayed his sympathy with the carpenter. "Maybe I just respect anyone those temple parasites are against. I saw his bravery. I've seen his brilliant mind at work. I watched as he turned the religious leaders into confused jackals with a cunning I never saw before—not even in the best thieves or the shrewdest merchants. I tell you, Caleb, this one is different."

"I agree," Caleb retorted sarcastically. "I have seen what he has done to you. He has taken away from you the ability to discard sympathy, maybe even your ability to see through the falseness of his words and actions."

Dismas found that he could not even argue with his young student. "Never mind me," he finally said. With patience he forced a smile and tried to change the subject as he called out, "Let's share the gold and live as we always dreamed we would."

Forcing himself momentarily to forget his injury, Dismas whirled around toward the table only to stop in midair to grab his leg and groan. At the noise, several customers glanced toward the two thieves, but quickly returned to their wine and private conversations.

From inside his robe, Caleb brought out four or five small coin purses and several crude leather bags. Into these would go the divided loot of the night before.

Although they were close friends and aware of their mutual admiration of each other, they did not trust each other when it came to money matters. In fact, one of Dismas' first lessons to Caleb came when, after an unusually fruitful day in the marketplace, the master thief took two gold coins belonging to Caleb. When faced by the younger man's accusation later, Dismas admitted to the theft by saying, "Caleb, my boy, there is a dividing line between friends and strangers. That line is built of two things—silver and gold." Caleb never forgot the lesson.

With the bag of stolen money on the table between them, the two thieves kept wary eyes on those in the inn—and each other. Over and over they repeated, as they pushed coins of equal value first to one side of the table, then the other, "One for you, and one for me. One for you, and one for me."

To keep Aram's customers from becoming overly curious, when the divided coins piled up on each side of the table, they would stuff them into the smaller bags and start over.

The more they counted, the more the pace of their counting quickened. In less time than they thought it would take, they reached the bottom of the big bag. Finally they were ready to count their new and individual wealth.

After a few minutes, during which the tinkling of coins repeatedly drew glances from other patrons, Dismas finally looked up, and with a tone of disbelief, murmured, "Caleb."

"Yes," responded the greedy thief, his teeth gleaming through his black beard.

"Do you realize we have enough money here to buy passage to Egypt and enough above that to purchase land and cattle there?"

"Land? Cattle? Are you crazy, Dismas?" Caleb glanced up then returned to his counting. Almost immediately he stopped to look at Dismas. "You talk of work, and you know that's not for us. Instead, why not go to Joppa and live like kings?" Caleb's eyes took on a faraway look as he continued, "We could sleep with a different woman each night and let the ocean breezes cool us after each of them." Suddenly his face came alive again. "Dismas! Where's your lust for living? Cattle, my foot! Unless you've become too old, let's enjoy our fill of women and wine."

Dismas' arm flashed out to grasp Caleb's beard, which he twisted viciously. "You doubt my manhood?"

"I—I did not say that," Caleb denied. "I just fear for you."

"Why should you fear for me?" Dismas asked irritably, maintaining his firm grip on the beard.

"I fear that through your encounters with that madman at the temple your lusty heart might be changed from what it was into something different."

Dismas again cruelly twisted Caleb's beard. "Stop goading me about my feelings for that man. You can't seem to comprehend my words when they are spoken civilly so I'll explain the only way you seem to understand." He yanked Caleb's head forward until their two faces were just inches apart. "Now hear me. Any more snide remarks about me or the carpenter and the only gold you'll enjoy is a single coin I put in each of your eyes before I bury you."

The old thief's voice took on a softer and more deadly tone. "Caleb, I love you like a son, but just one more smart remark about this Jesus or me and I'll—" Caleb swallowed deeply as terror and shock froze his face into a twisted shape. "I'll kill you."

Dismas released his strangling grip on the choking man and Caleb quickly jumped to his feet and began scraping the remaining coins in front of him into his outstretched robe front. When this was done he rubbed his chin, then looked at the hairs which came out in his hand.

In the wake of his finest robbery, a time when he should have been overcome with joy, Dismas felt his shoulders slump and his face drop forward until it was hidden from Caleb. In a voice choked with regret, Dismas murmured, "I'm sorry. I don't know why I did that. I can only say that this Jesus is someone I do not understand. I see in him a victory of some sort, one that would surpass the achievements of Alexander. At the same time, I see in him something so deeply tragic I could cry for him." Dismas swallowed deeply, "Caleb, I'm sorry. I'm in pain."

Finally the old thief raised his head to see why his student had not spoken, to see if he had quietly gone. When their faces met, Dismas saw something he had never seen on Caleb's face before—especially not for him. He saw pity.

Caleb too saw something he could not remember having seen before—tears rolling down the cheeks of a sober Dismas. It was not that Caleb had never seen his master cry before, but only when sympathy was needed to accomplish a theft, or when his teacher was so drunk he cried for almost any reason. These tears were different. Dismas was overcome with sincere grief, at a time when

186

he should have felt rich and happy.

"Caleb, I hate that man—the carpenter. I hate him for what he is doing to me—to us. I even hate myself for allowing it to happen." Dismas looked back down at the several stacks of coins in front of him as he absently continued, "Whatever curse he has placed on me, you should know it is not painful. His talk of a new kingdom, being kind to one another, and such as that, has caused me to ask if what we did last night was the right thing to do. Caleb, for the first time in my life, I doubt myself and the life I live."

Dismas looked up again, hoping some answer for his confusion would come from his friend. None did.

Dismas, despite the pain it brought, pulled himself to his feet. "Caleb, take the gold—all of it. I don't want it anymore. I just want to find that mysterious man and ask him to explain what's wrong with me." As he said this, he began to shuffle toward the door, using tables and stools as braces. After a few steps he stopped, turned, and said flatly, "And I don't really know what I want him to tell me—or why."

Caleb still said nothing. The shock and hurt he felt showed on his face. As he watched, the sleeves of Dismas' filthy robe billowed out with the raising of the old thief's hands, palms up. "I only know that all of my miserable life I have looked for something and no matter what I found, no matter how wonderful it seemed to be, I am still an unhappy man."

Dismas let his hands fall limply at his sides and his shoulders sag, giving him the appearance of being much older than he was. With his head cocked slightly to one side, he wailed, "Caleb, maybe from him I can find the solution to what it is I am really looking for."

Suddenly, and using a term Caleb had never heard his

teacher use before, Dismas almost cried, "Caleb, my son. I must go. Please forgive me."

Ignoring Aram, Miriam, and the inn's customers, all of whom stared at him, the old thief—the man known in every alley of Jerusalem as the man with vinegar in his veins—limped from the room. He had turned his back on more gold and silver than the pair had ever held in their hands before.

Out of instinct, a bewildered Caleb looked down at the small bags of coins on the table, then stuffed them into the crook of his arm. He quickly realized he could not carry the heavy money, so he rushed over to Aram, who stood behind the filthy counter picking his teeth. There Caleb plopped the bags in front of the startled inn-keeper before breathlessly hissing, "Listen you spawn of a scorpion, I know to the smallest mina how much money is here. Guard it with care and I will reward you greatly. Steal even one coin and Dismas and I will choke you with your own bowels."

Before Aram could reply Caleb whirled and raced across the room and into the brilliant sunlight of the morning. As far as Caleb was concerned, Dismas had gone mad and the young thief felt obligated to help him.

As desperate as he was to catch Dismas, the unwritten law of thieves forbade Caleb from shouting his master's name loudly in public. For this reason Caleb frantically looked in both directions along the already crowded street, hoping to catch even a fleeting glimpse of Dismas. The milling crowd to the left seemed to flow too evenly in both directions to have been disturbed by the pushing of an injured and mad man. For this reason, and because he saw men and women in the opposite direction grumbling as if they were recently shoved, Caleb ran to the right.

The younger thief could not help grin as he listened to irritated people curse the man who had so roughly jostled them in passing. Caleb knew too well that Dismas, when intent on going somewhere, had little respect for anyone but his victim, soldiers, or his assistant.

Dismas, blindly pushing his way along the street as if he owned it, had no idea where to find the carpenter. He just knew he had to look.

Minutes later Caleb saw his friend and master ahead of him, but he knew that it would be useless to try to stop him. Instead, the young thief walked a distance behind.

Dismas had become thirsty and, out of years of habit, reverted to the thief's way of obtaining whatever was desired. He saw a water seller approaching with a goatskin water bag slung over one shoulder and two brass cups clanking against each other from a cord suspended from the opposite shoulder.

Nearby was a blind man, seated along the street's wall. He held a small bowl containing three Greek drachmas, one of the smallest coins in the city.

Easing his way to the blind man's side, Dismas leaned over, and as if to place a coin in the man's bowl, thumped the bowl's bottom with one finger. The thump caused the bowl to drop sharply. As it did, the three tiny coins leaped into the air where Dismas, by simply turning his hand over, caught one of the coins in midair. The other two coins fell noisily back to the bowl's bottom.

"May God bless all of your remaining days," the blind man droned, as he had done so many times before. He was unaware that he had been robbed of one third of his current wealth.

With the drachma in hand, Dismas turned to the water seller and motioned he would like a full cup. The carrier pulled the bag around in front of him, yanked the wooden plug from the end of the bulging goatskin, and carefully poured. Dismas gulped down the water, made a face, then continued his search. Before going but a few steps, a hand gripped his arm, and he turned. It was Caleb. Without a word, the pair continued to walk along the street, their steps brisk despite the growing crowd and Dismas' accentuated limp.

After a few minutes Caleb gently inquired, "Do you know where you will find Jesus?"

"No."

"Where do you plan to look?"

"I thought I would begin at the temple. It is possible that he's there again teaching."

"That's as likely a place as any," Caleb agreed. "We could inquire. Possibly one of the beggars could tell us where he is today."

"I don't feel we should ask about him. He might be wanted by the authorities, or in danger."

"As you wish, Dismas," Caleb replied as casually as he could, but he was still very confused. He wondered how Dismas, the greatest of thieves, could change in such a short time. In a city where prophets shouted at every street corner, Dismas used to watch them come and go and his only interest was the purses of those who listened to them. Now, when the poorest of the lot came to town, Dismas suddenly acted as if finding the man was all that mattered. Poor Dismas. Age must be affecting his mind.

Suddenly a new thought struck Caleb. Deep down he knew it was not the truth, but it was the solution he wanted to believe. Dismas' curious actions must have resulted from his fall. With that excuse Caleb forced himself to relax a little; Dismas' madness would pass.

The pair pushed through the crowd as the heat, stench and dust grew insufferably dense. Despite this they

190

walked as if they were alone on the street, always pushing people aside and plunging on.

Finally they neared the temple. Even though the streets widened and the crowd thinned, their exertion getting to this point had been unrelenting and their efforts made both men breathe heavier. Ahead of them was the wall surrounding the temple courtyards. Looking at it, something struck Caleb as strange. The top part of the wall was brilliantly new and the lower part, commonly called Solomon's Wall, was dull and drab. He had looked at the wall most of his life but had just noticed the difference in its colors. The bottom part was the last remaining section of the ancient wall built by King Solomon, son of David. It was revered by all Hebrews—all except him and Dismas. They passed it and then climbed the gentle stairs which led to the huge new building.

As they climbed, two men dressed in common clothes walked toward them. Dismas and Caleb instantly recognized them as two of the twelve who normally accompanied the carpenter. Caleb squinted suspiciously, but Dismas lit up as if he was about to meet old friends.

When Dismas hailed them, the pair of strangers raised two limp fingers, as was the custom for greeting used farther north. The men stopped to speak with Dismas, but before a word could be said, Caleb saw his opportunity and quickly stepped to the side of one of them, as if to talk. Making sure he was pressed tightly against the man, Caleb cooed, "God's blessings, brothers."

As soon as he had greeted them, his fingers quickly ran around the girdle of the first man. Finding nothing, he shifted his weight and checked the girdle of the other.

Dismas saw and disapproved of what his friend was doing. The older and more experienced thief stepped deftly between Caleb and the two men. "Aren't you two of the carpenter's twelve?" Dismas did not give them an opportunity to answer before adding, "If you are, can you help us?"

"How can we help you?" one of the men asked.

By this time the excitement inside Dismas was about to explode. "Tell me, where can we find your Jesus at this time of day?"

At the words "your Jesus," the men glanced at each other apprehensively before one of them noticed the speaker's injured leg. When they saw it, they assumed he was but another wanting some cure so one of them replied, "At this moment we're not sure." The taller of the men continued, "He sent us to find a woman carrying a water jar at the lower well. That was quite some time ago, so we aren't sure ourselves where he is now."

"Have you no idea at all?" Dismas excitedly whined.

"Sometimes he teaches by the well."

"Which well might that be?" Dismas pressed.

"The one north of the temple—the one which feeds the Pool of Bethesda."

"Do you mean the place where the cripples and sick gather and wait for ripples in the water to cure them?" Dismas asked incredulously.

The men smiled, then one answered, "That's the one . . . near there."

Hearing this, Dismas clinched his lips tightly, bowed low, and started to leave. Caleb smiled at his master's bow. Usually such a gesture from Dismas meant the old thief had made the one to whom he bowed much poorer. Caleb was now sure the reason why he had found no purses on the men was because the master thief had beaten him to them.

Looking down at Dismas' open hands, Caleb was shocked as he realized Dismas had made no move toward the men. The young thief's shock became even greater when Dismas tucked both of his hands into the pit of his stomach and once more bowed low. As he did, from his mouth came the words, "May God truly bless you."

Turning away Caleb once more followed his master as he set off, hobbling down the street.

Finally they left the main street, walked along several narrow streets and alleyways, then turned into another wide street—one where the crowd thinned considerably.

Dismas' anxiety grew more evident by the minute. He was more irritable with the people who stood in his way as he hobbled along. Even though there was plenty of room to sidestep them, Dismas shoved everyone to one side. He met their scoldings with vulgar motions and returned complaints with occasional threats.

Minutes later the men reached the Bethesda Pool and began looking for the crowd which always seemed to follow the Galilean. It did not take them long to find him. When they did, it struck them how the many men and even a few women stood listening respectfully. They were not noisy, as most crowds are, but quietly hung on the words the carpenter spoke as if each syllable had special meaning for them.

Since the crowd was on the distant side of the pool, the two thieves made their way among the farmer's tiny stalls, which seemingly were everywhere in the city.

The stalls were not permanent. Each man operating his meager business from one of them had carried it into the city on his back that morning. By law he would carry it back to his home that night. This was easily possible because each stall was little more than a skeleton of branches covered on three sides and the top by woven reed mats.

Dismas and Caleb, on their way to where Jesus spoke, walked past stalls featuring melons, dates, figs, grain, and dried fish. As the pair neared the large group of people, they saw Jesus standing in the center on one of the steps which circled the second of the five landings surrounding the pool.

As he always seemed to, he taught softly, sympathetically, simply, and with few motions of his hands or head, except for the occasional upward motion of a pointing finger.

As the men drew nearer, Caleb's confusion at Dismas' attitude gave way to mild disgust. Dismas, with an attitude just the opposite of his friend's, grinned in a way normally reserved for one who, after a long separation, sees someone he loves. It seemed to Caleb that Dismas, at any moment, might rush up and throw his arms around the Nazarene as though he were his father.

Caleb was jealous, but he was also afraid. The look on Dismas' face caused the younger thief to hang back intentionally. If his master lost self-control, it would not only be embarrassing, but it was dangerous for thieves to stand out, even in a gathering as large as this.

Jesus had obviously been talking for quite some time before Dismas and Caleb arrived. His talk was not without distractions because several temple priests stood in the front row of the crowd. They were deliberately keeping the people from becoming too interested in what the Galilean said.

Although Dismas had pushed himself almost half way through the throng, Caleb did not venture in so deeply. Instead, he stayed near the rear, anticipating the ever present trouble he hoped would not come.

Jesus had a frown on his face. It was more a look of concern than displeasure, even though the heckling of the priests gave him much cause for unhappiness.

Jesus looked into the faces staring at him and, as if pleading with his listeners, said, "For a little while yet, the light is among you. Walk while you have the light that the darkness may not overtake you." He cocked his head downward and slightly to one side, the look of concern still showing. He paused as if seeking the right words.

Looking up again, he continued, "He who walks in the darkness does not know where he is going. While you have the light, believe in the light that you may become sons of the light."

Just like the day before, Dismas was bewildered. He heard Jesus say one thing but to the old thief, the words meant another. The light Jesus spoke of was not the sun or lamps. The light he told of was himself—both as a promise and almost as a threat. Dismas understood Jesus actually to mean that he and his teachings would be the light to guide anyone who would believe in them through all of life's darknesses so those darknesses would hold no terror. There was the promise.

At the same time Dismas realized that Jesus had said that if a person knew of him and his teachings—and did not believe in them, darkness, doubt, worry, despondency, and death would be his inheritance. This seemed to be the unspoken threat.

For the old thief who lived from day to day without any distinct purpose in life,there was yet another message. It came in the words, "He who walks in the darkness does not know where he is going." In full agreement with the speaker, Dismas nodded his head. The words fit him uncomfortably. Many times he had wondered where his life led. For what reason had he been born on this earth? Most of the time Dismas just forced the thought away because it was too disturbing, but it never completely left him.

Next, Dismas considered the words in relation to his friends and the company he had always kept. He thought of Miriam, the hard-working harlot; Caleb, the self-seeking thief; Aram, the greedy one; and his many drinking and carousing companions over the years. It was plain that, along with Dismas, they too wandered in the darkness about which Jesus spoke—whether they would admit it or not.

It was as if the man, who was many years junior to the old thief, was able to see a person's life and evaluate it in terms of worth—and Dismas, unhappily, felt his life did not amount to much.

Inside, the thief wrestled with himself over Jesus. As he stood staring at the rough-featured, but gentle-looking man, he wondered, *A man? Just a man? I don't see how he can be just a man and know all that he does.* How could he speak so authoritatively about things no carpenter could know—unless he is what others say he is—the Son of God. Didn't even his name, "Jesus," mean "God saves?" Hadn't He performed feats no other man would dare dream of trying? Weren't the mightiest of all the Jews, the Sadducees terrified of him and his friend Lazarus, whom he raised from the dead?

Dismas' thoughts were momentarily distracted as he thought of Lazarus. When Lazarus entered Jerusalem with Jesus three days before, the Sadducees freely let it be known that they intended to send him back to death again. They had to do it so he would not provide the walking evidence that being restored from the dead was possible. After all, the biggest difference between the competing Sadducees and Pharisees was that Sadducees did not believe the dead would return to life and the

Pharisees believed they would.

Dismas became slightly weak in his knees and elbows as he wrestled within himself over the man he looked at. He wanted to believe what the man said because in his words were real promise and hope. With all of his heart Dismas wanted to believe, but his past life, the evil he had done, lived strong in the aging body. He felt that to succumb to such thinking would be to open the door to ridicule from his friends. It would be to admit that what he had believed before was wrong and to believe would change his life to something he was not sure he wanted.

Just a man? No. This Jesus had to be more than that, but what? Certainly others had claimed to be messiahs, and they proved false. Yet, this man was different from all of them, Dismas reasoned. The others came praising themselves and asking for wealth. This man came praising only God, explaining how all people could eternally have a special peace, love, and kindness from God. He asked nothing in return except that people should listen to him and believe in him. A small price.

As Dismas thought of these things, he had missed some of what Jesus said. He was jolted back to awareness, however, when he heard him say, "He who believes in me does not believe in me, but in him who sent me. And he who looks upon me looks upon him who sent me."

A muffled, "Ooooh" went up from the whole crowd. Some people, including Dismas, took a small step backward in shock at what they heard.

Jesus had publicly spoken the words which could condemn him. He said what Dismas now strongly suspected to be true, but fought desperately not to believe. Jesus had said to believe him was to believe God. To see him was to see God. In effect, that he was God—here on earth—in man's form and body.

The old thief's mouth dropped open, then his breathing began to come in short gasps. "See me, see God. Hear me, hear God." That was what Dismas knew Jesus had said.

Did he realize what he had done? Was He fully aware of what he had just said? Questions raced rapidly through the old thief's mind. Over and over the same questions came. Amid them a gnawing fear gripped Dismas—a fear for Jesus.

Looking around to see what effect the words had on others, Dismas saw that the importance of what was said had registered on others too. Some were shocked. Some were overjoyed. Others were offended. From all sides the word "blasphemy" was whispered time and time again.

On the faces of the twelve, and a few others, was a look of sadness. They knew what such words would do when the priests, who now shoved their way through the crowd, reported them to the high priest and the temple officeholders.

Although Dismas was astounded to hear the very thing he suspected being spoken aloud, he felt that Jesus, in his seemingly fathomless wisdom, knew exactly what he was doing.

Above the heads of the crowd, the expression on the speaker's face showed that his words were bitter ones for him to say. It was as if he already knew the outcome of his announcement—as if he expected to be condemned by everyone, even those who, just three days before, had shouted "Hosanna" as he entered Jerusalem.

Dismas was again distracted as he thought of the word "Hosanna." It was a cry which had rang from the throats of many thousands of people when Jesus rode into the city on the white donkey. It was an old Hebrew word, a prophetic word, which meant "save now." It was a word used by King David in the songs he sang in praise to God. It had been used during home and temple rituals for centuries. Some psalms were written as praise following Nehemiah's rebuilding of the temple when the Jews returned to Jerusalem from Babylon's slavery. Back then they felt they had been "saved." Just three days ago, while shouting "Hosanna," the descendants of those same Jews looked on Jesus as the one to free them again.

Now the echos of the hosannas had died out. The hero of the people had not raised up a sword, but had lifted his arms for peace—always peace—and had, just seconds before, spoken words which could destroy him.

Dismas felt a tear trickle down the side of his face. "Jesus, Jesus," he said, saliva slipping from the corners of his mouth and his throat constricted and a deep sadness overwhelmed him. "Why did you, who looked on me as someone just as good as others, have to expose yourself to those who would destroy you?"

A curious look from the man standing next to him made Dismas realize he had spoken aloud. He quickly wiped the side of his face with a dirty sleeve and coughed to cover his embarrassment.

When the crowd settled down from the excitement of what had been said, Jesus concluded his talk. His listeners didn't know it at the time, but this would be the last time they would hear Jesus speak directly to them.

"It was as light that I came into the world, that everyone who believes in me should not remain in darkness. And, if anyone hears my words and does not keep them, it is not I who judge him. I did not come to judge the world—but to save sinners."

Like heavy hammers, the last words slammed into the whole crowd—especially the old thief. Looking around, he saw that the impact of Jesus' words was not wasted.

Everyone whispered and gestured to someone else, but the old thief just stood and stared.

He came to save the world, Dismas thought. *To save the entire world? Rome too? If his words are true, he is, indeed, the anointed one—the Messiah*. It was as if Dismas had become paralyzed; he could not move.

Finally, the old thief turned to look at the Greeks, who still stood before Jesus. As he watched them, the impact of Jesus' last words seemed to have several meanings. Dismas had been fully exposed to Jesus—God in a man's body. He realized now that the true word of God was offered to be accepted or rejected. Dismas did not want to choose.

In saying "the world," Jesus had aimed his words at his Greek visitors as representatives of all non-Jews. Until this time, as far as Dismas knew, the Galilean had directed his teachings only to Hebrews. This time he included the world, as represented here by the Greeks.

In saying, "I did not come to judge the world—but to save sinners," Jesus had invited all people to him. None were now excluded from the mercy, grace, and gifts of God as presented by this man. Unlike the gods of other religions, Jesus said he had come for "the world"—all of it.

As Dismas watched Jesus conclude his talk and begin to step down from where he had stood to talk, the old thief felt a heavy tug on the back of his mantle. Jogged from his thoughts, he turned and saw it was Caleb, who had worked up enough courage to penetrate the crowd in search of his master.

"Dismas, you fool. Let's get out of here." Caleb's irritation at the master thief for having forgotten his usual cautiousness to listen to a wandering carpenter left the younger man more than just angered—he was afraid.

"You know full well that if anything happened to bring the guards, there is no way for you to escape. Even now both of us are trapped if they appear."

Like a nervous wolf the younger man looked warily past the crowd for soldiers and listened for the ominous clank of armor. Seeing and hearing none, the irate young man began to lead Dismas from the milling bodies.

As they pushed and sidestepped their way back toward the street which ran through the market, Dismas shoved his way ahead until he walked in front of Caleb.

They had taken only a few steps past the outer edge of the crowd when someone behind them screamed, "Thief! Stop that thief!"

Out of instinct, the two men whirled and instantly dropped into a semi-crouch. They expected that at any instant many hands would seize them. By experience, Dismas had surveyed his surroundings as his body turned. He saw that there was no way to escape the crowd. If he ran down the nearest side street, he would be trapped against the pool wall.

As an alternative, he looked to see who called out the words, or if there were soldiers near him. He was surprised to see that the accusations were not aimed at him, but at Caleb.

The accuser was Hiram, the merchant, the man whose home they had robbed the night before. He was not more than twenty feet away from Caleb, pointing his leathery finger and screaming at the top of his shrill and piercing voice, "Thief! Stop the thief! Thief! Stop the thief!"

Dismas and Caleb did what all men with guilty consciences and the feeling they are about to be captured would do—they ran.

As a team, they pushed men and women alike to one

side, using more strength than either of them realized he had. Several of the men who had stood listening to the carpenter turned, saw what looked like an opportunity to gain a reward, and bolted after the fleeing pair.

It was no real race for Dismas. His injured ankle throbbed with pain and slowed him to an awkward lope. Caleb had turned to run without looking, and in doing so stumbled over a bundle of sheepskins which had been placed near him by an innocent owner. Caleb fell heavily, but, with the agility of the young, bounded back to his feet again and sprinted through the surprised people.

As they rushed into the nearby street, Dismas and Caleb glanced over their shoulder at the men chasing them, then ahead, only to see two Roman soldiers blocking the street not thirty feet ahead of them.

One soldier turned his rectangular metal shield on its side to protect himself and his companion. The other dropped the point of his spear until it rested on the shield's upper edge, pointing at the fleeing thieves—at throat level.

Caleb, who was traveling faster than Dismas, could not stop his momentum and collided headlong into the soldiers, knocking both to the ground. The spear point narrowly missed him, but the soldiers, acting by reflex learned in many skirmishes, clutched at the fallen thief and quickly subdued him.

Dismas, forced by his injured ankle to run with an ape-like gait, was unable to stop his forward motion quickly, so he threw himself violently against the mud wall. Now, instead of turning to run from the soldiers to save himself, he went against his instincts and turned to help Caleb.

The two soldiers were atop the now helpless man, one holding his wrists and the other lying on him. There was no way Caleb could fight back and the armor of the soldier on top of him mashed the flesh of his cheek into his teeth. He tasted blood as the soft tissue inside his mouth was gouged and torn. His fruitless struggle went on only seconds before the hands which held his wrists were torn away.

With his hands free, Caleb violently rolled his body, trying to throw his second captor to one side. The action removed the soldier's metal chest plate from Caleb's cheek, but the Roman was too well trained at fighting simply to be cast off. He clung to the young thief as if it was he who could not get free.

With the pressure off his face, the flushed young thief looked up to see Dismas struggling with the other soldier and screaming like a mother defending her child.

Both men knew their lack of combat training left them at a disadvantage; any chance of escape would have to come quickly. For this reason Caleb strained every muscle to lift the man on top of him sufficiently to allow him to roll away. From there he intended to leap free and again begin running.

The Roman felt himself being lifted, and when the Jew beneath him rolled away, rage caused him to want to kill rather than capture. His bloated Roman pride was being jeopardized. By habit he drew his short, deadly combat sword.

Above Caleb and his captor, Dismas pushed against the soldier who clutched at the old thief's mantle. Fear gave Dismas a strength he would later look back on with amazement.

Using a trick he had sprung on several men as a novice thief, Dismas first pushed against the soldier, then suddenly jerked him forward. As he did this, he stuck his leg in front of the Roman's legs, tripping him. The man pitched forward, releasing Dismas to free his hands to stop his fall.

Instead of the grunting and clatter of armor, as was expected, the soldier Dismas tripped, fell onto his companion just as the lower soldier drew his blunt sword. The falling man grunted, then let out a gurgling scream before his tensed body relaxed and slumped down.

The remaining three men all knew what had happened. Dismas and Caleb stared at the fallen man and the bright red triangle which was the tip of the sword. The blade had passed through the guard's stomach and now stood like a three-inch, colored ornament perched in the middle of his hunched, leather back.

The other soldier, accustomed to the sight and sound of death, did not take time to stand and stare. Instead he scrambled to his feet, yanking the sword from his friend's body as he rose. When he had reached a crouching position he swung the bloody sword gently before him. As he waved it, tiny flecks of blood splattered on the street, the back of the dead man, and even on the front of Dismas' and Caleb's robes.

Even after the sword was removed from the dead man, Dismas and Caleb stood and stared at the body in horrified fascination. Their stare changed only when their eyes shifted to a dark red line which snaked from under the slain man. It slowly wound its way through cracks and ripples in the street's dirt.

Soon four more soldiers came running up, their armor slapping against their legs and clanking with each step. Their spears all pointed at the obviously stunned and subdued thieves, who now stood with their mouths agape and their arms limply at their sides.

Dismas became aware that across the body from him, Hiram stood screaming. "See the amulet around the

204

young one's neck? See it? It is the very same one stolen from me just last night. See it?" The old man's voice cracked as it climbed higher in pitch with his excitement. "It was a gift from the queen herself. Given to my wife. See it? The queen will identify it. I want those men. . . ."

He did not finish what he was saying because the leader of the soldiers slapped him sharply across the face. After he silenced the noisy merchant, the Roman growled, "Shut your mouth, you old swine. Do you not see that a Roman has been killed?"

Hiram sputtered as he tried to apologize, and still cautiously and quietly accuse Caleb.

The red line of blood crept further along the street and Caleb still stood staring at it. Next to him, Dismas felt himself becoming cold, very cold. The pain in his ankle and the shock of what happened were too much. Dismas fainted. He felt and heard nothing more.

8 WEDNESDAY
AFTERNOON

Dismas' eyes fluttered open. He smelled the musty dampness even more than he felt it. Lying flat on his stomach on the cold, damp stones, he could see little more than the bumps on the floor's uneven stones. Each stone looked like a small and distant mountain peak from his prone position.

It was not until he opened his eyes that he felt the throbbing in his head. With each beat of his heart painful pressure caused his head to feel bloated.

After a few seconds of lying still and trying to focus his eyes, Dismas realized that the pounding would not quickly subside. Slowly he tried to sit up, only to learn that chains kept him pinned down. He gently strained to turn his head enough to look behind him, but the pulsating shafts of pain flashing through his head caused him to frown, then relax.

Inches from his head was a crude stone ramp which slanted upward. It was as wide as the room itself, and made of the same stones as the walls and floor. By rolling his head a little more to one side, Dismas saw that the ramp ended at the base of a narrow, slotlike barred window which continued on up the wall another two or three feet.

The experienced old thief knew he was in a dungeon. It was not a new experience, but in his many years traveling the shady fringe between freedom and prison, he thought he had seen most of them. This one was different from the usual drunkard's pit; here he had been put in chains.

He focused his eyes on the small window more than ten feet above his head. The wall was more than two feet thick. He quickly surmised that this prison had been built for dangerous men.

As he stared at the window a short snicker escaped his lips. He thought it odd that bars would be built into the window narrow enough that not even a child could slip through. It did not occur to him until later that the window was built as it was to keep outsiders from passing weapons to those inside. Dismas was not thinking clearly. Without lifting his head, he again closed his eyes and slipped into a fitful sleep, only to be rudely awakened perhaps an hour later.

A scream came from down the unseen hallway. It was the mournful, agonized wail of either a woman or a very young man, for it was high-pitched and more of a screech than a yell. The sound startled the old thief and gave him an acute awareness of his cell, the chains, and the acrid odors of mold, urine, and years of hidden and untended defecation.

No light illuminated his cell except what slipped

through the narrow window and a tiny square hole in a door, which was on the inner side of the room. Dismas couldn't tell for sure from the light what time of the day it was. But the noise from outside, filtering through the stale air, told of sellers barking their wares in the heat of the afternoon.

It was odd, he mused, that from this cell voices sound so unusual. To Dismas the sounds were just as if they were filtered over the city walls, as if they came from someone calling across a large lake. The voices were clear, but weak.

Lying very still, Dismas tried to discern any sound which might tell him who had screamed, or why. No further noise came from inside the prison. Through the window, and from what seemed like a great distance, he heard a clear tenor voice almost singing, "Chicken. Chicken. Buy your roasted, salted chicken." A much closer voice repeatedly croaked, "Goat's milk. Goat's milk." On the last "milk" the seller's voice rose sharply.

After squinting his eyes to contain the pounding he knew would come when he tried to sit up, Dismas slowly and gently raised his head. Finding the movement almost painless, he rolled onto his side. His chains were not attached to the floor, but ran only from one dirty wrist to the other.

After raising his arms to examine his bonds, Dismas grunted in disgust. Finally he put both hands against the floor and lurched into a sitting position. As he moved, he felt his muscles protest. He was stiff all over from lying in one position too long on the wet floor.

In the gloom of the dirty cell, about twenty feet away and against a far wall, Dismas made out the shape of a man's body. Straining to see the form's face, he finally recognized Caleb. The young man's beard was matted

208

by the same dried blood which was crusted on his face.

Seeing that his friend did not move, Dismas' eyes quickly shifted to stare at the young thief's gently rising and falling chest. *At least he isn't dead,* Dismas sighed, greatly relieved.

Next he scanned the rest of the room to see if they shared quarters with anyone else. They were alone.

After exploring the dismal cell with his eyes, Dismas' gaze eventually returned to Caleb. Alarm came over the master thief. What if the blood covering the boy's head and beard came from a fatal wound? Leaning over until he was once more on his stomach, Dismas quietly inched his way across the slimy floor to his friend's side. He lurched into a sitting position, crossed his legs, then, with the tenderness of a new father picking up his baby for the first time, he raised Caleb's head from the stone floor. Just as gently as he raised it, Dismas lowered the blood-caked head into his lap.

A cut, which started just below the scalp line, ran across Caleb's forehead, over the right eye, and continued back into his hair. Just to one side of the cut was another one which ran downward, slightly cleaving away Caleb's right ear. The cut across the forehead looked like a gaping, swollen mouth, which told Dismas that it was not from a sword, but from a tremendously heavy blow.

Caleb moaned as he tried to raise one arm. It fell back to the floor as limply and as meaninglessly as it had been raised.

"My friend. My boy, my son," Dismas moaned softly as he began to rock back and forth. Turning his head toward the ceiling, he begged, "O God, if You are there and can hear me, please don't let him die." Once more the old thief looked down at the dirt and blood-caked face in his lap. Despite the foolish feeling praying gave him, a tear slipped down the old thief's cheek and splashed onto the face of his friend. "Oh, Caleb. Don't die and leave me." He rocked several minutes before continuing in a loud moan, "What, oh, what have we done to end up in such a mess?"

As Dismas talked, Caleb's eyelids fluttered, then opened. In a weak voice which revealed the dizziness he felt, Caleb croaked, "Master. What—what have we not done to get here?" A small smile flashed at the corners of his mouth before he again shut his eyes, then lifted one hand to feel his cuts.

Instinctively, Dismas reached out and grasped Caleb's groping hand. As he did, Dismas whispered, "Hold still, Caleb. Your head is badly cut. The bleeding has stopped, but it will start again if you disturb it."

"What happened?"

"I hoped to learn the answer to that question from you. The last thing I remember is fire shooting through my bad leg." It was the first time since the fight with the soldiers that Dismas had even thought about his injured leg.

"Caleb, how did you come to such a bad end? The last thing I remember was a wall of soldiers coming at us with spears." Dismas smiled. "Knowing you, a good fight followed—one in which you could have been killed. I would bet you fought knowing full well you'd lose."

"Yes, I. . . ." The strength of Caleb's voice indicated that he felt better, but in an effort to force him to rest more, Dismas interrupted.

"Caleb. My Caleb. Why do you think Romans walk the streets of Jerusalem rather than Hebrews walking the streets of Rome?"

Dismas did not give Caleb a chance to answer. He

showed his relief at finding his young protégé alive and talking nervously. "It is because they are warriors and we—we are tradesmen. . . ." Dismas chuckled deep in his throat. "And some of us are in unusual trades."

Caleb tried to laugh, but his efforts turned from a grin to a grimace as the pain in his head kept him from enjoying the joke. He did not try to remove his head from Dismas' lap.

Seeing his friend's pain, Dismas again took over the conversation. "Do you realize that your feminine desire for a neck trinket got us inside this beautiful inn?" Dismas' arm made a small arc as he waved toward their gloomy cell. "Can you imagine it? We steal purses from right under the swollen bellies of Hebrews and Romans alike, and none of them are the wiser. Then a small amulet—not even from around some woman's neck—betrays us before we can even spend the money we took with it."

At that, both men, despite their discomfort, laughed aloud. It was the first time they had thought about the money they had left with Aram, and they were not overly concerned about it. Both men knew that when they were released from the prison, they would leave as rich men, for their fortune awaited them at Aram's.

Their congeniality was quickly silenced by the sound of leather-clad feet coming their way, each step cadenced by a raspy scratching of metal against metal. The pair seemed to freeze as they listened. They watched as a dim flickering light from some yet unseen lamp slowly lit the tiny window in the massive wooden door of their miserable cell.

They heard the bolt on the door thrown back and each man silently hoped that a guard would step inside to announce, "You are free to go."

211

As the bolt moved, Caleb quickly sat up and, with a crablike movement, scooted back against the wall. Dismas remained where he was.

When the door creaked open as widely as the wall would allow, a guard, covered from the top of his head to his waist with armor, stepped inside. No sooner had he done so than he spread his legs to stand balanced on the balls of his feet.

Despite his age, which was near forty, the ripples in his arms as he held the lamp higher told the prisoners he was more old leopard than old sheep.

"Who laughed?" he growled. Both prisoners remained silent.

"Who laughed?" he repeated. "I heard you from down the hall."

"We both did, excellency," Caleb whined. Dismas knew from the familiar tone of his comrade's voice that he was putting on the sympathy-seeking act of the underdog. Many times, when Caleb was a growing boy, Dismas had seen men of the world pass over the youth as they questioned men around him about a recent theft. The crime would be Caleb's, but by ducking his head, bobbing quickly up and down and with eyes wide in awe, talking in the same voice he now used on the guard, he would receive a pat on the head and be passed by.

"What were you laughing about?" the guard demanded.

With a hint of bravado in his voice, Caleb spoke for both of them, "We were just amused when we thought of what the judge will say when he learns two innocent men stand before him."

"Innocent men? Judge? Ha!" The tone of the guard's voice was ominous. Romans were not known for smiling at Hebrews, and the guard was grinning.

212

Dismas did not like what he saw and blurted out, "Why do you laugh, grand one?"

Putting his fists on his hips and leaning back, the guard sneered, then he snarled, "I laugh at your stupidity, Jew donkey dung." He turned his head slightly to one side and spit. "Do you really think you will come before a judge?" Do you think anyone held in Governor Pilate's dungeons ever sees a judge?"

"Governor Pilate's jail? Pontius Pilate?" Dismas asked. "What are we doing in his fortress? We are but simple thieves, not enemies of Rome."

At Dismas' words the guard lost his composure. He leaned down, almost even with his waist, and laughed long and loud. "Simple thieves!" Again he laughed. "Not enemies of Rome." More laughter. "Oh, you poor ignorant pigs. You, Dismas, are not a simple thief and besides, since when did such scum as you ever sway Roman justice?" The guard wiped his mouth. "I imagine you expect simply to be lashed a few times and turned loose."

The guard, weakened by his own laughter, staggered a step to his left, his arm darting up to steady himself against the wall. On touching it, he quickly sobered. After looking around for something on which to wipe his hand, and finding nothing, the smile left his face and he resumed his sour scowl.

"By the time we finish with you, the lash will be the least of your worries."

"But . . . but why? We have done nothing to offend the most magnificent procurator of Judea. We only stole a trinket from a Jew's wife." In Dismas' warped sense of reasoning he felt that by stealing from the wealthy, especially from Hebrews, the Romans would agree that no wrong had been done.

213

The guard viciously kicked the older thief in the face, sending him sprawling. "You kill a Roman soldier before the eyes of more than thirty witnesses, including another soldier, and now you tell me you are but a simple thief?" The sarcasm echoed in the man's last words, revealing a deep and bitter hatred.

As he wiped blood from a badly split and swelling lip, Dismas sobbed into the floor on which he lay, "Killed a soldier? Killed a soldier?" The memory of what happened near the pool began to focus in his memory. Dismas grimaced as the picture of the bloody sword tip sticking from the soldier's back returned.

"But we didn't intentionally kill him. He fell onto the sword of the other soldier. We had no weapons at all."

"Silence, you . . . you. . . ." The guard's rage left him at a loss for a name low enough to fit how he felt about the men on the floor before him. "Whether you did the actual killing or not, it was you who caused the death of a Roman." He paused. "And for that, you will wish a thousand times that you too were dead before that wish comes true!"

"What do you intend to do?" Caleb innocently whispered. The cowering in his voice was no act now; the brave young thief was afraid and it showed on his face.

Bending slightly forward and leering the smile of one obtaining sweet revenge, the guard slowly rasped, "Let me say this. If I were you, I would stand and move about. I would keep my hands at my sides as much as possible. Your freedom, except for what time is left to you here, is at an end."

The guard glanced toward the small window and back again. The evil smile again returned as he asked, "Have either of you been to the place called Calvary? The place where we plant our crop of Jews?"

"Do you speak of the place of the skull, Golgotha?" Dismas used the Hebrew name.

"I do."

"Yes, I have been there," Dismas ventured, scarcely daring to ask his next question. "Is that what they intend to do with us?"

The guard's gutteral chuckle rumbled out and swelled slightly as he screamed gleefully, "Yes!" Then he turned abruptly and left the cell, bolting the door loudly.

As the heavy *clank* of the bolt echoed down the hall, Caleb turned to Dismas and asked, "Is it really all that bad?"

"Yes, Caleb. At Golgotha the Romans crucify state criminals."

"Crucify? I have heard of it, but I have never seen it." The young man's body shook as a chill ran through him. "I hear it is almost too horrible to believe."

"It is worse. Some victims they hang on wooden crosses by driving large nails through their arms and feet to make sure they die quickly. Others they just tie on a cross and let them suffocate. Sometimes they tie men there, then build a small ledge on which he may stand. When this is done, the man stays there until he starves, and that sometimes takes weeks."

Terror had spread across Caleb's face, but he did not try to stop Dismas from telling him what he did not want to hear.

"If they want their victims to die quickly, they sometimes take a large mallet with a long handle and break their legs. That way they sag heavily, which hastens death."

Caleb finally found his voice, which was pitched higher than normal. "No! Dismas, tell me you lie just to scare me. Tell me you joke. Tell me. . . ."

"Silence!" Dismas snapped in his misery. "I do not lie, nor do I joke. It's true."

"If they hung you on a cross, why would they break your legs? Why don't they just let you die in peace?"

"You do not die of pain; you suffocate. When your legs can no longer hold you, and with your arms up as they are, you sag and can no longer breathe."

"Oh, my God!" Caleb wailed softly, burying his face in his hands. "Dismas, save us." Sobs caused the young man's shoulders to jerk. Caleb was no longer the flippant, carefree thief. In him Dismas again saw a young boy—one about to be punished and crying before the rod fell.

Tenderly Dismas reached out, put his arms around Caleb's shoulders, pulling his head over. Holding the young man's battered head with his right arm, the old man began to run the fingers of his free hand through Caleb's dark hair. He whispered softly, "There, there. Don't worry so." In a voice void of honesty he continued, "I don't believe the guard. He was just trying to scare us. He was just enjoying a Roman joke."

A sob momentarily choked him but Caleb blurted out hopefully, "Do you really think so, Dismas?"

"It may well be."

Caleb turned, and in the dim light, saw that Dismas did not believe his own words.

"O God," Caleb moaned before leaning away from Dismas and putting his face against the cold, slimy wall.

Several hours passed before the two men moved. Both were consumed by their own thoughts—the older thief thinking of his past and the younger man imagining all of the things he would never do.

The silence was broken only occasionally by gasps escaping from one or the other of them, usually followed

216

by a mumbled, "Oh no," or "This just can't be."

The vacuum of time pressed in on the pair. In what may have been hours or only minutes later, both men stiffened. More footsteps clanked down the hall. The new steps were light—the steps of a much younger man.

Dismas and Caleb sat upright, their eyes open wide, staring toward the tiny window in the door. The light in the room was so dim by this time that to look anywhere but at the window was almost useless; the setting sun now denied light through the small wall window.

The footsteps paused long enough to allow the man on the other side of the door to once more throw the bolt. The protesting door opened. This time it revealed not the veteran soldier, but a young smooth-cheeked lad.

As the newcomer raised his lamp high in an effort to locate his prisoners, he asked in halting Hebrew, "Where are you?"

"Here," the two prisoners answered in unison.

"Do you want food?" The young guard asked.

At that question both men realized they had not eaten for many hours and were hungry and thirsty. "Yes, mighty one. We need food and drink," Caleb humbly replied.

"I've brought bread and water. It's not much, but it's better than nothing." The soldier's tone was almost apologetic. As he said it, he pulled a corked gourd and one large, flat bread cake from under his coarse cape.

Dismas, instead of waiting for the soldier to hand him the gourd, started to rise, but the pain in his injured leg caused him suddenly to groan and fall heavily back to the floor.

The innocent-looking soldier was unable to see clearly in the darkness so he reacted as a soldier should to the noise of Dismas' fall. He nimbly leaped back and, in midair, drew his sword in a way which left no doubt that he could use it effectively.

"Hold!" he shouted. "I have orders to cut the tendons in the backs of your legs if you make so much as a motion to escape. Have no doubt that I will do it if I must."

Dismas, squeezing the aching leg which had given way on him, gasped from between clenched teeth, "Young warrior, we hope only to escape death. We have done no wrong against Rome, but we are told we must die."

"I know nothing of this," the soldier said, his sword still swaying threateningly in front of him. Slowly he stood erect from his combat crouch, the position to which he fell when he drew his sword. Seeing he was not about to be attacked, he returned the sword to its sheath. "I only know that you were sentenced without trial tonight. Then it was later decided you should be tried with another man before Governor Pontius Pilate."

"Another man? What did he do?" Caleb asked.

"I don't know. I just heard that from the man who suggested your trial be set. He said that it was probably a movement to break our monotony here. I can tell you that the last time that same man used those words, 'break our monotony,' what happened was really amusing. It was when a high-placed and drunken Egyptian was caught urinating on a statue of one of our heroes, Aurenius Gaelus. When the governor heard of it, he forced the offender to sit on the statue throughout his trial. To make it more meaningful, Governor Pilate had the man lashed one stroke on every fiftieth word spoken during the trial. The man died before it was over."

The young man leaned against the open doorway. "The governor seldom presides at a trial unless the person being tried is high-born. Are you two high-born, but disguised?"

218

Dismas winced slightly at the way the soldier casually spoke of the Egyptian's trial and death as amusing. He felt the soldier was saying that anyone coming before Pilate was guilty just for being there.

Caleb, his voice suddenly that of a slave, a person low-born, answered, "By the gods, no! We are not high-born."

"That seems to be true," the soldier mused. "But I imagine that since you are to be examples for the city's other thieves, Governor Pilate feels it would be more effective to sentence you himself."

Dismas' face lowered dejectedly toward the floor as he murmured, "Yes. It's much better that Pilate sentences us to death. How could we be 'good examples' if done otherwise?" A brief silence fell over the trio.

"Tell me." The young soldier squatted down, faced the chained men and seriously said, "I am told you are the greatest of thieves. Why do you do it?"

"Do you ask why we steal?" Dismas asked.

"Yes."

"We steal because it is our business, our trade, just as yours is to be a soldier." The young Roman's flattery gave Dismas sufficient courage to speak firmly.

"But it seems strange," the soldier countered. "We Romans have gods to obey, just as you must obey yours, yet you steal when your God says you shouldn't. Why do you do it?"

"As I said, it is the way we make our living."

"Yes," the soldier pressed, "but by your law it is wrong to steal, and yet, out there," he jerked his head toward the city past the cell wall, "it seems that half the city is made up of thieves."

At that Dismas' lifelong temper flared briefly. "That's not true. The blundering, heavy-handed animals caught time after time trying to steal bread or other meaningless things are not thieves. They are just hungry, or have some other reason. They are not true thieves." He stopped talking when he saw the young Roman was grinning. The soldier was amused by the older man's obvious pride in a trade considered sinful practically everywhere. Dismas' quickened spirit faded as rapidly as it rose.

"I still do not understand why Caleb and I must die for what happened. It was just a mistake—an accident. You know it, I know it, and I am sure Pilate knows it too."

"That may be," the young man agreed, "but Governor Pilate, like Herod, is besieged by complaints from your victims and the victims of others of your trade. From the opening of the Passover season the complaints have come without ceasing—so many that it was decided to show the people that thieves will no longer be tolerated."

"But stealing is not a capital offense, and what happened to the soldier was just an accident."

"Possibly, but a Roman died and that's why Governor Pilate said that even the slightest resistance to arrest would now be grounds for death."

Dismas could not believe his ears. "You mean it's not just Caleb and me?" He gestured toward Caleb and himself. "Do you mean everyone who even tries to escape arrest will be put to death?"

"That is right. You are but the first." He added, "The rest will not be honored with a trial. Only you."

Dismas looked at his young friend. Astonishment covered his face. For three generations the men of his family made their livings at a profession they considered an art—something of which to be proud, not something shameful. Now he was hearing that it was no longer a cat-and-mouse game with the authorities, but had been turned into a life-and-death event.

220

The old thief knew it was possible for isolated cases of injustice to take the lives of men in his trade. But this—this was an open order to kill those who tried, as had their ancestors, to avoid capture fairly. Such a thing even went against the Roman tradition of the hunter and the hunted. Dismas was thoroughly shocked.

As the youthful guard stood up once more, Dismas looked at him and softly asked, "Is there no chance at all that our sentence can be other than death?"

"None," came back the flat answer.

The guard pulled the door open, nodded slightly, and left as he had come. The door clanked noisily, then its bolt, and his body armor as he padded down the hallway. The light went with him, leaving the prisoners in darkness.

Minutes passed before either man spoke. Then Caleb started sobbing and fell forward to the floor. Dismas knew there was no consolation for the fear that gripped his friend. Dismas felt it too.

When Caleb's sobbing let up, Dismas tried to talk with him. "Are you all right, my friend?"

"Yes," Caleb gulped.

For the next two hours the men talked, plotted fruitlessly, and gave up each idea almost as soon as it was conceived. Finally Caleb said, "Dismas, I thought I heard in the attitudes of our guards that you are an even more respected thief than I thought. They seemed to look on you as possibly Judea's greatest thief. Is that true? Are you?"

Dismas' vanity would not permit him to deny the compliment, so he answered, "I'd like to think that's true." He paused, then added, "Under our present circumstances, I can now tell you some of my past which probably cultivated such a reputation."

With this introduction Dismas leaned forward and scraped up dirt from between the stones. Putting it in his hand, he rubbed his fingers together, allowing the dirt to sprinkle through. A serious look came over his face as his mind went back to times, places, and events he had forced from his thoughts before.

"Caleb," he began, "you wondered how this Jesus fellow could so affect me. Well, there's a reason for it that began almost forty years ago, when I was but a small boy.

"I remember squatting behind a large, gray rock and feeling the smallness of my size. At the time I was only around four feet tall and could not have weighed more than seventy or seventy-five pounds.

"It was quiet out in the desert, so very quiet. I remember the one particularly quiet, moonlit night when I was introduced to my father's work. That night was broken only by an occasional rustle of pebbles, stirred by the feet of my father's men. Some of them wore sandals, but most didn't. I was up on the side of a hill, and all my father's men were hidden behind rocks scattered throughout the gully below me.

"The brilliance of the silver night was lit by a moon so large and bright that it seemed unreal. Moons like that can only be found in the desert. Anyhow, it was my first robbery and I was very scared.

"I had been told to watch for prospective customers, and since we had positioned ourselves in a wadi which ran north and south, I watched toward the north.

"Oh, yes, Caleb. At that age I had the eyes of a sparrow. I could see the wart on the nose of a farmer's wife before others in the group could even see the wife." Dismas heard Caleb chuckle in the dark. Despite the slight interruption, Dismas' thoughts of his first venture

222

into lawlessness continued to spill out.

"In the dim distance, out on the plain, I could make out the tiny shapes of something moving far away. It looked like a man leading a skitterish donkey. The animal, as I remember, was loaded only with people and no other goods. I could tell little more from such a great distance. Since my job was only to watch and report, I whistled a soft tune I had been taught by my father. With it I signaled the distance and number of people coming toward us. It took me many months and slaps on the head to learn that whistle. With it I signaled well when I had to."

Dismas stopped to demonstrate with a low whistle which went up, then down, in pitch. "That meant almost a mile away." Next he gave two low-pitched sharp whistles, "That meant only two or three people. Animals didn't count, since they could not fight back."

With the demonstration of signals over, Dismas went on.

"It was usually cold at night on the desert, but that night I shivered in anticipation, not cold. I saw those two people coming our way and I shivered. I certainly would not have admitted it then, but I squatted down and tucked the open bottom of my cloak around and under my bare feet trying to stop my shivering. Anyone who says he is not scared during his first robbery is a liar."

Caleb broke in again, "I thought you said it was just one man? Now you say you saw two people coming toward you."

"That's how it turned out—two people—but let me go on."

Taking a deep breath, the old thief continued, "Anyhow, on the other side of my rock, far down the crumbling sides of the wadi, my father and his six cohorts waited. As I said, they were well hidden behind the bolders which were scattered around the floor of the abyss, near the wadi's mouth.

"I remember how funny they seemed to me. When I peeked over my rock, and I remember it clearly, I all but laughed. Every time they shifted positions, no matter how slowly or carefully they did it, they looked like desert lizards—alive among the lifeless rocks, yet not moving enough to draw attention to themselves.

"They were some of the worst men in the world. At least, they were the worst I had ever met, but they were experts at their work. You know, Caleb. The ditch where we did our work that night is between here and Debir, to the south. It was called the Red Ditch by the merchants of Jerusalem."

"Why?" Caleb asked.

"Actually, in this city the place had two names then. It was called the Red Ditch because of the blood so many merchants and servants and slaves spilled there."

"What was its other name?"

"I'm coming to that," Dismas said curtly. "To the people living outside the law it was just called the Ditch of Death."

Caleb blurted out innocently, "I've heard of that."

Dismas, in a rush of pride over the fact that his friend had heard of the place, and what took place there, gushed back, "Good."

"Tell me more," pleaded the young thief.

"It was there that Ezra Bar Nameth, my father, sent many Romans—"Dismas lowered his voice to a whisper. "And others—" His voice rose again. "To their end. Yes, sir, that was the very spot where those who sucked golden blood from Judea met real justice."

Dismas did not explain that patriotism had little to do

224

with the business that night. He did not mention that his father took what he wanted from Roman and Jew alike. He did not explain that all, rich or poor, were fair prey for his father. Dismas had never challenged his father's motives, because what his father did was something which, simply, always had been done. Dismas just accepted it as a natural way of life.

It was evident that Caleb, as he listened to the tone of Dismas' voice change, that the old man was no longer in Pilate's black dungeon. The young thief knew his companions's mind had returned to his childhood and the scene of his first robbery. Caleb listened dutifully and carefully despite his fatigue, afraid that any movement or sound might stop his teacher from telling of his secret past.

"Since coming to the gorge more than an hour before, and several other times that morning, I wished that I had not asked my father to take me along. Chills racked my small body—chills of fear which knotted every muscle I possessed. Even before we left our home, I was fighting fear. Out on the rim of that gorge my fear was no small thing." Dismas stopped talking for an instant. His face took on an even more faraway look, though it was unseen in the prison's darkness, and he breathed deeply through his mouth before continuing, "Oh, how I gritted my teeth to keep from being sick. I was so scared that several times I tasted the cheese and goat's milk I had eaten earlier. Our work lay ahead of us—and I wished it was over."

Dismas' story was not the fantasy of an old man; it was all true. In great detail the older thief told Caleb of his initiation as a professional thief.

Minutes after young Dismas had squatted to fight his terror, he could not only see the unsuspecting travelers clearly, but he could even hear the clicking of their donkey's hoofs, as he carefully picked his way along the stony path.

Walking ahead of the animal, the man kept his head turned toward the ground. On the donkey's back sat a woman, apparently the man's wife, who appeared to talk to a small bundle she held.

Ezra, Dismas' father and the leader of the waiting bandits, held himself and his men in check until the intended victims were practically on top of them. When the travelers were close enough for Ezra to hear clearly what they said to each other, he stood, raised his spear above his head, then stepped from behind the large rock which had hiddden him. He shouted a resounding, "Hold!"

With that as their signal, the other men rose from their hiding places and showed their weapons. Dismas' father slowly stalked toward the couple.

The young boy could see that even though his father was a husky man, and looked even bigger in the moonlight, the man leading the donkey was equally as large. Both men wore simple clothing.

As Dismas' father neared the stranger, the man stopped his donkey and raised his right hand in a form of salute. Then, with a look totally absent of fear, the stranger said, "God's peace, my brother."

"My brother!" Dismas' father spat back bitterly. "I am not your brother, and I don't know where you intend to go—but you have already reached the end of your journey."

The man lovingly rubbed the donkey's head as a slight frown crossed his face. He said, "I don't understand. If you intend to rob us, you can see we have nothing of value, except this donkey. By your dress I can see you are

226

not Romans, so why is this the end of our journey?"

It appeared that the stranger was not going to fight, so Dismas' fear quickly changed to excitement. He slid down the steep slope to hear better what was being said. In seconds he was behind his father, but kept near a large rock, which could quickly shield him if necessary.

Ezra looked the man up and down, ignoring his question, before asking a question of his own, "So you have nothing of value and fear no one but Romans?" A laugh boomed from the huge bandit, who then mockingly asked, "What did you do to the Romans? Not bow low enough? Run away from the tax collector? Fail to register for the head count? Just what was your terrible crime— brother?" He spit out the last word more bitterly than any of the others.

Before the stranger could answer, a voice from the nearby men growled, "Kill them and let's move on." The speaker was Jedah, a swarthy man who looked more Egyptian than Hebrew. The dark man then began swinging his sword and walking forward.

Jedah, the bloodthirsty one, was a killer. Ezra knew it and did not trust him. Several times in the past weeks Jedah had done things without first asking, and had even sneaked an unfair share of the group's money when he thought no one was looking. Ezra knew all of this and he saw this demand to kill as another attempt by Jedah to encroach on his leadership.

Shoving his spear into the ground just inches in front of Jedah's toes, Ezra growled, "Until you become leader, I will make the decisions."

Jedah, not fully realizing how close he stood to Ezra, angrily turned his head to find his face close enough to that of his leader that he could smell his foul breath. Both men stood with eyes blazing. Like two curs circling

227

before combat, Ezra and Jedah all but growled at each other. Ezra, to complete the scene, prodded, "And when a swine like you becomes a leader, I will kill myself; you won't get the chance, Jedah."

Seeing that he was about to lose all respect in the eyes of the other men, Jedah hissed back, "You could be saved that effort, Ezra."

The brilliant white teeth of the bandit leader flashed from his suntanned face, which was made even darker by the long, unkempt black hair and beard completely surrounding it. Letting his eyes shift to Dismas, who was now pressed against his protective rock, Ezra decided to goad Jedah all the way. "To remove all misunderstanding, Jedah, I will show you what value I place on your advice, opinions, or threats."

Turning to his young son, but keeping his eyes on the killer, Ezra extended his hand and beckoned for the boy to approach. "Come here, my son!" Ezra commanded. As Dismas came hesitantly, the big leader loudly said, "I want you to take your first step as—" he turned his full face toward Jedah. "As the future leader of these cutthroats. What do you say should now be done?"

Jedah gritted his teeth, but glared silently into Ezra's eyes.

Several seconds passed before Dismas spoke. He knew his next words could result in someone, even before he bakes the loaf."

Looking back at Jedah, who still glared at him, the bandit chief continued, "You check if the woman has anything of value, Dismas. I will examine the man."

Dismas, sensing that lives still hung in the balance, ran to the woman and found himself looking into two of the deepest, warmest eyes he had ever seen. For an instant he just stared at her, surprised that she was not frightened as other women might be. She smiled at him.

Seeing the young boy's confusion at what he should do next, she said, "We have but three things of value—our son, our donkey, and this." She handed him a very small leather bag.

As he tugged at the bag's string, Dismas was unaware of his father's approach. Without warning Ezra whacked the small boy across the back with the wide, flat tip of his spear, sending burning pain up and down his body.

The blow knocked him against the woman's feet, which hung down along the donkey's side. Turning to face his father, Dismas leaned back and rubbed his stinging back against the animal's warm flank.

"This was your first decision," his father growled as he snatched the tiny purse from his son's hand and yanked it open, "but it is still my robbery."

No sooner had Ezra said this than the contents of the purse spilled into the open palm of his hand. "God's beard" he exclaimed. "One silver mina and three silver shekels." Turning to look at the man at the head of the donkey, Ezra laughed, "You, stranger, are even poorer than we." Looking down at the coins again, he just shook his head.

"My brother," the man quietly said, "before you do us harm, which I feel you intend to do, I must tell you that God sent us on this journey."

At this the other men, who until now had remained silent, began whispering to each other. Their look said they did not like what the man said. One of them blurted out, "You say God sent you? Was that after too much bad wine—or does He visit you often?" The man's question was asked as an attempt at joking, but it was forced. No one laughed.

"He came in a dream," said the stranger sincerely.

Dismas, like the others, didn't like what he heard. It upset him. Everyone in the whole band of robbers knew of the legends surrounding their trade—especially the one about men with demons in their heads which drove them mad. It was said that those who killed a person so afflicted received the demons themselves; it was called "the assassin's inheritance."

As the men mumbled to each other about this unexpected turn of events, Ezra just stared suspiciously at the stranger.

Dismas, in his innocence, turned back to the woman. Reaching up as high as he could stretch, Dismas tried to pull the coarse cloth from the baby's face, but he could not reach it.

Instead of the woman pulling away, as he expected, she held the bundle down so he could see without stretching. As she turned the cloth away from the child's face, the baby turned his eyes away from his mother, stopped sucking his lips, and fastened his burning eyes firmly on Dismas. As the men looked questioningly at the father, Dismas fell prey to the infant.

Dismas stood transfixed. The eyes into which he looked were like two glowing coals in a black night.

"Father," Dismas said softly, not taking his eyes from the child, "We should let them pass unharmed." Dismas tore himself away from the baby's gaze to look at his father. Almost as if in panic, he chirped in his high-pitched voice, "Father! We must let them pass."

A look of disgust came to Ezra's face as he asked, "Now, just why should we do that?"

"If they are poorer than we, our purses gain nothing. If the Romans do seek them, we are kindred, of a sort, and—" Dismas threw a quick glance at the woman's husband. "And if God visits this man, or if he is just cursed

230

with madness, his death could leave us with much more than we seek."

Waiting for the meaning of his last statement to take its effect, and taking a deep breath, the boy concluded, "I say that since they move away from the soldiers who could do us harm, they should be allowed to go in peace."

"God's beard, boy. You either have no stomach for the kill or wisdom beyond your years." His father shrugged his bulging shoulders and, as if resigned to the decision, sighed, "In either case you have made your first decision and I will not violate it." Glancing at the stranger, who was looking into the twinkling starlit sky and mumbling to someone unseen, Ezra grumbled, "Go quickly."

"No!" screamed the bloodthirsty Jedah. "We have a right in this decision, too, and I say kill them."

Ezra, jerking the point of his spear up and shoving it against Jedah's throat, leaned forward. The hulking leader barked, "So you want to see blood do you? Tell me again, Jedah. Do you insist on death, or do you honor my son's first decision? Your wrong choice could bring a welcome relief from your challenges of me."

Jedah gasped through clenched teeth, afraid to move, "No, Ezra. Whatever you say. You are the master."

"I'm glad to hear that," Ezra hissed, as he slowly removed his spear from the terrified man's throat. Jedah knew he had been but a muscle's flex from death.

Before the stranger had a chance to move away, Dismas turned back to the woman. She again held her child down for him to see. As the young boy looked once more at the baby's face, he murmured, "Oh, most blessed of children, if ever there comes a time for having mercy on me, then remember me and forget not this hour."

Dismas did not understand the events of the night, not

231

even his own words. He just knew those tiny eyes demanded the decision he had made, and that the unusual child would, somehow, not forget.

The woman whispered so only Dismas could hear, "If ever we return to our home in Nazareth, you are welcome. Ask for the home of Joseph, the carpenter. It will be a long time from now, for we must flee to safety from King Herod, but the time will come someday." Before she could say more, the donkey lurched forward and the woman and child went with it.

Later, back in their camp, which was nothing more than a barren cave, the joy Dismas felt as he watched the travelers go their way was quickly stifled. Although his father felt the disappointment of having gained practically no money, the men of the band were in a dangerous mood.

Unlike other nights, when the women fed them, and before the sun baked the outside world, the food did not leave the men sleepy and satisfied. This day they were not gathered together as usual, but instead, moved away from Dismas and his father and mother to whisper among themselves.

Occasionally, Dismas caught snatches of their conversation and knew that his decision to free the travelers had made them angry. Jedah and his unceasing complaints were the spark which fanned the flames of discontent.

After the mumbling and grumbling had gone on about an hour, Jedah, the killer, stood up. He said a few more words to the other men, who had built a separate fire to gather around, then sauntered over to where Ezra squatted.

"Ezra, we did not like what happened tonight. It was wrong for you to have your mongrel son speak for us. It

232

was foolish and an insult to us as men.''

Ezra did not leap to his feet and scream, as Dismas expected. Instead, he rose slowly—very slowly—and never took his eyes from the fire. When he was fully erect he towered about four inches over Jedah. Like a striking snake he whirled, grabbed the front of the killer's mantle, and began to shake him like a rag. ''Insult you as men? Men? Who among you is a man?''

It was plain that Ezra was not talking to the others, only to Jedah. For months, ever since the killer joined the band, Jedah had opposed most of Ezra's orders—never openly as he had just done, but mockingly, when things did not go as planned. It appeared that the boil which festered between the two men had reached a head.

As he shook Jedah, Ezra continued to rave, ''Who do you think you're speaking to? I don't need you. I could gather better men from Jerusalem's Lepers' Hole. I keep you only because you do as you are told.'' With that he threw the shocked man backward into the rest of the men—and their fire. Ezra's eyes, now just narrow slits, glared at the men, giving no indication of mercy. The group of thieves scrambled away from him.

The big leader's thundering voice dropped to a deep-throated hiss, ''If any of you dislike my decision today, stand on your feet—'' He paused to look around. ''Stand for the last time.'' It was the second occasion in less than three hours that he had threatened his men.

As Ezra finished his challenge, he jerked a knife from some hidden place in his girdle and waited. For almost a minute he silently looked over his men, then spat at them to show his contempt. Without a word he turned and squatted again before his fire.

Instead of remaining tense, as if anticipating an attack, the big bandit chief grabbed a huge, greasy bone and

233

began to gnaw on it. His hunger was not real, but another symbol of his contempt. He told them with actions that, as cowards, they were nothing to fear.

Dismas, now a little arrogant in his father's strength, rose from his place and went over to the man. "I too challenge you to think and act as men, because none of you—" He had not finished his sentence before Jedah's rough hand streaked out and struck him across the cheek. The blow was so strong it whirled the small boy around and dumped him in a heap at his father's feet.

Instead of the explosion Dismas hoped for, Ezra casually glanced at him, then went back to his bone. Dismas knew then that his father had little parental love for him, if any, only a pride of ownership.

Turning away so that Ezra would not see the tears which gushed to his eyes, Dismas pressed his stinging cheek into the cool dirt. In such a position he could see his mother's feet padding around the cave, but no one could see his face. He felt that she too held no love for him. She didn't even stop to see if he was injured.

After a few moments Dismas turned his head around and put his other cheek on the back of his hand. Across the cave's uneven floor he watched the face of the man who had struck him. A wave of the most intense hatred he had ever felt swept over him.

Jedah, a stocky, full-bearded Dannite, had killed scores of men in his lifetime. He frequently brought various women into the cave only to send them away when he finished with them. He was the only member of the band who, almost nightly, drank himself into a stupor. From the way he was now acting, this night would be no exception.

While the fires burned themselves out, but before the morning sunlight rose above the desert's edge, Dismas looked cautiously around the room. The boy had decided to repay Jedah for the blow he had delivered and the humiliation which came with it. The small boy looked around to see if everyone was sleeping. He heard snores as they erupted around him and saw bodies wrapped in skins and rags, but there was no movement.

Without a sound, the boy inched his way to his feet, pausing as he rose to insure he was not heard. When he was on his feet, he tiptoed to the side of the now drunken and snoring man who had struck him. Near Jedah's drooling head, and glinting in the fire's last flickering light, was the sword with which the killer had so frequently slain helpless travelers.

Dismas knelt and grasped the sword's handle with both hands. As he struggled to his feet and began to pick up the weapon, he was surprised at its weight. He strained as he lifted the deadly weapon from the ground. He clutched it to his chest, point down.

Once more he looked around the room to see if anyone was awake. All were still except for his father who with a loud snort rolled over in his sleep. Dismas gasped slightly when his father moved. The boy held his breath, hoping the big bandit leader would continue to sleep.

Seeing that Ezra had just rolled onto his back and again breathed easily, Dismas looked down at Jedah again. Ever so slowly, and scarcely breathing, Dismas eased his small frame above the sleeping killer. As he straddled Jedah's head, he gripped the sword handle so tightly his fingers felt numb. He took a deep breath and raised it higher and higher. As the weight of the lethal instrument rose, the boy's arms began to shake.

Finally, Dismas looked down to make sure the keen point of the weapon was directly above the sleeping man's throat. When he saw that it was, he put his entire seventy pounds behind his movement and slammed the blade down as hard as he could.

He heard the *thuck* the blade made as it went through the man's neck and into the dirt below. He watched as Jedah's unseeing eyes popped open and his hands clutched the thick sword blade as if to choke it. Blood squirted up from the man's throat and from both hands as they squeezed the sword's honed edges. No sound had been made except that of the sword as it ended its deadly trip. Jedah's mouth opened and closed as he tried to scream, blood flowing out one side as he did, but he did not make any sound at all.

Leaving the weapon impaled in Jedah's neck, its handle standing silently upright, Dismas tiptoed out the cave's door to vomit. When he had finished, he crept back inside and lay down in his usual spot. As he had reentered the cave he saw that his father grinned broadly through his thick, black beard. Since Ezra's eyes were closed, Dismas could not tell if the leader knew what had taken place or if he was enjoying a good dream.

After dawn, Dismas awoke to the shouts of angry men. "Kill anyone you like," one of the voices said, "but you don't kill your own men."

"Who says I killed that harlot's scab?" Ezra shouted. "Do you think I'd wait until he slept to kill him? Do you think I would kill, then sleep beside my victim? Such a thing would take more of an assassin than I," his father countered.

"If not you, then it must have been another in this room," one of the men reasoned. "I know Jedah did not stab himself with his own sword—not that way—and none of us hated him this much. Only you."

As Dismas sleepily sat up, one of the men glanced at him. The look of a man thinking the improbable came over him. "But him! He hated Jedah that much."

"You mean you think a nine-year-old boy could do such a thing? Don't make me laugh."

"Is he not your son, Ezra? Yes, I think he could do it. In fact, I think he did."

"Boy!" Dismas' father barked. "Come here and tell these braying jackasses you did not kill Jedah. Show them you do not have the strength to do such a thing." Ezra then added, his tone taking on a disgusted ring. "Nor do you have the stomach for killing."

Dismas climbed to his feet, but stayed at a distance from the clustered men. He made his way around his father's fire to stand by Ezra's side. What they had not noticed was that the boy put himself between them and the cave's opening, in case he had to flee to escape their anger.

As everyone looked at him, Dismas took a deep breath, looked around the circle of tense faces, then said, "I may be young but not too weak to lift a sword. I did it." Nodding toward Jedah's body, which still lay as Dismas had left him, he blurted out, "I killed Jedah with his own sword. That one. And I stuck it through his neck just as I wanted to." The boy braced himself for flight. "I did it because he struck me." Dismas began to cry. "And I would do it again."

His outburst brought a look of shock to everyone's face except that of his father.

"Well," Ezra beamed, allowing his voice to express mock surprise, "at least for those of you who felt my son to be a coward when he freed those people earlier, you may want to reconsider."

Before anyone in the band could raise a protest, or even move, Ezra continued, "I, your leader, said I was not assassin enough to kill, then sleep beside the slaughtered. Now I see in my son a leader who may someday challenge Rome." Pride radiated from Ezra's face.

"That may well be, Ezra, but he killed one of us," pointed out one of the men. The speaker gestured toward Jedah's body. "And he's as dead as if a Roman had done it. I say that revenge for Jedah's death is beyond your leadership. It is ours."

"You say nothing. I say you are just vermin."

"We do not challenge you, Ezra. To do so would be to slap fate's face, but your son is another matter. I suggest you quickly teach him to fight. By killing his own, he now stands alone. The day will come when he will need a friend, but with such a sin as this, no man on earth would befriend him." Dismas' father just snorted.

The boy now felt that his father would stand up for him, but the talk of having no one stand up for him later sounded almost like a curse and it scared him.

"You blame me for killing a killer? Why do you not spit on him?" Having seen his father's pride, Dismas again began to feel a little arrogant and angry. "No. The innocent and defenseless you will kill; so, why become angry when a man like Jedah is killed? He was nothing." Dismas was but a boy, but the type of life he had led throughout his childhood had forced a man's thoughts on him at an early age. He continued, "I will go if my father sends me, but I'll not run from any of you." But he was still positioned to break for the cave opening if any of the men made a move to grab him.

"Who said anything about leaving, little mosquito?" His father turned to the unhappy men. "Take that carrion out to the vultures." With that order, Ezra lay back down on his coat of hair, ending further conversation.

Seeing that further objection would be fruitless, the

238

grumbling men tied a rope around the man's neck, removed the sword, and dragged Jedah from the cave.

The women, like Dismas' mother, were prostitutes with no place to go. They had watched and listened to the talk, expecting an exciting fight to start. When everything ended peacefully, they disappointedly returned to their sewing, cook fires, and other duties. Life in the camp returned to normal.

Dismas again went to his father's fire, lay back down, and idly scratched a louse which gnawed at his armpit. He closed his eyes as if to sleep, but in his mind he again clearly saw the disbelieving, hostile eyes of Jedah as he had died.

As Dismas watched the mental image of the dead man's eyes, they were replaced by another pair of eyes. The new ones were the innocent, trusting, demanding, and knowing eyes of the baby he had seen earlier. They were the eyes of a child too young to know anything, and yet the eyes of one who knows everything. Both pairs of eyes haunted him, yet they haunted in completely different ways.

The noise of snoring yanked Dismas back to reality from his childhood memories. Shaking his head slightly, he remembered where he was—a prisoner beneath the fortress of Pontius Pilate, below the street level of Jerusalem—and condemned to die.

The snoring belonged to Caleb, who had listened until nervous exhaustion claimed his consciousness.

As the old thief stared unseeing into the blackness of the cell, at the place he knew Caleb was resting, a single tear ran from his left eye, along the side of his nose, and was finally lost in his moustache. "Caleb, my friend. You are all that I have now. Of all I have seen, done, or had, you sorry human being that you are, have been the brightest spot in my life."

Dismas went on mumbling aloud. "I once feared that curse of my childhood, the curse that I would someday have no friends at all. It was wrong; you saw to that. Sleep well, Caleb. Become used to it, because we will soon sleep the long sleep together."

Dismas lay down beside his friend and student. After several minutes, he too slept.

9 THURSDAY MORNING

With dawn came the heat. The prison was as hot as the desert. The temperature was so high the prisoners lay on the sweltering, but somewhat cooler floor. In the hallway their armor-clad captors, dressed in what acted like ovens, were even more uncomfortable than those they guarded.

Although the dungeon filth was almost beyond description, most prisoners chose to lay on the floor rather than to sit up. Just inches above the stone floor the temperature was hotter by as much as twenty degrees.

As miserable as the heat was, it was not without compensation for prisoners. The day's rising temperature dried the tears, spittle, vomit, and blood which were so much a part of prison life.

Dismas and Caleb had fallen asleep in the corner of the cell most distant from the tiny street window.

241

Through the narrow window flowed the day's new light and heat so they slept until well into the morning. Sleeping conserved body moisture, which in turn permitted even more sleep. Retaining moisture was important because water was brought only twice a day by the guards—once at noon with the prisoners' only cooked meal, and again in the late evening, with stale bread.

To Dismas, it seemed he had no sooner fallen asleep than he awoke. Like most men in Pilate's prison, Dismas did not like the time he had to spend awake. To be conscious meant only that a man was acutely aware of his misery. Sleep, on the other hand, was like a drug; it temporarily erased troubles, chains, and prison walls.

Caleb, unlike Dismas, slept on. From the way he had begun to lick his dirty lips and swat aimlessly at the relentless flies, Caleb too would soon awake.

After one particularly loud snort, the young thief reached up to wipe his lips only to stuff one end of his moustache into his mouth. When this happened, his eyes snapped open and he bolted upright, into a sitting position. Coughing, he crouched to defend himself from the unseen attacker he felt to be there.

Dismas, who was four or five feet away, laughed at his friend's confusion and strange actions.

After Caleb had shaken his head and spit the encroaching hair from his mouth, which took three or four disagreeable tries, he looked sheepishly at Dismas. He snorted again and then smiled the embarrassed smile of one who feels foolish.

"Good morning, you young whelp," Dismas joked, trying to sound more cheerful than he was.

"Ungh," Caleb grunted in response as he slowly turned his head to look around the dismal cell. "It looks no better than before," he complained.

242

"Did you expect to wake up in the arms of some sweet, young girl and have a cup of wine beside your bed?"

"No. It's just that this place looks and smells no better than it did last night."

"It could be worse," Dismas muttered as he tugged at one of his ear lobes. "We could be chained to a wall, or placed in solitary confinement."

After a short silence, Caleb said, "Dismas, I'm sorry I fell asleep as you talked last night."

"That's all right. I said nothing of interest anyhow."

"Oh, but you did," Caleb insisted. "I had no idea that, as a boy, you felt as unwanted as I have always felt."

"Maybe that's why I bought you. Maybe I saw myself reflected in you." Both men were silent as Dismas closed his eyes and rested his head back on folded hands.

Then Caleb began clawing desperately at a biting louse deep in his crotch. "I heard what you said. You know, about the killing and such as that. Something about your past still puzzles me though."

"What's that?"

"Why did you change from robbing people to being a thief? From what you said, you were really destined to be the leader of your father's men."

Dismas smiled. "Maybe I'm just an artist at heart. My life as a thief all started after I came to Jerusalem." Reaching up, the older man began stroking his beard from his chin down to the beard's tip. He looked toward the ceiling and seemed almost to pick up his tale where he had left off.

"Let me see. It was when I was, oh, thirteen or fourteen years old. For more than three years after old King Herod the Great died, all covered with sores and screaming his life away, things had not gone well for my father and his men. Taxes had risen until money was so

243

scarce all across Judea that it worried everyone. People no longer took pleasure trips, even journeys they previously considered routine. Merchants no longer shipped great quantities of goods as before. If asked why, they would openly and bitterly tell you, 'Why try for profit? Either Herod or Caesar will just take it from you.' "

Dismas slowly slipped back in time. He explained that even caravans from countries not hard-pressed by taxes were fewer, but bigger. The increase in caravan size was for safety's sake. Hard times were on Ezra and his small band.

"It would take a small army to rob such caravans, and I refuse to be a jackal, following caravans hoping a camel or an ass will eventually drop out. That I will not do," the old robber had frequently told his men. But deep inside he was worried. He knew times would not get better, the way things were going in the country. They could only get worse.

Men of Ezra's profession could still have a measure of success by striking at the small caravans which passed between cities. Unlike long chains of camels, which snaked their way across the desert, the caravans between remote Judean villages were small and had few guards. This was because they were usually only one or two days from the protection of the city. Their masters felt that threat to their safety was less to worry about than the cost of many guards.

Although the smaller caravans usually carried a cargo of domestic goods—food, local wine, oil, cloth, tools, and other things of little immediate value to anyone who had to travel swiftly—each usually had at least one fat purse. It would normally be carried by a single agent who was hired to buy and sell for several merchants, instead of each merchant doing the job for himself.

244

The agent was the man Ezra wanted to meet. Several obstacles stood in his way, however. He had no way of knowing when or where the caravans were to leave, or by which route they would go. He didn't even know the types of cargo being moved. Most important, he had no way of knowing which of the caravan's men would be the merchant's agent—the man with the heavy purse.

Ezra felt like a blind man with ambition. He knew what he wanted to do and he knew he could do it well— if he only knew when and where to do it. He did know one thing for certain; on several occasions he had over-looked a well-disguised money carrier. This fact ate at him, but he would never admit to anyone that it had happened.

The biggest threat to men of Ezra's occupation was that caravans between cities traveled routes guarded by small Roman forts which perched like vultures atop the scattered hills. The forts were strategically placed so that small bands, such as Ezra's, had little chance to attack without being seen and chased away or slaughtered before they could complete the job.

To counter these obstacles would mean the difference between success and failure for a robber band, and the crafty old leader thought he had the solution.

Late one night, after Ezra and his men had huddled around a fire several hours, Dismas was summoned to his father. The boy was no longer small but had entered the age of the uncontrollable voice and gangling legs. He was far from being a mature man, but was no longer looked upon as a child or trusted by the men. They had not forgotten Jedah or the way he had died. This, to Dismas, was a real compliment.

"Dismas, you have seen that things do not go well for us. We are no longer the lions, but have become vultures forced to pick bones where we find them. Because of this, we must try something we have never done before." His father took a resigned breath and tilted his head to look at his fellow robbers from under furrowed brows. "We want you to be the central person in our plan," he continued.

Looking around the circle of faces staring at him, Dismas saw doubt in every eye.

"I want you to be the eyes and ears of our group," Ezra said, his voice holding more hope than conviction. "Dismas, in the past we relied on fate to bring the game to us, but fate has failed us. If we could know caravan departure times and their routes, we feel we could again prosper. Do you think you can tell us of these?"

The young lad could hardly believe his ears. At a time when most boys still enjoyed games or worked with the women, he was being asked to become a member of the band.

It was incredible—for years he had begged to join them only to be rebuffed. Now they came to him.

"What must I do? How can I discover their plans? When I do, how will I tell you of them?" Dismas had more questions to ask, but he was afraid that voicing them could lead to his dismissal.

"These things we will discuss later. Do you think you can do it?"

"Father, I will do my best," Dismas said solemnly and honestly.

"Fine." Ezra turned to the men, dusted his hands to show he considered the matter closed, and sat more comfortably. With the other men, he began to discuss the details of using Dismas and the information he would provide.

Later in the evening, when the other men had settled

down in various parts of the cave with their wine and women, Ezra came over and sat down beside the excited boy to explain what had to be done.

"First, we must find a place in which you will be lost in the crowd—a place through which many of the caravans pass or have their beginning. I think—" Ezra tapped the tiny bare spot of skin between his graying beard and his lower lip, using his right thumbnail to mark time. "I think that Jerusalem is the place for you."

Again Dismas was stunned. Jerusalem! The city of King David! The center of the world! And his father had spoken its name as if it were just another oasis in the parched nothingness Dismas had always known.

"Yes, boy. I will send you to Jerusalem as one of the army of beggar boys who clog its streets. I will give you the name of a man there, a man who will show you the city, ways to enter and leave it after the closing of the city gates, and where and how you can gather the information we will need. Listen, Dismas. Although this man knows the ropes, he is not to be trusted—not in any way. If it were otherwise, I'd hire him instead of sending you. Trust him with no more than your name."

Ezra looked down at his folded legs, then leaned forward and picked up a small twig. As he drew diagrams in the dirt floor, he continued, "If his method fails, you must obtain the needed information in any way you can. For this reason you must first meet caravan tenders and through them seek answers. I leave all of that up to you."

Dismas felt his own disappointment because his father expressed no fear for his son's safety. All Ezra seemed to care or think about was the information which would be sent his way, and the money he would gain from it.

"How will I live? What about money? Food? A place to stay?"

"You must make your own way and fend for yourself."
Seeing that his son was disappointed, Ezra quickly
explained. "After all, if you had money, clothes, and a
place to stay, who would ever believe you were a mere
beggar? No. You must live as other beggars live."

Grudgingly, Dismas accepted this cruel logic. "When I
learn of the caravans, how will I pass the news on to
you?"

"That part I will take care of. Each day a blind man
sits before the Dung Gate. Beside him will be a staff, a
bowl in his hand, and beside his staff a bag of his personal belongings. You must tell him all that you know of
the caravans before midday."

"What good will it do to tell a blind beggar?"

"Boy, you give me no credit," Ezra snapped. "Each
day I will have a man watch the beggar from nearby. If
the bag of rags is large, I will know a rich caravan will
leave the city that day. The staff will point away from the
wall in the direction the camels will go. If the crook of
the staff is pointed away from the wall, many guards will
be protecting it. If the crook is toward the wall, there will
be few guards."

"How will he tell you which man carries the
merchant's money?"

"When he picks up his begging bowl, he will raise and
lower it as he and other beggars do when asking for alms.
The number of times he raises and lowers it will be the
position of the man with the fat purse."

Dismas was surprised at the thoroughness of the
simple, but efficient method of communication.

Ezra cautioned, "Don't think what you are to do will
be easy. It won't. You must not only be wise; you must be
cunning. You must remember all that you see and hear,
and, above all—" The old leader spaced his next words.

248

"Keep—your—mouth—shut."

"But of course," Dismas answered smuggly.

"Don't be so sure of yourself, you smart suckling. Do you even know what the Romans would do to you if they learned you were a member of this illustrious group?" His father laughed gutterally as he looked evilly around the walls of the cave. The watching men smiled as they heard Ezra's words.

"I imagine things would go badly for me," Dismas mumbled.

"Badly? Ha! Have you ever seen a person, other than our man Cliphas, with whom the Romans have dealt?" He waited for his son to answer, knowing the boy had no answer.

"Sometimes they cut off fingers, one joint at a time. Sometimes they scourge you with thongs tipped with lead until your bones are the best part left of you. And if you are lucky, they garrot you—put a cord around your throat and twist it. When they do this, they choke you until your eyes pop from their sockets." Ezra paused to let Dismas fully absorb what he said. "This is payment for those who make mistakes." Suddenly Ezra corrected himself, "No. It is payment for anyone who makes even one mistake."

"I do not plan to make mistakes," Dismas defended.

"They are never planned."

"All right. I now know the payment for carelessness and I am prepared to avoid it."

"One final thing," his father cautioned. "Let me also warn you of this. I speak before the others when I say, if you betray us, any of us, every man in this band will have my order and full blessing to hunt you like a dog. If you betray us, you had better pray that the Romans get you instead of us."

"I would expect no less for treachery," Dismas replied, "but I also expect payment according to the risks I take." The boy swallowed deeply, then cleared his throat in hopes his voice would not crack. "I will accept nothing less than a full share."

From across the room several voices yelled, "No! Absolutely not." They were quick in their response, but one man stood to speak for all. He was known as "The Bull," a huge Philistine slave, who had not only murdered his master, but an overseer and two fellow slaves as well, when they tried to stop him from escaping. "Why should we divide a full share with a whelp? Even yours, Ezra?" Fire was in the man's eyes.

Dismas did not give his father time to speak. He turned to the Bull and asked, "How well do you fare now, Bull?" Dismas took a half step backward before he spit out, "I don't ask more than what is fair. Let me earn my worth. If my eyes and ears do not furnish what you need to stop your hunger and add to your purse, let hunger be my share also. When you profit from my work, then profit should also be mine."

The Bull stared stupidly at the boy. Dismas' reasoning could not be rebutted. With a loud grunt and no further objections, the big man sat down.

Turning to his father, Dismas asked, "How will the blind beggar be paid?"

"That is my worry," Ezra grunted.

"And me? How will I be paid if I cannot have money?"

"Your share will be brought to you once each year, but you must put it away until your job is finished." This arrangement seemed suitable, so Dismas asked no more questions about it.

Before the week was over Dismas was on his way north

to Jerusalem. As he trudged along, he enjoyed the fact that the wadis became fewer and fewer. After a few days the greenness of his surroundings stood out in his eyes, as did the terrain, which became more and more hilly. Eventually these gave way to small mountains, which, to a boy of the desert, were anything but small.

As he walked along the dusty roads he eyed with great suspicion all others who traveled his way. The other travelers, walking or riding donkeys, paid little attention to him, other than to suspect him as much as he suspected them. Despite the weariness of days of walking, Dismas' pace quickened each time he pictured the whiteness he knew the Holy City would have. Jerusalem. Jerusalem. Dismas could not keep from repeating the name over and over as he plodded along.

One morning, having risen just as the sun came over the horizon, Dismas walked to the crest of a hill. From there, gleaming in the golden glare of dawn, lay the Holy City in all its wonder. The young boy just stood staring at it, unable to believe he was actually looking at Judea's capital city, Jerusalem, the crossroads of the world.

Finally, and without losing sight of his destination, he once more started toward the city. Dismas was somewhat surprised by the town. The early morning sun gave the city the appearance of being white. Oddly, however, it was also a light yellow, like the desert.

Instead of covering the whole horizon, as he expected, the city was smaller than his imagination had made it. *That's what happens when you listen to thieves*, Dismas thought, as a smile crossed his face. He hitched up his food bag, repositioned his makeshift water gourd, and continued on his way.

By nightfall the young boy was making his way along the foot of the Kidron Valley, which bordered the city wall on the east. Ahead of him, and to the right, he saw the potter's diggings and some ovens. On the far side of that, atop a slight rise, he made out graves and burial vaults.

Dismas decided that the graveyard would make a safe, if not a comfortable lodging place. In his superstitious mind he knew that to live among the dead was to invite disaster. Since disaster was to be his companion for as long as he was in Jerusalem, he felt he might as well face it immediately. He headed for the cemetery.

In a matter of minutes he located a small crypt built atop the ground and with room in it for an average-sized man. After pushing aside the improperly mounted stone door and crawling inside, Dismas spread the wool cloak his mother had made for him years before. There, amid the dead, he lay down for his first night at the Holy City. Slowly the sun slipped down behind the city wall, which towered above the graveyard. Behind that, the town became draped in night, bringing loneliness with it. For the first time since his father proposed that he become a spy, Dismas felt alone, like a tiny island surrounded by hostility. The young boy tried to console himself with the thought that he was probably the only person in all the city who knew the feelings of a sacrificial lamb.

Night and the long journey finally took its toll; Dismas slept as the dead—among the dead.

With dawn came the sound of diggers and their slow, telltale *chuch—chuch*. The sound came from picks tearing into the hard ground. When Dismas first opened his eyes, he snapped upright. *Where am I?* he wondered as he looked around, only to realize he was in a burial crypt. He bit his lip to keep from screaming. Quickly falling back to steady his shaking and to insure that he could not be seen, Dismas lay still until the panic left. When it had passed, the still frightened boy quietly pulled himself across the smooth stone floor to the door, only to find the sun quite high.

Across from the cemetery, heavily ladened donkeys picked their way across the valley floor to and from the city. Dismas saw, toward the direction from which the sun had come, an olive grove on a hillside. Behind the crypt where he hid, he could also hear the diggers talking.

As they hacked at the claylike dirt, they complained. "Alizah, do you think the king will ever have enough gold to finish the temple he has started?"

Chuch! The man's pick dug into the dirt.

"Only when all of us are dead."

Chuch!

"Watch your words. Choose better ones even when you speak words other people think."

Chuch!

"How can a man watch his words when his family is always hungry, just because Herod wants Roman marble instead of the stone from our mountains? He is even more mad than his father was."

Chuch!

"Alizah, your bile-covered tongue is going to be your death someday. At least say what you must so that only I can hear it."

Chuch!

Standing straight and putting one hand to the small of his back as he stretched backward, the older of the two diggers said, "My tongue may be a danger, but what is death to those who are already dead and just happen to still breathe?"

"Arguing with you is useless because what you say is true. As a young man I had nothing. Today I am old and

253

I have even less. Between the Romans and Herod, God is fortunate to get my soul. Who knows, Rome or Herod may yet demand that too."

Chuch!

With the workmen's complaints still bouncing from one man to the other, Dismas eased himself from the crypt, leaving his cloak on the floor. He slid the stone back into place, then slipped into the stream of people making their way into the city. There, his filth would make him invisible to the mass of uncaring eyes.

At the gate, guards poked into bundles, searched people, and asked questions. When it came Dismas' turn, the guard just wrinkled his nose and took a deep breath as he sneered at the rags the boy wore. Dismas' garments were matted with dirt gathered during years in the desert. His search of Dismas was nothing more than a disgusted look, so the boy quickly pushed through the gate.

Glancing around him Dismas thought, *Here I am, finally at the world's center. I'm really in Jerusalem.* He felt like shouting, but restrained himself.

Around him, on all sides, he saw men dressed in fine clothes brought from many parts of the world. Most of all, Dismas noticed the odors. Back in the cave the only smells he could remember distinctly were those of moist dirt, sweaty bodies, greasy meat cooked over a smoky fire, and, once each week, the aroma of bread baking.

In Jerusalem things were different. Here Dismas learned how much his nose had missed. Mixed with the dusty smell of blowing dirt were the heavy scents of sweet temple incense, boiling sugar cane, baked goods of all descriptions, and, in contrast, an occasional whiff of fresh camel dung.

Dismas' first day in Judea's capital city was spent wandering the streets. Hour after hour he curiously peered into each shop. Sometimes his gaze was met with the smile of a proud owner, and sometimes by the angry wave of a hand as the shop owner shrilled, "Away! You, filthy beggar boy, go away."

The first few times this happened, Dismas made mental notes of the shop's locations so that later, when his father's men were his to command, he could return and cut the owner's cruel tongue from his mouth. Maybe he would chop off the man's hands too. However, before the day was over he'd had so many such encounters he could no longer remember which was which, or where they had occurred. Finally, Dismas just shrugged off such verbal abuse as the product of men even more unhappy than he.

Even before midday the young boy was hungry. It didn't take long for him to realize that unlike the desert, where hunger could be stopped by finding a tasty lizard or bird egg, the city provided few opportunities to eat unless one had money.

The boy's first efforts to beg resulted in failure. Next he tried tears, but this too proved fruitless. After several attempts for sympathy by telling sad tales of being lost, or abandoned, he gave up. Seeing a heavily loaded fruit cart nearby, he decided to employ a trick he had often used on his mother. Stopping the peddler to ask the price of his fruit, Dismas examined three or four oranges. As he did, he dropped several of the fruit to the ground. After apologizing for his clumsiness, he retrieved all but one of the oranges, which he left under the peddler's cart. He replaced the fruit he had retrieved, then waited nearby until the peddler pushed the cart away. Quickly he darted forward, scooped up the lone, small orange and enjoyed his first food since arriving in the city.

255

Wiping the sticky juice from his hands onto the front of his stained mantle, Dismas strolled casually along the streets again, bumped by men as they made their unseeing way from one place to another. He was jostled by peddlers, women carrying water jars on their heads, and even by protesting animals as they were led along the jammed streets and alleys. The city was heartless, and Dismas thoroughly enjoyed it. He smiled as he sauntered along. The atmosphere was like home—cruel, and he knew how to deal with it.

Finding an unoccupied niche above a low ledge which ran along the base of a building, Dismas crawled up, squatted, and watched the people.

As he allowed his eyes idly to pass over the bobbing heads, Dismas saw a young girl balancing a large bowl of huge oranges on her head. As she glided past him, Dismas took the opportunity and snatched the other half of his meal without even rising from his squatting position.

After peeling the orange and tossing the skins into the street, he relaxed in his cool, but exposed seat and spat orange seeds through compressed lips. After the treatment he had received all morning, he hoped each seed would strike and stain the rich robes of the pitiless people passing by.

His little game changed from amusement to pain once. Just as he squirted an orange seed, a hulking and richly dressed merchant stopped, looked down at the offending seed sticking to his sleeve, then viciously struck Dismas across the face with a ring-clustered hand. The blow spun the boy's head to one side with such force it left him dazed. When the instant of dizziness lifted and his eyes once more focused, Dismas saw only the man's back as he strutted on up the street.

He screamed an oath after him, but the man did not

bother even to look back. Tears ran down his stinging cheek and he was angry with himself for allowing such a thing to happen. He had relaxed his guard.

"That is another man I will kill," he mumbled, straining to stand on tiptoes. He wanted to see the man's features, wanted to remember what he looked like. The man disappeared in the distance and Dismas had to settle for just seeing his broad back.

Finally he again squatted back down on his ledge and crossed his arms over his upraised knees. When his cheek and pride stopped stinging, he went back to watching the crowd lazily.

Before many minutes passed, the boy's eyes fell on a short, middle-aged man, who had a frown so deeply planted on his face that it caused the boy to smile. Finally Dismas laughed out loud at the comical appearance it gave the small man.

Ahead of the frowning man walked a huge and seemingly prosperous merchant, complete with a heavy, pendulous golden chain swinging from around his neck. The boy's eyes widened as he saw the wrinkled little man deftly reach around the rich man's swollen belly and remove a leather purse. The merchant had carried it in one of the folds of a highly ornate girdle. Dismas was particularly awed by the way the old thief had so easily taken the money without even having looked at his victim.

As an expression of admiration lit his face, Dismas pursed his lips and blew out air in a manner which, if he had tightened his lips, would have been a whistle.

The little old thief had not changed the intensely thoughtful expression on his face, and had made no effort to run from the scene of his crime. Instead, he gave the merchant a gentle push and made his nonchalant way around him. Encountering several other people walking ahead of him, the accomplished thief elbowed his way through them, putting several bodies between himself and the man he had just robbed.

Dismas then saw the art of thievery for the first time and it was not a crime to him, but a highly polished skill—an art to be admired. Dismas saw the man come into sudden wealth with hardly any effort and he liked what he saw. From his stone perch the boy looked over the bobbing river of heads, trying to observe the route taken by the thief. Quickly seeing that this was impossible, he dropped to the street and tried to follow. He felt he had to talk with this most gifted man.

If he would teach me his skills, I could be rich, Dismas convinced himself. *If I could do that I would no longer need my father or his men.*

Before the boy had traveled a hundred yards he knew that the wily thief had escaped him. It seemed as if the man had just vanished. *He has probably ducked into one of the many doorways along the street,* Dismas reasoned.

The boy was disappointed and it showed on his face as he stopped chasing the little man. Dismas made a brief, but futile, search of the nearby shops before shrugging his shoulders and returning to his ledge to try again begging for food or money with which to buy food. Hunger would not allow him to dwell on his disappointment.

At his young age he found that women were more likely to give what little money he needed. He eventually learned that the most likely women to approach were ones with silver in their hair, with children or grandchildren around his age.

This day, with just enough money to buy a single loaf of bread, he made his purchase and walked toward his cemetery home.

The crowds were starting to thin out and Dismas again felt a little lonely. Before he reached the edge of town, two ragged boys, each about Dismas' own age, darted by. As they passed, one screamed directly into Dismas' ear, causing him to crouch protectively. Bent over, he failed to protect his bread from the second boy, who deftly snatched it away from him and ran around a nearby corner. Dismas' disillusionment, on this day of failure, deepened. Here, on his very first night in God's city, he would have to go to bed hungry. It was something he could not remember having ever done back at the cave.

As things turned out, Dismas learned he had made a bargain with his father which could not be kept. Within two weeks of his son's arrival in Jerusalem, Ezra was dragged to death behind a Roman horse. Not only was his last raid on a caravan a futile one, it was fatal—for every member of the band.

To top off the tragic news, Dismas later learned that one member of the group, and he never learned who, became a traitor when his captors began to tie his hands and feet to four separate horses. The man had disclosed the location of the cave, where all of the women, including Dismas' mother, were also slaughtered. The man gave away the secret as his last words, just before the four horses |to |which he was tied, were driven in opposite directions, tearing his limbs from his body.

The boy had been sent to the city to become one of the crowds of orphaned beggar boys as a disguise. In but two weeks, it had become real. Dismas felt even worse knowing the bloodletting of his father's men and their women occurred on the first raid they had made using information he, Dismas, had sent to them.

With a determination given only to youth, Dismas decided he would simply find the little old thief, learn the wonders of his art, and remain in Jerusalem forever. Seldom were such loose plans to be so completely fulfilled.

The next morning Dismas reentered the city, and just as before, a disgusted guard waved him through the gates rather than to touch him, even to search.

Before leaving the crypt where he slept, he left what he knew was a very puzzled gravedigger. Since his life was now to be that of a thief, he stole the gravedigger's lunch. It was just a half loaf of bread and a piece of cheese, but in the place of the dead, the digger was sure to wonder which of the local "dwellers" would have need of food.

Back inside the city's gates, Dismas watched the formation of caravans. Observing their coming and going, he enjoyed the sport of all young boys—dreaming of faraway places and imagining what riches the long lines of camels and donkeys might carry.

Every week small caravans left Jerusalem for Gibeah, Jericho, Mizpah, Gibeon, and other northern cities. Some of these places were located so close to Jerusalem that Dismas was tempted to follow them.

The boy was caught between temptations; if he went with a caravan he would visit new places and see new sights. On the other hand, if Jesus Barabbas and his men, who were rumored to number in the thousands, raided the caravan, it could mean serious trouble. If, during the battle, he should be killed, or worse yet, captured and thought to be a caravaneer, the shame would be unbearable. He was a robber and a thief, not a caravaneer.

Not many days passed before Dismas sat once more on his familiar ledge. Again he felt the touch of what the desert people believed so strongly in—fate.

Around midday, as he lay slouched back against the building's cool wall, he lazily looked out across the bobbing faces passing before him. Suddenly he sat bolt upright; the little, old thief he had searched for was walking his way. As the stranger bustled along, Dismas saw that he wore the same offended look as before. Also as before, he seemed to ignore everyone around him.

Afraid that anyone watching might see him staring at the thief, Dismas pretended to be asleep, but instead, peeked through his almost closed eyelids. The little man only blustered along like everyone else, he seemed to have a destination in mind. His face did not look downward, as would a man who wandered aimlessly. Instead, he glared into the distance. He seemed intent on something far down the street, and forged ahead toward it.

Dismas thought to himself, *He probably has game in sight and is about to pluck it.* Without taking any chances on losing the man, Dismas dropped from the ledge and followed as closely as he dared.

The enchantment of the idea of simply picking his fortune from those around him filled Dismas' mind. He felt that for a man to be an accomplished thief would be like a farmer ready to gather in a crop of gold. A really good thief would have constantly ripe fields coming to him to be harvested.

For the next several hours the boy padded along behind the little thief, stopping when he stopped, and walking only when he walked. All afternoon and until late in the evening, the pair wandered the streets, one moving as if with a destination, while unknowingly pulling a boy-sized shadow along behind him.

They wandered westward, as far as the outer walls of Herod's Palace, north past Hezekiah's Pool, then east again toward the construction site of the huge temple.

Long after the sun had set and the gates were closed, but before the dogs began to roam the streets, Dismas saw his opportunity to talk to the man. He just had to ask if he might learn the art of thievery.

The old thief had stopped, stepped back into a dark doorway and, without surrendering his frown, leaned back to rest.

"Sir, may I have a word with you?" Dismas whispered through the side of his mouth when he had reached the doorway.

"Yes, my lord," the man responded before his eyes skittered over Dismas' filthy rags. When he saw it was but a beggar boy, the man's tone suddenly changed to that of irritation. "What business could you possibly have with me?"

Dismas looked in both directions to insure no one was in earshot, then moved into the doorway too.

Without hesitation, the anxious boy blurted out, "Many days ago I watched as you relieved a wealthy merchant of his purse without arousing him. I want to learn to do that."

"You lie, you miserable cur," the man retorted defensively.

"No, I do not lie. You see, I too am a thief, of sorts." He took a deep breath. "But I have never seen anyone as masterful as you."

"Shut your lying mouth, you . . . you. . . . You are wrong! I am a stonemason by trade. Be gone before I call a guard," the old man bluffed.

Without giving him a chance to protest further, Dismas grabbed the old thief's hand and thrust it into the light of a torch which flickered from a nearby wall. "Those," the boy said as he held the man's hand high, "are not the hands of a mason. I have seen your hands work, and they are the hands of an artist—the hands of a master thief from whom I truly want to learn."

The man was startled, but impressed by Dismas' bravado. Flattered by what he heard, the thief knew the boy was sincere. "I must ponder what you ask, young lion. I will meet with you later and give you my decision."

"Yes. Certainly. But before you decide I am a lamb to be shorn, I must tell you that I am more akin to you than you suspect." With that, Dismas stepped from the doorway's shadows and looked both directions along the near deserted street. Although it looked vacant in both directions, Dismas still whispered, "You can usually find me at night in the burial crypt of Chlorias the dyer, in the Kidron, and alone." The boy smiled at the shocked look on the old man's face. "Don't worry. I don't like living with him any more than he does with me, but still, he has never objected to my company." The boy turned and walked into the night.

Dismas' story of his boyhood was interrupted by a piercing scream which echoed along the prison corridors. The scream was not high, but told of extreme pain.

Caleb and Dismas glanced at each other, a puzzled and worried look on their faces. Before they could comment, the scream came again. This time, instead of the voice lasting long seconds, as it had before, it quickly trailed off to silence. As it diminished, it took on the sound of a man gargling with water.

"My God!" Caleb mumbled. "What creature from hell could make such a sound?"

"It was not a creature from hell," Dismas mumbled, "but one on his way there. I've heard that sound several times before."

"What was it?" Caleb asked.

"That sound came from a man now dead. It is the sound given when Romans put a rope around a bound man's throat. The rope is loose when it is put over his head. Then a stick, one about a foot long, is put through the rope. The stick is turned, twisting the rope tighter and tighter until the man strangles. Death can be as fast or as slow as his tormentors desire."

"My God!" Caleb gasped.

"God is one person who has nothing to do with what just happened," Dismas muttered. His voice sounded completely defeated.

Before they talked again, a loud thump from down the hall announced that food was being brought to them. Neither Dismas nor Caleb were hungry. They still pictured in their minds the scene of a man being choked to death, but they also knew this was their first chance to get much needed water.

A guard, accompanied by a slave, entered the cell. As the guard watched, the slave filled their bowls with gruel. Next, he slopped water into a small pail near the door. Caleb, after the jailer left, told Dismas he had seen maggots squirming in the mush, so both men passed up their meal in favor of several deep swallows of the tepid water.

It was near noon and the heat was so thick breathing was a cruel necessity.

10 THURSDAY
EVENING

It was well past midday when Dismas and Caleb awoke from the nap that followed the water they had so eagerly consumed as their noon meal. Their sleep had fallen over them, not so much from fatigue as from the heat, which hung like smoke on a breezeless night.

What moisture they had drank three or four hours earlier, seemed to have drained from them during their sleep. Both men's tongues stuck to their lips when they tried to lick the dust from them.

Seeing a way to take some of the misery off them, Dismas reached over and none too gently poked at Caleb's knee. "Boy. Come with me and do as I do. It will help."

Without waiting for the confirmation of his instructions, the older man awkwardly scooted across the floor until he was near where the two of them had sat when the guard had come with their noon food.

Before doing anything more than just moving across the room, Dismas waited for Caleb to come. Reluctantly the younger man dragged himself over beside his teacher.

Pointing to a spot in front of him, Dismas said, "There's water on the floor here. You may not be able to see it, but I remember the guard's slave spilling it there when he filled our bowls." Then he added appreciatively, "Maybe he knew how desperately we would need it in this heat."

Motioning Caleb to copy him, Dismas leaned forward and began to rub his sleeve around in a circle on the floor and deep into the cracks. Caleb followed suit. He was not sure what his old leader had in mind, but he had faith in his judgment.

Seconds after they had begun this strange action, and still holding their sleeves from inside their robes, Dismas raised his arm and began rubbing the sleeve over his face and neck. When Caleb tried it he realized what Dismas was doing. The sleeve had soaked up considerable moisture. Even though it was not as good as a drink of water, it cooled him and lessened his thirst somewhat. The trick was as much a surprise to Caleb as when Dismas had taught him to wear his woolen cloak even when the hottest days of the year were upon them. The woolen garments, like sponges, absorbed perspiration which, when struck by even the faintest of breezes, acted as an efficient cooler.

After they had repeated the rubbings several times, and were convinced that further hope for wetness was useless, both men lay back and waved their still damp sleeves over their heads and close to their faces. They tried to gain whatever cooler air they could generate.

266

"Dismas?"

"Yes," the old thief half grunted.

"How did you actually get into stealing? You are so masterful at it; you seem to have always been the best. How did you get that way?"

"I was about to tell you that earlier."

"Oh yes, you were describing the little old man with the worried look. Who was he anyhow?"

"Before I go into that," Dismas replied, "let me begin where I left off. I told the old thief that I slept with the city's dead, which was something he did not like. Anyhow, that same night he came to the crypt and called to me. I saw him coming and it was all I could do not to laugh at him. He was clearly frightened, but even more, he was not sure that I was actually there.

"As he called among the graves—" Dismas stopped long enough to hang his head and chuckle softly. "I remember it clearly. The look on his face said he felt utterly foolish. All crouched over, he crept around hissing, 'Boy. Where are you, boy?' Then he would mutter something like, 'If that confounded boy got me out here doing this just as a joke, I'll kill him. I'll steal the eyes from his head and stuff them into his nose. Boy! Where are you, boy?' Caleb, you should have seen him."

Again Dismas stopped talking to laugh, but this time he did it loudly, and even had to wipe tears of laughter from his eyes. Caleb grinned too.

After a few minutes of dwindling laughter, each man burst out laughing again, only to end with contented sighs. Dismas went on, "He was a funny sight."

Before allowing his friend to ramble on, Caleb interrupted, "How did you get outside the gates at night? The gates were closed?"

"It is true, they were closed, but for a beggar boy, getting outside them at night is easy. As you well know, wild dogs are thick outside the walls at night. A few of them even get inside the city when the hour is late. Outside, however, mixed with the dogs are hyenas, which can bite your arm off with a single snap. As for me, for a guard to allow wealthy persons to venture out at night and get injured could bring trouble. For a beggar boy to ask to go out, if the hyenas ate him, the world would be better off. The first guard I asked to let me out did so with a smile on his face. I'm sure he thought I would be killed and eaten. Anyhow, that's how I left the city at night. I simply asked."

"I see," said Caleb, somewhat amazed, "but what about the thief? How did he get out?"

"As I said, he came to see if I really slept in a crypt. I have no idea how he got outside, nor did I ask, but there he was."

"What was his name?"

"David. David of Antioch."

"David of Antioch? Why, I've heard of him. Wasn't he the one who lost both hands to the ax before starting a school for young thieves?"

"Yes, he's the one. After losing his hands he went on to make an even better living than before through his students, which included me. At least he did for a while."

Caleb, fascinated by the idea of a thief with no hands, chuckled, "I heard he was even caught stealing a holy lamp after he had lost both hands."

"Don't laugh—, it's true. He's the man I'm talking about and I was the leader of his group of boy thieves."

Caleb was obviously impressed. With a half smile on his face," he commented, "He must have been a wonderful person."

"Well, that's hardly the right word to describe David.

He wasn't an easy teacher. In fact, he was selfish, cruel, and many more things which are anything but wonderful. I must say one thing for him, though, no one ever knew more of our trade or was a better teacher."

Dismas stopped long enough to pick his nose thoroughly. After he had carefully examined his nasal findings, he leaned back and stared up toward the ceiling. A look of contentment spread slowly over him as his boyhood memories returned. He again smiled gently and cracked the caked dirt around his eyes.

"Oh, I'll have to tell you how he began my training. It was the next evening after we met. He had me move from the crypt into the old chariot stall he called home.

"My lessons began as a series of instructions, just as yours did. He started by telling me something I never forgot. He said every man I'd ever meet walked the streets expecting to be robbed. For this reason, the intended victim was always on guard, even imagining hands upon his purse which did not exist."

Dismas leaned forward, picked up a straw from the floor and stuck it, dirt and all, between his teeth before continuing. "He told me that because men were so alert for thieves, I would have to be better than perfect. He said I had to dispel the victim's apprehension before or during the time that I struck. That's why, Caleb, you have always, or nearly always, seen me either jostling or talking with the person I robbed. I never tried simply to lift a man's gold, not that I couldn't do it that way, mind you, but that's what he expects to be done. Instead, I always did what he did not expect."

"Yes, Dismas, that's as you taught me, too."

"And until we left stealing to become killers, it never failed us, did it?" Dismas did not wait for an answer.

Reaching up and rubbing his forehead with his

fingertips, he began rolling tiny balls of dirt off. He kept it up after moving his fingers to his neck and face.

"You know, Caleb, that old man would stick a gold coin in some hidden place on his body and then make a mark on the floor near a creeping shadow. If I could not find and steal that coin by the time the shadow reached his mark—mind you, have stolen it from him—he would pick up a small bag of coins from the table and hit me across my head.

"Each time he did that, he'd say, 'You want gold to come to you? Then do it by making sure it arrives painlessly. Any other way is disgraceful and not worth it.' Caleb, that man could take a girdle and roll it as a Hebrew, Phoenician, Greek, Roman, or even as an Egyptian might do. He could even roll it as a woman would. He learned them all, so he could practice on them, and he never missed."

Glancing toward Caleb, who listened intently, Dismas continued, "He even showed me how merchants would hide coins under their scrotum or weave them into their hair or the hair of their wives or mistresses. Not only did he know all of these things, he knew how to relieve the owners of the coins too. He demanded that I master all of that too."

A bit hurt, Caleb inquired, "Why then, master, didn't you teach all these things to me?"

"Because they are of little use, if any at all, these days. With the Romans as they are, merchants no longer use such tactics because Rome will protect them—so they seem to think at least.

"David even went so far as to burn my fingertips with a hot knife blade so they would be sensitive enough to feel what coins a purse contained even without opening it. That man was a hard one, have no doubt of that."

270

"It sounds like he was little more than a slave master," surmised Caleb.

"That's exactly what he was, a slave master bent on two things. First, he wanted to make rich men poor; second, he wanted to make sure his students made victims of other people, not the other way around."

Dismas thoughtfully rubbed the side of his head before softly saying, "Caleb, old David made me train from dawn to dark every day for more than two years before he let me lift my first purse. In his own peculiar way, I think now, he cared about me. He was determined to make me his living monument." Dismas shook his head slowly and dismally before letting his eyes dart around the cell. "Little did he know I would come to this sad end." Blowing his breath out in a half sigh, Dismas continued, "Oh well, I guess each man reaches the end of his rope some time. You and I just happen to have reached ours here and now."

A brief silence fell over the two men. It was broken when Dismas continued recounting his past. "Yes, Caleb, old David was quite a man. Did you know that he lost his hands in Damascus?"

The younger man shook his head no.

"It happened on two separate occasions, both of which stemmed from hunger. David had gone to Damascus to relieve a certain camel dealer of more gold than you can imagine. Not only did David miss the man, but disease had forced almost everyone from the streets.

"David eventually got hungry, but when he went into the streets and found food, the officials arrested him for violating their curfew and for stealing the food he was eating when they caught him. For this they cut off his right hand with a broad headsman's sword. The captain of the guard warned him that a second offense could cost

271

him his head, but in less than two weeks, when he was caught a second time, he only lost his other hand. After that, he left Damascus forever."

Dismas lay back and folded his hands behind his head. "It was then that the master thief came to me instead of me to him. For more than a month we gathered boys just like you, Caleb—boys to teach how to steal. From that point on, things were good for everyone. Dismas coughed lightly, "Yes things were better."

"What happened to David?"

Dismas looked long into Caleb's face before saying, "You might say I killed him."

The shocked look on Caleb's face made it plain that he did not believe what he had just heard. For an instant his mouth opened and closed, like that of a fish, before he blurted out, "You what?"

"I killed him. He was an old and bitter man. He was made bitter by his dependency on me and others like me. At the time, I was a young, hotheaded man who was being browbeaten harder and harder all the time. One day, as usual, after we purchased some large items, I had to carry them back to our home. All the way from the market to where we lived he cursed and swore at me. Several times he called me an idiot, then—" Dismas looked down into his lap. "Then he said I was fit only to be food for the pus-licking dogs of the streets. That did it."

Unable to look Caleb in the eye, Dismas went on, "About the time he said this I went blind with rage. I let his abuse pass until we had again returned to the streets.

"We had not gone far before I saw a Roman war chariot, one of the biggest I've ever seen, speeding down the narrow street. What I did then was a simple thing. As the other people on the street pushed and shoved to get

272

out of the chariot's way, I stuck my foot in front of David's feet. He fell forward and under the huge wheels. I still remember him screaming one loud 'NO!' as he stuck the stumps of his arms out, trying to stop his fall. An instant later he was sliced in two, as cleanly as a butcher halves a sheep. He never knew what happened."

Caleb was stunned. His mouth hung open, a look of total disbelief on his face. After a few seconds of awkward silence, he grunted, "Why?" Not getting an answer, he cleared his throat and almost shouted, "Why, Dismas? You said he was someone you greatly admired."

"That's true, or at least it was true until he lost his hands. Then," Dismas spat over his shoulder, "he became like a gambler who could only lose. He hated everyone and everything, and that included me. No, Caleb, I don't feel badly about killing him. Some might say I didn't kill him—that the chariot did. I only know that if I had not—" Dismas did not finish what he was about to say. From outside the small window of their cell came the shouts of a large crowd. As they listened, the yelling became louder.

Both men, moving like crabs crossing a sandbar, scampered up the inclined stone wall to the tiny window. From this point they were at street level. For the most part, all they could see, once the crowd reached them, were dirty feet and ankles. When they pressed their cheeks against the bars and looked to the right, they could see a slight break in the mob. Through the opening they could see what all the excitement was about. Far down the street they saw the carpenter, Jesus, surrounded by a surging, yelling mob.

When the two thieves realized who it was, their reactions could hardly have been more different. Caleb moaned in disappointment and Dismas' excitement showed in his tighter grip on the bars. He had the look of a drowning man clutching at a log.

As he clung to the bars, Dismas noticed that the feet below the rust-colored wool robe worn by Jesus stopped directly in front of him. Looking only at the feet, each housed by a sandal of the simplest kind, Dismas first muttered, then shouted, "Soon!"

He repeated the word, only to have Caleb ask, "Soon? What do you mean, Dismas?" Dismas did not look away from the feet. "You've met that fraud before," Caleb scoffed. "And look where you've landed."

Dismas released his hold on the cell bars and tumbled to the bottom of the stone incline. As he gained his balance and untwisted his robe, he found Caleb hovering over him. This time it was not disgust, as he had heard in the question before, but was genuine concern, "Are you all right?"

Dismas rolled into a sitting position at the base of the steep wall. This time, instead of snapping at his questioner, the old thief just raised his eyes until they met Caleb's. "I honestly don't know. I just don't know."

It was plain that his friend was not just unsure of himself—he was frightened.

"Caleb, that mysterious man is either a devil or a god and I don't know which. I only know that he is special—very, very special."

"What do you mean, Dismas? He's just another of the many prophets who come to Jerusalem. We talked of this before. We even agreed on it.

Making a chopping motion with his hand, Dismas groaned, "I know what we agreed on, but we were wrong. I've seen this man's bravery and it's not of the usual kind. I've heard him teach and he's not like other rabbis. He doesn't tell everyone they are damned to hell

274

and recite ancient quotations at them. No, he tells them that there is hope for even the worst of men."

Almost as an afterthought, Dismas added, "Caleb, he doesn't even ask for money." The last fact was a true mystery to the two thieves. Man's greed for money was the common denominator among all ordinary men. Jesus' utter disregard for it left many Jews, who were accustomed to religious leaders asking for money almost without ceasing, in awe of him.

"This man is more—much more. I don't know how that is, but it's true. I know it as sure as I'm here." Dismas had worked himself into an excited sweat, so he dabbed at his forehead with the sleeve of his cloak.

He stood and began pacing and wringing his hands. The chains on his wrists clanked noisily as he walked from one side of the hot cell to the other and back again. Caleb sat staring at his friend. He was unable to understand what had upset the old thief so quickly and so deeply.

"I tell you, Caleb, what you just saw and heard worries me more than it does you. He never says a word to me, not a single word, but his slightest look, even his presence, causes me to feel him near to me, even as if he were inside of me. Each time I've met him, I've known that something would happen between us, and very soon. I don't know what it is or how it will happen, but it will. Soon. Possibly right in this prison—I don't know."

"That's it!" Caleb exclaimed, "That must be it. He must be the new king of the Jews and he will get us out of here. If he is truly a magician, as some say, maybe he'll just set us free. Maybe that's what he's telling you, that soon he will get us out of here," Caleb offered hopefully.

"No, that's not it at all. He's trying to tell me something much more important."

"More important? More important? What could possibly be more important than living? More important than getting out of here?"

"I don't know, I tell you. I know it sounds insane, but that's exactly what I mean. It's more important than life and getting out of here."

"You are insane, Dismas! What could be more important than life?" Caleb wailed.

"Don't ask me!" Dismas shouted back, throwing both hands into the air and whirling around.

"Dismas. Oh, Dismas," moaned Caleb as his whole body seemed to sag. "You've lost your mind."

"I don't know, my friend," said the older thief. "Maybe I have, maybe not. Maybe our pending death has warped my senses. I only know that what he has in mind for me will happen soon, whatever it is."

After several minutes of silence, broken only by deep, jerky inhalations of air, Dismas whispered, "I'm sorry, Caleb. I had no reason to shout at you. If I hurt your feelings, I didn't mean to."

"I know that—and it didn't hurt me. I just fear for both of us," Caleb murmured.

Dismas closed his eyes and an agonized look crept over his face. In a voice like that of a person mourning a death, he wailed, "Oh, if only I could but understand. Oh God. God, help me."

Caleb scooted closer to his friend and compassionately put his arm around the older man's stooped shoulders. Dismas bowed his head and dug both grimy fists into his streaming eyes.

"What's left for you to understand, Dismas? Old master, there's little time left for either of us to mourn. We understand that we are thieves. And we were caught at our work, only to be condemned unjustly to die. We understand that we may have days, or just minutes to live. What else does someone in our position need to understand? What more really matters—to us?"

Dismas looked directly into the face of his friend. Through moist eyes, with tears causing small clean stripes to appear on both cheeks, he stared. Finally he answered Caleb. "I don't know what I want to understand. I only know that this man, this Jesus of Nazareth, sees me in a way no other man sees me—not even you. He sees me in a way—I don't know—he sees into my mind, into my innermost soul, and he does not condemn me for what is there. Instead, his gaze penetrates so deeply that he looks past all the rottenness that others can see in me. I can actually feel his sympathy for me. It's as if he was saying, 'You poor man. God loves you. He can clean you up inside and make you a new man.'"

"But he's never said a word to you."

Dismas wailed, "I know that! But still I know he—he—he loves me. He loves me honestly, openly, freely. He loves me and I cannot understand it. I'm afraid of it. I am afraid to accept it."

Dismas, his face still twisted from crying and his chin quivering uncontrollably, looked at Caleb with a puzzled expression. "Caleb, no one ever cared about me as he does. Even you, my best friend, my son, you care for me in your way. But even with such care as you have, you never loved me the way he does. I can understand your kind of love, why it is and how it is, but this man really loves me—oh, I don't know how to explain it. He just loves me stronger, more deeply, and in a different, a clean, rich way—in a way so different and wonderful that it is beyond our understanding." Dismas paused, then asked, "Do you know what I'm saying at all, Caleb?"

"No" was his flat reply.

"Of course not. How could you? I don't even know what I mean myself."

Caleb couldn't imagine what Dismas was talking about, but the younger man felt his cell mate was losing touch with reality, and it irritated him. "No, I don't understand. Why should that man love you?" he mocked. "We're nothing but thieves—and liars. You're a killer and an adulterer. How could he love you?"

"I don't know," Dismas responded huskily. "But since I first saw him last Sabbath, I have wondered if I was losing my mind. At that time, and again today, he looked into my future through my eyes—without saying a word he did it. He gave no gesture, spoke no word, but he told me that he and I have something to do together, and soon. Oh," Dismas cried, "it's driving me insane."

"That I can see and fully understand," Caleb snorted cruelly.

Eventually the younger thief looked out the window to see night racing in on them. He shrugged his shoulders and muttered fatalistically, "Well, if your feelings are right and something is going to happen between the two of you, so be it. If it doesn't happen before you and I die of Roman justice, it won't matter. You may want to ponder it more, but frankly—I am tired and want to go to sleep."

With that announcement, Caleb padded his way across the room to a small, sparse pile of much used straw, where he fell heavily and stretched out.

Dismas saw that his friend's eyes were open and staring at the ceiling. He knew that with death so close at hand, he shouldn't burden his friend with more doubts and confusion.

Finally Dismas lay down too. Several hours later both men slept.

278

11 FRIDAY MORNING

Midnight Until the Third Hour

Moaning, broken only by deep, gasping sobs, came from the small window above the prisoners' heads. The sounds were not loud or wheezy, as would be made by a drunken man who had fallen into the street. Instead, they were slow, steady, and quiet, coming as if from a man who was utterly inconsolable.

Dismas was the first to be awakened by the sound. In the blackness he listened for almost a minute before his mind began to clear. At first he thought it was one of the more miserable inmates of the prison. He soon realized the sound was not from the prison at all, but from outside its walls.

When he finally became aware of this fact, he awoke fully.

"Caleb," he whispered.

279

Since his friend did not seem to hear his call, Dismas clutched his chains to his body as tightly as he could to keep them quiet. Then, moving silently, he scooted across the floor through the darkness until he reached Caleb's side.

"Caleb," he again hissed. "Do you hear that?"

Grunting irritably at being disturbed in the middle of the night, the younger man grumbled, "What is it you want now, Dismas?" His gruff tone was ignored by the older thief, who was only interested in the crying above him.

"Listen!" Dismas quietly urged. The sobbing and moaning continued to filter through the window, just as it had done before.

"It's someone crying," Caleb said flatly. "What's so unusual about that in here?" Caleb had not even raised up to listen. Instead, he merely cocked his head up a few inches from the crook of his arm, where it had been cushioned, then almost immediately dropped it again.

"But it's not coming from the prison," Dismas explained. "It's someone on the street."

"So someone's crying outside," Caleb huskily mumbled. "He's probably drunk, or was rejected by some shapely sleeping companion."

"I don't think so, Caleb. Listen. That's not wine talking, and no man would be so disheartened by a woman's scorn."

"If you think not," Caleb chided, hoping Dismas would leave him alone, "why don't you ask him what his trouble is? Better yet, tell him to cry somewhere else so we, the condemned, can weep for ourselves. It's more fitting that we lament being chained rather than having to listen to a free man crying in the night air."

Although he was apprehensive, Dismas felt Caleb's

idea had merit. He crawled to the top of the ramp and pulled himself to the window, using the bars as a hoist.

Once he reached the small opening and had a firm grip on the bars, to insure that he would not slide back to his starting place, he next peered out. By the light of a distant and dim torch, all he saw was a small part of a thick woolen robe, below which were stretched the hairy legs of a very large man who wore sandals. The stranger apparently had not heard him for his moaning and crying continued unabated.

"What's wrong out there?" Dismas called in a subdued voice.

The moaning stopped long enough to allow the man to sob thickly, "Who speaks?"

"It is I— from the prison window below you. I am a prisoner awakened by your sorrow."

Dismas heard the man sniff several times. Finally the stranger changed positions, leaning forward until his face dropped below the top of the window, low enough for both men to see each other in the dim light. It was Peter, one of Jesus' twelve, and the one to whom Dismas had talked during the carpenter's temple rampage.

"Peter!" Dismas exclaimed in complete surprise. "Why do you suffer so?"

"Do I know you?" the big fisherman asked, not recognizing Dismas.

"Yes. We met in the courtyard of the temple several days ago—when all the excitement took place there. You may not remember me, but I was the one who insisted your master was a madman."

"Oh, yes," Peter said as another deep gulping sob interrupted his breathing. "I have disturbed you, and I'm sorry. I thought that here, on the edge of the city, especially along the fortress wall, I would be alone."

"It's all right," Dismas offered, then again asked, "Why do you suffer so?"

Peter hesitated a few seconds before replying. Then he moaned loudly, "It's because I don't deserve to live."

"I don't understand. When I last saw you, the light of happiness and the security of the future shone in your eyes. From the way you spoke then, no power on earth could defeat you. What happened to change that?"

The big man closed his eyes, bowed his head, and from the way the muscles in his jaw and temple tightened then relaxed only to flex again, Dismas knew he was in great mental agony. "I betrayed my master. I not only deserted him in spirit. I denied even knowing him when he needed me most."

Another deep series of sobs wracked the man's body. When the outcry passed, it gave way to more whimpering moans from deep within him.

"Deserted him? When he needed you most?" Dismas tried to absorb and interpret what he heard. Finally he asked, "Is Jesus dead?"

"No, he lives, but I am dead now. I died tonight within my soul." Peter opened his eyes and turned his head until he faced Dismas. "I don't know what crime placed you in prison, but I tell you this, if God offered me a chance to change places, deeds, and sentence with you, I would seize the opportunity. You have undoubtedly transgressed against Caesar, but whatever you did is but a gentle thought compared to my sin."

Dismas did not understand what the man said. If Jesus was still alive and Peter was free, what could cause the big man to be so deeply troubled?

"Tell me what happened, Peter. Why are you suffering? Possibly there's something I can do, though I don't know what it could be."

"There's nothing anyone can do," Peter insisted. "But possibly my sin will enable you, brother, to suffer your punishment with greater courage." The big man took a deep and quivering breath as he sought to compose his thoughts. "About three hours or so ago my master, two other members of our group, and I were in the Garden of Gethsemane, across the Kidron from the city. There the Lord Jesus had asked us to pray with him. Even then—" Peter broke down and sobbed several times before swallowing and continuing, "Even then I failed him. He had told us this was to be the beginning of his greatest test. We knew we were to give him comfort as best we could. We failed. When we arrived at the large rock, the one beside the twisted young olive tree with the bloated trunk, my friends and I found ourselves worn out, almost as if drunk from fine wine, so we lay down to wait his call— and we slept. Whatever suffering he had to endure, we failed him. He had to face it alone. Alone, all alone, because we—I failed him."

Seeing that the big man wanted to shift from his cramped position, Dismas allowed him to do so by breaking in, "I'm sure he understood your weariness. He's unlike you, Peter. His strength seems to be more than that of most men, even greater than someone as strong as you."

"You're right. I know he forgave me for that, but that was only the beginning. After he woke us we again slept, then again. When he woke us for the third time, we saw a large crowd coming toward us—many of them carrying torches." The big man covered his face with his hands.

From between his fingers came a high-pitched moan which originated deep in his throat. It quickly faded and he lowered his hands. "The crowd was mainly temple soldiers." Peter, his sobbing now sporadic, again shifted positions, then wearily continued. "When the first of the soldiers neared, their leader, a middle-aged centurion, asked if anyone could identify which of us was Jesus."

Peter shut his eyes before shaking his head, trying to force the bitter thought from his mind. He took a deep breath and went on, "From behind the centurion came one of our own—Judas." The big man paused.

"I saw him," Peter said, "and thought he had come to stand beside us. But no. He even walked over to the master and kissed him in recognition. Then the soldiers walked straight to our Lord. Before he was taken, I drew the knife I used on reeds when I fished near the lake banks, and I silenced one of those who was shouting. He was a servant of the high priest. I cleaved the man's right ear cleanly from his head."

"Good for you!" exclaimed Dismas gleefully.

"No, brother. Jesus was quick to tell me I had done wrong. The fact that I had not heeded his teaching of gentleness upset my master. I had not loved the man, my enemy, as I was taught. Instead, I did him harm— a harm the master quickly righted."

Dismas interrupted, "How do you right it when a man's ear has been sliced off?"

"For him it was easy. He just picked up the severed ear and replaced it on the man's head. Then it became just as it was before being cut."

"Impossible," Dismas protested.

Peter, slightly hurt by the old thief's doubt, and thinking Dismas to be a believer in Jesus, countered, "You know of the master's power. I speak the truth."

"Go on," Dismas urged anxiously.

"When my Lord rebuked me, I became frightened and fell back among the trees. It was then that the soldiers put their arms through those of my Lord's and

284

marched him through the crowd and into the city."

"Do you know what happened to him after that?"

"I'm not sure exactly what happened, but Caiaphas had him taken to the temple, where he and his scribes and the elders had liars waiting to accuse him." His sobbing interrupted the story at this point. "They spit in his face, slapped him, and even beat him—my master, Jesus, the Christ, they mistreated this way. It was terrible."

At that point, Peter broke down completely and cried as if his heart had shattered.

Dismas knew he couldn't console the big fisherman, so he didn't try. Instead, he rolled from his side onto his stomach, still keeping a tight grip on the bars. from behind him, Caleb sourly asked what was taking so long.

"I'll tell you later. Right now, be quiet," Dismas ordered sharply.

Peter's wracking sobs waned, but his eyes were still blurred with tears. "It was there that I did forfeit my soul out of fear. I was given God's true strength by Jesus; he had even called me his rock. I was supposed to be the strongest in the faith that he is the Messiah, the genuine Son of God—and I broke." Peter stopped talking long enough to moan, "O my God, my God. Forgive my cowardly weakness. O my God, in Jesus' holy name, please forgive me." The big man dropped his head and slowly shook it from side to side before lowering it to his forearm.

After a few seconds he lifted his head again to take a deep and trembling breath.

"The master told me I would deny him three times before the rooster crowed this morning. I knew that could not be, and I told him so. Yes, I was sure I would never let him down. And yet, he, God's own Son, knew it would happen."

"You did it, Peter? You denied even knowing him?"

"Yes. Just as he had said. It happened when they took him to be questioned."

"Who did the questioning?" Dismas asked.

"The Sanhedrin, the lawmakers," Peter answered. "When they questioned him, I went to the courtyard outside and below their chambers. I tried to learn of his fate. While I waited there, I became afraid. People all around me were so angry, so hostile, so full of hate. I was just afraid."

The big man hesitated, as if gathering his thoughts. "In not more than a few minutes, three different people asked me if I was a follower of Jesus. As proud as I have always been to make such a claim, I told all of them—all of them—that I never knew him at all. Three times!" Peter's voice once more began to rise. "O my God! Why couldn't I have shouted, 'Yes! I'm his. I have him as my Messiah and you who hear me can have him too.' No. I cursed him, and swore I did not know him. I left him alone among the wolves."

From deep in the big fisherman's throat came the spirit-wracked moan Dismas had first heard.

Before the moan fully erupted, Dismas knew that for possibly the first time in his life, his own heart reached out for someone else unselfishly. At a time when he normally should have pitied only himself, he now felt sadness for the big man in the street. Even when sympathizing with Caleb, who was as close to him as a son, part of his sympathy was for himself. He not only feared what would happen to Caleb, but feared that whatever it was would also happen to him. He feared that whatever might cause Caleb to leave would only leave him, Dismas, alone.

"Peter," Dismas whispered fervently, "don't condemn

yourself. Jesus knew what you would do. And he forgave you even before you denied him."

The big man stopped moaning to consider what he had just heard. Despite the darkness, the big fisherman stared at Dismas, carefully studying his face. He slowly, ever so slowly relaxed. He took a deep breath, suddenly looked up at the stars, then back at the old thief.

"I believe God speaks through you, brother. Now I think I understand why the master announced my treachery, my denial, without malice." He licked his lips. "It is as you say. He did know I would do this dreadful thing. And he loved me in spite of my sinfulness." A frown came to the big man's brow and he asked, "How can he love anyone that much?"

Dismas thought about the question before he answered. "It may be an example to others that temptations will come to all of us. What is it he called you? His rock? He knew that even the strongest of his followers would weaken, but through the faith he talked of, they could again stand strong." Seeing that Peter was taking heart, Dismas kept talking, "I've heard that Jesus taught that God's forgiveness is almost limitless if you asked for it in the right way and in the right spirit." Dismas quickly thought of his own past, "I'm sure God forgives much."

"Not 'almost' my brother. God forgives absolutely everything—without exception—to those who truly believe in Him. Not only that, God doesn't forgive through my master's teachings, but through my master himself."

"Then there's your answer," Dismas said cheerfully. "You're still his rock, but you weakened and fell, just as he knew you would. Now, through your faith, you must stand, also as I am sure he knew you would. You must

again stand, not for yourself, but as a sign to others."
Dismas quickly let his voice fall until he whispered.
"Others—such as I."

"Praise God! My brother, you are a light in my darkness. You have been blessed to speak God's words to me."

Dismas was shocked by Peter's outburst. "Peter, God doesn't speak through me. He doesn't even know I exist. You are his rock—I am but a thief."

Peter frowned slightly, then asked softly, "What is your name? I don't even know your name?"

"I'm called Dismas." Then, as if he were suddenly ashamed, he added, "Dismas—the thief."

Peter paused a few seconds before pointedly asking, "Dismas, my brother, do you believe that Jesus is the Christ? The true Messiah?"

There it was. Dismas was now forced to face the question he had so desperately evaded—the question he was even afraid to ask himself.

His grip on the bars tightened as his thoughts jumbled. To himself he asked, *Can I, a thief, an adulterer, murderer, and liar, the walking, breathing symbol of everything evil, believe that my life, from my very birth, has been totally wrong? A life which was only a wretched mistake? Can my life be salvaged for some worthwhile use?* Peter's words, "Do you believe?" thundered in Dismas' mind.

He had seen Jesus confront centuries of religious belief and, in effect, say to his followers, "The old is past and I am sufficient to complete it." He had watched the Galilean defy the practices of the temple and reverse the verbal arrows of Judea's most learned men. He had even seen him perform miracles which staggered the mind. If there was a hell, as everyone believed, could Jesus yank the soul of Satan's most proficient sinner, Dismas, from its gates?

The old thief desperately wanted to believe the man could do this thing. He wanted it more than anything he had ever wanted before.

"I do," Dismas responded to Peter's question, even though he retained doubts. Lying came easily to Dismas' tongue.

"Do you believe he can take all your sins from you? All of them? And put a new heart within you?"

"I do."

Peter reached out and clasped Dismas' fingers with his own. "Bless you, Brother Dismas. If what you say is truly what you believe in your heart, God welcomes you into His heavenly and eternal family. For your faith, God rejoices." Peter stirred and Dismas knew he was about to leave.

"Friend," Dismas pleaded.

"Yes," Peter responded. "Is there something you wish of me?"

"Yes, yes," Dismas gushed, frantically trying to delay the big man's parting. "Would you do something for a dying man?"

Peter's huge body once more relaxed into the dirt. He looked with pity through the bars into the old thief's face.

"Dismas, Dismas. Don't let your voice betray you. You sound as though you still fear death. There is no eternal death for those who believe. Jesus promised this. Through your admission of faith in our Lord Jesus, you are now free of death's eternal grasp." Peter put his hands over his face and rubbed vigorously as he tried to wipe away the sticky tears which had caused the gleaming lines which streaked the front and sides of his rugged face. "What is it you need of me?"

The strange compassion Dismas had felt for the big fisherman earlier had swung momentarily to the last person on earth he would have believed he felt concern for at a time like this—Miriam.

"Peter. In the inn of Aram there is a girl— a woman. She is called Miriam—a servant girl." Dismas took a deep breath and renewed his grip on the bars. "Someone needs to care for her." The straining prisoner knew his words were completely out of character for him. After all, he was Dismas, the man to be feared, the man without fear—the man who now cared for the well-being of another.

"Peter. The girl is alone. She is alone even more now than when Caleb and I were able occasionally to give her a coin or two. Peter, she is—"

"Don't worry, Dismas," Peter interrupted. "I believe I know of whom you speak. She's the one at Aram's inn who has—" Peter tried to find the right words. "The one who's had such a hard life—the one with the tired, sad eyes, is she not?"

"She is, well, she is like all the others I know, except she is kind and gentle." Dismas was at a loss to describe Miriam accurately. "She's just Aram's servant girl. The only one he has."

Peter smiled tenderly. "Yes. I know who you mean. She's the one." Peter nodded his head slowly as if approving something. "She came to my brother Andrew, after we had left from the supper with our Lord last night. Andrew told me of her—that she'd been a woman of the street, just as was Mary of Magdala in her earlier life. But that doesn't matter now." Peter looked down then back up. "Andrew sent her to Bethany to join Mary and Martha, the sisters of our brother Lazarus. They will provide her a place to live as long as she wants to stay."

Dismas was puzzled. "Doesn't it matter that she was a woman of the streets? She can't call back what she has given. She's no longer pure."

"Jesus makes all things pure to those who come to him. Her sins, like yours, are no more. They are blotted because when she accepted our Lord, God accepted her. Like the sacrifices in the temple, He only accepts the purest of hearts. What the body did before is of no consequence."

"But what of her lost virginity?" Dismas was having a hard time understanding all of this. "What of the many transgressions of temple law? Can it just go away as a wisp of smoke?" Dismas' questions now came as a flood. His concern for Miriam was being replaced by a frantic hope for himself. "What if she had been a thief?" With this question the old man was desperately serious. "What if she—no. Could—" He was having a difficult time choosing his words. "Is there any way Jesus could remove guilt and blame for such as that?"

"Yes," replied Peter matter-of-factly.

"And drunkenness?"

"That too."

"And . . . and . . . and murder?" Dismas now spoke only of himself.

"Jesus is the master of life and in life there is love. Now, I speak of real life, not just breathing existence. I speak of the kind of life so easily found in Jesus and his teachings. As I said, there is love in real life. In love there is forgiveness—even for murder if the sinner turns to God in his heart and forsakes his old ways." Peter breathed deeply. "When a sinner turns to God for forgiveness, his soul is purged of greed, and lust, and self-love. His heart becomes fit again for God to live in.

291

When that truly happens, greed, lust, and the rest no longer have a place in him."

"But what about the person who wants to love God and Jesus but is afraid of failure? Afraid that he will return to the ways of the past?"

"When a man once bathes, does that mean he shall remain forever clean? No. So it is with submitting yourself to God. To remain fit for Him, and none of us are that fit, except for God's grace, we must bathe in submission to His will each day—each hour. No matter how filthy, how corrupt, how far down a person has gone, it takes but a single bath in submission to God to be again cleansed—as long as that person's heart is honest in his submission."

Peter again patted Dismas' clutching fingers. "Fear not, Dismas. Miriam has begun her new life with us and is also experiencing the peace and the love of God. Last night she became one of us."

Again the big man shifted his weight. "I must go now," he mumbled, "and you must seek God through prayer."

"But . . . but, I don't know how to pray," Dismas stammered. He didn't want the big fisherman to leave.

"Just open your heart fully to Him, in thought or word. Don't think you will make a fool of yourself, for it is not man but Almighty God to whom you talk. It doesn't matter what words you use, or whether they are eloquent, just say what you feel, that's all. Nothing more. He will hear you and will answer—I am certain of that. If you have need of Him, just ask. Ask in Jesus' name as was commanded and whatever you need will be given to you."

"But," Peter cautioned, "when you ask, be sure that what you desire will be pleasing to God, not just to your-

292

self. His will must always be first. Also remember, you must expect Him to answer your prayer—not necessarily with what you want, but with what you need. He knows that better than you."

The big fisherman looked down the dark street and without glancing back at Dismas said, "Good-bye, my brother, from this moment on—" Peter turned his face to the old thief. "Forever and ever, may you rest in God's love and merciful grace—according to your faith."

Dismas was keenly aware of Peter's earlier words, "If what you say is truly what you believe in your heart," and now his parting admonition, "Rest in God's love and merciful grace—according to your faith," burned into his mind. In his desire for a savior, Dismas knew what he wanted, but he could not differentiate between what he wanted to believe and what he actually believed.

As if he were urgently needed elsewhere, Peter bounced to his feet, turned, and taking long, quick steps, disappeared into the dark night.

Despite the fatigue he felt in his arms, Dismas clung to the bars for several minutes after the fisherman left.

He stared across the dim street, the torchlight causing shadows to flicker along the cobblestones, which were at his eye level. He felt the colder night air and thought about what had been said. Finally, releasing his grip, Dismas allowed himself to slide slowly down the rough stones to the cell floor below. There the odor of the prison quickly brought his thoughts back to the reality of where he was and what lay ahead. At the bottom of the incline he squirmed around until he lay on his back. He did not bother cushioning his head with his arms, but stared up unseeingly into the cell's blackness.

"Well?" Caleb impatiently probed. "What was so important that it kept you up there so long?" Caleb was still

293

hurt because Dismas had spoken so sharply to him earlier.

The old thief did not answer immediately. He was confused. He had committed himself with words to be a follower of Jesus, but he knew differently, or he thought he did. He wanted to believe, just as he had said, but how could he know that Jesus was what others said he was? He wondered, *Can the master thief of Jerusalem ever believe the things that this prophet taught? Can I really love other people, the ones I've spent a lifetime hating?* Dismas had told Peter he believed in Jesus—and possibly he could believe in him, but he was not sure. He had even accepted "God's blessings" from Peter, when all of his life he had felt God was just the crutch on which people leaned when they reached the end of their abilities. Dismas had always believed God was used by the powerful and wealthy as someone to blame when fortune turned against them. God, he had also felt, was a weapon used by priests against the weak, the fearful, and the superstitious.

Was God real and totally different from all of these things? Had His words been perfect—but corrupted over the years by those who claimed to speak for Him? Dismas wanted to believe in a God who could give a man the strength and courage He had given to Jesus. He wanted to have something to hang onto as did Peter and the others. Dismas' human nature wanted a God who, when needed, would be near enough to turn to and trust, but he was not certain he could accept anything he could not see or touch. He knew Jesus was different from other men, somehow. He knew the man was above the things which seemed most important to other men, but was he what people claimed?

People prayed for release from sickness, taxes,

Romans, and other things, and didn't always get what they prayed for. But then maybe it was as Peter said, a person receives what he actually needs and nothing else.

Shrugging, then blowing out a forlorn sigh, Dismas turned his head to one side and tried to erase the confusion which clouded his mind. A moment later he remembered where he was and that he was not alone.

Turning to Caleb, the old thief finally told him what he had learned at the window. "The carpenter from Nazareth, the one called 'master,' was arrested and the priests are trying to have him killed."

"Is that true? Well, it's as I expected," Caleb responded. He yawned and said casually, "It seems this is the season for celebrating Hebrew freedom by killing as many innocent Jews as possible—even though our laws forbid such a thing at Passover."

Dismas flung back, "It's just that type of legal breaking of our laws which angered the Galilean so—the temple laws being changed to fit the whim of the priests."

Ever since he encountered Jesus, Dismas had changed and it bothered Caleb. The young thief understood when his friend and leader ranted against the temple and its hypocritic leaders. He recalled how Dismas used to speak of the God of the Jews in the same tone and derisive manner he referred to the many gods of the Romans, Greeks, or Egyptians. Dismas' respect had never been high for any of them. However, the coming of the carpenter had changed all of that. Dismas now seemed to have gained respect for the unseen God of the Jews. It was certain he felt deeply about this Jesus. This complete change of attitude of his—to Caleb—was unnatural and something to worry about.

Caleb was quiet several seconds before he asked, "Was

that all this Peter had to say? Who is he anyhow? I mean, is he a rich or powerful man?"

"He is the mountain of a man among Jesus' twelve, a Galilean fisherman of some position, I hear. Judging from the way he carries himself and the way he acts and talks, I would say he was an influential man in his city." Dismas' mind shifted, "Peter said he was afraid when the master was arrested."

Caleb was quick to catch his possessive reference to "the master," rather than "his master," when Dismas referred to Peter's words.

Caleb did not respond to Dismas' statement, but instead asked, "Dismas, do you believe this Jesus is the anointed one for whom we have looked so long?"

Caleb was not trying to gain knowledge. Instead, he was trying to see just how far gone his master's mind might be.

Twice in one night, almost within the same hour, Dismas had been placed in the position of deciding whether or not he believed in Jesus and the things he taught. Whether he replied yes or no, Dismas felt he would be lying to himself and his friend. "Is he the anointed one? I am not sure at all what he is." Then he stuttered, "I . . . I . . . I know that he is more than a common man, as we know men to be. I have tried to compare him with all of the people I have known in my lifetime and I find no one with whom he can be compared. I tried to tell myself he's only a country carpenter who does not realize the power of money, fame, and glory. That doesn't work either. He just turns all of that aside and is still more powerful, famous, and rich than most—oh, not in gold or silver, but in other ways. He's rich in knowledge and a peace of mind which almost shines from his face." Dismas was weighing his own thoughts as much as talking to his friend.

"Caleb, two days ago I actually thought that anyone who gave him more than a casual thought was insane. Now I know that anyone who does not take him seriously may be missing something that nothing else can replace. I don't know what it is, but he is something great. That I know. I feel it."

Caleb did not smile. The change in his master was evident. Even his speech reflected a changed attitude. Not only did he refer to the carpenter as "the master," but now he said the man was "something" great, not "someone" great. Did Dismas really think this Jesus was above other men? Possibly even above Herod or Caesar? Was the greatest thief in all Judea succumbing to the magic the Galilean seemed to have? Caleb felt his master was crumbling.

On the other hand, he and Dismas were condemned to death, so what did it matter? Maybe the old man's mind was simply being numbed by fear.

Listening as Dismas talked, Caleb knew the old thief's mind was as sharp and clear as ever. He was just more intent. It was as if Dismas, who was still talking, was obsessed by this Jesus.

"A messiah? What is that?" Dismas asked. "All I know is that he is someone whose strength we saw at the temple, but what we saw was but a drop from His well of strength."

"How can you think so?" marveled Caleb skeptically. "He possesses none of the things you and I have tried to gain all of our lives. He has no riches or position—nothing like that." Caleb hoped the thought of wealth and power would pull Dismas back to his former greedy self.

"Maybe we've spent our lives seeking the wrong things," Dismas responded. "Did you ever consider that?

Maybe we should look at the sun instead of our feet—or purses. Perhaps we should look for eternity, rather than just at today."

"Certainly. But how can that buy a woman's passion? How can Jesus topple kingdoms by saying 'I love you' to beggars, cripples, and mobs? How can he have the comforts of life teaching peace and not taking the things he wants from those who will not give it?"

"These things are of no concern to him, Caleb. You and I see only what is within our narrow sight. He sees into men's souls and looks into kingdoms far greater than what we are even able to imagine. You and I are but grains of sand while he is the stars and earth rolled into one."

"You're crazy. He's just a man."

"Oh, no. Oh, no!" Dismas shook his head violently. "This man divides the now from the forever. He knows too much; he's too confident to be a fraud—he's—Oh, I don't know what."

"Well, if that's true, what's he doing upsetting priests by telling everyone that what they have believed over the years—what their fathers, and their fathers' fathers believed—is garbage? And that he, apparently, knows better."

"He did not say that!" Dismas protested. He paused, then asked, "What does he accomplish? Maybe it's just as he said. Maybe he's saving the world." Dismas did not give his young friend a chance to interrupt. He couldn't see Caleb in the darkness now, but heard the young thief take a deep breath as he prepared to launch into another tirade. "Caleb, would you say the world in which we live is a good place? No. Would you say peace and contentment are available to all of us just for reaching out and accepting them from God? No. But this man

298

talks of hope and the power of love to triumph over evil. He says he has come to light man's darkness."

"But how can you believe that?" Caleb protested. "Anyone could say such things. Besides, what's he supposed to be saving the world from? The Romans? He hasn't even addressed them. Maybe he's afraid of them. The temple jackals? If so, why do they arrest him and not the other way? Do you have peace and contentment here in prison?"

Dismas was surprised by Caleb's attack, but he answered him the best he could. "What you say is true about a mortal man claiming the things Jesus claims, but have you seen or heard anything to challenge his words as you have with others who made such claims? I haven't. As for the rest, Caleb, this man doesn't care—" He snapped his fingers. "Jesus doesn't care much about the things of this world. He plans for another world, one which is far greater and beyond our minds." Then Dismas seemed to correct himself. "Oh, he cares about our earthly well-being as long as we're building his new, spiritual kingdom. As for the Pharisees holding him prisoner, you and I have seen the most brilliant of men try to catch him in the shrewdest of traps—and they failed. If they have arrested him, it is undoubtedly because he allows it."

"Oh, Dismas. Will you see things as they really are? Come out of your trance. He's just a man. A sly one, yes, but just a man." Caleb was obviously frustrated. "I didn't see him come with his armies to be the Messiah we all expected." Caleb smiled in the darkness as he threw out the challenging statement used so often by so many Jews since Jesus entered Jerusalem.

"That's right," Dismas agreed. "We turn away from him just because he doesn't do things as we would have them done. Look around you, my friend. Of the many things we have done, the things we have built, the things we have created, how many are of any lasting value? None. Maybe we should do what he tells us. Maybe things would then change."

"But, Dismas. If it's as you say, if he's really the Messiah, come to save us from our tormentors and ourselves, what makes you think he cares about such scum as us? We've broken practically every law of this land, especially hundreds of the temple laws. We've even broken the ones this Jesus says we should obey. We've lived such bad lives most other criminals won't even associate with us. Why would he, if he's what you claim, have anything to do with us?"

"Because he loves us. No other reason."

"Ooohhh!" Caleb wailed in disgust. "He loves us?" he exclaimed incredulously. "He loves us? that's no explanation."

"It is when you look at it like this." Dismas took a deep breath. "You and I have repeatedly heard him refer to God, who is someone very real to him, as Father, haven't we?"

"Yes, but. . . ."

"Doesn't it seem logical that if we refer to God as Father, then we must be His children?"

"Yes, but. . . ."

Dismas was not giving Caleb a chance to stop him. "And doesn't it make sense that a father would love his children?" The older thief still wouldn't wait for an answer. "If you were a father and your son came home and told you he had stolen money, lied, mated with harlots, and had drank himself senseless, what would you feel—if you were a respectable person?" This time the old thief waited for an answer.

300

"Probably nothing," Caleb sneered. "But if I was a positioned father and really loved my son, I imagine I would be unhappy with him."

"Exactly. You wouldn't hate him—you wouldn't turn away from him. You'd just be unhappy with what he did. You'd love him no less. Isn't that right?"

"I can't deny that."

"Well, that's exactly what Jesus has been telling us. I don't understand how I know these things, but I feel deep inside that he has told us this and much more. Oh, not in the actual words he spoke, but in the meanings of those words." Dismas looked down as if groping for words. "Caleb." He hesitated again.

After a long pause he began again. "Caleb, he has said that from our childhood each of us searches for meaning in life. Some seek for it in riches and power, but these things do not last. He has tried to tell us that even though he is known as a carpenter from Nazareth, he is more. He has taught that somewhere in another dimension of time and life, is a place so magnificent we cannot even comprehend it." Dismas' enthusiasm made his voice rise, so Caleb hissed through his teeth to quiet him. He quickly lowered his voice, but went on.

"He said he is a light which can show us the way to that peaceful kingdom of his if we will but follow him. Just before you and I were arrested he said that in him we see and hear God, the God of our forefathers."

"Did he really say all of that?" Caleb could not swallow all the master thief was trying to feed him.

"He said that and much more."

Dismas again paused, this time to take a straw from the floor to chew on. "There's something else I felt he was trying to say to me, but I'm not sure what it was."

"Maybe it was that he will yet end our misery."

"Oh, of that I feel certain, but I don't know how."

"Do you mean that he'll rescue us from this cell?" Caleb asked.

"No. I wasn't speaking of that kind of misery. I think that because of him, the wrongs that you and I and everyone have committed will melt away—at least that's how Peter feels it happens, or something like that. I think so too."

"Come now, Dismas. How can all that we stole be returned? How can the words we have spoken against the Jewish God be pulled back?"

"I don't know, but I'm sure he can do just that. He may not repay copper for copper, but as he told the priest when he asked for the coin at the temple, those things are Caesar's and not of any real interest to him."

Dismas continued seriously, "I have frequently mocked that I had no soul, and if I did, it was not worth saving. Jesus makes me feel that my soul is my most priceless possession. Maybe in spite of all I've done in my worthless life—maybe, just maybe—I'm still worth saving. And he said he came to save the whole world. Caleb—I'm part of that world. Maybe he meant me too, and you."

Dismas said the last words in a voice which almost begged his friend to agree with him. Dismas wanted Caleb to believe what he said more than anything.

"My friend, my old master. You go ahead and believe like that," Caleb sneered. "I'll put my hope in Roman justice, such as it is."

"I will believe that," Dismas whispered to himself, more with hope than faith. He turned away. A few seconds later the old thief muttered, "Let's sleep now."

Dismas was not ready to sleep, however. But he was glad to stop talking so that he could think about the many confusing things Peter had said. He wanted to think through his own ideas. He wanted to think of what Jesus had said. Was Dismas correct in his interpretation? Was he right in what he was trying to believe? Would it be better just to let the Romans kill him without hope rather than to hope in vain? Was Jesus something special—or was it just that he wanted him to be?

Before he could collect his thoughts, he could hear the faint hum of Caleb's shallow breathing. The younger man had already dozed off again.

Neither of the men confined in the prison cell learned that Jesus was sent to Pilate, who refused to give him a trial for several reasons. Foremost, Pilate looked forward to spending the day at his nearby mountain retreat, outside the stifling city. It was a trip he planned early in the day, just after sunrise, if the carpenter did not interfere with his plans.

The second reason was that Jesus, in whom he could find no guilt at all, was accused of blasphemy. Rome had no interest in blasphemy against a Jewish god; this was an internal problem of the Jews.

Finally, when he learned Jesus was from Galilee, Pilate quickly directed that the man be taken to King Herod, who ruled Galilee as well as Judea. Pilate was procurator of Judea, Samaria, and Idumea, not Galilee.

Not long after Pilate's servants had awakened him so he could prepare for the trip to the country, Jesus arrived, only to be sent to Herod's palace. Slightly more than an hour later, on Herod's orders, Jesus was once more back at the procurator's fortress. This time he was not accused of blasphemy, but was charged as an insurrectionist against Rome. As Pilate well knew, the man's accusers wrongly said the Galilean had proclaimed himself king of the Jews and urged the people not to pay taxes to Rome. Like it or not, the case now fell to Pilate, who was tempted summarily to set the man free just as an example to King Herod and his arrogant temple priests. He didn't do it because Rome already had enough complaints about his governing.

This time, when Jesus arrived at the governor's fortress, he was taken to the south porch, which overlooked the temple's north wall. He was no longer dressed in coarse wool, but wore a beautiful and expensive robe—an evil gift of mockery given by an evil king.

The Third Hour

Caleb's sleep and Dismas' contemplation on what he and Peter had discussed were broken by the loud talk of several men clanking their way down the prison's hallway. As the sound came closer to where the terrified pair crouched, they began to tremble. They knew their time had come, but were afraid of what was sure to lay ahead.

A light appeared in the small window of the door just as the bolt was thrown with such force that its noise echoed through the room. The door crashed against the cell wall and a lamp was held high in the hallway. Dismas and Caleb shrank back as four or five armor-clad figures stalked into the cell.

These soldiers were not jailers, as had been the others. They were equipped with shields and spears. "All right, swine, to your feet and come with us," snarled their leader.

Before either prisoner could voluntarily rise, they were yanked to their feet—Dismas by one arm and Caleb by his hair.

Nothing more was said to them. Instead, the soldiers roughly pushed and prodded them along the narrow and seemingly endless corridors. Finally they reached a set of worn stone steps which led upward. Above them was a huge stone, which served as a lid for the stairway. As the men began to climb the steps, the stone above them was raised by someone and they looked up into the faint, pink light of the coming dawn. Panic overcame them, but there was no place to run.

On the first step, Caleb tripped and fell forward, catching himself with one hand. As he lunged forward, the guard marching behind him apparently anticipated such stumbling. He immediately slammed his shield into the back of the younger thief's head. Caleb cursed from the pain, but staggered to his feet. Both men continued their upward climb fearfully.

As they emerged through the opening where the huge stone had been, they found themselves overlooking a courtyard. It was not the street, as they had expected, but a stagelike porch slightly above and a large crowd of people, most of whom were Judeans. Dismas knew by the size of the mob at this early hour, that most, if not all of them, were paid to be there.

Seated on a thronelike stone chair between where they stood at the rear of the porch and the mob whispering below them, was a man Dismas and Caleb had only seen from afar. He was a man they had hoped never to meet face-to-face—the Roman procurator of Judea and Samaria, Pontius Pilate.

He was not an old man, as Dismas had guessed from his rare glimpses of him. He appeared to be in his early forties.

Dismas and Caleb expected the worst from Pilate. During his time as governor, Pilate had not only proven himself ruthless, he had bungled most forms of governing except control by force. He had antagonized the Jews

305

by entering Jerusalem time after time bearing the graven images of Caesar on his standards. Rome had repeatedly reprimanded him for slaughtering thousands of Samaritans without just cause. Mercy was unheard of for any accused person unfortunate enough to stand before Pilate.

Taking his eyes from the procurator, Dismas saw that two other prisoners stood on the porch with them. Across the widest expanse of the platform, surrounded by six guards, stood a chained hulking giant of a man. He wore animal skins and was almost completely covered with long, graying hair. The wild looking man was slobbering from his slightly open mouth. In his eye, and directed toward everyone, was a look of hatred.

Standing behind and slightly to the right of the overdressed Pilate was Jesus. Seeing him here surprised both of the frightened thieves.

Just as when they had first seen him, Jesus had his head bowed and his eyes closed. The look on his craggy face, unlike that on the men around him, was stoic, but terribly sad. Dismas saw by the carpenter's face that what took place around him had little, if any effect on him. Pilate spoke.

"Citizens of Jerusalem. I have asked you before, but I ask again, what do you want me to do with Jesus?"

The governor listened patiently as the mob, which numbered more than one hundred persons, called out, "Crucify him! Crucify him!"

The din of the screaming faded when Pilate looked down at his lap in disapproval, then raised his head to glare at them.

At dinner the night before, Pilate had told his wife, Claudia, of the priests' intentions to arrest and convict the carpenter. Pilate had thought it all to be a big joke.

To him it was strange that a religion, whose followers were subdued by fear, would itself be afraid of one of its followers.

He told Claudia what he knew of Jesus, and in the telling, said, "I came all the way from Caesarea with hundreds of soldiers to keep the peace during their Passover. The only sign I find of trouble is a penniless vagabond who preaches no fighting, no money, no resistance, obedience to any form of government, love even of one's enemies, and other ridiculous things."

Claudia, surprisingly, announced that she already knew of the man and, in disguise, had even gone to hear him speak. She confirmed what Pilate had heard, then warned, "Pilate, have nothing to do with that righteous man. You have no cause to fear him, but you may regret the outcome of any association you have with him." Pilate could not escape her words as he disgustedly looked at the jeering mob milling before him.

Tilting his head back so he could sneer down his nose, Pilate mockingly drawled at them, "In him you say you find fault, but I find none." He hesitated, then in a quick bark, which startled his listeners, he snapped, "You accuse this man—" He waved a limp hand toward Jesus, who did not even look up. "You accuse him of inciting others to refuse payment of taxes to Rome. You say he claims to be your true king." Pilate allowed his voice to take on an approving sound, "And yet, during my questioning of him in the Praetorium, he did not seem treasonous. He seemed courageous. He neither admitted to your accusations, nor did he deny them."

Pilate looked around, "I say I find no fault in him." Grumbling rippled across the listeners.

Pilate looked around once more before standing and swaggering slowly along the edge of the porch. "Nor do I say he is innocent," he continued. He looked up, sneered again, and bitterly spat out, "No doubt his determined accusers assail him more from greed and from jealousy than from fact."

Turning his back on the mob and looking toward the ceiling, Pilate once more yelled, "What do you want?"

As if directed by a leader, the crowd responded, "Crucify him!"

"But what did he do?" the governor pleaded.

Without waiting for an answer, he sauntered back to his seat, plopped himself carelessly down, and yawned, "Your law says on the day of the Feast of Passover one prisoner shall be freed."

"For this reason, which of these prisoners—" Pilate made a sweeping motion toward all of the prisoners. "Which of these shall I release?"

As one, the mob cheered, "Barabbas. Barabbas. Give us Barabbas."

Only then did Dismas and Caleb realize that the hairy beast of a man across from them was the vicious, but famous bandit and insurrectionist, Jesus Barabbas, leader of the thousand. The two thieves stared openly at him.

When his name was shouted, Barabbas broke into a wide grin—his blackened teeth exposed through his matted beard. He grinned not only because he was to be freed, but because he thought the people chose him out of fear, even when he was in chains. He did not know his selection was but a service bought and paid for by priests whose only interest was the death of the carpenter.

With a wave of his hand, Pilate signaled for Barabbas' release, then motioned for a large, silver pan of water to be brought. Clamping his jaw tightly as he spit to show his disgust for the decision, Pilate first washed his hands, then dried them on a towel held for him. In this symbolic act, and in his own eyes, Pilate had washed his hands of any guilt in the condemnation of the innocent Galilean.

Pilate normally gave no thought to the deaths of Jews or Samaritans, but to kill any man for absolutely no reason other than the pleasure of others—Pilate had no stomach for such an act. Even the gladiators were allowed to defend themselves from death.

Pilate took a last look at Jesus. The silent prisoner stood as if meditating, his strong face emotionless.

Unknown to them, the trials of Dismas and Caleb had also been held, even though there had been no mention of them. They had been found guilty without an accusation, judgment, or sentence—guilty, without a word.

Since there was nothing more for him to say, Pilate strode from the porch to a waiting chariot. Seconds later he was on his way to his country home, fresh air, and the ever-present fawning, adulating guests.

As the dust rose from the chariot wheels, Barabbas bounded from the porch into the waiting crowd and the guards began shoving Dismas, Caleb, and Jesus back down the open hole in the porch floor.

The two thieves stumbled their way down the stone steps and, instead of returning to their cell, were roughly herded into a large barren room directly under the porch used for their "trial." Jesus received no better treatment behind them.

The room, which was more than fifty feet wide and one hundred feet long, had a fairly low ceiling, Its floor, like those of the prison cell, were of rough, hand-hewn stone. This room, they learned from listening to the soldiers guarding them, was called the common hall. It was where condemned prisoners were tortured before being executed.

Because they preceded Jesus into the hall, Dismas and

Caleb felt that if torture was to come, it would involve them first. For this reason, when they reached the center of the room, their heads hung and their nerves twitched in anticipation and fear.

Instead of blows from whips, or worse, the captain of the guard ordered the thieves to one side of the room. As they were yanked aside, Jesus was shoved to the center of the floor. All the time this went on, other soldiers, each wearing the colors of Pilate's own Praetorian Guard battalion, filed into the room from various doorways. Each door led to a different part of the fortress, or opened to the street.

From the laughter and threatening manner of the men, as well as the cruel smiles on almost every face, Dismas knew that what was about to be done to the quiet carpenter was more heinous than usual.

When the whole room was packed, the captain of the battalion walked over and stopped directly in front of the Galilean. After glancing around the walls of faces, which stared in anticipation, the captain loudly barked, "Ho, Lord Jesus. How can it be that Governor Pilate allowed you—" Again he looked at the nearby men as he sarcastically continued, "You, the king of the Jews, to go dressed in rags—in the cast-off clothing of Herod? Why? You are the one who should be dressed as the king." The captain motioned to someone behind him and two nearby soldiers sprang forward. They stooped to grab the hem of Jesus' robe and, in a swift, flowing movement, whisked it over the prisoner's head, leaving him naked except for his thin sandals.

Jesus raised his head and looked around. He appeared to hope to see even a single sympathetic face among the jeering soldiers. There was not one, so he again lowered his eyes to stare at the floor. Oddly, he was not tense, as most men would be, but seemed to be resigned to whatever fate was his.

Dismas, standing in a half crouch with his hands drawn up along side his face in terror, saw the look on Jesus' face and he felt himself being strengthened. The old thief marveled to himself, *How can this man, who has done nothing more wrong than to expose evil and offer people the peace of God, stand so quietly surrounded by such hate?*

Next to Dismas, Caleb was hunched over in a full crouch. The panic which gripped the young man was such that even to look up was now beyond his will.

Dismas looked from Caleb to Jesus. The difference between the man who put his faith in Roman justice and the man who trusted in God was astonishing. It caused Dismas' mouth to open in amazement.

The captain of the guard, instead of allowing the soldiers to take advantage of the unprotected man's nakedness, waved them back and brought out a robe of pure scarlet. Its colors were almost alive, even in the dim light of the packed room. The arrogant officer stepped up and draped the robe over Jesus' head. As its folds settled, one of the biggest men in the room stepped forward and gleefully asked, "Captain, sire. May I use my skills now?" As the man's last word sounded, his lips split into a pathetic grin. Sadistic laughter bubbled from his mouth. The sound was more than cruel. The laugh began low and quiet, then, like a winter wind, rose in volume and pitch until it shrilled like the laugh of a hysterical woman. He was drooling at the corners of his mouth and his massive jaws opened and closed as he waited, eyes ablaze, for his leader's approval.

Stepping to one side, the captain mumbled, "Do as you will, Petrimus."

311

At that, the big man first jerked the red robe roughly over Jesus' head, then shoved his victim toward an iron ring set in the floor.

Another soldier came forward with a chain and manacles. He laced the chain through the floor ring before attaching it to the manacles, which he clamped onto the prisoner's wrists.

With this done, the Galilean was so stooped by the shortness of his shackles that his hands and ankles almost touched.

The apelike soldier strode to a whip rack set in the wall and removed one of the biggest instruments of torture. The whip handle was almost as thick as a man's wrist and had many thongs, each four feet long and tipped with half-ounce lead weights to insure that sufficient flesh would be ripped away.

"How many, my lord?" the grinning brute asked of the captain in obvious anticipation.

"Begin and I will tell you," the sullen leader replied.

Without delay the soldier jerked the whip up and back to full arm's length. His sudden move inadvertently laid the lash across two of his own group, bringing them howling to their knees. The man with the whip hesitated only long enough to glance at the men he had accidentally flogged before bringing the lash down across Jesus' back with crushing force.

With the first stroke, blood appeared across the crouched man's back and the whip's lead tips tore chunks of skin from his chest and under his arms.

Like a man doing a graceful exercise, the huge, gloating torturer again raised the whip and viciously smashed it down, only to raise it again—and again—and again.

As the whip hissed through the air, then cut into the helpless man, Dismas could not bear to watch. Instead, he

312

closed his eyes tightly and turned his head to one side. He could hear each blow and the instantaneous grunting of animal approval from the onlookers. Dismas flinched each time the whip landed.

In his lifetime the old thief had felt the Roman lash but once—when a royal chariot crashed its way along a street. The chariot had a whipsman riding ahead of it clearing a path. That time, in but a single blow, Dismas had received two deep cuts, both of which left blue scars along his right shoulder. He knew from that one blow that strips of flesh and muscle were now being cut from Jesus' body in a way no man could silently endure—yet no sound came. Dismas expected screams and the begging for mercy, but there was neither. The old thief felt like screaming and begging for the Galilean, who now seemed to be beyond pain.

"Beg. Beg!" Dismas whimpered under his breath. He thought to himself, *Maybe just one word will cause them to stop sooner*. The old thief's eyes squinted in sympathy for the agony he knew Jesus felt. "Beg! Beg!" He began to sob. Still Jesus gave no sound.

Some of the soldiers followed the lash with smiling fascination. Others had disgusted looks on their faces, and still others stood by with the blank stares of men too numb to care.

The last group had seen so much death in battle that it had lost its attraction. Some had been too long at isolated outposts. Deaths they had caused, seen, and heard had extinguished the spark in their souls—the spark which made men laugh and cry. These men were no longer able to do either.

Through all of this, through each searing stroke of the ripping, slashing whip, Jesus remained silent. Not even an involuntary outcry escaped his lips from the excruciation he could not help feeling. His patient silence dulled the entertainment the soldiers had come to see and hear. It had affected Dismas to such a degree, instilling in him a conviction that God strenthened Jesus, that he kept gasping for air. He was unable to exhale all of the air from his lungs before his astonishment caused him to gasp again, and again. His lungs felt as though they would burst and he wanted to scream—but he couldn't. His brain screamed that what he watched could not be happening—but it was.

Finally, after countless strokes of the whip, the captain of the guard wearily, and in a bored tone, drawled, "Enough, enough. Hold—or you will kill him. And you know what Governor Pilate would do if that happened before we carried out his exact sentence."

Dismas felt his breath whoosh from his mouth. The horror, the madness of that lash was finished. Now fear again crept back into him. The old man expected that it was now his turn to serve as the target of the drooling giant who now shifted from foot to foot, laughing at his friends when he flicked blood and pieces of skin from the whip onto them. Dismas' fear once more caused him to crouch.

As Dismas remembered the Nazarene's courage under the lash, his thoughts, oddly, began to give him courage too. Dismas forced himself to stand erect as he turned to look pityingly at Caleb. The proud, carefree young man, whose only love in life had been self-gratification, was now the picture of a crushed, terrified, fear-devoured child. At that instant, Dismas knew that his newfound strength and courage came from Jesus, the man who was just humiliated, but not beaten in spirit. Dismas had no doubt. His courage was not of his own doing.

Through his mind, like a ringing bell, came the words,

"He who hates his life in this world will keep it to life eternal."

He looked back at Jesus, this time not with pity, but with quiet awe. Jesus, the naked, bleeding man chained to the floor, was not to be pitied, but loved, even adored—yes—even worshiped. Could it be that he was what all men searched for? Was it in him that life, real life, could be found? Dismas was not certain.

As if in slow motion, Jesus gradually slumped to the floor. There he lay, face down, a mixture of blood and perspiration smeared on the floor under him, and he seemed to be asleep. As he lay there, his back rose and fell; he was having great difficulty breathing.

A young soldier noisily pushed his way through the crowd. In his hand was a bucket of brine, which he poured over the prone man's back and head. The soldier poured the water as if he were putting out a campfire. When the searing liquid splashed onto him, Jesus opened His eyes wide in an effort to bring them into focus. He then shut them again and lay deathly still.

As the man with the bucket left to get fresh water, the soldier who had chained his prisoner to the flooring leaned over and, in two smooth motions, removed the manacles.

Dismas stood staring at the man on the floor. Blood oozed from hundreds of scarlet lines across his back, shoulders, and legs. After a few seconds the old thief could stand it no more. He was afraid, almost to the point of vomiting, but he just could not let the good man lie there any longer. Although he expected to be struck down as soon as he moved, Dismas stepped forward to help Jesus to his feet. To his surprise and relief, his move did not draw so much as a look from anyone. They were too busy gawking at the cut and bleeding man to pay any attention to Dismas. Jesus seemed not to notice who helped him. As Dismas raised the weakened man to his feet, the young soldier returned with the fresh water.

With Dismas supporting him, the Galilean, his eyes closed, slowly rolled his head back. He opened his eyes and looked pleadingly toward the low ceiling. For the first time since his punishment began, the man's face showed deep anguish. As Jesus stared up the soldier began to pour the fresh water onto him. It splashed on his face then ran into his beard and over his now mutilated body. The bucket of brine had caused his wounds to burn terribly, but Jesus had uttered no sound. The fresh water seemed to revive him.

While this was going on, several men had drawn a table into the room, then placed a low stool on its top. As they did this, they shouted, "If he is a king, we should treat him with honors." With a yell one of the men snatched the scarlet robe from the floor and draped it sloppily over the prisoner. Shoving Dismas back to Caleb's side, two other men grabbed at the robe and then threw it over Jesus again. No sooner was this done than strong arms seized the weakened man and lifted him, feet first, toward the table top.

As Jesus was being carried to the table, the Roman officer was handed a circle of braided thorn vines of the type which grew thickly around the city. Turning, and as his men held the prisoner firmly, he jammed it viciously onto Jesus' head, causing the thorns to go deeply under the man's skin. The spines were rammed so deeply that removing the crown would have ripped wounds all the way around his head.

Once the weakened man was lifted onto the stool, another soldier stuck a thick, stout reed, such as was used by camel drivers to swat flies from their beasts, into the

316

prisoner's hand, giving him the appearance of a grotesque king holding an equally grotesque scepter.

As if on cue, all the men in the room, except Dismas, Caleb, and the officer, fell to their knees laughing, hooting, and shouting, "Hail to the king! Hail to the king of the Jews." Laughing at their joke, the men climbed slowly to their feet again.

Seeing that the entertainment was all but over, the soldiers started drifting out the same doors through which they had come. Several of them reluctantly stayed behind as guards. These men, all of them disgruntled at being on duty while others were free to leave, yanked Jesus from his makeshift throne and spitefully took their frustration out on him. One of them spit in the defenseless man's face and another snatched the reed from his limp hand and began to slash him about the face and shoulders with it. The one who had spit on him looked at the cloak his captain had donated and snarled, "Damnable cur, you are not worthy of so fine a garment." Taking care not to tear it, he pulled the scarlet robe from the man and in its place he tossed Jesus' original rust-colored wool robe back to him.

When Jesus looked down and saw that he once more had the cloak his mother had so lovingly made for him years before, he tried to pull it over his head but was too weak. Dismas again went to his aid. This time he was joined by Caleb.

As they gently slipped the rough woolen garment over Jesus' head, they took care to hold it as far from his many cuts as possible. They knew that the slightest touch of wool against the cuts would cause new pain for the already pain-racked man.

The captain of the guard had watched all of this with a measure of patience. Now that it was dawn, and would

317

soon be time for his relief, he had to complete his assignment. To make up for lost time he irritably ordered that the prisoners be taken outside and given their crossbeams. The order was quickly obeyed.

As the men left the hall and entered the same courtyard in which the crowd had stood for the trial, only a few spectators remained. Stepping through the door, each man had a sign hung around his neck—signs which announced the nature of their crime. Dismas looked down at his and even though he could not read, he knew the words said "Thief—Murderer." The same markings were on the sign around Caleb's neck.

On Jesus' sign the markings were different. As soon as it was draped over the man's head, the Roman soldier looked at the sign and read aloud, "Well, well. 'This is Jesus, the king of the Jews.' A fitting sign to tell these cowardly Judeans what happens to men of ambition."

A few steps away two soldiers grunted as they lifted a fifty-pound wooden crossbeam onto Caleb's shoulders. To keep from dropping it, Caleb had to wrap his arms under and behind it, then place his hands on its top. When he did this, the same soldiers quickly wound ropes around Caleb's arms, lashing them to the beam. Once the ropes were wrapped around fifteen or twenty times, the young thief was shoved to one side.

It was Dismas' turn next and the same procedure took place. The older thief staggered when the beam dropped onto his shoulders. When the ropes were secured, he felt numbness coming into his fingers almost immediately. Soon the carpenter's beam was in place too and the captain of the guard signaled it was time to leave. Jesus led the gruesome parade, followed by Dismas, then Caleb.

Before they had cleared the courtyard Dismas felt the crossbeam cutting into his neck and his arms began to

318

ache. Each of those first steps seemed as if it would be his last, but he remained on his feet, forcing one foot in front of the other.

In his discomfort, Dismas struggled with the many questions he had about the man ahead of him. Jesus had proven his strength at the temple—he was probably stronger than all men. Why did he not use his strength to break away and flee to the wilderness? With but a touch he could cure the blind, heal the lame, and raise the dead. Why did he not call on such power to take away the wood which was now his yoke?

Dismas knew all of these things could be done at will by this man, yet he endured the pain, humiliation, and degradation. Why?

If he didn't want to harm his tormentors, why did he not just soften their hearts? Swallowing deeply, the aging thief struggled ahead, planting a foot firmly, then shifting his relentless burden so he could move the other foot forward. Again, then again.

As he slowly and painfully lurched up the dusty street, he began repeating, "Why? Why? Why?"

Many times he tried to raise his head to see the back of Jesus, whose legs he was forced to watch stagger from side to side ahead of him. The crossbeam Dismas carried kept him from raising his bowed head.

Dismas watched the blood matting the back hem of the Galilean's robe and running down the calves of his legs. It spoke of an agony thousands of times worse than what he and Caleb felt. The beating had increased Jesus' agony manifold. Dismas knew that the whipping was so painful that many men escaped the cross because the lash killed them first.

At the same time he marveled at how Jesus was able to withstand such torture, the old thief felt blessed that the late hour had kept him and his friend from the whip. The pain now in his shoulders and neck and arms would not allow him to appreciate that blessing more.

Step by torturous step, led by the Roman captain and followed by six soldiers, the small, pitiful caravan made its slow way through the rising and falling Jerusalem streets.

All along the way the prisoners felt eyes staring, even though the beams kept their heads bowed, blinding them to what took place beside them. The eyes reflected many attitudes. Some just stared from simple curiosity. A few eyes were tightly shut with tears flowing from them, openly expressing the sorrow they felt at seeing their hope for freedom, Jesus, being led away to die. Some wept just because their Lord suffered so.

Several times along the way Jesus stumbled and fell— sometimes only to one knee, but on at least two occasions he fell all the way down. Finally, Dismas heard the captain tell someone in the crowd to carry Jesus' crossbeam. As the order was given, the tiny line of men stopped, giving relief to the prisoners. Ahead of him Dismas could tell the crossbeam was being transferred to new shoulders, but he heard no complaint. Instead, he soon saw new legs—legs with dark skin, darker than those of the Galilean—legs which were almost black.

Once the exchange of the crossbeam had been made, the parade of sorrow pressed on. Up hills and down them, up and down steps, the tearful procession went on its way. Dismas and Caleb expected the journey to seem like the shortest of their lives because any remaining minutes were all that remained of their lives. Instead, the trip seemed as though it would never end.

Many agonizing minutes later, the line of men trudged through the northeast gate of King David's city and began to climb a rocky path, one complicated by ragged stones on which the prisoners had to step. the high steps required Dismas' entire waning strength to push himself upright. With each one the old thief thought his legs would not support him, but they did. After each upward move, another and more difficult step remained to climb, then another and another.

Caleb did not recognize the path, but Dismas knew it. It was the last ground between them and the place of the skull—Golgotha, or as the Romans knew it, Calvary.

After staggering up and over an unusually massive rock and onto a patch of soft grass, the captain thickly barked, "Haaalt!" Dismas left his breath out at the pause. Almost immediately he felt hands guide him and his crossbeam roughly across the grass.

Before him was a freshly dug hole in which stood an upright beam of the same thickness as the one to which he was tied. As he stared at it he was spun around to face the direction from which he had just come.

He stood still, but terror almost caused his knees to buckle.

Without any ceremony, the six soldiers placed two long poles under Dismas' crossbeam and lifted him from his feet and far into the air. His weight, pulling down on his shoulders, caused his breath to gush from him as if he had been suddenly struck in the stomach. His crossbeam was placed atop the upright beam where, behind him and standing on a ladder, a Roman carpenter waited. With no more than a dozen stokes of his hammer, the worker-of-wood drove several large nails into both beams, securing them tightly together.

As the man climbed down from behind Dismas, Caleb too was hoisted into the air and his crossbeam placed on top of an upright beam identical to the one on which Dismas was hung. Looking to his right, Dismas saw the Roman carpenter climb up the ladder behind Caleb. Then dropping his head, Dismas only heard the nails being driven to secure Caleb's cross.

Dismas felt his tortured lungs laboring for air, which failed to come. His arms felt as though they were being torn from their sockets, which in fact, they were. Despite this, Dismas was surprised that he could not feel death coming. He knew he was dying, for his head was swimming from dizziness, but he did not feel the excruciating pain he expected to come with death.

So far he had not said a word, but instead, rolled his head again to the right, his jaw slack and his mouth open, gasping for air. Lifting his eyes slightly he could see and hear Caleb openly cursing his tormentors, even though his breath came in shallow gasps. Dismas thought, *After all, what more could they do to Caleb now?*

Below the two thieves, Jesus was about to endure a more hideous death. Soldiers had removed his wool robe and taken the crossbeam from the shoulders of the black man chosen to carry it. Naked, Jesus stood quietly watching as his crossbeam was nailed onto another beam, one much longer than those on which Dismas and Caleb hung.

Once the Galilean's cross was made, and without a single word being said to him, Jesus was seized by the soldiers and thrown down roughly onto the center of the cross. even though he offered no resistance, his arms were forcefully spread wide.

When Jesus' arms were flat on the crossbeam, the soldiers placed their knees on the muscle of one of his arms. At the same time the Roman carpenter put the tip of a huge nail, one of the biggest Dismas had ever seen, on Jesus' wrist. With but a single, powerful, ringing blow of his hammer, which he slammed down from over his head, the man drove the iron spike cleanly through the wrist and deep into the wood below. Two more quick, but lighter blows and the nail was securely in place.

Jesus did not scream or make any sound. He simply jerked his head forward, eyes shut tightly, with his lips open and pulled back over two rows of even, white teeth. The pain he suffered clearly showed in the tendons of his neck. They stood out as though he lifted an abnormally heavy weight.

The soldiers and the worker quickly shuffled to the other arm and the scene was repeated. Blood now flowed freely over the wooden cross.

Finally, the man with the hammer moved to Jesus' feet. Placing one foot on top of the other, he began to drive a third huge nail. This one he pounded and pounded until Jesus' feet were mashed, cruelly forcing the suffering man's knees to bend outward in front of him.

"No! No!" Dismas tried to scream, but the sound came out more a wheeze than a shout. From one side came a rippling snicker when unfeeling onlookers heard his outcry.

The old thief, in his pain, ignored his discomfort as he thought, *Passover. The high, holy days. A time to appreciate being freed from oppression. A time when the very best lambs are sacrificed to God that man's sins may be forgiven and lives started anew.*

Instantly his thought began to take on new form. A look of understanding slowly replaced the look of pain which had been on Dismas' face. Over and over the words came back to him: *Holy—best lambs—Jesus—sacrifice—so God will forgive.*

As if someone spoke them, Dismas could hear Jesus'

words, "I have come to save the world."

"Jesus. Jesus. O my Jesus!" Dismas muttered, incapable of making really loud noises now due to lack of air.

Dismas was finally convinced, beyond doubt, of the identity of the man on the cross nearest him. Now at last he was sure of his feelings about Jesus.

As the mystery of what he had sought became clear, Dismas, without looking up, began to feel what the blind man and the cripple at the temple had experienced. He felt the power of Jesus surge into his inner being. Even without the touch of his master's hand, Dismas could feel the weight of his sins being lifted and he was astonished. Dismas felt his guilt being removed, and a cleansing renewing his soul. A lifetime of evil was dissolving within him and the old thief knew why. It was just as Peter had said it—a thing so simple, so magnificently simple, he had not been able to accept it before. All the most evil man in all Jerusalem had done was believe that Jesus was the true Son of the living God. Nothing more.

Dismas knew his soul was clean now, clean for the first time since his early childhood. On the cross, steeped in pain such as he had never known and but a breath away from death, an ever so slight smile came to his face.

With the mystery of mysteries solved, Dismas thought, *I'm not dying now, even though my life is slipping away. Now it is as my master taught—now I live—finally.*

Slowly and with great effort, the old man turned his eyes to the form on the cross ahead of him and slightly to his right—to Jesus. Dismas knew all of the debts he owed to God were being paid by his suffering Savior, the lamb now being sacrificed.

"No," he gasped. "No." Dismas cringed at the suffering he saw. "Oh, no. His torment is too much," the old man wheezed.

324

Dismas knew that Jesus was suffering for all men—Roman, Jew, Greek, thief, drunkard, owner, slave—none were left out.

Still staring at the side of Jesus' head, the suffering old man felt a great sadness mixed with his great joy. Dismas' joy came from finding his God and himself. The sadness he felt was because the price, the lamb of God, was so high. The crown of thorns, which had been so cruelly jammed onto Jesus' head, was still there, but the blood which oozed from the punctures made it appear as if he perspired blood. Dismas shuddered. He could not bear to look anymore. He closed his eyes and cried. His consciousness was slowly leaving him.

When his sobs abated, he weakly raised his head once more. He could hear jeers coming from a group of priests who stood at Jesus' feet. They shook their fists, laughed, and made fun of him.

As the priests chattered and gestured, a soldier put a cloth dipped in a solution on the end of one of the long poles used to lift the thieves to their crosses. He held the cloth to Jesus' mouth. Instead of wetting his lips, the suffering man shook his head and turned his face away. The soldier, showing little concern, shrugged his shoulders, lowered the cloth, then dropped it limply onto the ground.

The soldiers, except for the unsmiling captain, who now stood nearby intently studying Jesus' face, were unmindful of what went on around them. They had spread his thick, seamless robe out before them and casually cast lots to see who would keep it. The gamblers knew that such a heavy woolen robe, when washed clean, would bring good wine money.

Dismas next looked beyond the priests and soldiers. He had a difficult time focusing his eyes, but when he

325

did, he could recognize many of the people who had gathered around.

To one side, standing respectfully, were an old woman and a man Dismas did not know by name but recognized as one of the twelve. The face of the woman beside him showed a grief so deep, so intense, that she seemed unable to cry. Dismas thought, *This must be the Savior's mother. No other could suffer so.*

Further back he saw Peter—mighty Peter. The big fisherman stood with his arm around a woman Dismas first thought just to be another of Jesus' followers. Her face was covered by her hands and deep sobs shook her shoulders. Dismas thought, *How wonderful it would be to be loved so deeply, so fully by someone—to have someone care that you die. More than that, to have them care that you should live.*

The pain-racked old man watched how Peter stood strong and straight, with two glistening streaks running down his massive cheeks.

As he stared, Dismas realized that even Peter did not fully understand why Jesus had to suffer as he now did. "Keep faith, Peter," Dismas sighed.

The girl with Peter, still sobbing, opened her hands and Dismas felt his breath escape him. It was Miriam, the servant girl! She had come to mourn Jesus, her newfound Savior. Their eyes met for a moment and he knew she was also there to mourn for her old friends, Dismas and Caleb.

As his eyes swept around the mourners, Dismas too was sad. It was not caused by the consuming fear of death still felt by Caleb, but regret that he would never be able to tell others of the gift of love God had given him. Dismas, deep within himself, felt calm and secure. It was a feeling alien to him; he felt peace and knew it was possible only because of the man nearest to him.

As his life slipped from him, Dismas again looked at Peter's face and remembered the big fisherman saying that true peace could be gained through Jesus. Dismas thought, *How truly Peter spoke.*

The old thief's thoughts were cut short as Caleb shouted at Jesus.

"You destroyer of the temple! You fraud who say you can again rebuild it in three days! Save yourself. If you are the Son of God as you claim, come down from your cross—and take us with you."

At these words, the serious atmosphere that had begun to settle over the small execution hill seemed to break. The priests and elders of the temple, who stood around Jesus' feet, began to laugh and a few clapped their hands in amusement. One of them whined, "He claimed he could save others, but he can't even save himself." The speaker lifted the edge of his priestly robe and shuffled self-righteously away from the foot of the cross.

Caleb, realizing he had the attention of those around him, was desperately trying to gain quick favor. His trust in Roman justice had earned only the fear of death, which now ruled the young thief. To keep the attention of the priests, Caleb mockingly pleaded, "Save us—if you can."

Dismas, his vision heavily blurred and now barely conscious, could stand no more of the taunting directed at the man he now knew to be the actual Son of God. He slowly turned his head toward Caleb, his friend, his companion, his son, his brother. As his head rolled over, he rested his cheek on his shoulder and, using what he felt was the last of his now feeble strength, took a shallow, raspy breath.

As strongly as he was able, his breath exhausted in

short gasps as he spoke Dismas thickly commanded, "Be
. . . still . . . Caleb. Don't you . . . fear . . . God? Can't you
see . . . we are under . . . the same . . . sentence as he?"
Dismas felt his head dropping and he was unable to stop
it now.

After an instant of rest, he again strained to fill his
lungs with the morning air, but succeeded only in gaining the slightest trace of breath. "And we . . . are guilty . .
. where he . . . did . . . nothing." Dismas felt he could
speak no more.

Caleb and the others saw that Dismas had but seconds
to live and was unable to speak above a whispered hiss.
Again they fell silent.

The weak old man helplessly watched a drop of saliva
fall from his open, gasping mouth.

With a final gigantic effort, he lifted his head enough
to turn his eyes toward his new Lord. As he did, he recalled the word "soon." Now he knew the meaning of
the word which had puzzled him before. Jesus had
known Dismas would find forgiveness for his sins and
would go to the cross with him. Jesus, a week before,
knew their destiny would be together—"soon."

In a voice barely louder than the mouthing of silent
words, Dismas whispered into the blackness, "Lord, remember me . . . when you . . . arrive . . . in . . . your . . .
kingdom."

His eyes could no longer see and his lungs were no
longer able to pull in life-giving air. Even the sounds
around him were fading rapidly.

In his mind a light had began to glow. Just as approaching thunder gradually swells as it makes its earth-
shaking way ahead of a storm, the light inside Dismas
slowly became brighter as it replaced the blackness
which had threatened to engulf him.

Before the dying thief gave up his spirit, as if from a distant place, he heard the gentle voice of Jesus, the Christ, calmly reassuring him, "Dismas, this very day you will be with me in paradise."

"This very day," Dismas tried to whisper back, but the words would not come.

A peaceful smile spread across Dismas' face as his head slumped forward for the last time.

David F. Barr was born in Seminole, Oklahoma, on August 29, 1931, the third son of an oil field worker. During the next seventeen years he led a gypsy-like life, moving from one oil field to another, eventually living in a total of thirteen homes located in five towns in three states.

As if such wanderings during his youth were not enough, after graduating from Centralia (Ill.) High School in 1949, he joined the Air Force. There he continued roaming to remote Alaska, North Africa,

Europe, the Orient, and Southeast Asia, as well as criss-crossing the United States many times.

After retirement from the Air Force in 1969, like Dismas, the subject of *This Very Day*, he resisted believing in Jesus Christ. When he could no longer deny the undeniable, his life took on a new and better meaning. He wanted to do something "worthwhile for the Lord."

His finances gone and having had to leave his wife, Lois, and three children, Paula, Douglas, and Shirley, in Texas, Dave took a new job in upstate New York. There he began laying the groundwork, then writing *This Very Day*, a tale he calls "the story of everyone—in one way or another."